A PRINCESS OF WIND AND WAVE

THE FOUR KINGDOMS AND BEYOND

THE FOUR KINGDOMS

The Princess Companion: A Retelling of The Princess and the Pea
(Book One)

The Princess Fugitive: A Reimagining of Little Red Riding Hood
(Book Two)

Happily Every Afters: A Reimagining of Snow White and Rose Red
(Novella)

The Princess Pact: A Twist on Rumpelstiltskin (Book Three)

A Midwinter's Wedding: A Retelling of The Frog Prince (Novella)

The Princess Game: A Reimagining of Sleeping Beauty (Book Four)

The Princess Search: A Retelling of The Ugly Duckling (Book Five)

BEYOND THE FOUR KINGDOMS

A Dance of Silver and Shadow: A Retelling of The Twelve Dancing
Princesses (Book One)

A Tale of Beauty and Beast: A Retelling of Beauty and the Beast
(Book Two)

A Crown of Snow and Ice: A Retelling of The Snow Queen (Book Three)

A Dream of Ebony and White: A Retelling of Snow White (Book Four)

A Captive of Wing and Feather: A Retelling of Swan Lake (Book Five)

A Princess of Wind and Wave: A Retelling of The Little Mermaid
(Book Six)

A PRINCESS OF WIND AND WAVE

A RETELLING OF THE LITTLE MERMAID

MELANIE CELLIER

LUMINANT PUBLICATIONS

A PRINCESS OF WIND AND WAVE – A RETELLING OF THE LITTLE
MERMAID

ISBN 978-1-925898-16-3

Luminant Publications
PO Box 203
Glen Osmond, South Australia 5064

melaniecellier@internode.on.net
http://www.melaniecellier.com

Cover Design by Karri Klawiter
Editing by Mary Novak

For Greg and Ber,
for your dedication and insight

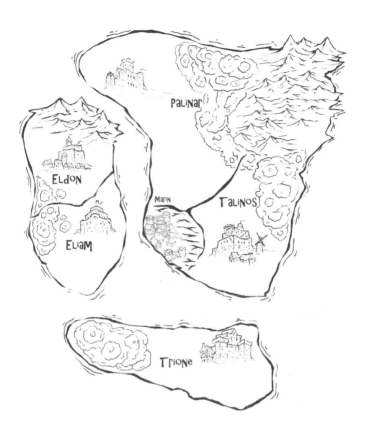

Palinar

Eldon

Eliam

Marin

Talinos

Trione

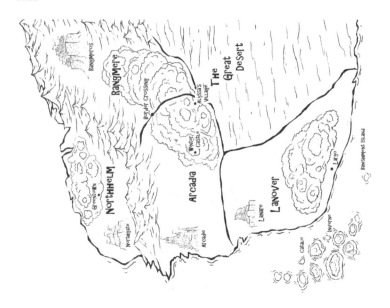

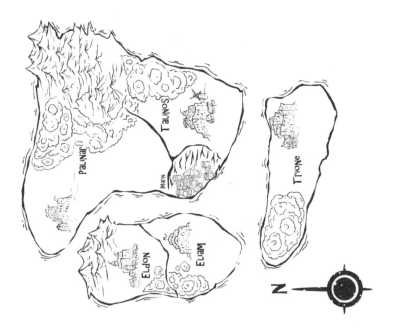

PART I
THE SEA KING'S PALACE

CHAPTER 1

a large curved shell, its pale pink interior bleaching into soft ivory, rolled off the shelf beside me and plummeted toward the floor. Without thought, my hand dove out and caught it, saving it from smashing against the stone beneath my feet. But I barely had time to grin at my improved reflexes before the ocean bed itself began to roll and pitch.

Splintering crashes filled the air as I scrambled beneath my desk to escape the flying projectiles that had once been the rest of my extensive shell collection. I had grown last summer, and my legs barely fit under the small piece of furniture. I folded in on myself, one hand gripping one of the desk legs while the other still clutched the single shell I had managed to save.

My ears strained, trying to hear any sign of the barrier collapsing and the ocean crashing through. But I knew the effort was futile. If the bubble that surrounded us did fail, hearing it a second in advance would do me no good. My desk wouldn't be enough to protect me if the entire palace was crushed.

But the movement slowed and stopped without the appearance of so much as a trickle of water. I eased out of my hiding spot to survey the ruin of my room. Pieces of shell lay scattered across the floor in every direction, and both of the chairs had tipped sideways, one of them breaking in the process while the other was now decorated with sprays of black squid ink from the inkwell that used to sit on my writing tray. The tray itself had disappeared from its haphazard home on my desktop. One of the curtain rails had also come loose, tipping soft folds of light green curtain into a tangle on the floor.

Only my bed appeared untouched, although a second look showed it no longer sat straight—apparently having bounced a few inches during the tremor. I gave a single rueful glance at the intact shell in my hand. No reflexes could possibly have saved all this destruction.

Energy coursed through me. I knew I should feel sorrow for the destruction of my collection, but I felt only guilt for the lack of any sadness. My shells were my only connection to the mother who had died when I was three, each one of them collected by her before I was born. I should have been crushed to lose them. But instead I felt something I horribly feared was relief. I had tried to love them—for Mother's sake—but in truth I had always hated their smug, smooth shapes. A good mermaid princess would love such a collection of the treasures of the sea. But I had never been a good mermaid princess.

I gave myself only a moment to think despairingly of the collection I did love—the one in my *other* room—before I gently set my remaining shell down on the middle of my bed and rushed out the door. This tremor had been the biggest one yet—by far. Now Father would have to listen to me—whether he wanted to or not.

I had barely made it a few steps down the long hallway before I had to stop, however. Grabbing a convenient length of heavy material, I beat out the flames that had started consuming a rug of rich blues and greens. Only when the fire was out did I guiltily notice that I had extinguished it with a tapestry depicting my grandfather's great victory over an orca. It was one of my father's favorite decorations, and I had listened to him regale us with the story of the orca's attacks on our fishing parties, and the creature's subsequent defeat, many times.

After a hasty examination of the material, I concluded the singe marks were barely noticeable and returned the tapestry to where I had found it—in a crumpled heap on the floor. Thankfully a hurried look along the corridor in both directions revealed that only the one lamp had come loose from its moorings, something for which we could all be grateful. It was dim in the streets and buildings of Merrita, and our lamps were plentiful in number and always burning. Our people would have enough to do in the wake of this tremor without being called upon to put out a large number of fires as well.

I hadn't made much more progress toward my father's study when I was once again distracted from my purpose. A head, made startling by the streaks of blue through the blond hair, popped out of a doorway.

"Isla!" my sister cried. "Are you hurt?"

I gave her an exasperated look. A moment of consideration would make it clear I was uninjured, but it was just like Avalon not to bother looking for herself. She stepped into the corridor, and I was relieved to see she looked to be equally unharmed. But seeing her brought Waverly forcibly to mind. The sister closest to me in age—the one between Avalon and me—had a special raised reading nook in her room that she accessed with a ladder. It was, strangely enough, the only place in her room not covered in books—and it was also her favorite place to be.

"Have you checked on Waverly?" Avalon asked, as if reading my mind. "I was just on my way to her."

I didn't bother replying. Instead I took several steps back the way I had come, pushing through our middle sister's door without knocking, Avalon on my heels.

"Waverly!" I called, halting just inside.

The last time I saw her room it had been an ordered chaos of books. Now it was just plain chaos. Books spread across every inch of floor, several layers deep. But my sister was paying them no attention, her focus instead on her window which looked out over the city.

A chill swept over me.

"What is it?" I gave up on trying to find a better way inside and clambered over the books to join her. "The barrier hasn't failed, has it?"

"What?" She turned to me, startled, her eyes wide. "No, of course not! That couldn't happen!" She looked back at Avalon who was still lingering at the door. "Could it?"

I bit my lip and said nothing, scanning the streets instead. My opinion wasn't a popular one, and Father had forbidden me from speaking of it. Spreading baseless fear, he had called it. And now that my case looked stronger than ever, I found myself reluctant to reply. Waverly was a year older than me but a great many times more timid, and I shied away from the fear in her eyes now.

My own examination of the streets below showed no flooding, no rising seawater coming to wash us away. It did, however, reveal what had caught her attention.

I gasped. "The Hall of Meetings!"

My words were enough to spur Avalon forward, and she soon joined us at the window. Together, we looked out over Merrita.

The palace was located at the highest point of the vast city, and winding streets spread out below us, lined with stately buildings made of white stone and decorated with shells. The Hall of Meetings stood on the other side of the city to the palace. Its vast bulk usually dominated the view with its distinctive iridescent sheen from the unique, polished shells that covered its walls, a mimicry of the ever-present sheen of the surrounding barrier.

It still commanded our attention, but no longer because of its grandeur and bulk. The building had collapsed, one of the walls crumbling inward and taking most of the roof with it. Silently we looked from the view to each other. No great meeting of the merfolk had been called, so the building had most likely been empty. I hoped. But that did little to ease the shock. The Hall of Meetings was a symbol for our kingdom and the unity and voice of our people. It stood across from the palace—nearly as imposing as the white marble edifice that was our home—to remind our Family that we served the people and not the other way around. And now it had fallen.

I stumbled back across the books. I needed to speak to Father. Avalon and Waverly had no real need of me, and our older three sisters didn't have rooms in this wing. No more distractions lay between me and the royal study.

When I finally reached it, however—thrusting the door open without ceremony in a way I had often been censured for in the past—I found it empty. I let out a frustrated sigh. Of course it was. My father would not linger here given such happenings.

After a moment's indecision, I hurried back out into the corridor, ignoring the books and papers the tremor had scattered across the study, and made for the ornate audience chamber that opened off the vast throne room. It was my father's preferred location to hold meetings too formal for his study but too small for the throne room itself.

I knew I had guessed right when I found a guard at the door. Captain Sawyer had never had much patience for me, and he narrowed his eyes when I came into view, his face telling me not to try bursting into this room. But my own expression must have shown him I would not be put off, and as a princess I outranked him—something I had always suspected was the root of his issues with me. Stiffness in every line, he turned and rapped on the wooden panels behind him.

"Princess Isla," he called through the closed door.

I didn't wait for further permission, brushing past him and pulling on the door handle. Inside I found my father facing the windows, just as Waverly had done. This room had an even more impressive view of the city, designed to impress supplicants to the throne, although none of them were in sight now.

Only one of my sisters was present—Oceana, my father's heir. Her husband, Lyon, stood by her side, along with General Nerissa—head of all the Merritan guards and the king's right-hand officer. I saluted her, and my father pretended not to notice. He had been the one to block me from ever becoming a true guard, and he hated it when I copied their mannerisms. But he clearly wasn't willing to fight about it right now.

"You've seen the Hall of Meetings?" I asked. It wasn't really a question. "And you felt the strength of that tremor. You must believe me now!"

"It is hardly the first tremor Merrita has withstood," Father said, his voice calm and steady, despite the slight creases on his face.

"Exactly!" I hurried forward to join him at the window, staring up at him imploringly. "They're getting worse. And now the Hall of—"

"Enough." He cut me off, his voice harsh. "If you cannot see that now is not the time for your outlandish theories, then you have even more to learn than I thought. I have told you before that Merrita has stood through even worse shakes. You are too young to remember the one that rocked us when you were three, but I will admit that I felt grave concerns. Who knows what rash action I might have taken if I had not been so soon distracted by even more grievous concerns?"

I bit my lip. I knew what event had distracted him. My mother's death.

"Time passed," he continued, "and I found that Merrita continued to stand. And here we are still, fourteen years later, the barrier as strong as ever. Don't think I don't know what's behind these wild theories of yours. I know about your fascination with the surface, and it is time you stopped letting such childish dreams drive you. We must focus on what is before us. We are fortunate indeed that no one was inside the Hall when it collapsed, but we are still receiving reports of damage and injury from across the city. Our people need us to be focused on restoration and healing, not creating panic and fear over nothing."

My hands balled into fists as I pushed aside the tears that threatened to well up at his humiliating tone.

"But it's not nothing." I tried again. "It's a message. And what stronger message could there be than the Hall of Meetings?"

"It had been showing cracks for some time." General Nerissa spoke in her usual measured tone, but she gave me the slightest of shrugs, an apologetic grimace flitting across her face.

I looked at her imploringly, silently begging her to stand up for me as she had in the past, but she shook her head slightly. She had already offered to have a risk report prepared on the tremors some months ago. And my father had refused, saying that the general already indulged me enough, and that he wouldn't have me spreading my wild ideas among the guards next.

"Exactly," my father said now with a sigh. "And the official in charge of such reports failed to pass that information on to me. But one of the prices of being king is that it will not matter whether I knew or not. I failed to repair the Hall, and now it has collapsed."

"It must be rebuilt," Oceana said, "before the people begin to whisper that the throne no longer cares to hear the voices of the kingdom."

My father nodded, frowning down at me before sighing and laying a hand on my arm. "Our Family must be strong and united in this time, Isla. And you are a part of that."

I bit my lip and looked away. So I had been wrong. Not even a tremor big enough to collapse the Hall of Meetings was enough to make my father consider the possibility that our ocean sanctuary might be tearing itself apart. Why was he so determined to stick his head in the sand?

But I knew the reason. Down here he was the king of the ocean. Down here we had been safe for generations. Whereas up there...up there we would be refugees in a land that had become foreign to us.

Father seemed to take my silence as acquiescence because he turned back to Oceana and the general.

"How close are we to a full accounting of the damage?"

"We're still waiting on reports from the furthest districts," General Nerissa replied. "I've dispatched guards, but it will take them time to make a full tour. And if they find anyone trapped, it will take them time to organize rescue teams."

Her words pierced through my frustration.

"Have there been any fatalities?" I asked.

"None that we know of," Oceana said quickly. "But as you just heard..." She spread her arms wide and shrugged.

"Can we help?" I ask. "Can I help? If there are people trapped—"

My father cut me off. "If there are people trapped, then we have plenty of guards to assist them. Real guards."

I glared at him, but Oceana spoke before I could.

"It might be a good idea to let ourselves be seen. We can walk the streets and visit the hospital. Let our people see that we hold them in our hearts regardless of which buildings stand or fall."

"Wise words, Your Highness," the general said. "I concur. And I will accompany you. Perhaps we will meet some of my guards coming back with reports."

They all turned to leave, and I trailed behind until my father paused in the door and looked back at me.

"Not you, Isla. You stay here. You have made it clear you can't let your wild imaginings go, and I don't need more things to worry about right now."

I gasped. "But Father—"

"I said *stay here*, Isla." And with that he pulled the door closed behind him.

I stared at it in shock, tears once again stinging my eyes. How could he say such a thing? Did he really think I would cause trouble by talking of my theories when our people needed practical help? I loved them, too. It was the only reason I had been arguing for months that we needed to prepare to leave. If we waited too long and the barrier failed...

"Oceana will make a good queen one day," said a voice from the far corner of the room. "It was a good idea to go out among the people."

I whirled around, only now realizing there had been another person in the room the whole time. He stepped forward out of the shadows, a lazy smile on his face. I glared back at his handsome features and tall, well-muscled frame.

"Yes, I am very well aware that Oceana is everything I am not," I snapped.

He raised his brows, his expression of surprise suggesting that it hadn't occurred to him that his words might be taken in such a way. But the glint of amusement in his eyes told a different story.

"Oh, and I suppose you find it all too easy to live up to your older sisters?" I said in response to his unspoken words. "I'm sure that's why you were hiding in the shadows." It was like him not to put himself forward in such company. I was only surprised to find him here at all.

"Maybe you should try hiding in the shadows a little more often, Isla."

"I can't hide when—" I pulled myself up short when I saw the gleam in his eye and groaned. "Really, Ray? Do you have to bait me today of all days?"

The twinkle turned into a full grin. "I consider it my solemn duty as your uncle to bait you on all days."

I collapsed onto a low sofa that had previously sat against the wall and now stood slightly off kilter, thrusting into the room.

"Sure, old man," I said. "I can see how those extra three years and all those Family responsibilities have really worn you down."

He sat down gracefully beside me, the grin still firmly in place.

"See, that's your problem, Isla. You should have more respect for the bonds of family. Like me. I know better than to try to measure up to sisters twenty and thirty years older than me—sisters who are a deceased queen and a general. It's called wisdom. You'll gain it one day, no doubt."

I picked up a cushion which had fallen to the floor and smashed it against his face. "Yes, when I reach your venerable old age, I'm sure. But for now, I'm seventeen and intend to make use of my youth and vigor."

"Of course you do." He gave an exaggerated sigh. "So where are we going?"

CHAPTER 2

*I*f I wasn't wanted out in the streets, at least I could check that those within the palace itself were all safe. But I soon found that even here no one seemed interested in my assistance. More chatter than usual filled the corridors, but the servants worked while they talked, restoring everything to order.

Neat piles of broken items stood outside doorways, and guards assisted where larger furniture had fallen or structural damage was suspected. I soon gave up on being useful and decided to check on my family instead.

I made for Oceana's large suite—located in the same wing as our father due to her position as heir. Both my sister and her husband were out on the streets, but my young niece and nephew might appreciate some company after a scare.

Ray followed behind me, his slightly mocking eyes burning into my back. Or maybe that was just my imagination.

It turned out my other four sisters had all had the same idea, so Ray and I entered to a crowd. For half a second I thought Oceana herself had already returned, but then I recognized Waverly. With her long, dark hair, everyone constantly commented on how much like our oldest sister she looked. Just as they noted Avalon's resemblance to our second sister, Coral—at least until Avalon started dyeing her hair in outlandish colored streaks.

While I watched, Waverly separated herself from the crowd and pulled herself up into a deep window seat, curling her legs beneath her and opening a book. I hid a smile. Of course Waverly had brought a book with her.

"Isla! There you are!" Avalon bounded over, her blue hair standing out in the crowd of heads. "Everyone's been asking me where you are." Her voice turned petulant. "I don't know why they're asking me." Her eyes fell on Ray behind me. "Oh, you're here too."

She turned and flounced away without a further word. I looked back at Ray, trying to suppress a smile.

"I take it she still hasn't forgiven you for stopping her the other night?" I asked.

He shrugged, his calm untouched. "I don't try to keep up with Avalon's moods. No one would guess she was nineteen and not fifteen with the way she bounces around."

I considered being offended on my sister's behalf but couldn't muster the emotion. Not when Ray was right. And not when she owed him too, for all her sour attitude. She thought it was merely chance that Ray had been the guard on duty at the door when she tried to sneak out a week ago to attend some wild festivities at one of the younger noble's mansions. But I knew he had swapped shifts especially so that he could be there to stop her.

Not that I'd known at the time why he asked for the swap. If I'd known Avalon meant to sneak out, I would have tried to stop her myself, not that she ever listened to me. I only heard about the attempted excursion afterward when Avalon complained for two straight days about her miserable luck that Ray of all people had been on duty at the side door. She was used to half-charming, half-ordering her way past all the other guards.

I hadn't given him away—he had chosen the simplest and

least involved way to deal with the issue, and he wouldn't thank me for telling Avalon the full story. I did, however, tell her that she'd had a narrow escape since the guards had raided the party. Nerissa had received a tip that a number of young mermen who had been raiding some of the fishing parties for amusement were to be in attendance, and she had wanted to give them a fright and teach them a lesson.

Even Avalon had been forced to admit what a disaster that would have been. Father would have been beside himself with fury if she'd been hauled back to the palace by guards for attending an unsanctioned party with a group of troublemakers. But apparently that didn't mean she'd forgiven Ray for blocking her exit that night.

She claimed that the party had been arranged by one of the younger Delaneys—a cousin of our brother-in-law Lyon—and that it therefore couldn't have been that bad. She also claimed that Ray was only jealous because he hadn't been invited— possibly because he was a Vasant, but more likely because he was a stick-in-the-mud. What she didn't mention was that she was always irritated with Ray for one thing or another, almost certainly because she resented that he spent more time with me than any of his other family members, and Avalon had never liked me getting too much attention. Personally, I wished I could pass it all on to her. I had never appreciated so much scrutiny, but she could never be convinced of that.

"She'll have to forgive you eventually," I told him. "Most likely when she wants to make use of our connection to the guards. The only reason she wanted to go to that party is because she hasn't had a chance to wear that new dress she designed. The one with the shells that Father hasn't quite decided if he approves of yet."

"I have no idea what you're talking about," said Ray.

I rolled my eyes. "I'm sure. There's no point pretending with me. I know you're aware of everything that goes on around here.

Why do you think I went to you when I wanted to be included in guard training?"

Ray pressed a hand to his chest. "What? I'm shocked and hurt. I thought it was because of the paternal care I have always shown toward you as the youngest of my nieces."

I snorted, but another voice spoke before I could, addressing Ray.

"One day, Nereus, you're going to meet someone who doesn't stand for any of your nonsense. And, personally, I can't wait to meet such an exemplary young lady. If I'm very lucky, she might even turn you down." Coral had a wistful smile on her face, as if envisioning such a golden future.

I grinned and gave her a hug. Oceana had always been occupied with matters of state, as well as making an appropriate political marriage and producing further heirs. Which meant when my grandmother passed away when I was six, my second sister, Coral, had been left to do the mothering of all of us younger ones. And she had never been afraid to wield the three extra years she had over Ray.

I glanced around at the rest of the room. Coral's husband was apparently occupied elsewhere, although Marine, my third sister, was here with her fiancé. At seven, six, and four years older than me, I had always had a different relationship with Oceana, Coral, and Marine from the one I had with Avalon and Waverly, only one and two years older than me. But that didn't change the fact that every one of them saw me as the baby. And, not surprisingly, none of them were looking to me for comfort.

In the midst of a disaster, I was of no particular interest to anyone—except to make sure I didn't get in anyone's way. It was entirely possible that even Ray was following me around purely because he had been instructed to keep an eye on me. He would certainly never tell me anything of the sort. He liked to complete his duties with a minimum of effort and fuss—a quality that meant a few of the older courtiers and nobles were actually taken in by the lazy air he exuded.

I let myself drift away from him in the small crowd, my thoughts finally turning back to my second room. My hidden room. If no one needed me here, then no one would mind if I left.

I slipped around the largest of the three storage sheds that huddled to one side of our shell sculpture garden. The sculptures were works of art, mosaics of shells, large and small, shaped into beautiful creations and nestled into the winding paths of the rocky outcropping which guarded the rear of the palace. And with the shifting, shimmering lights of the barrier behind them, I could almost see the beauty. Waverly certainly enjoyed coming here to read on one of the many benches that had been cunningly inserted among the sculptures.

But I couldn't spend more than a few minutes here without feeling a horrible sense of wrongness. The palace should be bordered by real gardens, lush and green—a place of life not this barren rock. But while we had deep wells of fresh water which burbled from the solid rock of the seabed, we lacked the necessary sunlight to make surface plants grow.

The ancient history books told me it had been a true garden once, before Merrita had sunk beneath the waves and come to rest here. And, if I closed my eyes, I could picture it. Not like the great forests of kelp, or the colorful vista of a coral reef, but a true garden. With the sun on my face and the wind in my hair and the softness of grass beneath my toes.

It was a daydream I could not share with my sisters. I had tried once, and Avalon had scoffed at me, asking what I knew of grass beneath my toes or wind in my hair. I had nearly let my tongue run away with me, but Waverly had saved me from such a mistake by joining in with a scolding of her own. She had reminded me of our great fortune to be protected beneath the waves, safe from the harsh sun and destructive wind.

"With the barrier around us, we do not burn or freeze, and no storms come to knock down our homes," she had said.

"And there is no life," I had muttered back, saved by her words from allowing Avalon to goad me into saying something far more revealing. Something disastrous.

"If it's life you want," Avalon had said, turning back to the mirror to admire her hair, which had been pink that day, "you can find more than enough of it outside the barrier."

And that had been enough to cause Waverly to shudder and drop the conversation altogether. My bookish sister didn't like wearing her tail or immersing herself in water and avoided it as much as possible. She was more than willing to sacrifice contact with plant life in exchange for the stability and comfort of life behind the barrier.

I didn't bring up the topic again. At least not with them. But I couldn't entirely keep my thoughts to myself, either. And so Ray knew my secrets. Or at least some of them.

As I strode through the barrier behind the shed where no one could see me, I reflected that it was a good thing my uncle didn't know all my secrets. He was far too fond of using the ones he did know against me. When I had protested in hurt the first time he did so, he merely shrugged and told me that I should have known he always used the easiest path to achieve his aims.

"If you didn't wish me to use your secrets against you, you shouldn't have told them to me," he had said.

I had called him a horrible name and given him the silent treatment for a week. He hadn't appeared in the least discomposed, and I had been forced to forgive him as soon as I needed his help convincing my aunt to allow me to join a patrol going out in search of a leopard seal that had been giving our fishing teams some trouble.

And since the insufferable boy was invariably proved to be in the right every subsequent time he lorded his knowledge over me—much as he had when he prevented Avalon's attempted excursion—I had limited myself to token protests after that. But while my burning desire for the feel of the wind and the sun needed an outlet at times, this secret was more personal. I carried it close and felt no desire to invite anyone else in to share it with me.

As my body passed through the shimmering bubble that surrounded our city, a tingle started at the tip of my hair and swept down my body. By the time I had registered the press of water against my face, the tingle had already passed my head, leaving me transformed in its wake. I took a breath, and somehow—impossible though it was by all logic—it was air that filled my nose and mouth, although it had been water I sucked in. The dark water around me lit up, as my improved eyesight allowed me to see through the depths as if through a sunlit day, no sting of salt water burning my eyes.

And before I could do more than bob once in the water, the tingle reached my waist, and I could feel a more significant trans-formation taking place. My legs sprang together, locked against each other as my skirts turned to green scales. I had loved to watch the process as a child, fascinated by it, but I was too focused on my goal this time to do more than pause for the beat it took before my tail had fully formed. I had passed through the barrier so many times in my seventeen years that I no longer needed to think about the matter at all. I knew exactly how long I must wait before giving a single flick of muscle and fins to propel myself forward through the water.

I curved to the left, pushing upward slightly, but not rising above the level of the outcropping of rock that, on the Merrita side of the bubble, supported the sculpture garden. On this side it was mostly barren, an empty stretch of sea visited by few. The deep ocean was a dangerous and lonesome place, and when merfolk spent time in it, they did it in groups for both companionship and protection. Only the guards had the necessary training and permission to roam the seas alone.

No doubt this was why all traffic through the barrier happened where its bubble caused the abrupt ends of the east-west road—the places named by the history books as the East and West Gates. Although, when we were children, Avalon had claimed a different reason for the command that all traffic must pass through the old gates. She had enjoyed terrorizing Waverly and me with stories of the early days after Merrita sank when the occasional careless Merritan had passed through the barrier above the level of the sea bed only to plummet to their death on the other side. I was fairly certain she had made the stories up. The edict, however, was real.

Which was why I had needed to find a place that was hidden and private on both sides of the barrier for my unauthorized passage into the ocean. The fishing teams and the guard patrols that protected them regularly traveled east to the colder waters of the vast, unmapped ocean and west to the great kelp forests and coral reefs of the more temperate waters surrounding the kingdoms of the land. But here, behind the northern palace, I was alone.

I didn't need to search for the dark smear of the cave opening. I had been here too many times to have trouble finding it. Some days I regretted how short a distance I had to swim to reach it, closing my eyes and twirling my way through the water, enjoying the feeling of weightlessness and the way the liquid moved against my skin. I couldn't indulge in such fancies when I was on sanctioned swims, not when they were always in the company of the guards I had trained beside.

When I was young, Coral had occasionally latched onto the idea that I hated swimming and tried to convince me of its benefits, as she did with Waverly. She didn't understand that it wasn't swimming I disliked but being trapped beneath the ocean, and my efforts to explain had only ever horrified her further. Swimming at least felt free compared to the stifling restriction of our undersea bubble, but most Merritans saw the two states as too closely linked to be separated in such a way.

Today I was too worried for such foolishness as undersea dancing, however. I kept my eyes focused on my goal, powerful strokes of my tail pushing me toward it in less than a minute.

And then I had reached the opening, and I was inside. Just past the cave mouth, I encountered the shimmer of the barrier, hidden from the outside by a twist of rock. I had nearly missed the cave the first time I passed this way, and I was sure no one else knew of its existence—a pocket of air on the Merritan side of the barrier, surrounded on all sides by stone and accessible only through the cave mouth located on the ocean side of the outcropping.

I pushed myself through the barrier. This time the tingle started at the tip of my tail, rushing upward as my scales fell away and my legs separated, my feet stretching for the ground to catch myself before my whole body had even made it through. By the time my lungs were ready to once again gulp in regular breaths of air, I was staring around in dismay.

I had told myself I was ready to find a scene of destruction, but the reality of it hit me hard anyway. I had spent so many hours arranging and sorting my treasures—each one painstakingly discovered on one of the occasions I managed to slip away from a patrol—and now it looked as if one of Waverly's dreaded storms had found its way in here. Smashed pottery and ceramics littered the floor, books lying both above and below the shards, their pages strewn open at awkward angles.

The cushions that had kept me comfortable as I pored cover to cover through each of the books many times—looking for information about life on land—had escaped unharmed, merely tossed into odd positions amid the jumble. But everything else had come crashing to the floor from the many shelves I had painstakingly carved out. I had followed the natural lines of ridges in the rock walls, but it had still been hard work.

The books looked mostly salvageable, but my favorite of the dresses had caught on something and now had a large rip down the bodice. I gathered the books, piling them into the small, watertight chest I had originally discovered them in. It now sported a large dent in one corner, but it didn't look as if the waterproof sealing had been damaged. Despite my father's insistence that nothing was wrong and nothing could endanger the barrier, it would ease my mind to have them in there, protected against further tremors.

But as I worked, sifting through my scattered belongings, I searched for something that mattered more to me than anything else inside my personal treasure trove. Something made of steel instead of paper.

CHAPTER 3

*T*here.

I dropped the book I was holding into the chest without looking and rushed over to where the tip of a scabbard poked out from underneath a crumpled pile of cotton. Pushing the material aside, I retrieved it and the roll of leather beside it.

Shaking off one of the cushions, I sank down onto it and carefully unrolled the oiled leather. The sword that appeared in my lap shone with the reflected light of the barrier, the strange iridescence glinting against its sharp edges. I slid it into the scabbard and rose to my feet, buckling it around my waist. As the familiar weight settled on my hip, I let out a soft sigh. My head had told me it was an unlikely item to be damaged in a tremor, but I couldn't shake the strange itching worry that drove me to make sure.

Pulling it out in a single, smooth motion, I gripped it in two hands and lunged forward, as if against an unseen opponent. The move—as familiar to my body as walking or swimming—faltered as my feet caught on a dented pewter jug. I only just caught myself, nearly coming to grief on my own blade in my efforts to regain my footing.

Quickly I returned the blade to my scabbard, shaking my head at my own foolishness. Now was hardly a time for waving around weapons. There was clean up to be done here, just as back in the city. And here there was no one to help me.

Dropping to my knees, I returned to the task of clearing and sorting debris, but I didn't unstrap the belt and scabbard. Even when I kept tangling myself in it, I stubbornly kept it in place. It was a foolish conceit, and I knew it. But today of all days, I felt the need for the reminder it brought me.

Here, in the glittering undersea kingdom of Merrita, I fit nowhere. My father considered me a nuisance—and a dangerous one, at that, with my foolish ideas. My sisters liked me well enough, but they didn't understand me, and with so many of us, each had been able to find a more compatible companion. The court thought I was far too interested in training with the guards to be a good princess, and the guards knew I was too much a princess to ever be a guard.

"They can see straight through you," Ray had told me once, his tone suggesting he had no emotion wrapped up in the matter himself, either way. "They know you're only playing at being a guard because you find it more interesting than spending time with the court. They know you begged for your honorary position among us so you can have an excuse to join patrols outside the city."

"You always include me in your patrols," I had pointed out.

As one of the youngest ever captains—beaten only by his older sister in her meteoric rise to general twenty years ago—Ray often led patrols.

"Of course I do." He had looked mildly surprised. "Just think how you would plague me if I did not."

I had flushed at his words, a hot defense rising to my tongue, but he gave me a knowing look, and I swallowed it down. Because he was right. Ray himself had covered for me many times when I had slipped away from my designated patrol.

Not that I had any other choice. I had worked so hard, spending as many hours at training as any other guard recruit and from the same age of thirteen. At first I had hoped I might find a place to belong among them, thinking that the duties and freedoms of a guard might satisfy the restlessness inside me. But I soon learned they would never accept me, not truly. I still worked just as hard, however, because I had glimpsed the true value of their position. All my efforts had been designed to prove to my father and aunt that I should be allowed the same freedom as a trained guard—the freedom to roam the ocean alone.

I had felt so hopeful after my aunt convinced my father first to let me train and then to let me join the patrols alongside the other recruits when we all turned fifteen. And at the beginning it had been thrilling to roam further than the well-escorted pleasure trips I had taken previously with my sisters. The king of the ocean allowed his daughters far less access to its vast reaches than the rest of his subjects enjoyed. Even the children were allowed to venture out to explore further than us, which most of them did on a daily basis in laughing clumps escorted by indulgent parents and alert guards. And those not inclined to exploration still attended regular, supervised lessons in the yellow reef or on the edge of the kelp forest. My sisters and I had only ever been given one lesson a week actually in the water.

My aunt had attempted to talk about it with him once, but I hadn't been surprised at her failure. She carried the same grief he did—his lost wife was her lost sister—so she could understand his concern for his daughters too well. I had hoped she would have more persuasive power when the other recruits were awarded full guard status at sixteen, but she failed then as well.

My father had repeated his words to me when I approached him myself after Aunt Nerissa delivered the news.

"You are a princess of Merrita, Isla, though you seem determined to forget it. You should *have* a guard, not *be* a guard. It is one thing for you to play at joining patrols, but a full guard has authority to undertake missions solo or in pairs. And you are mightily mistaken if you think I will ever let you outside the barrier with any less than a full patrol of guards."

I had been too angry to think clearly, lashing out at him in my disappointment.

"I worked so hard, but you can't even see it! I know you wish I was like Waverly—shunning my tail altogether aside from our annual royal procession."

He had shaken his head, impatience filling the lines of his face.

"You are a mermaid, Isla—I would never wish to take your tail from you. But you do not need to be a guard to enjoy the ocean."

"No. But I need to be a guard to—" I had caught myself just in time, but the damage was already done.

His expression turned keen, his eyes boring into my face.

"You need to be a guard to what, Isla? Tell me what it is you have worked so hard for all these years."

I had let my tears spill out then, using them as a shield and an excuse to run from the room. But I knew it was too late. He would never be convinced now.

The tears had still been streaming down my face when I ran to Coral, and she had stroked my hair as if I was six and not sixteen and told me not to take it so hard.

"You know it has nothing to do with you, dearest," she said. "It's because of Mother. He still blames himself for only sending two guards with her the day she died."

I had stilled, black despair washing over me. She was right, of course, and a part of me had always known it would turn out this way—as much as I had told myself otherwise. I had few memories of my mother, but I remembered the dark cloud that descended on the palace after her death.

My aunt had been as grieved at the loss of her older sister as my father had been at the loss of his queen, and she had led the guards on a deadly mission without thought for her own safety.

And when she finished, no dangerous sharks remained anywhere within our seas—all of them killed or driven off to distant waters. She had won her place as general, and I had been able to hold onto the hope that my father would eventually relax some of his fear for his daughters.

But clearly he had not, and I had been goaded into revealing that I was driven by something other than a desire to be a guard. But still, it would have been worse if I had finished the sentence. Then he might have refused to ever let me past the barrier again.

Here, in the privacy of my hidden room, I let myself speak the words I had bitten off back then.

"I need to be a guard to explore the surface."

Hearing the words aloud sent a forbidden thrill down my spine. Not even guards were permitted on the surface of the ocean, and few guards even used their freedom to pass through the barrier alone. But it was all I had dreamed about since long before my first royal procession. If I could have accessed the ocean freely—without guards to stop me or report me—the surface would have been the first place I went.

Only once a year did Merritans have permission to breach the surface. Once a year when representatives of every Family in Merrita walked through our city, then swam through the ocean, and then floated on the surface behind the royal family in a great procession as my father symbolically declared his continued mastery over the city and every part of the sea.

Royal children joined the procession from their fifteenth year, and it had been agony to wait as each of my sisters surfaced before me. When my turn finally came, I had been overwhelmed. The great sky—vaster even than the ocean—the warmth of the sun, and the light…everything was so bright, the colors so vivid. But the procession always surfaced far from the land, and I had longed to explore further, to see ships and the shore itself.

I had known better than to ask such a thing of my father. The kingdoms of the land were even more dangerous than the open ocean. They were places filled with such darkness and evil that our ancestors had been forced to sunder themselves from them— beseeching the High King and his godmothers to protect us.

I had often wondered if those distant ancestors could possibly have guessed how he would respond. Surely they could not have dreamed that he would honor their allegiance to his ways by sinking their island beneath the waves, giving them tails, and erasing their existence from the minds and histories of the remaining lands. But such it had been.

Or so we were told. All I knew, as I floated, half raised from the water, my face turned up to the sun, was that such a place as the surface could not be evil in itself. Not when it contained such beautiful light. Generations had passed now since we had fled the other kingdoms. Perhaps the time had come to explore the rest of the world again?

But my sisters were horrified at the suggestion and made me promise to never speak a word of such things in front of our father. A promise I had nearly broken when he refused to let me become a guard.

I grimaced and threw the last of the broken pottery into a corner. It would take a long time to replace my carefully accumulated treasures. If I had been a true guard—able to come and go on my own instead of being forced to do no more than tag along on occasional patrols—I could have rebuilt much more quickly. It chafed that I was limited to slipping away from patrol whenever I could manage it—a feat that would have come to my father's attention by now if Ray hadn't been covering for me.

Or maybe he was covering for himself.

His first time leading a patrol after becoming captain, he had been assigned me and two other fifteen-year-old recruits. And I had been accidentally separated from the rest of them. I found myself sinking into the memory, pausing in my clean-up efforts as I relived the moment I had already relived so many times before.

We were attempting to move along a whale who was disrupting the efforts of one of our fishing teams, and I found myself on the opposite side of the beast to the others, out of sight. When the creature finally swam on, I found I had traveled beside it far further than I initially realized.

There were many ways I could have attempted to orient myself in an unfamiliar place, but it was only weeks since my first inclusion in the royal procession, and the sight of the sky and the sun played endlessly through my mind. And so I shot straight toward the surface. I had read about how the sun could be used to tell direction, and I hoped it would be excuse enough to cover me if anyone discovered me there.

But when I burst from the water, there was no sign of the sun whatsoever. For a moment confusion and fear filled me, a swell of water bursting in my face and pushing me back below the surface again. But a single flick of my tail was enough to send me back out into the air again, and this time I realized what I was seeing.

Clouds. But not the fluffy white balls that had been floating through the blue sky on procession day. These clouds didn't look like something I longed to sink into. These clouds looked heavy and dark, a solid wall of gray and black blocking off any sight of the sun.

And with the sun had gone the delicious warmth and the effusive light, although I could still see well enough. Instead, an invisible force pressed against the exposed parts of my body—like a current but made of dry air instead of water. I shivered, my wet skin pummeled with the cold and with tiny droplets, as if the entire sky had become a giant fountain like the one in front of my father's palace where the mer-children played when there were no patrols free to escort them past the barrier.

It took several moments for me to process and understand such new sensations. Wind. Rain. I had read the words in books, but the reality was so much fuller and more intense than I had been able to imagine. I had laughed at the land dwellers' dislike of mere splatters of water, but I hadn't understood. This wasn't the gentle embrace of the ocean; it was an assault.

Another word came to me. Storm.

I let myself rise and fall with the swelling waves, catching their rhythm and flicking my tail to keep myself in time with it. Despite the cold, a grin spread across my face at the unexpected wildness of it all.

I don't know how long I would have remained there if an incongruous flash of brown hadn't appeared between two distant swells. Before my mind fully comprehended what I was seeing, I was already driving myself through the waves. I ducked below the surface, swimming fast without the waves to contend against.

Beneath the water, my mermaid eyes saw easily through the gloom of the storm, and I picked out the hull of a ship in the distance. All thought of my missing patrol was long gone as I sped after the vessel.

I popped out of the water beside it, realizing my mistake as soon as I emerged. A wave caught me and attempted to dash me against the wood. Diving beneath the water at the last moment, I swam to the other side, breaching the surface at a safer distance this time.

She was beautiful, this ship—like in form to the two wrecks I had seen on the ocean floor, but also unlike in every way that mattered. They had been empty shells, disintegrating into the ocean around them. A ghost of the land dwellers consumed by my father's kingdom.

But this vessel was proud and strong and alive. She danced across the surface, both embracing and defying the sea at the same time. And at her prow—standing on the rail, laughing into the storm—stood a boy.

Without conscious thought, I felt my body rising further from the water as if I could propel myself all the way up into the air, to meet with the lithe, golden-haired figure. And in that moment, I couldn't have told you which of us belonged to the sea and which the land—only that we both belonged to the sky and the storm.

And then the boy turned, as if to talk to someone behind him, just as a fresh wave smacked against the hull. He swayed, and for a second I thought he would catch himself, but then he was plummeting toward the ocean.

He twisted as he fell, stretching his arms out in front of him to pierce the water in an elegant dive. A laugh burst unbidden from my lips, and I dove beneath the water myself to join him.

But as soon as my mermaid vision took over, reality swept over me. No laughing merman swam to meet me. Instead bubbles and thrashing limbs seemed to fill the water in every direction. This boy was a land dweller, and he could not join me here beneath the surface.

Panic overwhelmed me, but my two years of training leaped to the fore, pushing me to action in the face of danger. With two flicks of my tail, I was at his side. Looping my arms under his, I tugged him up toward the surface.

For a second he fought against me, and I barely managed to maintain my grip, but then some part of him seemed to recognize that we moved toward the air, and he went still. We burst out into the storm once more, and he gasped, sucking in a deep lung full of air. A band around my own lungs seemed to ease.

He sucked in a second breath, nearly going under again as a wave tried to tear us apart. I held on tighter, my tail keeping us both afloat.

A fresh spray of water from his hair flicked across me as he twisted, his eyes meeting mine. For one breathless second, the storm disappeared, and once again I couldn't remember who wore the tail and who wore the legs. I only knew that I had truly seen him, and he had seen me. And I would never think of the land dwellers in the same way again. Because there was nothing evil in this boy's eyes.

Then a wave crashed over us, and he coughed and gagged, and

panic returned. I glanced around wildly. Where had his ship gone?

Already it had outstripped us, the storm driving it forward at a fast clip. I could see shouting figures swarming along the rail, no doubt looking for the boy. It hit me suddenly, what should have been in my mind from the beginning. This was no mere breach of the rules in order to place myself by the sun. I had swum with a ship, seen land dwellers—held one in my arms. For many generations my people had been hidden beneath the waves, and now I was at risk of revealing our existence to the kingdoms we had sought to escape.

Cold rushed over me. I was a traitor to my own people. Had this boy seen my tail? What was he thinking about my impossible presence? And what would he say to his own people when I returned him to the ship? Because even in my horror, I knew any other course of action was unthinkable.

All of a sudden, a memory from my childhood filled my mind. I could hear the incredulous laughter of my sisters as my grandmother read us ancient stories from before Merrita ever sank beneath the waves. Stories that warned humans of the beautiful creatures of the ocean who sang the song of the depths.

Oceana had scoffed while the rest of us laughed, pointing out that in all our generations ruling over the seas, our patrols had never seen any sign of such creatures. But did this boy know that? Had he heard the ancient tales?

I pulled him up over another wave, tugging him now in the direction of his retreating vessel. And as we swam, I opened my mouth and sang. I used no words, instead pouring everything I loved about the waves and the wind and this boy himself into pure notes which spilled effortlessly from my lips.

The boy started, his eyes growing wide and locking on my face. He lay limp in the water as he watched me, apparently realizing any effort to assist in our progress would only hinder me. I could feel the desire to speak rise within me—to ask his name and tell him mine—so I swam faster and sang harder, desperate to keep myself from completely losing my head.

A faint splash sounded over the storm, and the boy yelled into my ear.

"There! A rope!" He lifted his arm, pointing, and I realized we had caught up with his ship.

I let him go, sinking immediately out of sight, desperate not to be seen by any more land dwellers. For half a second he sank beside me, but I twisted, my perfect vision restored, and put my back and shoulders beneath his feet. He pushed off against me, arrowing toward where the end of a rope pierced the water.

And then he had hold of it and was gone. Faintly I thought I heard him call something—but whether to those pulling him aboard or to me, I didn't know. And I couldn't risk surfacing again to find out.

I had saved him. He would live. That would have to be enough.

Ray found me some time later, swimming slowly, as if dazed, although I had taken no physical hurt. Still in shock, I poured out the story to him, and watched a second set of eyes widen as they fixed on my face. How flat and brown these ones looked beside the green of the boy's eyes.

And then slowly his expression had registered, breaking through my shock. And then his eyes looked anything but flat— leaping into flame as he gripped my shoulders.

"That never happened," he said. "You must never speak of it again. To anyone. Do you understand me?"

I swallowed, my fear returning. I had broken our most important rule, and I had done it when he was supposed to be watching over me. If anyone found out, we would both be in enormous trouble.

Slowly, I nodded. Yes. He was right.

He slumped slightly, his body relaxing. "Yes," he murmured, as if to himself. "We will both forget, and it will be as if it never happened."

But it had happened. And I could not forget. And, sometimes, when I caught a certain look in his eyes as he watched me, I knew he had not forgotten either. The idea to escape my patrols—and the knowledge of how to do it—had been planted, and sometimes I caught the ghost of guilt on his face, as if he knew he bore some responsibility for it all. Or perhaps just that he feared my father might see it that way.

But Ray didn't know everything. He didn't know that in the struggle with the waves, the boy's sword belt had come loose. And he didn't know that before he found me, I had retrieved the weapon from the depths and hidden it in the pack I carried.

I stroked the hilt of the weapon, the image of its previous owner as clear in my mind as it had been that day. He might have lost his weapon to the storm, but he had kept his life.

And this was why I could not give up my childish dreams of the surface. This was why I clung to a sword that wasn't truly mine. Because I had found the place where I belonged. And it had been with one of *them*.

CHAPTER 4

ears filled my eyes, and I thrust myself through the barrier, letting the water of the ocean wash them away. I had trained with the sword for an hour, letting the familiar movements that I had diligently copied from one of my books calm me. Thoughts of the boy from the storm had filled my head, as they always did in such moments. It comforted me to know that someone out there in the world understood me. It hadn't taken more than a look to know that he saw deeper into my heart than any of my family had ever bothered to look.

And now my anger and frustration had given way to sadness. This hidden room had been my sanctuary, but I would never be replacing the lost treasures. I had let my emotions drive me back to the girl I had been for so long—the girl who dreamed of the surface, and the golden haired young man, and a place she felt truly at home.

But I hadn't been that girl for many months. There had been small tremors for years, slowly building in severity, although my father refused to acknowledge it. Several months ago a bigger one had hit, and not long after, I had slipped away from a patrol and stumbled across a deep fissure in what had once been solid seabed. I could hardly make an official report, but I had told Ray of my discovery, and the next day he had arranged for a patrol to pass by. The crack was gone.

I accused him of taking them to the wrong place, but when he took me himself a week later, I had to accept that it was gone. For another week my mind had been at ease. Until another tremor struck, and I found another fissure. This time I didn't find it by chance, having gone looking as soon as I could. When it, too, disappeared, I knew something strange was occurring. Something far outside the experience of anyone in Merrita.

And so I had done the most logical thing and called for the assistance of someone outside Merrita. My godmother. It was my first time attempting to call her, but I never doubted she would answer. Coral had often told stories of her appearance at each of our Christenings. Yet she did not appear.

One by one, I pleaded and cajoled my sisters into making the same attempt. She did not come for them either.

That night I took the issue to my father for the first time. He pushed my concerns aside, saying that if the cracks had been so close to the city, then no doubt the magic of the barrier had forced them closed. Proof, he said, that it was as strong as ever, and we were in no danger at all.

As for my godmother, he seemed to think she might have more important things to do than answer the calls of a princess caught up in foolish dreams.

I had gone to my grandmother's rooms that night, wishing she was still with us to offer her counsel, and hoping for some measure of comfort in the familiar place. Instead I had found the counsel I needed, after all.

My grandmother had been the keeper of the stories, the one to read to us in our mother's absence, and stacks of books still sat around where she had left them. Everyone had loved her too much to think of changing her room, and I suspected I wasn't the only one to slip in here alone from time to time in search of comfort.

In her favorite book, placed on the small table beside her bed, I found a story she had read us only once. It gave an account of the time when Merrita sank beneath the waves. My father had said I was too fascinated by it—already I had been showing signs of my longing for the surface—and forbidden her from reading it again, but I devoured it eagerly now.

It had been written by the queen of Merrita at the time, and the beginning was filled with her fear at the way the other king-doms were turning from the ancient ways of the High King. But that fear turned to wonder and uncertainty as she recorded the way the ground shook and opened up, the deep fissures closing again. Those who dwelled in the scattered homes and villages of the island gathered in the great capital—and just in time. With a great roaring sound, the entire island sank into the sea, with the capital city enclosed in a bubble that sprang up to protect it.

A great deal was lost, she reported, and even in the capital many buildings did not survive. But all of the people were saved, and many of their possessions with them. *And what we have gained cannot be measured*, she wrote. *I only hope the godmothers are right, and that my children and my children's children are among those who get to enjoy the era when merfolk dwell in our waters, and Merrita rules over the ocean, protected from her sister-kingdoms of the land.*

I took the book straight to my father, but he claimed he had no time for ancient tomes. And even my sisters looked doubtfully at it and pointed out that it didn't actually say that our protection beneath the waters wasn't meant to last forever, or that tremors were always a warning from the godmothers.

But each time I read it, I grew more certain. The High King had sent tremors then so that our people could be gathered and ready. And now he was sending them again. But why? Why was he preparing to withdraw our undersea protection from us?

Kingdoms of the land was a familiar phrase. But sister-kingdoms? We no longer thought of them that way—as a family that had been rent asunder, in need of reconciliation. And yet that was the way she spoke of it, as if she knew the old ways would be reestablished and merfolk would not always rule beneath the waves.

And she had spoken of all that was lost. Of the years it had taken them to adapt and rebuild. How they had learned to harvest the kelp, and the fish oil. How her own son had discovered which undersea plant could be cured in such a way that when pulled on, it sprang back, creating a sling that turned our tridents into deadly projectiles.

The High King had protected them, but he had not shielded them from every consequence. Instead he had sent the warnings, the shaking of the land to tell them to gather and prepare. They had heeded him then, but in the generations since, it seemed our people had lost their way. No one heeded the warnings this time.

If the barrier failed now, before our city had risen again from the waters, some of our people would survive in their mer-forms. But how many would be crushed as the buildings collapsed under the sudden pressure of an ocean of water? Our city and our possessions would be lost. And without our books, our knowledge and history would be gone. Those who emerged would do so as a tattered wreck, a people without home or past, not fit to take their place among the kingdoms of the land.

Now when I escaped patrols it was to search for further proof, for new fissures, for anything that might convince my father Merrita was in real danger. And I requested to join fewer patrols now, spending my time in the palace library or in my cave, reading everything I could find on the time before we sank and the ancient ways of the High King, trying to find some indication of where we had lost our way, something I could show my father to prove we were in danger of losing our protection.

My father needed to take action before it was too late. We needed to send emissaries to the surface, to search for habitable land we might call our own. And we needed to be salvaging as much as possible before the barrier failed. If we acted now, we could do much to prepare our people for the great change that was coming.

I had no time for chasing ships or finding treasures now.

My thoughts consumed me, and I paid little attention to my surroundings as I swam upright through the barrier, my newly formed feet reaching for the ground before the feeling of pressure had left my head.

"You always look like you're breathing a sigh of relief when you do that, you know," a familiar voice said in a conversational tone.

I gasped and whirled, my heartbeat rising and then falling again when my eyes confirmed it was only Ray.

"When you come back through the barrier, I mean," he clarified, as if his comment was the source of my confusion.

"What are you doing here?" I asked, ignoring his words.

Was it any wonder I felt the pressure of so many miles of water above me? I had learned to ignore it when I was in the ocean, but I always noticed the relief of its absence when I passed back through the barrier and resumed my human form. I never spoke of it, though.

I had assumed everyone felt it until I mentioned it once to Avalon. She had been in a particularly bad mood, and had laughed at me, calling me defective and saying that no true mermaid felt the pressure of the ocean.

I had run crying to Coral that time, too, since I had been only six. She had comforted me, and scolded Avalon, but when my tears had dried, she had admitted she felt no such pressure. I had never mentioned it again.

"Waiting for you," Ray replied, unaffected by the way I ignored his initial topic.

I looked back toward the barrier, unable to keep the alarm off my face.

"Yes," he said, "I know you have some sort of hideaway back there. And no, I don't know exactly where it is. I've never looked." He paused. "But what I have always wondered is why you bother with the whole charade of the guard patrols if you've found a spot to sneak through the barrier unnoticed."

I put my hands on my hips and glared at him. "First of all, it's not a charade. I always make sure I help out for just as many shifts as I escape. Which is more than any of the other nobles or royals do. I took three shifts last week alone helping guard the children while they took lessons at the yellow reef. And I helped train a new fishing team in how to wield their tridents the week before."

Ray raised an eyebrow, and I rushed on before he could criticize me further.

"And secondly, you know I can't go exploring unless my sanctioned departure has been registered at one of the official exits. It would be too risky. If one of the merfolk see me out there after I've slipped out the back of the barrier—if anyone from the entire kingdom gets even a single glimpse of me roaming out in the ocean without the excuse of having lost my patrol—then you know word would get back to my father."

"And then he'll never let you so much as leave the palace again," Ray said, matter-of-factly.

Something in his expression told me that he understood how that would kill me. Just the fear of it had always been enough to keep me from giving in to temptation. And it always was tempting to go exploring after I slipped out past the sculpture garden—but I never went further than my secret room where no one could see me.

I examined Ray's face. Maybe it was care for me more than concern for himself that kept him silent after all.

"Exactly," I said, my irritation gone.

He watched me for a moment, as if waiting to see if I intended to bite again, and then he spoke, revealing his real reason for lying in wait for me.

"Thankfully it seems we escaped any deaths. And even the damage is less severe than initially feared—except for the Hall of Meetings."

"Great," I muttered, my bad mood returned.

Ray continued on. "But you're right that it was bigger than the others, and I just went for a swim."

I looked up sharply, pinning him with my gaze.

"Another fissure? You found one?" I tried not to sound too eager.

He nodded. "The largest I've yet seen."

"And you reported it?"

He nodded again. "I went straight to my sister. You know she takes your concerns seriously, Isla. But she also said it wasn't the opportune moment to raise it with the king."

I scoffed before frowning at him. "And what of you, Ray? You believe me, don't you?"

He paused. "I believe something is happening, certainly. I don't know if it's meant as a warning or not, but the fissures are new—and that concerns me." He paused again. "And I believe that King Morgan is both an intelligent man and a good king. You should speak to him again—at a more opportune moment, as Nerissa would say."

I bit my lip. This had hardly been the first time I tried talking to my father. But Ray was right. The tremors might have been happening on and off for years, but this last one had been a big one, and Father hadn't mentioned anything about fissures in the past tremors. Surely once the initial shock and activity had died down, he would be able to see that. I just needed to get through to him somehow...

"Isla?" Ray called to me, and I realized I had already begun to walk away, too deep in thought to realize I had left him behind. I turned with a questioning look.

41

"Coral said if I found you, I should tell you to get your head out of the clouds and make sure you're ready for the ball tonight."

I knew my family had always known of my tendency to get lost in my daydreams—even if they didn't know where I disappeared to do it—but his words still shocked me.

"The ball? They're going ahead with the ball?"

Ray shrugged. "There were no deaths, and it was felt it would send the wrong message to cancel it."

"Of course it would," I muttered under my breath, already starting to move away again. "We wouldn't want anyone to think anything was *wrong*."

"Oh, and Isla," Ray called, pulling me up again. "She said if you're not ready on time, she'll let Avalon pick your dress."

"What?" I glared at Ray in Coral's absence while I tried to suppress a flush of embarrassment. How dare my sister send such a message through Ray—even if he was my uncle? Did every single person in my entire family think of me as a child?

"Consider it the warning of a friend," Ray said. "Avalon looked entirely too delighted at the idea."

"Ugh, I can imagine." I shook my head. On no account would I let my fashion obsessed, and sometimes vindictive, sister choose my clothing for a public event. Especially not when she was still angry with me for siding with Ray over her attempted escape.

"I suppose I'll see you there," I said grudgingly.

"Oh goodness, no," Ray said with a twinkle in his eye. "I have patrol tonight."

My own eyes lit up, and I took a step toward him.

"Oh no." He held up a hand to ward me off. "Not even my excessive charm and influence can get you included in it. The royal family is hosting a ball, and you're a princess, remember?"

I spun around without another word and stomped back toward the palace, already running through my wardrobe in my mind. If nothing else, at least I would choose my own dress.

CHAPTER 5

"*V*ery nice," Waverly said, surveying my dress. She gave a second nod for the simple and elegant arrangement of my auburn hair—pulled up onto my head in soft twists.

With a look almost of reluctance, Avalon nodded her agreement. Although she couldn't resist adding that she would have done a better job if I'd let her choose my wardrobe. Since she herself was wearing a gown that appeared to be made up of an endless number of soft fluttering strips of material—in a blue as intense as that of a blue tang fish—I had no qualms in disbelieving her superior selection skills.

She noticed me looking and twirled on the spot, the strips fluttering out around her. "Isn't it gorgeous? It matches my hair." She flicked her long locks which she was wearing down to better show off the blue streaks.

"That, at least, I can't deny," I whispered to Waverly, who tried to swallow a snort of laughter.

She was regarding Avalon's gown with some concern. "Is it… decent?" she asked at last.

Avalon grinned even wider and spun again. "Well, is it?"

This time both Waverly and I gave the dress our full attention, and after several rotations we both had to admit that there were simply so many of the strips that no matter how they fluttered and moved, they revealed no glimpses of any skin beyond.

Avalon smiled in triumph at our expressions.

"This time Father can't complain."

"No, only good taste will," I muttered to Waverly, and Avalon glared at me.

"You might be willing to look merely respectable, but I want to stand out." She marched for the door of my room and left, closing it firmly behind her.

I looked down at my own purple gown which floated around me in soft layers of tulle. It was a reworking of an old dress of Marine's, and I thought it looked elegant enough. I had never owned a new dress, of course, not with five older sisters and no source of fabric other than the occasional cargo lost from a ship.

"Don't worry, you look charming," Waverly assured me. "She's just jealous because she overheard a couple of the older courtiers saying they hope you mean to sing tonight."

I groaned. "That's the last thing I feel like doing."

Waverly frowned at me reproachfully. "Everyone has had a terrible shock today, Isla. The least you could do is sing."

"Why don't you sing then?" I asked.

Waverly pulled back, wide-eyed. "Oh no. No one wants to hear me sing!"

I considered pushing the matter further but decided against it. Waverly hated being the center of attention, and it wasn't fair of me to tease her when she wasn't the cause of my frustration. She did have a beautiful voice, though. All six of us did. It was just my bad luck to be stuck with the sort of voice that only came along once in a generation—or so I was told. Personally, I thought Avalon sung almost as well—and she was a great deal more interested in performing, so I wished everyone would direct their requests in her direction, as she clearly desired.

Two hours into the ball, however, I could see that I wasn't

going to get out of the responsibility that easily. At least seven members of the nobility had requested I perform, including both my brother-in-law Lyon's mother and his grandmother. And since they were Delaneys—one of the most powerful Families in the kingdom behind only the royal Family and Ray and my mother's Family, the Vasants—I knew my father would wish me to honor their request.

Still, I tried to put it off, lingering near the ballroom's famous clear crystal wall and gazing across the palace grounds to the shimmering barrier in the distance. But seeing the wall—an ancient gift to our kingdom from my Family's godmother—only reminded me of everything that was going wrong now. Far more than could be fixed with a song. When my aunt approached, I let myself groan.

"Please, please tell me you're not here to ask me to sing as well. Or order me to as my general."

Aunt Nerissa laughed. She was dressed in an elegant gown that still allowed her the full range of movement and which was adorned with the sash that showed her rank and displayed an impressive number of medals.

I sighed. My formidable aunt had fought to make a place for herself and had succeeded beyond anyone's dreams. I only wished I could fight my way to where I belonged too. But it wasn't so simple for me. It was clear at this point that nothing I did was ever going to convince my father to let me go to the kingdoms of the land.

"Don't look so glum, Isla," she said, her voice low and slightly husky from a lifetime of shouting orders. "It's a song, not an execution."

"You know they'll never let me get away with only one."

She chuckled again. "You remind me a little of me at your age, you know."

I shook my head. "That's a lovely compliment, aunt. I only wish it were true. But even if it was, you weren't burdened with being a princess. By my age you were already a full guard and well on your way to becoming the youngest captain ever."

A shadow crossed her eyes. "No, but at seventeen I had an aging father for my general and an older sister who was queen and had just given birth to my second niece. I know something about pressure and family expectations."

I winced. I knew how hard my aunt had fought to win the respect she now enjoyed; I hadn't meant to belittle her efforts.

My grandmother had told me once about the intertwining history of our families, from before my parents' marriage. She had spoken with grief of the long years she had waited when it seemed she couldn't have a child, and the joy throughout the kingdom when she finally bore King Donovan a son—my father.

"A Vasant general had served the Rennon royal line for generations, and Jason was the general in those days," my grandmother had told me. "A younger man than your grandfather, and as fine a soldier and advisor as anyone had ever seen. Such bravery and strength." She smiled, her eyes going cloudy, as she remembered the youthful images of those now passed away.

"His wife was pregnant the same year, you know. And the people hoped for a son who might be raised to take his place, a friend and advisor to the young prince." She had shaken her head and smiled, her whole face brightening. "But he had a daughter, and everyone saw at once that a daughter was even better—for then she could grow up to be their queen." She winked at me. "A friend and advisor of a different kind."

I had wrinkled my nose, unimpressed with the idea of being betrothed from birth. But my grandmother seemed so delighted with the arrangement that I didn't voice my disapproval.

"Of course, everyone hoped the general's wife might go on to bear a son to succeed him," she added. "And many were greatly disappointed when no further children were forthcoming."

I had frowned, confused. "But General Jason did have more children. Aunt Nerissa and Uncle Nereus."

That made her laugh—the sound like ringing bells. I had always loved my grandmother's laugh.

"They came later, child, though I'm sure it's hard for you to imagine a world without them. And, indeed, when your maternal grandmother fell pregnant again after ten long years, the people thought the general might finally get his son." She had paused, the distant look back in her eyes.

"But instead he got Aunt Nerissa," I said, my young, eager voice interrupting her tale. "And she was better than any boy. And now she is general like her father was before her."

My grandmother had smiled and stroked my hair. "Better than any boy, indeed, my dear one. Although she had to prove herself. And by the time the old general's second wife finally bore him a son in his old age, he already had three granddaughters from his oldest daughter. As perfect young princesses as anyone could hope to see."

I had lost interest after that, bored with such ancient history, but the whole story flashed through my mind now. I should never have suggested my aunt knew nothing of the constraints of family or the struggle of knowing you were born for something more than the role others had assigned you. She had fought and proved herself to all her doubters.

I straightened and realized with a flush of embarrassment that she had noticed my moment of abstraction, her expression one of tolerant amusement.

"I'm sorry, aunt. I shouldn't have spoken so carelessly."

She clapped me on the shoulder. "You are young, Isla, and the passions of youth are strong."

I flushed and looked away. In her own youth, my aunt had worked tirelessly for the good of the kingdom and for our people. She hadn't allowed herself to be distracted by foolish emotions. I wanted her respect, not her forbearance.

"Isla! Sister!" Avalon's voice sounded over the crowd, and I spun around, still off balance.

My sister stood on a slight platform beside the small orchestra, which had fallen silent. The two musicians closest to her gripped their precious, ancient instruments tightly, as if they feared the interloper in their space might bump against them and cause damage. Avalon seemed oblivious to their discomfort, waving for me to join her, a smile on her face, although she didn't look happy to my familiar eye. She was clearly seething beneath the surface at the courtiers' insistence that I be the one to sing.

"Oh no," I said under my breath, backing away a step.

But Lyon's grandmother, Elda—head of the powerful Delaney Family—and his mother, Fina, were standing only steps from Avalon, and they joined her in waving me forward. My wild glance flew around the room, only to land back on my aunt. One look at her face, and I knew I had no choice but to go forward. She expected me to obey my father, and he had said we needed to remain united and to keep the people calm and happy. And apparently my role in that was to perform whenever I was asked to do so.

I wove through the crowd with heavy feet, moving slowly. When I passed Elda, she smiled at me.

"You sing so beautifully, Princess. Thank you for helping us all to put today's misfortunes behind us."

I nodded at her, trying to keep a pleasant smile on my face, despite my instantaneous reaction to her words. Help put today behind us? That was the last thing I wanted to do. The kingdom needed to wake up and see the danger we were in before we lost any lives.

I had never felt comfortable in the role Avalon seemed to want—the performing princess, an admired ornament of the court. And regardless of what my father thought, I did no good for our people by doing nothing but sing. I had chosen to learn to fight instead, and even though I had not found a home among the guards, I could still fight for my people. They were all in danger, and here I was with the chance to warn them. I would make my father listen, as Ray had advised.

My father would be furious, of course. Who knew how he might punish me? But I could show my courage, as my aunt had done so many times.

As I stepped up, Avalon stepped down, giving me a sisterly embrace as we passed.

"Well, sister," she whispered, her tone making it an accusation. "It seems it's your voice the people want to hear."

I took a deep breath and turned to face the expectant crowd. Avalon might be wrong about that. But while they might not want to hear what I had to say, they needed to hear it.

"People of Merrita," I said in a loud, ringing voice. "You have asked me to sing. But I cannot do so. Our kingdom is in danger."

Gasps ran through the crowd, and shocked whispers broke out in every direction. I pushed on.

"Our kingdom is in danger, and I vow before you now that I will not sing again until our people are safe on the surface."

"The surface?" someone in the crowd called out. "It is beneath the waves we are safe."

I shook my head, ignoring the unnatural warmth that had settled around my throat. "We are no longer safe here. You have all felt the tremors, and today was worse than ever. Cracks are opening and closing all around us. None of this is natural. Look to your history books. It is a warning. The godmothers have deserted us, and our protection is failing. We must rise to the surface while we still can."

"No!" called out a high, breathy voice. "This is our home."

"Our place is beneath the waves," yelled another, a slight tremble of fear in his tone.

I looked around but couldn't identify the speakers. A rush of desperation filled me.

"We can survive on the surface—as we did long ago." My

words rushed over each other now. "But only if we are prepared. We must prep—"

"SILENCE!" My father's voice roared over the crowd, and all conversation instantly ceased.

He stood in the doorway of a back reception room, and I realized he had not been in the room when I began my speech. My palms began to sweat, and heat raced through me as the enormity of what I had done crashed over me.

"The barrier will continue to protect us, as it has always done," the king said in a voice that sounded far more authoritative than mine had done. "No one is asking you to abandon your homes. Soon the Hall of Meetings will be rebuilt—grander than ever before—and the tremors will be forgot. The sea has sheltered us for generations, and it will shelter us still."

He paused, and if anyone disagreed, they didn't speak up. Then his eyes turned to me, their expression terrible.

"Isla," he said. "You will come with me."

CHAPTER 6

I stepped from the platform, using every ounce of self-control to keep from trembling as I walked through the crowd. They parted before me, giving me a direct line to my father, but I kept my face lowered. I couldn't bear to see their expressions.

My father remained by the door to the reception room, waiting for me to enter before him. As I stepped past him, he nodded in the direction of the musicians, and music filled the vast ballroom again. But the sound was swiftly muted as the door closed behind us.

I finally looked up, my eyes widening as I realized I was alone with my father. So even my aunt was not to be included on this occasion. Clearly whatever he wanted to say to me wouldn't bear an audience of even his closest advisor.

Finally I did tremble, afraid to be alone with his anger and disappointment. All I could see now was how I had betrayed him, although that had never been my intention. I had done what he most feared and had expressly forbidden—spreading my ideas and, with them, fear—and I had undermined him in the process.

If only Ray hadn't been on patrol. He would have found a way to stop me—somehow. Because it was as clear as the crystal walls of the ballroom that this had not been what he meant when he encouraged me to keep trying.

"I'm sorry," I said, my words tumbling over each other in my hurry to speak before my father did. "It just came out. The people need to know the truth, they need to have time to prepare, they need—"

"No." My father's hand sliced through the air, cutting me off as if he were a conductor and I a well-trained musician.

For a moment we stared at each other, both of our breaths rising and falling faster than usual. And then he seemed almost to crumple in on himself, and that was somehow harder to bear than his anger had been.

"What the people need," he said, his voice quieter now and weary, "is for their *king* to lead them. For their king to find a way through, no matter how troubled the waters. What they don't need is a seventeen-year-old girl with only half the picture disobeying orders, stirring up trouble…" his voice dropped so low I could barely hear it "…and making foolish vows."

"Father, I—"

"Have I ever told you that you sound like your mother when you sing?" he asked, bringing tears to my eyes.

"No." My voice trembled. "I've heard she was a beautiful singer, and occasionally someone has said my voice reminds them of her, but not many people talk of her to me. I guess they think…"

He shook his head. "They think it might cause you pain, especially since you have so few memories of her of your own. But I should have known better. Together we could have remembered —because I know neither of us ever forgets her absence. I could have helped make her real for you."

He sank down onto a chair, rubbing a hand across his face. "I should have told you that you sound *exactly* like her, and that your singing voice is the most beautiful sound in the world to me." His hand dropped. "And now I shall never hear it again. You stood in the crystal ballroom of the godmothers and made a vow, and it cannot be broken. Go on, try to sing."

"I…" I could still feel the lingering warmth around my throat, and I knew instinctively it would do no good to make the attempt.

"Try!" he said, his voice harsh and loud again.

I swallowed and opened my mouth, attempting to sing a lullaby—the only song I remembered my mother singing to me. A harsh croak emerged that bore no resemblance to song.

My father turned his face away, but I dropped to my knees in front of him, my purple skirts billowing around me, and took his hands.

"But it doesn't have to be forever, Father," I said. "It won't be forever. You will lead our people to safety on the surface, and you will hear me sing again."

"Oh, Isla." He looked at me again. "There is so much you don't know."

"Why won't you even consider that I might be right?" I asked, despairingly.

He stood abruptly, nearly sending me toppling backward, and strode over to a tapestry on the wall. I recognized it easily—a sister piece to the one I had singed, depicting the battle with the orca from a different angle.

But my father paid the tapestry itself no heed, pulling it aside as if it was a curtain and revealing a recess halfway up the stone wall behind it. I scrambled to my feet and moved to join him with tentative steps. I had lived in this castle my whole life and been to countless receptions—both formal and private—within this room, but I had never known anything lay behind the tapestry.

From the recess, he pulled a small wooden casket, decorated

only with a single, large ruby above the elaborate lock. His hand fumbled at his neck and withdrew something else I had never seen—a long metal chain with a small golden key on the end.

I stood at his shoulder now, watching as he inserted the key and opened the lock, pushing back the lid. Inside, resting on purple satin, lay a large conch shell. But it was unlike any conch I had ever seen. In place of the pink blush that usually spread from the inside of the curved shell, gold gilt spread instead, although I could see no ridge to separate it from the smooth surface. It was as if the conch itself had been created that way, with the gold already inside.

My hand reached forward instinctively, but my father pulled the chest back.

"Don't touch it," he said sharply. "This is my most valuable and dangerous possession."

Carefully he lowered the lid back down, re-locked the chest, and returned it to its hiding place. When he turned back to me, his face was set in stern lines.

"You wish me to believe that what you did back there was merely rash thoughtlessness." He gestured back toward the ballroom. "Well, now is the chance to prove it. I have trusted you with my greatest treasure—you must never breathe a word of its existence to anyone."

"Father, I wouldn't—"

He gripped me by both shoulders, his hands firm and his eyes boring into me.

"No one, do you understand me, Isla? No one can know of this shell or its hiding place."

I nodded, hesitated, and then spoke. "Of course I won't say a word to a soul. But...Father...what is it?"

He sighed. "That is the royal conch. Royal blood, royal conch —that's what the godmothers told my ancestor." He looked tired again. "It is my responsibility to bear, and mine alone. As it will be Oceana's after me."

"Does it…do something?" I asked, no less confused than before.

My father stared at me blankly for a moment, as if he didn't understand the question.

"Yes, of course it does something. If I blow into that conch, Merrita will rise again from the sea and take her place among the kingdoms of the land."

I fell back, gasping, my hand flying to my throat.

"You! You hold the power to restore us to the surface with our entire home intact?" I raced forward and gripped his arm with both hands. "But Father, that is wonderful! This is the answer to all our problems. You must blow it before our barrier fails us."

"No." He spoke sharply, frowning down at me. "We have no proof the barrier is failing. Our Family has been tasked for generations with keeping our people safe until it is time to rise again."

"But surely now is the time," I cried, letting my hands drop. "The High King has sent us warnings, just as he did before Merrita sank. Here is the proof that we were always meant to rise —I don't understand how you've been denying the warnings all this time when you knew about this artifact."

"It is time you finally accepted that you are the one misinterpreting the message," my father said. "I can see now that it was foolishness to keep the truth from you—even though it was motivated by love and a desire to shield you. You're far too stubborn." His voice dropped. "Just like she was."

I gaped at him. "You mean you do think the tremors are a message?"

He shrugged. "I think it's a real possibility. As a king I must consider all possibilities, and the tremors have certainly served such a purpose in the past."

"But…I don't understand. You keep saying that I'm wrong, but you actually believe me? That makes no sense."

"I said I believe the tremors may be meant as a warning. I didn't say I agree with your interpretation about their message.

In the past, the tremors warned us that the surface was no longer safe for us. And when we sank, my ancestors—and now me— were entrusted with keeping our people securely beneath the waves until the surface should once again be a place of light and love. I will not be the king who raises us prematurely and brings our great kingdom to ruin. If the tremors are a warning, then they are a reminder to me of the danger that lurks at the surface. I nearly made a mistake and rushed to the conch fourteen years ago when the first big tremor hit. But the tremors died down again immediately, bringing no terrible threat in their wake, and I realized the danger of such rash thinking. I will not go from king of the seas to the bringer of darkness."

My brow crinkled, my brain trying to absorb the shock of what he was saying. "Darkness? What are you talking about?"

"You're so young," he muttered, as if to himself. "I must remember how young you are."

Despite myself, I stiffened. But I managed to bite back the words of protest that rose to my lips. And after a moment of heavy silence, he went on.

"Surely you cannot imagine that we would have continued down here all this time with no concept of what might be happening above the surface?"

I frowned. "But it is forbidden to go to the surface—except for the annual procession. And we always surface far from land on those occasions."

He shook his head. "It is forbidden except by royal command."

My mouth fell open. "Royal command? You mean you send people up to the surface?" I couldn't keep an eager note from creeping into my voice.

"No, Isla," my father said roughly. "Don't even think about it. I will never give you permission to go to the surface—and you should not desire it. It is a dangerous job." His eyes narrowed. "And you needn't think of going to your aunt or your uncle. I will not be moved on this, and your aunt wouldn't even consider making the attempt. She has a heavy enough heart choosing guards for the missions as it is. A number of them have been lost."

"Lost?" I drew in a sharp breath. "Is it so very dangerous, then?"

"The kingdoms of the land have not turned back to the ancient ways as we have always believed they eventually would. Instead they have become even darker and more evil. There is a darkness there that you could never understand, my daughter, sheltered as you have always been here beneath the waves."

"But—" I cut myself off before I mentioned the golden-haired boy who had laughed at the storm. I had looked into his eyes and seen only light. It could not all be as bad up there as my father feared.

But he had just given me his trust—I could not confess to him in this moment that I had been to the surface. And not just been there, I had actually interacted with a land dweller.

"You will have to trust me on this, Isla," he said. "It is as bad as anything I have ever imagined. Rulers so full of evil that they have brought curses upon not only their royal line but their entire kingdom. Famine, poison, corruption…Whole kingdoms lost to creeping infections of the heart and mind that leave the people empty, mindless shells."

Bile rose up to burn my throat at the picture he painted of the world I had always longed for. It couldn't be true. It couldn't.

"The princesses of the land are not as protected as you, my daughter. Why, one princess of your own age was only recently forced into a betrothal with a prince so cursed they call him the Beast."

I tried to picture myself in that poor girl's shoes and shuddered.

"And now you have told our people to be afraid." My father straightened, a sterner look returning to his eyes. "The Delaney

Family has already challenged me on this—it is not the time to be agitating public feeling in their favor."

"Challenged you?" I gasped. "You don't mean your rule?"

"No," he admitted, "it's not as bad as that." He hesitated, something in his mood souring even further. "I have taken steps to ensure it will never come to that." He regarded me coldly. "You know nothing of the compromises and negotiations that come with the crown, Isla. With these tremors to disturb our peace, I hold everything in a delicate balance. People are nervous. Conflict between our people has always been the greatest fear of the crown, given we are all trapped down here together. I cannot allow you and the Delaneys to spread fear and a false hope that may lead to the kind of desperation we must at all costs avoid. The godmothers are warning us that the surface is not the solution to our problems, which means we must find solutions of our own."

"Couldn't you tell the Delaneys—tell everyone—the truth about the current state of the kingdoms of the land?" I asked, trying to think of a way to fix my error.

My father shook his head firmly. "Certainly not. My goal is to minimize fear and panic, not increase it. There are many who would fear the ocean is not enough to keep the darkness from finding us."

My eyes widened. "And is it enough?"

My father paused, his eyes focused on something I couldn't see.

"We must hope so." His attention returned to me. "But as you can see, it's a delicate situation."

I winced. And I had blundered in, anything but delicate.

"You must learn you cannot just do as you like, Isla," my father said. "I have trusted you with our greatest secret so that you don't do anything else to upset the careful balance I must wield. And though you have wrought a greater punishment for yourself than any I might devise, still I cannot simply ignore such behavior."

My hand fluttered to my throat, and for a moment he looked regretful before he hardened himself.

"For the next year, you will remain inside the palace. In that time you might find some other skill to replace your lost voice. You have always been an elegant dancer, perhaps—"

"A year?! Father, you cannot—"

"Don't test me, Isla." His voice held steel. "Or I shall be forced to make it two years. You may return to your room now. I do not think you are fit for company tonight."

I opened my mouth to speak, closed it again at his expression, and ran from the room.

My feet flew over the stone of the corridors, my heart thrumming so hard, I thought it might burst.

A golden conch. Darkness infecting the kingdoms of the land. My father's angry, betrayed face. My father's broken-hearted face as he said that in my singing, he had heard my mother again.

I burst into my room, slamming the door behind me and leaning back against it. A year. *A year!* An entire year in which I was apparently to improve my dancing—so I might entertain the court in another way, I supposed. Tears stung my eyes. It didn't matter if I didn't want to perform for the court—that was my assigned role, and I was supposed to meekly accept it.

I reached instinctively for the hilt of my sword, seeking the comfort of its presence and my memories. But of course I wasn't wearing it. It was wrapped safely, tucked away inside my hidden room.

I straightened, my tears drying instantly as the face of the golden-haired boy filled my mind. My father had never seen the land dwellers for himself, as I had. Neither had my aunt—she would not leave her post for the time such a journey would take. They were relying on the accounts of others—and the more I thought about it, the more I could not believe they had been given the whole picture.

My father had just said I had no role here beside ornamentation—and the court already had five beautiful mermaid princesses. They would have to be ornamentation enough.

I rushed to my wardrobe and threw it open. Rummaging around in the bottom, I pulled out a canvas bag. Throwing only the essentials inside, I worked at a feverish pace. My father hadn't set any guards to watch me or sent anyone to lock my door behind me. He didn't know of my more rebellious adventures.

But at any time, he might think better of it and rectify his mistake. I paused, my stomach writhing. Or perhaps Ray would hear what I had done and be so horrified and disgusted at me that he would tell my father everything.

And then I would no doubt have an armed escort day and night. I flew back into motion, stripping off my ballgown and replacing it with a simple shift. It was the only unadorned piece of clothing I owned.

I didn't pause in the doorway of my room, pulling the door closed firmly behind me. I had never belonged here—not like my sisters did—but I could still help my people. My father believed the tremors were a warning to him about the darkness on the surface. But why would he need such dire warnings when he had not considered blowing the conch in fourteen years?

He feared the darkness finding its way here, and what if he was right? But also wrong. He thought the tremors gave the same warning as generations ago—darkness is coming, and safety lies beneath the waves. But their original message could be interpreted a different way. What if they said, as they had back then, that darkness is coming, and we must seek a new safe haven?

I would find the boy, and I would find out the truth about the darkness. I would make him tell me how he and his people remained safe from it. I would make him tell me how we, too, could be safe. And then I would return and lead my people up to the surface. It was my one chance to make things right.

But both my certainty and my headlong flight came to a standstill in the middle of the shell sculpture garden.

"Ray." I stared at his tall figure, leaning casually against a sculpture. "What are you doing here?"

But I already knew the answer to that question. "Don't try to stop me. I know I made a mistake—lots of them, probably—but this is my one chance to make it right. I can't explain it all right now, though. I have to hurry."

"I don't remember asking for an explanation," Ray cut through my babble.

He leaned over and picked up a canvas bag of his own which had been hidden in the shadow of the sculpture. I gaped at him as he slung it over his shoulder.

"Although I am curious to find out if I'm finally to see this secret hideaway of yours," he said.

"You're not angry with me?" I asked cautiously.

He sighed. "If I was angry every time you did something idiotic, I would exhaust myself on a regular basis. You've always been the most infuriating child I've ever encountered. But we're family. I think you know that while you may officially be my niece, in truth you're more like my sister than my actual sisters ever were. And I believe you have the good of our people at heart. So I'm coming along, whether you like it or not. You have a unique ability to infuriate people, and someone has to make sure no land dweller is inspired to violence against you."

I couldn't help grinning up at him. "I'm touched, Ray. So much familial love. I might almost think you liked having me around. Except I'm perfectly well aware you only put up with me because you decided a long time ago humoring me is less bother than attempting to hinder me."

He grinned back. "Ah, see how well you know me? Why wouldn't I want you on all of my patrols? Who could resist such an obsequious underling?"

I gasped in outrage. "Underling? I'm a princess, remember!"

"Are you?" He gave me a mocking look. "And here I thought you were just one of my guards."

I narrowed my eyes at his reminder of all the times I had begged him to help me gain acceptance from the other guards.

"What you are is impossible," I said. "Come or don't come. I don't care. But I'm not waiting around any longer."

And with that I turned and strode through the barrier.

CHAPTER 7

$\mathcal{I}$ had to stop at my hidden room, which rather cramped my grand departure. But dramatic gestures had always been wasted on Ray.

He did look around my room with interest, though. The piles of broken pottery got only a cursory glance, but he spent a minute flicking through the spines of the books before eyeing the sword I had unwrapped with extreme misgiving.

"No one in Merrita has trained to fight with a sword in generations," he said. "I have a terrible suspicion one of us is going to end up getting skewered."

"*I've* been training with a sword," I replied, casting a last wistful look around the room. There was no point trying to take anything else.

"Somehow I'm not reassured," he said.

I gave him an exasperated look as I carefully wrapped the sword back up in its oiled leather and squeezed it into my water-proof bag. "We can hardly erupt from the sea carrying tridents, now, can we? We might as well advertise where we come from."

"Perhaps," he said. "Although I'm not so sure it will mean anything to the land dwellers."

I forced myself to lead us back into the ocean without a backward glance for my haven.

"I know the godmothers told our ancestors we would be erased from all minds and histories," I said, once we were both in our mer-forms. "But if we've been sending regular scouts up all this time, surely someone must have let slip about our existence by now?"

Which meant I hadn't needed to be so secretive when I rescued the boy, after all. The thought rankled.

"Those scouts are a rather interesting matter," Ray said slowly.

Something in his tone made me twist around to give him a searching look.

"You didn't know about them? I thought you must have chosen not to tell me so that I wouldn't bother you to help me get selected."

"Oh, I certainly wouldn't have told you if I knew," Ray said promptly. "But I didn't know. Not until tonight."

I resumed swimming but glanced back at him, understanding dawning.

"You would have gone yourself if you'd known."

"Of course," he said simply.

"And that's why you're coming now."

"I'm coming now to look after you." He paused, a twinkle showing in his eyes. "But I will admit to a little curiosity."

I suspected there was something more than curiosity. Most people would probably have agreed with my father not trusting important information to his baby daughter, but Ray was a different story. He was a captain of the guard, and the heir apparent to his sister. Everyone expected he would be general one day. His sister shouldn't have kept something like this from him—although I could understand why she had. She must have known he would immediately volunteer himself, regardless of the danger.

But apparently tonight had been enough for her to confess the truth to him—no doubt accompanied with an account of my outrageous behavior. And he had immediately taken action. Did he feel betrayed by her? It was hard to imagine Ray of all people acting out of rebellion, but it made me feel better about my own actions to think that might be his reason.

My father and my aunt would be angry, but I felt only relief. It was a weight off my shoulders to know I wasn't venturing into the unknown alone. And when we came back with the solution to Merrita's troubles, they would have to believe Nereus, captain of the guard, even if they didn't want to believe the baby of the family who always had her eyes turned to the surface.

At some point during my musings, Ray had taken the lead. I made no protest, falling in behind him. Ray had always been the kind of captain who led from the front on patrol, so the positions felt natural. I stayed alert, however, ready to guide him if necessary. I had a lot of experience at sneaking away from our kingdom.

As time passed, however, I began to suspect that I wasn't the only one who had ventured further afield than I had any real right to. Not once did I need to speak up or point out any potential danger spots.

It was late, and with the ball underway there were no pleasure parties and few patrols out roaming the seas, but we still proceeded with caution. Ray skirted the yellow reef entirely, leading us on a weaving path that avoided all of our fishing grounds. We did swim over the closest wreck, secure in the knowledge that no children would be darting through the sagging doors or open portholes at this time of night.

I gave it a lingering glance, a thrill racing through me despite the tempestuous emotions of the day. How empty and lifeless it looked now that I had seen the real thing. Would that be what life on the surface was like? So much more vibrant and alive than my imagination had painted it?

But a shiver swept over me almost as soon as I finished the

thought, my father's words returning to haunt me. Was the surface actually far worse than I had imagined? I pushed both possibilities from my mind. I would know the truth soon enough.

The burst of energy from the shocks of the night had worn off long before we reached the edges of the territory usually traversed by our people. But I had trained with the guards for the last four years—and Ray for longer than that—so neither of us faltered.

Twice we took shelter from passing merfolk—once behind an outcropping of rock, and once behind a small patch of kelp. Only when those encounters were far behind us did Ray resume our abandoned conversation.

"I asked Nerissa about the danger the scouts posed in terms of exposure," he said without losing his focus on our path. "And it turns out that the godmothers protected us from ourselves as well as the other kingdoms."

"What do you mean?" I put on a spurt of speed so I could swim beside him.

He gave me a slight frown but didn't order me to fall back. Perhaps it had occurred to him that we weren't on patrol—we were far outside any official guard duties, in fact—and I outranked him. I almost chuckled at the thought. No, I didn't think that would have been more than a passing thought in his mind—if he thought it at all.

"Apparently," he said after a moment, "while on land, we are bound from any speech regarding Merrita or our tails."

"Even to each other?"

"Any speech at all, they said."

I frowned. "That might be limiting."

Ray turned to look at me fully. "Well, that sounds ominous. Is now a good moment to ask what exactly it is you have in mind for this grand adventure?" He quirked an eyebrow. "And please tell me this is not just some lovelorn quest to find your golden-haired storm boy."

I flushed. I must have been dazed indeed when Ray found me after the storm if I'd mentioned the boy's hair.

Ray groaned. "We are going looking for the boy! It's not too late for me to go back, you know." But he didn't slow in his forward progression.

"I am hoping to find the boy—or at least his people," I added in a rush. "Did Aunt tell you what the scouts have found up there?"

All humor dropped from Ray's face. "Why do you think I couldn't let you go alone?"

A rush of gratitude filled me.

"I am grateful, you know," I said softly.

He glanced across at me.

"I know, Lala," he said, using my sisters' childhood nickname for me. "But we're family remember—and this is what family does for each other."

For a moment I felt the sting of guilt. My father would see my flight as a betrayal. But then I remembered him suggesting I could spend a year improving my dancing, and the sensation fell away. When I returned, he would realize I had been right and that it had been love not betrayal that drove me.

Ray gave me a strange look but didn't question my thoughts.

"So you do have a plan, then?" he asked instead.

I bit my lip. It wasn't much of a plan if I was honest.

"My father spoke of a darkness, but I didn't see anything like that in the boy. I'm hoping that means his people have found a way to protect themselves from it. If we can find them, and find out how they've done it…"

"Then maybe we can protect ourselves, too," Ray said, thoughtfully, "if we're eventually driven up to find a home on the land."

I opened my mouth and then closed it again. Clearly Nerissa still hadn't told her brother everything. Ray didn't know my father held the key to raising us from the depths at will. But he had said he trusted me, and I would not speak of it even to Ray. I would keep what trust I could.

"So he told you who his people are?" Ray asked, his tone gently mocking. "While you were towing him through the waves and singing an aria?"

"Not exactly." I drew out the words, adding an apologetic grimace.

"What a surprise." Ray didn't look in the least concerned, however.

"But I've been thinking about the map," I said. "And I think we should head for Trione."

Ray considered my words for a moment. "I can only assume you have a map in that waterproof trunk of yours because I know the Merritan maps don't include the kingdoms of the land." He paused. "Not the regular ones, anyway."

I jumped on his words. "You've seen full maps, too, then? Do you think I'm right?"

"It's hard to say with certainty, but it seems as good a guess as any."

I nodded, eager to explain my reasons. "First of all, I've spent quite a bit of time working out where I was when I surfaced into that storm. And I'm fairly certain I was near the eastern coast of Trione. Plus, they're the only island. Now that Merrita is gone, anyway. So it makes sense that they might have escaped this darkness." I tried to keep the concern out of my voice. "Don't you think?"

"I would like to think the darkness was stopped by something as simple as a stretch of open water," he said. His voice said he didn't believe it, however.

But neither did he refute my points. And by my calculations, he was leading us toward the eastern coast of Trione.

"There," he said suddenly, pointing across me. "That current is heading in the right direction. If it doesn't veer off, we might actually get there by tomorrow."

I followed his lead, and we were soon being swept along too fast for easy conversation.

~

We stopped to sleep eventually, curled in among some kelp where the great plants could keep us from drifting away as we slept. They would also keep us hidden from sight if pursuers somehow managed to catch us—a possibility neither of us had spoken aloud but I knew was on both of our minds.

When I woke it was with a start and a thrashing that disturbed the kelp around us. A moment later orientation came, and with it, embarrassment. I had never slept in my mer-form before, but as far as I knew, neither had Ray, and he hadn't woken in such a manner. At least I didn't feel stiff, the cradling water having been much kinder to my body than the rocky seabed would have been.

We resumed travel with a minimum of conversation, neither of us mentioning our grumbling stomachs. Merfolk couldn't eat in our mer-forms without suffering crippling stomach cramps— the reason our people had never spread further than Merrita and the seas which surrounded it.

But all thoughts of food disappeared when the seabed began to noticeably rise. As the ocean above us became shallower and shallower, a corresponding mass of nerves and excitement rose inside me, more potent even than my hunger.

And stronger than everything else was the face of the boy from the storm. I had brushed off Ray's words, claiming it was only the boy's people that I wanted to find, but I admitted the truth to myself. I had come here for him, just as I had dreamed of doing for two years.

Color appeared before us, quickly growing closer. I recognized it easily as a reef, although it was an unfamiliar one. Bright fish darted through the rough, knobbly formations, a blue tang catching my eye and reminding me with a brief pang of my sister. Had our flight been discovered?

Resolutely I put my home from my mind. It didn't matter now —it was too late for them to stop us. The decreasing depth combined with the reef told me we had neared our destination at last.

Ray and I swam side by side as we passed over the coral, careful not to touch any of it in passing. Even in our mer-forms we weren't immune to the poison some corals released.

But soon enough we were across, the water deepening again into a flat lagoon. I dove instantly toward the bottom, running my fingers through the sandy base. The grains were fine, and my fingers sank into them in a satisfying way. I could only imagine how the land dwellers must enjoy wading and swimming in this warm, calm water.

The thought had no sooner crossed my mind than I spun myself around, looking rapidly in all directions, sudden fear gripping me. But my sharp eyesight could see no sign of thrashing legs disturbing the water. For the moment we were alone in this peaceful bay, or at least in this section of it. The lagoon stretched far to my right, curving out of sight.

Seized with a heady, giddy rush of delight at such a surreal moment, I spun again and again, twirling upward through the water, my hair twisting around itself. When I opened my eyes and saw Ray's expression, a giggle erupted from my mouth.

"Sorry," I gasped, giggling again. "It's just that it feels so glorious here—it's so light without the pressure. And so warm!"

Ray frowned. "What do you mean pressure?"

I bit my lip. I was letting my excitement get to my head. I'd forgotten it was my sisters and not Ray who knew about this particular oddity. I shrugged, trying to pass it off as inconsequential.

"Oh, just the feeling of all that water, pressing down on you. It gets worse the deeper you go. And it's cold down there. You've never noticed it? It's not painful or anything, just a mild discomfort."

Ray's eyes narrowed, his expression turning thoughtful. "No, I can't say I've ever felt such a thing. And to me this water feels the exact same temperature as the water around the barrier."

That took me by surprise. "Really? Exactly the same? How odd. It's much warmer, I assure you."

He shook his head, not returning my smile. "That sounds unpleasant. Maybe I'm starting to understand something of what constantly drew you back to the surface."

"Maybe." I shrugged again, not willing to go into the complicated mass of reasons why I had never been able to resist the lure of the waves and the sky—and the land dwellers.

"Well, we've reached Trione," he said after a pause. "What now?"

I took a deep breath. "Now we go ashore."

It turned out to be more easily said than done. I was used to transforming from my mer-form to my human one by swimming upright through a barrier. One of the earliest skills learned by mer-children was to pass through at just the right angle that your newly formed legs could step forward to smoothly take your weight.

But here the water grew shallower and shallower, crystal clear and full of tiny, darting fish. Soon we could no longer swim comfortably and had to position ourselves parallel to the sand. I reached my hands down and dug my fingers into it, propelling myself forward by walking with my hands as much as swimming with my tail. And soon enough, even that grew difficult. I glanced across at Ray.

"How much of us has to be out of the water for the transformation to occur?" I asked. "It won't stop halfway will it, leaving us with half a tail or something because we're partially in the water still?"

An even more horrifying thought occurred to me, my eyes

widening and latching on Ray. "We will transform, won't we? It's not the barrier itself that does it?"

Why had I never thought of this possibility before? I had spent years dreaming of the moment when I would step up, above the sea, and it had somehow never occurred to me that such a feat might be beyond my power.

I gulped. No. It had to work. What else would happen when Merrita rose from the ocean again? We would be land dwellers once more, no longer enclosed by the bubble or limited to our capital city.

I took a final deep breath with my mermaid lungs. There was only one way to find out. Pushing up from the sand, I straightened my arms, my upper half breaking through into the air. I gazed around with wide eyes while water ran down my face and dripped from my hair to the sodden upper half of my shift. The sun was bright and hot, the sand of the beach almost blindingly white. But I could still make out the lush green of vegetation beyond the sand.

For a moment I felt triumph. Then I realized I had felt no tingle. Looking down, I saw green scales shimmering beneath the water.

CHAPTER 8

*I*t hadn't worked. Horror washed over me. It hadn't worked. It was just like the times I had pushed my head above the surface back out in the open ocean. My tail remained.

I stared back toward Ray, his face visible through the clear water. But he looked merely thoughtful. After a moment his lips moved, but up in the air, I couldn't hear him. A moment later his own head emerged from the water.

"Try getting some of your tail out of the water," he said.

I didn't reply, too eager to try the suggestion. Twisting awkwardly into a sort of sitting position, I used the muscles in my tail to launch myself up, as if I could stand on the sand with my fin.

I shot upward, moving too fast, but all of my concerns fell away as the familiar tingle swept down from my head. I let out a gasping cry, and then I was teetering and falling, my body unpracticed at such a move, and my legs not yet formed enough to catch me.

I twisted as I fell, my hands thrusting out to catch me. They crashed down into the water, sending droplets spraying in all directions, and I realized that I now knelt on all fours in the shallow water of the cove. In human form.

For several long seconds I remained frozen in position, taking deep, glorious breaths of fresh air. Then a fish darted between my hands, and a splashing sound made me turn my head.

Ray stood beside me, his attention turned toward the beach. He wore the same leather guard's outfit he had worn when he confronted me in the sculpture garden of the sea palace, but it looked different somehow, here on the shore.

I gave a quiet sigh and found another reason to be thankful we had no audience. No doubt Ray had learned from my example and found a far more elegant way to manage the transformation than I had done.

But I didn't dwell on it for long, scrambling up to join him in standing upright. He gave me a mocking bow, his eyes glinting at me in silent laughter as he gestured for me to precede him.

I shook my head but stepped forward anyway. In three steps I had overtaken him, and in three more I had stepped out of the gentle lapping of the almost nonexistent waves.

I wiggled my toes and felt the sand beneath them before a more adventurous wave raced across the sand and foamed around my feet. I looked down at the white bubbles and laughed. How utterly strange and entirely captivating.

I stepped further forward, my feet sinking slightly into the wet sand and leaving indentations of my steps behind me. Soon I came to a strange line across the sand which I quickly realized was created by the wet sand meeting dry sand. I stared at it blankly for a moment before remembering what I had read of tides in my books. Perhaps this was the mysterious high tide mark I had seen mentioned more than once. How different dry sand was from wet sand. We had no appreciable amount of sand inside the barrier.

I turned with excitement to point it out to Ray, but he had already stridden past, wasting no time on such things as the feel of the sand beneath his feet. He stood, surveying the beach with a critical eye, as if looking for threats.

The warmth of the sun above me reflected back from the sand beneath our feet, cocooning us in light and heat. Nothing could seem further from the dark picture my father had painted of the kingdoms of the land. But appearances could be deceiving, and Ray was right to be on his guard.

Kneeling down, I unsealed my bag and carefully removed my wrapped sword. By the time Ray walked over to join me, I had already re-stowed the oiled leather and was strapping the belt around my waist.

I could see the light of misgiving still in his eye as he regarded my weapon, but he made no comment this time. He had refrained from bringing his own trident, but I could see all three of his usual knives in their normal places about his person.

Before either of us could speak, my stomach gurgled loudly, and he winced. I tried to remember the last time I had eaten, and failed. It must have been before the ball because I had been far too agitated to eat anything at the festivities. Thankfully Ray produced some dried fish and seaweed from his own bag, and we ate a quick meal standing in the sand.

I had barely finished when a strange beat reached my ears, growing rapidly louder. I frowned toward the trees that blocked my view further ashore in time to see movement. Several huge shapes burst out onto the beach.

I screamed, stumbling backward, and even Ray seemed frozen for a moment in shock. A human laugh sounded, rough and unpleasant, and my mind grasped what I was seeing.

These were not strange monstrous creatures—half-human, half-beast, like some land version of the merfolk. They were humans riding on the backs of...horses, I realized several beats too late. They must be horses. I had seen an illustration of one once, but the reality of it had taken me by surprise.

"Look what we have here," said the one who had laughed, pulling on leather straps that encircled the head of the animal. The horse slowed and turned, apparently in response to his movements.

The others following behind did likewise, and Ray and I soon found ourselves at the center of a moving circle of long legs, sharp hooves, and heaving sides. They were so large.

"He looks strong," said another one, eyeing Ray.

Ray drew one of his knives and stepped protectively in front of me in one fluid motion. But the first man merely chuckled.

"Perfect," he said, his tone turning brisk. "Let's scoop them up and be on our way."

Fear rushed through me, loosening the paralysis that had gripped me at the strange sight.

"The faster, the better," one of the other men muttered, casting what looked like a fearful glance up the beach toward where it curved away northward.

The leader eyed the speaker aggressively, jerking his head forward, and after a half-second's hesitation, the cautious one kicked his foot against his mount's side, breaking away from their circle to approach us. He wasn't as large as some of the others, and he looked almost reluctant as he slid down to join us on the sand.

Ray shifted slightly as if about to attack.

"I wouldn't try that," said the leader, dark humor in his voice. His eyes flicked behind us just as I felt an arm grab me around my waist and a cold point touch my neck.

"Ray," I managed to gasp, but it was unnecessary. He had already seen.

Indecision flickered in his eyes, before he glanced up at the ring around us. His shoulders slumped, and his hand dropped.

"It'll go better for you if you don't fight," the cautious man said in a quiet voice as he wrested the knife from Ray's unre-sisting hands. "They won't harm her as long as you cooperate."

I could do nothing but watch as he bound Ray's hands and beckoned for another man outside the circle to come forward and help him. The second man left his mount standing several paces away, leading forward an extra horse without a rider.

"Can you ride?" the cautious man asked Ray who shook his head mutely.

The man looked almost apologetic at that answer, but he didn't hesitate again as he and the second man hoisted Ray between them and slung him over the back of the free mount. He lay on his stomach, his bound hands dangling, and I realized with a sick feeling that I must be about to join him.

I could smell the sour scent of the man who held me captive, as if he hadn't bathed in weeks despite the enticing water only steps away from us. Father had been right about this place. Its beauty concealed only a rotting core.

I could barely choke back the tears. But when the cautious man turned to me, another length of rope appearing in his hands, he paused. This time the leader didn't reprimand him, all of the riders pausing, as he did, to look up the beach.

A distant sound—something like the beat that had preceded the riders' arrival—reached my ears, and it occurred to me that it must be the sound of horses' hooves. But I had no time to process this information before a challenging shout rang across the sand.

"Quick!" shouted the leader, as several of the men yelled, "Guards!"

Hope rose inside me at the word, but the leader gestured, and the man holding me moved too fast for me to take advantage of the moment. Dropping his blade, he spun me around and tossed me up into the air. For a brief moment I experienced the strange sensation of flight—like to swimming and yet unlike at the same time—and then I collided with skin and bone.

Most of me landed against the flank of the horse, but the rider managed to catch me beneath the arms and haul me up to join him. There was no place on the saddle for a second rider, and I lay awkwardly draped across the horse's back.

A flurry of movement surrounded me as the three men on the sand flung themselves into their saddles, and the whole group spurred their mounts into movement. For a dizzying moment, I could feel only the strange rocking sensation of the horse, and then renewed shouts from behind goaded me into action.

I no longer had a blade against my throat, and there had been no time for them to tie me. I exploded into movement of my own, thrashing and writhing, too off-balance to use any trained blows. But my elbow landed hard against the man's sternum, and the side of my fist collided with his face.

He cursed and pulled back, unbalancing us further, and I began to slip. As I went down, I realized my mistake, the sharp hooves of the horse flying terrifyingly close to my face. But it was too late to do anything but throw myself as far away as possible, curling into a ball as I fell.

I hit the ground hard, grateful for the sand which cushioned my landing. I allowed myself only a moment of assessment. Somehow, it seemed the hooves had all missed me, so I pushed myself up, suppressing a wave of dizziness.

My captor had come off with me, both of us left behind by the horse who was keeping pace with the rest of the group. The man didn't seem to have been as fortunate as me, a gash across his leg already starting to soak his clothes with red. But he still managed to stumble to his feet, looking after his disappearing companions.

I risked a glance in the same direction, hoping to see Ray following my lead, but instead I saw the leader glance back toward us. Anger crossed his face, but he didn't pull up or turn to come back. Apparently he meant to abandon both me and his own man.

Ray's head lifted, looking back toward me, and for a second

our eyes met. Then something flashed, and he slumped back down, hanging limply across the horse. The leader's arm pulled back, and I saw with relief that it had been the hilt of his dagger, not the blade, that he had driven against Ray's head.

A wordless yell from the man on the sand in front of me pulled my attention back to my own predicament. The pursuing hooves sounded loud now, and on the edge of my vision I could see churning legs and brown flanks entering our stretch of the beach.

But I didn't dare wait for rescue. Not with my attempted captor standing mere feet away, and no knowledge of who this second group of riders might be. My body responded instinctively, my feet planting firmly in the sand as I pulled my sword from its scabbard in one smooth movement.

The man in front of me backed away, eyeing me nervously, while several things happened at once. My eyes caught on a tall, golden-haired young man who rode his horse as if they really were one creature. He seemed to be leading the pursuing group, although one horse kept pace with his. It was ridden by a young woman with matching golden hair whose long, elegant skirts seemed somewhat at odds with the excited, martial look in her eyes.

"Make sure she's safe," the young man called, "I'll pursue the rest of them."

His sister—because it had to be his sister given their almost shocking similarity of look—just rolled her eyes, having already turned her mount's head toward me before he spoke. It was so like an interaction I could imagine having with Ray that in spite of everything, a surge of amusement and fellow feeling filled me.

The young man didn't slow his pace, but he turned in his saddle to gesture for two of the guards behind him to pull off with his sister. I didn't see which of them obeyed, however, because as he turned back, his eyes briefly landed on me.

For a second his eyes swept over me, still standing with my sword outstretched—and then our gazes met. Fear, relief, amusement, pain, everything fell away to be replaced with shock. It was *him*. The boy who laughed at the storm.

His eyes widened, too, my shock mirrored on his face, and then he had turned again and pounded away across the sand.

CHAPTER 9

$\mathcal{I}$t took several endless seconds for my immediate surroundings to come back into focus. By the time they had, the three newcomers had all dismounted, and my captor had surrendered to the two guards. The girl showed no interest in him, instead approaching me. She had lifted her long skirts, tucking them up somehow so they didn't trail in the sand, and bare feet poked out from underneath.

My eyes latched onto her toes, struggling to take in anything more relevant in the scene, my mind still jumping between an image of Ray's slumped form and the boy. But, no. Even in my one brief glimpse of him, I had seen my mistake. I had been thinking of him for more than two years as a boy, when he had grown into a man.

"Are you hurt?" The girl's voice, concerned and kind, broke through my haze. I must look terrible—disheveled, shocked, and dazed.

I forced myself to focus on her face. "A little bruised, but otherwise unharmed. Thanks to you."

The girl brushed my gratitude aside. "I only wish we'd been

here sooner. It looked as if you had a companion with you, although I didn't get a good look."

I nodded quickly. "Yes, my uncle. They took him—across the back of a horse. He—" I could hear my voice rising and gaining a panicked edge, so I cut myself off.

The girl laid a sympathetic hand on my arm. "My brother is pursuing them, as you saw. He will do all in his power to capture them and free your uncle."

I drew a steadying breath and nodded. I had trusted the boy I met in that storm enough to leave the ocean for him. I could trust him with Ray. I hoped.

"Where's Teddy?" asked a new voice, making both me and the girl start.

A child stepped into view. She picked her way across the sand toward us, having emerged from the trees directly across from where we stood. Her face suggested she was no more than ten, and her short skirts—tucked up as the older girl's were, but in her case rising above her knees—seemed to confirm it. Her figure was tall and lithe for that age, though, and she seemed unafraid of the odd scene that confronted her.

"Daisy!" The older girl spoke the name in a voice of long-suffering. "You're not supposed to be here."

The girl grinned. "I'm never supposed to be anywhere interesting. And I knew as soon as Teddy expressly forbade me from following you that you were off to do something interesting." She looked at the bound man standing between the two guards and then at me. "And I can see I was right."

The older girl groaned. "Teddy should have known better than to say something so foolish to you. I knew it as soon as he said it."

Daisy smiled at me conspiratorially. "He was far too excited to show any sense—which was another clue that I had best be off after you straight away." She adopted a world-weary expression that made me want to chuckle. "Brothers, you know."

"I'm afraid I don't know," I said. "I only have sisters."

"Well they can be just as much trouble as brothers," the older girl muttered, glaring balefully at Daisy, confirming that the three of them were family.

"Who are you?" Daisy asked, examining me with even more interest. "And why is he tied up?"

I looked quickly across at my rescuer, unsure how much she would want me to say about the attack. I expected her to tell her younger sister that it wasn't anything to do with her—that's what my older sisters would have said to me, I was sure. But the older girl seemed to have accepted the futility of such an effort, instead replying to the question.

"He's one of the raiders."

Daisy turned to him with a look of disgust. "Filthy traitor," she spat.

"Daisy!" The older girl looked horrified.

"But he is, Millie! And you know it."

So they were Millie and Daisy. And their brother was Teddy. I rolled the name around in my mind, deciding it fit the golden-haired, laughing boy of my imagination. And if their clothes and the guards were any indication, they must be wealthy or titled, or both. The children of the local lord, I decided, even if the younger girl didn't act like it. Perhaps this was a more remote part of the island kingdom.

One thing was clear, however. They represented the official, lawful part of the kingdom, and they were nothing like the men who had abducted Ray. Which meant I might be right after all in thinking there was more to the kingdoms of the land than the corrupting evil my father feared.

Daisy turned to me. "Then I suppose you must be one of their victims—or intended victims anyway." She looked me up and down with widened eyes. "Did they steal your clothes?"

"Daisy!" Millie looked mildly embarrassed. "I'm sorry, she says the most outrageous things." But her own eyes strayed to my simple shift, as well, and I could see the hesitation in them.

I had chosen it over my royal gowns in an effort to blend in and not draw attention to myself, but clearly I had chosen poorly. From their own clothes, I guessed that I looked to them as if I was wearing my underclothing only. Among the merfolk, simple clothing and single layers were favored by many since they dried faster when you returned through the barrier.

"Umm…" I said, stupidly, trying to think what I could say to cover up my blunder.

Daisy seemed to take pity on me, rushing on to a new topic.

"I like your sword. I've been begging and begging Teddy to teach me how to use one, but he keeps refusing."

"And thank goodness for that," Millie said with an exaggerated shudder. "Few images raise as much terror in my heart as the idea of you running around waving a sword."

Daisy scowled. "I would be an excellent swordswoman." She turned to me with a calculating look. "Will you teach me?"

My chuckle instantly died, and I quickly sheathed my sword, using the movement to hide my lack of response.

"Ha!" Millie clapped a hand against her leg. "She's known you for all of five minutes, and she already knows better than to agree to such a request." Her brow creased, and she turned to me.

"I don't think I ever got your name."

"Oh, it's…uh…Isla," I said, too caught off guard to say anything else.

Ray and I should have used the journey here to discuss how we would introduce ourselves, but we hadn't. I took comfort in the fact that they could hardly know the names of the sea king's daughters if they didn't even know of the existence of his kingdom.

Daisy glanced up and down the beach. "But where is Teddy? You never answered. And where are the others?"

"The other guards, you mean?" asked Millie. "They're with Teddy."

"No, I meant the other ones like her." She pointed at me. "The raiders never take people on their own—they always abduct more than one at a time."

"Efficient raiders—great," Millie muttered before directing an accusing stare at her little sister. "You've been listening at doors again if you know that."

Daisy just shrugged. "How else would I hear anything interesting?"

Millie appeared to restrain herself with some difficulty. "There was another," was all she said in the end. "Her uncle."

Daisy's eyes lit up. "That's where Teddy is then, I suppose. Chasing them down?"

Millie nodded.

"Do you think he'll catch them?" Daisy asked. "Should we be worried?"

I stiffened, trying to remember how many guards Teddy had taken with him. In the whirl of everything happening at once, I hadn't even stopped to wonder if he might be in any serious danger from the raiders.

But Millie shook her head. "He had more than enough—" She broke off, her head swinging around to stare down the beach. "Wait. Is that hooves?"

Daisy and I stared after her, a mass of movement soon becoming clear against the white sand. We all stood in silence, our attention focused on the approaching riders.

It didn't take long to pick out Teddy at the front of them, his dark horse taller and more elegant than the others, and his form straighter. But my roving eyes could find no sign of Ray. A whirling mass of tension sprang to life in my stomach.

Millie must have seen the same thing because she stepped quickly to my side, once again placing a reassuring hand on my arm.

"Don't worry," she said, her words low and fast. "The raiders must know this whole island intimately because they always manage to slip away, but we know they don't harm the men they take." She gave a sigh. "In fact, the men all seem to decide to join them for unfathomable reasons."

She directed a glare at the bound man standing a few steps away, and I followed her gaze. He was watching us with a wary expression. I looked between him and Daisy.

"Did you say they never take only one person? Do they usually take only men?"

Millie shook her head. "They don't seem so discriminating—they've even taken children and the elderly on occasion. But it's only the men who have been seen riding around at their sides."

"The man who bound Ray said they wouldn't harm me as long as he cooperated."

"Be quiet!" The man standing between the two guards went from sullen compliance to bristling hostility in an instant, and it took both of them to restrain him from lunging toward me. "Don't you say a word! They'll think I was the one to talk!"

He sounded desperate, his face twisted with fear as the guards wrestled him to his knees. Millie and I had both drawn back, but she stepped forward again, looking down at him with an arrested look. When she finally looked back at me, I knew what she was thinking.

"It would make sense," she said slowly. "Quite a clever plan in a way."

"Clever? Despicable, you mean," I said, my gorge rising, and my father's description of these kingdoms coming back to the fore.

"Oh, certainly," Millie said absently. "But the important point is confirming it, and then working out how to use it to our advantage. It rather changes everything. They must—" Her words cut off as she noticed her younger sister watching her intently.

"It must be considered," she finished, rather lamely.

Daisy looked as if she was about to take issue at this, but the approaching riders had nearly reached us, cutting off whatever she had planned to say. Teddy outstripped the others, arriving several lengths ahead of them.

He slid down from his horse's back before the animal had finished moving, landing lightly in the sand without losing his balance. His eyes were fixed on me, and with a thrill, I remembered the way his face had mirrored my own shock as he rode away.

Our eyes locked again, and if I had thought my stomach was writhing before, it was nothing to the fluttering thrill that filled every inch of me now. Finally, after all this time, we stood face to face again, our eyes locked. I could see the green of the ocean in his and make out every angle of his face. I was right that he had grown and changed, his face maturing in a way that was hard to pinpoint. All I knew was that I couldn't look away, although Millie started to speak.

"I see you didn't catch them. I've just been assuring Isla that the raiders won't harm her—"

But Teddy ignored his sister, reaching me at last and halting a mere arm length away. My breath caught as I tried to read the emotion in his eyes. The connection between us crackled and writhed, as bright and dangerous as a glow eel. At any moment it would consume me.

And then his eyes dropped from my face to the sword now hanging at my waist.

"Where did you get that sword?" he asked, shock and accusation in his voice.

CHAPTER 10

A bucket of sea water tipped over my head couldn't have more effectively doused my quivering nerves. It hadn't been me that inspired the shock on his face as he rode past, it had been the sword in my hands. The sword that had never really been mine because it had been his first.

"I...I found it," I managed to get out.

"Impossible," he said.

"Teddy!" Millie's scandalized tone reminded me that Teddy and I weren't the only ones on the beach. "Between you and Daisy you're going to bring dishonor on our whole family. Poor Isla must think we're utterly uncivilized."

"But Millie..." He turned to his sister. "That's my sword. The one Father gave me on my sixteenth birthday. To console me about Gabe going back to Talinos. I barely took it off to sleep that whole year, remember? I would recognize it anywhere."

"But you lost that sword," said Millie, her brow crinkling. "In the—" She broke off, her eyes widening.

"Yes, exactly," he said. "In the ocean, during that storm." He turned back to me. "Let me see it."

Trembling now, my mind racing as I tried to think how to

explain myself, I drew the blade and handed it to him. I had barely been on shore for an hour, and I had already given myself away. But if Ray was right, I wouldn't be able to tell them the truth even if I wanted to. What would they do to me when I refused to give them answers?

Teddy held the sword out, swinging it experimentally.

"Yes," he breathed. "It's definitely my sword." His eyes bored into me.

"Isla said she found it," Millie said dismissively. "And I don't see what's so astonishing about that. You lost it in the ocean, and flotsam from shipwrecks washes up on shore all the time."

"I'm sorry," I said quickly, desperate for Teddy to stop looking at me like that. Or maybe I never wanted him to stop. I didn't know what I thought, and it terrified me. "I didn't realize...I never meant to *steal*—"

"Of course you didn't," Millie said briskly. "And my twin is well aware of the laws regarding salvaging flotsam. It may have been his sword to begin with, but it's yours now."

Teddy, however, didn't seem ready to let the matter drop.

"But that storm drove us well out into open sea before the captain managed to turn the ship west to head back through the strait to Marin," he said. "And you know how sea water corrodes steel. But look at the condition it's in." He swung it again. "It doesn't make any sense."

He let the tip drop and stepped toward me, even closer than he'd stood before. I forgot how to breathe as I noticed how broad his shoulders had become and how much taller he was than me, although I wasn't short. Up close I could see that he had the faintest dusting of freckles across his nose.

"Red," he whispered, his hand reaching up to gently catch one of the long strands of my hair, wrapping it around his finger as his eyes roved over my face.

I tried to swallow, my mouth suddenly dry. This time there was no mistaking the hint of wonder behind his shock.

"Theodore of Trione," Millie's voice rang out. "Unhand her at once."

"I would call it more of an auburn, personally," said Daisy in a conversational tone, as if Teddy had been asking for an opinion on the matter.

Teddy let his hand drop, my hair slipping free, and stepped back half a step.

"What has come over you?" Millie asked, regarding him with both hands on her hips.

"But Millie..." His voice was low, and he seemed to be having almost as much trouble speaking as I was having breathing. "Her hair...the sword..."

Millie's eyes widened, and she held up her hand abruptly, cutting him off. "Oh no, you don't! I thought we'd moved past all that nonsense about your ocean girl."

My breath caught, and I realized I must have started breathing again after all. His ocean girl? What did that mean? Had he remembered me the way I had remembered my golden-haired storm boy? My heart was pounding harder than it had when the raider held his knife to my throat.

"We are nipping this in the bud right now." Millie turned to me. "Do you like to spend your time out in the deep ocean, Isla? Not in a ship, mind you, just cavorting through the waves? In the middle of storms?" I could almost hear the eye roll in her voice.

"I...uh..." I looked wildly between them. I had no intention of blurting out the truth, but I could feel my throat closing over anyway, as if to prevent any words that might come slipping out. The godmothers' enchantment.

"Precisely," Millie said, apparently taking my confusion as bewilderment at the question. "I once again apologize for my fanciful brother, Isla. He didn't used to be given to such wild notions."

But Teddy was still watching me, a light in his eyes suggesting he wasn't as convinced as his sister. Probably because he knew he had been rescued from the water by a girl—however impossible that seemed. He didn't seem to recognize me with the certainty I felt about him, but then he had been drowning at the time, blinded and winded by the waves as I was not.

"The girl in the ocean had the most beautiful singing voice," Teddy said. "Do you sing, Isla?"

Panic flared, and then I remembered. My hand flew involuntarily to my throat.

"No," I managed to make myself say. "I can't sing." The words hurt far more than I had ever expected them to.

"Nonsense," said Daisy, joining the conversation again. "Everyone can sing. The only question is how well they can sing. Teddy has always said his ocean girl has the voice of the sea itself. I think it's half the reason he's in love with her. But there's also every chance he's in love with a deathbed mirage, so I'm not sure we can take his word for it."

My heart seized at her casual use of the word love. Teddy loved me? I barely heard Daisy commanding me to sing so we could all get on with our day.

"I…" I gaped at her, my eyes swinging wildly between them.

"Don't worry," said Daisy cheerfully. "I myself am an incredibly enthusiastic and utterly terrible singer, so I can promise they've heard worse."

At any other time, her frank admission would have charmed me. But I was rapidly descending into some sort of panic attack, and I could barely think.

"Sing, Isla." Teddy's soft voice cut through everything else, and without thinking, I took a deep breath, opened my mouth, and sang.

Everyone present winced, and Daisy even slapped her hands over her ears, gazing at me open-mouthed. I quickly shut the sound off, appalled at the horrifying squawk that had come out in place of notes.

"I'm so sorry, I—" I buried my face in my hands, mortified, but not before I got a glimpse of the light disappearing from Teddy's eyes, like his emotions had been swiftly shuttered away.

"There's someone who sings worse than me!" Daisy sounded delighted.

I felt small arms encircle me and slowly lowered my hands.

"I love you," Daisy declared. "You're my new best friend. Come and live with us forever."

"Well, that answers that," said Millie briskly. "Hopefully we can now get back to the *important* matters at hand."

I tried to muster a weak smile, but my face didn't seem to be cooperating. Relief, that's what I was feeling. Definitely relief. Because Merrita's secret was safe, and these kind people weren't even upset at my not answering any of their questions. It only felt like heartbreak because I was so confused by the many emotions of the morning.

I almost had myself convinced until Teddy turned back to me with a closed, polite smile on his face and the pain started all over again. Teddy was in love with his ocean girl and, as far as he was concerned, that wasn't me.

"What are you doing here?" he asked Daisy suddenly, as if he'd only just registered her presence. "I specifically told you not to follow us."

"Yes, and a great deal of good saying that has ever done," Millie said dryly. "You would have done better telling her we were only going on a routine patrol and inviting her to join us."

"As if the two of you ever go on routine patrols," said Daisy with an eye roll. "I don't know why you would think me stupid enough to fall for that."

Millie shook her head. "To tell the truth, I didn't think the apparent sighting of the raiders was likely to come to anything. They've never dared come in so close before."

"I had an instinct it was real," Teddy said in a slightly superior tone.

Millie instantly snorted. "Ha! What you had was a burning

desire to go blazing off at the head of a squadron of guards. I know perfectly well you've been dying to do so ever since Father decided to put you in charge of hunting the raiders down."

Teddy looked like he wanted to argue this point, but after a swift glance toward the rest of us, he settled for saying, "Don't worry, I remember he put both of us in charge, not just me."

"Certainly," Millie said. "But I know better than to go haring off after any and every rumor."

"Yes," said Daisy in a deceptively amiable voice. "That's why you stayed calmly at home rather than leaping onto the closest mount despite not being dressed in a riding habit."

Millie flushed slightly and then laughed, the sound so merry it couldn't help but lighten my spirits slightly.

"Don't worry," said a deep voice in my ear. "You get used to them. Sort of."

The speaker was the only one of Teddy's guards to have dismounted. He looked older than the others, already well into middle age. An experienced captain, I suspected, assigned to keep an eye on the young twins.

I nodded at him, relieved my distress and confusion were being taken as a natural consequence of meeting the trio of siblings.

"I'm Captain Flint, by the way," he said, confirming my suspicion. "I'm sorry we weren't able to catch the raiders and rescue your...uncle, was it?"

I nodded, instantly guilty for allowing my mind to be consumed by Teddy while Ray was experiencing unknown suffering.

"For what it's worth," the captain continued, "I do agree that he's unlikely to be harmed. That doesn't seem to be their way, though they're ruthless enough. But they don't do things for no reason, and they see people as tools. And a dead person is of no value to them."

This time my smile came more easily, my relief at his words

prompting a more genuine emotion. Not that I hadn't believed Millie, precisely, but the words held more weight coming from someone who clearly had more experience.

The captain cleared his throat. "Your Highness," he said, and I jumped, the blood draining from my face.

But I had avoided all their questions! I'd escaped detection. How did he know?

I looked up and found he wasn't looking at me at all. He was looking toward Teddy. And I could see now that not only Teddy, but both of his sisters had turned in response to the captain's words. All four of them seemed oblivious to my internal panic.

"May I suggest we get the prisoner back to the palace before his friends decide to attempt a rescue?" the captain continued.

The palace. Not some remote corner of the kingdom then. No wonder Millie had said the raiders didn't usually dare come so close. My overloaded brain struggled to come to terms with the ramifications of this information.

Teddy wasn't just the wealthy son of some minor noble. He was a prince. Theodore of Trione, Millie had called him. Prince Theodore. He was a prince which meant any minute now he would ride away to his palace, and I would never see him again.

Because here in this kingdom, with my words and voice bound by enchantment, I was nobody at all. Worse than nobody, I was a stranger without home or people.

The reality of my situation hit me afresh. Ray was gone. I believed these young royals and the captain when they said they would keep searching until they found the raiders and freed him, but it didn't change the reality of right now. I was alone with nowhere to go and nowhere to stay. I had none of the local currency, and I could only imagine how it would be received if I wandered into an inn in my shift and tried to pay my lodging with one of the pieces of jewelry I had stuffed into my bag during my frantic packing.

I shook my head, trying to stay focused on what was

happening around me. Perhaps I could manage a word with the captain before they all left. He might be able to advise me on where I could go.

Everyone else's attention seemed to be on the captured raider who had stirred at the suggestion of rescue but didn't look hopeful. Millie gave him a measuring look before nodding.

"Captain Flint is right, Teddy. And Isla and I have come up with a theory that could prove of great importance in our search. But I don't want to discuss it here." She gave a significant look at Daisy.

"You and Isla?" Teddy looked back at me, his interest reignited.

The captain also threw me a look of surprise, but he didn't allow himself to be distracted. Without waiting for further agreement from the royals, he gestured for the two guards securing the prisoner to get the man up onto the back of one of the horses.

A guard came forward, leading two horses and a pony. Apparently someone had retrieved Daisy's mount from behind the tree line. Millie took her horse's reins and gave Teddy a look.

"Do you think you could return Isla's blade to her so we can get moving?"

"*Her* blade?" He sounded offended, but he was looking at his sister, not me.

"It may have been your blade once," Millie replied tartly, "but I think you'll find the scabbard is currently attached to her waist. So I suggest you hurry up and give it back to her. As well as having things to talk about, I—for one—am ravenous."

Teddy hesitated for only a second before turning to me and offering me the sword, hilt first.

"I'm sorry," he said. "I'm being very graceless. Of course Millie's right, and the sword belongs to you now. It's only because it has sentimental attachment, which I daresay seems most foolish given we're talking about a piece of steel."

His easy smile made me melt a little, and I reached for the

buckle. He had no idea how much I understood having an emotional attachment to a piece of steel.

"Of course you should have it, given it was yours first," I said, although it hurt a little to think of parting with it.

"Not now!" Millie called to us, stilling my hands. "The two of you can sort it out later. For now, we need to get moving. You heard Captain Flint."

"Yes, indeed," Teddy said. "And I hope you'll let me give you a ride. Just to show that I can be gallant, in the normal course of things."

"Give me a ride?" I asked, confused.

"You can ride with one of the guards if you prefer, of course," Teddy said quickly, looking rather downcast.

"I don't understand," I said. "Ride where?"

He looked at me blankly. "Why, to the palace, naturally." He glanced toward his sister. "Millie did say the two of you have some theory or other, didn't she? Plus we can hardly leave you here alone when your companion has been taken in such a manner. And practically within stone's throw of the castle, too."

Millie, now mounted, edged her horse closer. "Of course you must come with us, Isla. Didn't you hear Daisy? She intends for you to live with us forever."

She smiled, but the expression dropped away when she caught my apprehensive look. "Oh, I'm sorry, I was only jesting. Of course we don't mean to keep you prisoner forever or any such thing. I'm afraid I assumed from…" Her voice trailed away for a moment, and I got the distinct impression she was trying not to eye my shift. "I'm afraid I assumed you were a stranger to these parts. If I have it wrong, however, and you have a home nearby, or someone expecting you, we will arrange for your safe passage to them. But I still hope you'll join us for a meal first."

"No, you're right," I said. "I'm not from this region." I nibbled on my lip before letting my words out in a rush. "In truth, I'm not familiar with horses, and I've never ridden one before. If I look uncertain, well…he's very big!"

Teddy laughed, looking instantly contrite.

"Oh, I'm sorry! And here I am needing to offer you yet another apology. I swear I'm normally much better mannered. But I promise you, Waverider is much better behaved than his rider. He'll carry you gently, and I won't let you fall."

I couldn't resist such words. Nodding, I stepped forward and, at Teddy's invitation, rested a careful hand against the horse's flank. He felt soft and warm, his sides moving with his breath. His ear flicked toward me, but otherwise he remained motionless, seeming to know that Teddy wanted him to be particularly well behaved.

Teddy swung himself into the saddle with practiced ease, and a guard stepped forward with a polite nod to offer me cupped hands. I stared at him blankly, and he had to direct me to place my foot into them and use them like a step.

Once I understood what he wanted, however, it proved an effective tool, his hands launching me upward so that I easily gained the necessary height. And it was so very high.

I stared down at the ground uneasily. Stepping out onto the land had seemed like a big enough step for the day, and yet here I found myself already perched far above it. I reminded myself it was, in fact, my second time on horseback. But the panicked seconds draped over my captor's horse hardly seemed to count— and the conclusion of that ride was far better forgotten. At least for the moment.

Then Teddy's steadying hand went around my waist, and it was forgotten.

PART II
THE LAND KING'S PALACE

*W*e rode north along the curving sand of the bay, the lagoon sparkling, calm and blue, to our right while the rest of the island stretched out green and lush to our left. My waist burned where only the simple material of my shift separated me from Teddy's arm, and with my mind no longer on the animal beneath me, I found my body adjusting itself naturally to the swaying rhythm of the creature's walk.

As the beach curved, I realized that we had been at the southern end of the great bay that shaped the northeastern edge of the island. I could picture it from the maps—facing out into the open ocean. I hadn't imagined they would build their palace on such an exposed part of the island, but now that I knew about the protection of the reef, and the great lagoon it formed, I could understand why they had chosen such an idyllic spot.

The northeastern point of the island was a small peninsula, jutting out toward the southern tip of Talinos and creating a wide strait. Seeing the map in my mind, I realized it must be the strait Teddy had referred to when he mentioned their earlier journey to Marin. The journey that had encountered the storm.

In the distance, I could make out the shape of a large building, and I realized the palace must be built on the northern point of the bay, just before the peninsula began.

"Waverider likes you," Teddy said, breaking into my thoughts. "Are you sure you've never ridden before?"

"Quite sure," I said, a small smile pulling at my face.

We still had smaller animals—cats, dogs, chickens—in Merrita, but the larger animals, and the birds, had failed to thrive away from the sun and the wind. Unable to escape into the ocean as we did, they had stubbornly refused to breed and all died out within a generation.

"Were you and your uncle on your way to the capital when you were attacked?" Teddy asked. "Are you from one of the southern villages or the western forests, perhaps?"

I hesitated, wondering what would be safest to say. As crown prince, surely Teddy knew all the parts of his own kingdom whereas I knew nothing of the geography or customs of Trione. Already I had shown myself to be an outsider.

"Actually," I said, "we don't come from Trione at all. But we had heard your kingdom was a hospitable place, and we hoped we might find shelter here."

It felt better to speak the truth, even if I was leading him to false conclusions. I just hoped he would be satisfied with such a vague answer.

He just nodded, however, his chin brushing lightly against the top of my head.

"With all the recent turmoil, you're hardly the first new arrival to Trione." He straightened behind me, as if suddenly struck by a thought. "I suppose you come from southern Talinos. It makes sense that my sword would have washed up there. It's good to know that Talinosians are starting to venture beyond their own borders again."

There was a smile in his voice although I didn't understand his meaning. I didn't dare ask, though, afraid to discourage him from the conclusion that I was Talinosian. In the few short minutes I had been in their presence, I had already nearly come to grief. As much as I longed to pour out a stream of questions about the state of the kingdoms, I had no idea how to form them without giving away my ignorance—ignorance no true land dweller would have.

"But this is not the welcome you hoped for, I'm sure," he said, his voice turning gentle. "And on behalf of my kingdom, I am most sorry for it. It would be daunting for anyone to find themselves alone in a new place when they had expected to have a companion beside them. My family will be more than happy to accommodate you at the palace until your uncle is rescued."

"That is very generous, Your Highness," I said, a little doubtfully.

I could feel the relief of his offer all the way down to my toes, but I kept reminding myself that I wasn't a visiting princess here. Was it proper for me to accept such a generous offer?

"Excellent!" Teddy said, in a tone that suggested as far as he was concerned the matter was decided. I hesitated internally for a second longer before deciding to make no protest. I hoped to find answers in Trione, and what better place to find them than the palace? If I could only think of a subtle enough way to ask.

I looked up, toward the building in question, and my eyes widened.

"Oh!" The involuntary exclamation fell from my lips before I could stop it.

"It's beautiful, isn't it?" said Teddy behind me, taking my shock for admiration.

"Very," I breathed. And it was.

The palace sat on the very edge of the beach where the rocky ground of the peninsula began, extending down to the sand itself. It should have looked incongruous to step directly from sand onto white marble, and yet somehow it did not.

My eyes moved over the innumerable towers, both round and square, that seemed to make up the bulk of the structure. Their differing heights were crowned with cupolas of various sizes, some gilt by the hands of artisans and some by the sun itself glinting off their glass surfaces. But it was to the ground level that my gaze was inevitably drawn, settling on a long, straight wall of transparent crystal allowing a glimpse beyond at polished wooden floors and golden chandeliers.

"The crystal ballroom of the godmothers," I breathed, leaning forward instinctively and nearly toppling from Waverider.

Teddy's arm tightened around me, steadying me.

"Yes." He sounded proud. "It's our most famous feature. Everyone is always astonished when they first see it. Whatever my ancestors did must have pleased the godmothers mightily to warrant such a gift."

"It is...incredible." My voice choked over the word.

Sister-kingdoms, my own ancestor had written, and I had clung to her words. But I had not appreciated them as I did now, staring at an exact replica of my own home—but one that shone brightly against the blue sky, birds wheeling and screeching over-head as the sun brought the glass and crystal into glorious life.

This was how my own home must have once looked—and how it could still look again, if only I could convince my father to blow the golden conch before the barrier broke and the sea crushed it all. We, too, could live beneath the brilliant sun and the vast sky.

The line of horses turned away from the ocean, passing the ballroom to walk through enormous wooden doors that stood open, facing the distant trees. A short passage of stone opened into a vast internal courtyard, ringed on all sides by buildings, doors, and towers. I shook my head as I gazed around, unnerved by the uncanny familiarity of it all.

A man I assumed must be a groom ran forward and helped me slide down from Waverider's back. Emboldened by the uneventful journey to the palace, I even patted the huge creature on his shoulder and managed not to startle when he huffed and swung his head toward me.

Teddy, jumping smoothly down beside me, chuckled.

"We'll make a rider of you yet, Isla."

I smiled back at him. "I'd like that."

A harried looking woman appeared, scanning the milling people in the courtyard.

"Prince Theodore," she said, hurrying over to us. "I heard that Princess Daisy was—"

She broke off and lunged through a gap between two grooms, reemerging with Daisy's hand firmly gripped in hers.

"Why am I not surprised?" She looked heavenward with a despairing gesture. "You're supposed to be at your lessons now, Your Highness."

"I know," Daisy said, "but this was more interesting."

"It always is," the woman said tartly. "But might I remind you that I am employed for the sole purpose of conducting your lessons—and if no lessons are undertaken, I may find myself summarily dismissed. And then think how guilty you'd feel!"

Daisy actually looked somewhat subdued at this, turning toward the doorway that I knew led to the wing that held both the nurseries and schoolrooms. As the governess trailed behind, she threw a conspiratorial wink in our direction, and Millie laughed from behind me.

"Maybe if our old tutor had been anything like her, you might actually have paid attention in lessons, Teddy. She knows just what to say to make Daisy fall in line."

Teddy grinned, seeming to take this aspersion in good cheer. "Hiring her was certainly an inspired move on Father's part. I think she actually convinces Daisy to pay attention in half her lessons which is far more than the previous governess was managing."

I hid a grin. My own governess had doted on Waverly but

despaired of me, throwing up her hands entirely once I started training with the guards.

"Your Highnesses," said Captain Flint's gruff voice behind us, and I hoped no one noticed that I turned just as quickly as Teddy or Millie. "Might I suggest we adjourn to the map room?"

He gestured toward the opposite side of the courtyard where the guard barracks stood beside a wing filled with their store-rooms, offices, and meeting rooms. Or at least, they did back home.

Millie nodded but didn't step toward him, grasping me by the arm instead.

"We'll be there in just a moment, Captain," she said before tugging me almost at a run toward the main part of the palace which stood directly across the courtyard, facing the great gate.

I almost tripped on the stairs, but she didn't slow, barreling through the ornate doors. I had only a second to glimpse that they were carved with unfamiliar decorations—a point of diver-gence from my own home—before we were through the echoing entryway and into a long marble corridor.

My heart sank. Did she mean to deposit me in a room, excluding me from the meeting about the raiders? I could hardly argue with such a course of action, but I had received the impres-sion I was to be included. And with Ray's life at stake, I couldn't sit calmly by doing nothing.

But when she thrust open a door and pulled me into the room beyond, it was clearly not a guest suite. A pile of books sat on the small table beside the elaborate four-poster bed, and various brushes and pots lay strewn across the polished wooden dressing table. A young woman wearing a practical dress of dark blue was in the act of picking up a wrap and nightgown that had been abandoned in haste on the floor.

"Oh good!" Millie said, "I'm glad you're here, Sara. We're in a hurry."

"In a hurry, Your Highness?" Sara asked, cautiously, her eyes darting curiously to me.

"This is Isla," Millie said. "We've just rescued her from the raiders."

Sara's eyes grew round, and her expression more sympathetic. "How terrifying!"

"Yes," said Millie, barreling on. "And now Teddy and Captain Flint are waiting for us. But—" For the first time she hesitated.

"But she can't go dressed like that." Sara gave a brisk nod. "Of course."

I glanced down at myself and bit my lip. I had once again forgotten about the issue of my shift.

"Will any of my dresses fit her, do you think?" Millie asked, moving toward a door in one wall.

When she opened it, my mouth fell open, and I couldn't help following for a closer look. Behind the door was another, smaller room, and lining all of the walls were racks of dresses in every imaginable color.

"There are so many!" I gaped at them, my mind flying to Avalon. My sister would be beside herself in such a room. Glancing back around the big room, I noticed other differences from the rooms I had grown up in. The four-poster bed had filmy, gauze curtains, and the actual curtains, pulled back from the large windows, looked bright and new. As well as the bed, the side table, and the dressing table, Millie's huge room contained a desk, two wooden chairs, and a small sofa which sat beside another side table.

Everywhere I looked there was so much wood, so much material. It looked decadent and opulent compared to Merrita where only my rank afforded me a wooden bed and a single desk, along with a small handful of dresses. Seeing Millie's room only renewed my determination to see my people restored to their proper place on the surface where they could once again access such plentiful resources.

Yet again my shock was taken for the normal awe of a commoner confronted with a royal palace, and neither Millie nor Sara seemed to find anything strange in it. Instead they entered into a serious, but rapid, discussion in which they flicked through a dozen dresses.

"I think this one will fit well enough," Sara said at last, holding up a long dress consisting of an under layer of white cotton with an overlay of dark gold in what looked like a light brocade that was open down the front, revealing the cotton beneath.

Millie looked critically from the gown to me. "It will be short on you, Isla, since you're taller than me, but it's true that many of the ladies have this style designed that way. The parties with the younger set often spill out onto the beach, and it's easier if your dress isn't trailing against the ground."

"It's beautiful," I said, letting my fingers trace across the material. I grinned at Millie. "I don't care how long—or short—the skirt is."

"Excellent," she said. "Now let's get you into it."

Before I knew what was happening, Sara had my sword belt unbuckled and the two of them were wrestling the dress on over my shift which had thankfully long since dried in the sun and breeze of the beach. I could feel the lingering residue of dried salt, but I was hardly going to ask for a bath when we already had people waiting for us.

When I stepped toward a mirror, to admire the end result, I left a small dusting of white grains behind me on the rug. I frowned at them, wondering how I could have accumulated so much salt.

"Don't worry about the sand," Millie said. "With a beachside palace, we have teams of servants whose sole job is to sweep the insidious stuff up."

"The grains get everywhere," Sara agreed. "We're quite used to it. I'll have the rug cleaned up in no time."

Sand. That made more sense. There were so many things I'd never considered about life on the surface.

I only had time for a single glance at myself in the full-length mirror before Millie whisked me away. But this time I kept pace beside her, so she soon let my arm drop. We passed a number of servants who stepped out of our way but didn't look surprised at our headlong pace. The Trionians might dress more formally than we did under the sea, but in other ways they seemed as relaxed as their palace's beach setting suggested—an impression only reinforced by the feel of the corridor floor beneath my bare feet.

Millie led us toward the guard barracks by the fastest route, pulling up short before we reached them, however. Taking a quick moment to catch her breath, she looked back over her shoulder at me.

"This is the map room," she said, and then led us into one of the most incredible rooms I had ever seen.

CHAPTER 12

*M*y mouth dropped open, and I barely registered the other people in the room. Large maps, exquisitely illustrated, stretched across all four walls, and a large table in the center of the room held even more. A quick glance told me that all of the kingdoms of the land were depicted, but my steps drew me to the largest map, laid out on the table.

My finger traced gently over the spot on the beach where Ray and I had arrived and where the raiders had appeared, following their progress away from us along the beach. The whole of Trione was laid out here, with their palace drawn in its place, and all of their settlements, villages, and towns marked, as they had not been on the map I had in my secret room.

"The markers show where they've struck before," Teddy said, at my shoulder, pointing to a number of red wooden cubes scattered across the surface of the map.

He handed me an identical cube—about the size of my smallest fingernail—and I placed it carefully on the beach. My eyes roved across the rest of the kingdom, noting that while the previous attacks had occurred further away from the palace, they had no other obvious pattern.

"Do tell me if you can see something we can't." Teddy's voice sounded rueful. "We're starting to get desperate. These raiders emerged from nowhere six months ago and have been increasing in size ever since. If we don't do something about them soon, we'll have serious problems with the general populace."

"Your father must trust you—" I glanced at Millie, "—both of you—to place you in charge of finding and arresting the raiders." I hoped they couldn't hear the sour note in my voice as I remembered my father telling me to take up dancing.

"Now we just have to prove him right in that trust," Millie said in a subdued tone.

I looked at her serious face and felt an overwhelming desire to somehow be of assistance. Contrary to what my father had said, these royals had done nothing but protect and welcome me—a stranger in their midst.

"So what is this new theory you have?" Teddy asked, looking at his sister.

"Where's the raider that we captured?" Millie glanced around the room as if she thought he might be stashed in a corner somewhere.

"He's locked up safe and tight, ready for interrogating," Captain Flint replied. "But we thought we'd better hear what you have to say before settling on a line of questioning."

Millie looked relieved. "Good. Because we mustn't interrogate him at all."

"Not interrogate him?" Teddy stared at her. "We weren't proposing to start pulling his fingernails off, Millie! But of course we must see what information we can get out of him. Capturing him is the first real breakthrough we've had."

"No." Millie shook her head and looked at me. "Rescuing Isla was our first breakthrough." She smiled at me. "Tell them what you told me. About what the raider said to you."

Both the prince and the captain fixed me with a steady stare, but I had given far too many guard reports to be discomfited.

"They came out of the trees here, onto the beach." I pointed down at the map. "They had us surrounded before we realized what was happening. They seemed nervous about being so close to the palace and eager to be gone. One of them got a knife to my throat, and they demanded my uncle surrender."

My eyes narrowed as I recalled the scene. "The leader was vile, and the one who threatened me a brute, but many of the others..." I frowned and shook my head. "The man who dismounted and bound my uncle looked almost *apologetic* about it. The whole thing was odd. And he warned us, quietly, that we should cooperate—he told my uncle that as long as he did, I wouldn't be harmed."

"An apologetic raider? That's a new one." The captain rubbed his chin thoughtfully before giving me an uncomfortably piercing look.

Millie nodded. "And Daisy—who has clearly been listening at doors again, by the way—mentioned how the raiders always take at least two people in their raids. We haven't had a single report of a lone abduction."

Teddy looked quickly at his sister, understanding breaking across his face.

"You think they're growing so fast because they're abducting new members and taking hostages to keep them compliant?"

The captain raised an eyebrow, his gaze roving between us all.

"It's possible, I suppose," he said. "It would certainly explain some of the stranger elements of the case. Although it's something of a long shot if that's all the evidence we have of the theory."

"It wasn't just what the raider said to my uncle," I said. "It was the way the one you captured responded when I recounted the conversation to the princess. He had been compliant up until then, but as soon as I began talking about it, he attempted to physically attack me."

Teddy glanced at me in alarm, but I shrugged. "The guards

restrained him, of course, but the poor man looked positively desperate. He seemed to think that if I told you anything, the raiders would think he was the one to talk."

"Perhaps he fears retribution," the captain suggested.

"Oh, I think he certainly fears that," Millie said. "But the question is whether his fears are for himself. The raiders have kept far from the palace until now, and from Isla's report they were nervous today. I don't think he's afraid that the raiders could get to him inside our dungeon. Which means he's afraid they'll get to someone else. Someone they can access far more easily."

"And that's why you don't want to interrogate him," Teddy said. "You don't want to bring down retribution on some innocent member of his family."

Millie sighed. "Obviously we need information, but the raiders have taken children, Teddy. What if they're holding this man's children hostage and they harm them because of us? We're supposed to be helping our people, not hurting them."

The captain tapped one of the wooden blocks against the table, clearly deep in thought. We all waited, and after an extended moment, he spoke.

"I will handle the interrogation myself, Your Highnesses. I'll tell him that if he confirms the truth of what is going on in the raider camp, we'll make sure that the safety of his family is our first priority. I can spread a rumor easily enough that the raider we caught is being uncooperative and won't give any information."

Teddy nodded. "And we can keep up our current search patrols, as if we still have no idea where to look for them."

"Which we currently don't," Millie said dryly.

"Leave that bit up to me, Your Highness," the captain said briskly. "And we'll see what enlightenment our captive can give us."

Both Teddy and Millie nodded their assent, and the captain

left the room. At the door, however, he paused, glancing back at me.

"Thank you for your assistance, Isla. It is an uncommon person who can observe so closely and so rationally at such a moment." He nodded respectfully to the twins and was gone, leaving the three of us alone.

I had tensed at his words, wondering if he could recognize the guard training that gave me such skills. But if he had meant his words to be a subtle warning to his prince and princess, they didn't take it as such, beginning a quiet conversation about the search patrols currently on assignment.

I drifted away from them, not wanting to look as if I was attempting to eavesdrop on their words. It was an easy room to distract myself in, and I was soon examining the maps on the farthest wall.

It didn't take long for footsteps to sound behind me, however.

"Are you looking for your own village?" Teddy asked over my shoulder, a smile in his voice. "We have a map of Talinos over there." He indicated the opposite wall.

I shook my head quickly. "No, I was dreaming of all the places I've never seen—all the places I might one day go." I turned away from the map. "Foolishness, I suppose."

"No, indeed," Teddy said promptly. "There could hardly be a better time to explore all the kingdoms."

I frowned, taken aback. "Do you really think so?" I tried to read his meaning in his eyes. "But what of the darkness, and the curses…" My voice dropped low. "What of the Beast?"

Teddy nodded. "Yes, we have been fortunate here in Trione. And, of course, I can understand why some still feel hesitant about traveling far from their homes. Such things take time to heal." He smiled at me encouragingly. "But you have already shown yourself to be brave and adventurous, or you wouldn't have found your way here. I have no doubt you will see the kingdoms one day, if that is what you desire."

I bit my lip, confused at the way he talked as if my concerns were unwarranted while not denying the existence of the darkness, either. I tried to think of a way to push him for further information without revealing my own woeful ignorance. My eyes strayed back to the wall, traveling on to the next map.

I gasped, stepping forward, my hand reaching up to brush against it. What kingdom was this? It looked entirely unfamiliar.

"Father is proud of this room," Teddy said, his own pride evident in his voice. "It is the largest and most well-equipped anywhere in the kingdoms. So naturally he came home from the Tourney determined to update it as soon as possible. It's a good thing Duchess Aurelia is his sister. She knows of his obsession well enough and allowed him to include two of his map makers on their first trading voyage to Arcadia after the betrothal. It took our people months to travel to each kingdom and complete these copies, but Father considers it entirely worth it. *We must know our world*, he says."

My eyes flew ahead across the walls, picking out three more kingdoms I didn't recognize and one map drawn at a smaller scale that seemed to show a single land mass that included all four.

"The Old Kingdoms," I breathed, astonishment spreading through me. "You have maps of the Old Kingdoms."

Teddy gave me a quizzical look. "Your village must have a good memory. Old Albert calls them that—the retired Keeper of the Library at Marin, that is. But I'll confess, for all my royal education, I hadn't heard of them before the storms between us died, and the Marinese emissary returned with the foreign delegations."

I stood transfixed before the wall. Our people had fled the Old Kingdoms long ago, when they turned from the ancient ways and invited darkness into their lands. We had sought refuge in these kingdoms, and the High King had raised the storms to protect us. But now the way was open again. Was this the source of the darkness now spreading through these kingdoms? If so, then my father was right. The High King must have abandoned these lands too, now, and there was no refuge on land for our people.

"I think we've had quite enough of maps for one day," Millie said from the doorway. "And I think it's past time for a meal. Come on, you two."

Teddy crossed over to her with an eager step, pausing before leaving the room to glance back at me. I remained by the wall, my gaze fixed on their open, kind faces. I could see no more trace of darkness in them than I had seen in Teddy's face more than two years ago. It was becoming clear that there was a great deal more going on in the kingdoms of the land than I understood, and I wasn't ready to accept that nothing but darkness could be found here.

"Food sounds delightful," I said, turning my back on the maps and crossing to join them. "More than delightful, in fact."

My stomach gurgled, right on cue, and both of the twins chuckled before leading the way back down the corridor.

CHAPTER 13

They took me past the large royal dining hall, where my family ate their meals back home, and instead showed me to a much smaller room that my own family used as a sitting room. In Trione, however, the room had been fitted out with a dining table, and Millie explained that the royal family always ate here unless they were entertaining guests.

A midday meal had been laid out on a long side table, and an older couple already sat with half-full plates. I stopped short just inside the doorway and dropped into a deep curtsy because there was no mistaking their identities.

Millie glanced back, as if wondering why I had stopped.

"Oh! Mother, Father, this is Isla of Talinos," she said, and I flushed at the inaccuracy but didn't correct her. "Isla, my parents, King Edward and Queen Juliette."

"We rescued her from the raiders this morning," Teddy announced in what was clearly supposed to be a nonchalant tone.

"Yes, I've had a report from Captain Flint," King Edward said, and Teddy's face fell. "A pity they managed to escape, but capturing one of them is a significant advantage."

Teddy brightened again and looked about to launch into an

explanation of their plans when the door opened again, and Daisy entered. Millie gave her twin a significant look, and he subsided.

"Isla!" Daisy bounced forward and threw her arms around me. "My fellow terrible singer."

"Daisy!" Queen Juliette frowned, reprovingly, but Daisy was unquashed.

"She knows how to fight with a sword, and she's going to teach me," she said, looking sideways at her parents to see how they would take this news.

"What?" I said, horrified, with a quick look at the monarchs myself. "I never—"

"Please do not distress yourself," the king said, cutting me off. "We are far too familiar with our youngest daughter's ways to suspect you of making any questionable promises."

Daisy sighed and let me go, traipsing over to fill her plate with food while I still hesitated near the door. Millie glanced over at me.

"Come and serve yourself, Isla, I'm afraid we don't stand on ceremony at private family meals." When I still didn't move, her brow creased. "Oh, but don't be concerned, you're welcome here. The servants have long since finished their meal, so you couldn't eat with them anyway."

"As if we would send you to eat with the servants!" Teddy slid into a seat, carefully balancing his heaped plate. "You just helped us out immensely, you know. Plus, you're carrying my sword—which you wield like you were trained to it—and you give reports like a guard."

So he had noticed then, after all.

His eyes flitted to the dress I had borrowed from Millie and then quickly away. "Though you don't dress like a guard. In short, you're far too intriguing a puzzle to be relegated to the servants' hall."

I flushed. Every part of me thrilled at his assertion that he wished to keep me close, but my mind was also screaming that the last thing I wanted was for this family—of all families—to go looking into my secrets.

"I could have a tray in my room," I forced myself to say. "I hate to intrude."

"Nonsense," said Queen Juliette, gently. "There is no need for such discomposure. We are glad to have you among us."

There was nothing to do after that but drop another curtsy and murmur my thanks before heading for the table of food. My eyes widened as I surveyed it, so much of it unfamiliar to me. I took a small sample of as much as I could fit on my plate, ignoring only the several varieties of seafood. I did, however, throw a chicken leg on top at the last minute just in case I hated all the new food.

Daisy slowly filled her plate beside me, looking so downcast that I couldn't resist leaning over and whispering to her.

"I learned to fight with my sword from a book, you know. I didn't have anyone to teach me either."

Daisy gazed up at me with an arrested expression. "You can learn something like that from a book?" she whispered back.

I nodded and gave her a conspiratorial smile before turning carefully with my loaded plate. I didn't know if it was just that we were both the babies of our families, or if it was the sense of dissatisfaction with her place that I sensed from Daisy, but I couldn't help a fellow feeling.

My feet tried to pull me to a seat beside Teddy, but I sternly directed myself to one next to Millie, leaving Daisy to sit beside her brother. Except I quickly realized that put me across from Teddy which proved only slightly less distracting than sitting within hand's reach of him.

The food itself proved a worthy distraction, however, and I couldn't help but exclaim several times as I ate everything from bread to beef to a juicy orange. None of the merfolk would complain about returning to life on the surface once they had the chance to taste food like this.

The royals politely ignored my amazement, merely exchanging the occasional amused glance between them. Once again, I was saved by my apparent background as a commoner from a small seaside village. King Edward and Queen Juliette made polite, intelligent conversation, and I listened more than I talked—a feat that would have no doubt astonished my older sisters.

As soon as the meal was finished, Millie whisked me away, saying that since we had nothing useful to do except wait for a report from Captain Flint, we had better do something about my wardrobe. Part of me knew I shouldn't continue to accept gifts from these people, who thought my possessions had been stolen by the raiders, but the allure of a whole selection of new dresses was too great to ignore.

When we arrived back in Millie's room, we found Sara had somehow amassed a number of gowns which she had laid across Millie's bed. A couple of them I recognized from Millie's own dressing room, although several were of a simpler style than any of hers.

With startling efficiency, Sara had me in and out of every one of them, a young seamstress's apprentice tucking, and pinning, and humming to herself the whole time. She eventually tottered from the room, her arms piled high with fabric, leaving only a promise that they would all be returned as soon as possible.

I collapsed back onto the bed.

"Why is trying on dresses more exhausting than fighting off raiders?" I asked the ceiling.

Millie appeared in my line of vision, leaning over me and holding out an imperious hand. With a groan, I let her pull me to my feet.

"You have a wardrobe now, but you still need a room. And I've had an excellent idea."

She crossed over to a large tapestry which hung on the wall opposite her dressing room. It depicted a young queen, mounted on a horse with a sword held aloft. But I didn't have a chance to take in the rest of the scene before Millie pulled on it and the whole thing crumpled to the floor, the pole which had been holding it in place tumbling after it with a loud clang.

I winced, but Millie merely produced a key and opened the sturdy wooden door revealed behind the tapestry.

"This room is actually part of a full suite, but I've never had a need for the empty room. So it's furnished as a guest room. But it's such a small one that it only ever gets used when the entire palace is packed full for a special event with visitors from all the other kingdoms. And I realized it will be the perfect place for you."

She pushed the door open with a triumphant flourish only to have it catch against something on the other side.

"I'll get it," Sara said before dashing out into the corridor.

A moment later, I heard her in the other room. A thump and a clang were followed by the sound of something heavy dragging across the floor. Millie attempted to open the door again, and this time it swung wide to reveal Sara, her face flushed with exertion, and a heavy pile of material strewn across the floor behind her. Apparently the door had been hidden by a tapestry on both sides.

The opened door revealed a small, neat guest room decorated in forest green. I stepped through and looked around, aware that I was fortunate indeed to end up in such appealing accommodation.

"It's lovely," I said, my eyes on the window and the view of the distant trees. I crossed over to where sunshine streamed in and held my arms out, letting the warmth fall across them. "More than lovely."

"Sorry it isn't ocean views," Millie said with a grimace. "I used to have the room on the other side of the corridor, but I gave it to

Teddy two years ago in a moment of weakness." She gave me an exasperated look. "He likes to gaze out across the ocean."

My eyes widened as I grasped her meaning, and I quickly turned back to my own view to hide the pleasure on my face. While I had been looking up at the surface, he had been looking out to sea. But my heart plummeted a moment later when I remembered that he had no idea of my identity, and I was power-less to reveal myself.

"Don't worry," Sara was saying to Millie as she unsuccessfully tried to gather the huge tapestry into her arms. "We'll get a footman or two in here to get this rolled up and out of your way. The other one, too, since I assume you'll want the door accessible."

Millie nodded. "Yes, I think so. It could be quite handy if we get a call in the middle of the night to go after the raiders."

I hurried over at that.

"You mean, you'll ride after them yourself? And me?"

"Only if you want to," Millie said. "I just assumed with your uncle…"

"Oh, yes," I said quickly. "I would greatly appreciate being included."

"Father won't let Teddy and me ride with the search patrols," Millie added. "He says that's the sort of routine work best left to those trained for it. But Teddy made him promise we could be present for any actual raid on their camp."

She rolled her eyes. "Of course Mother made us promise not to put ourselves in any unnecessary risk, but I think at this point, the raiders are becoming enough of a problem that Father sees value in the crown being directly involved with their defeat." She grinned at me. "That's politics for you."

I nodded, but if I was honest, I'd never paid politics much attention. It was hard to find much interest in it when the surface lay so tantalizingly close, ready to be explored. But maybe if I had paid more attention, I wouldn't have blundered so badly.

A knock sounded on the door.

Sara dropped the tapestry and answered it, blinking in surprise at the footman on the other side.

"That was fast," Millie said in mild surprise.

"Fast, Your Highness?" The footman looked between Millie and Sara.

"However did you know we needed you, Bertram?" asked Sara.

"Needed me, Sara? Whatever do you mean? I've just come with a message for Her Highness. From Captain Flint."

"Captain Flint?" Millie almost jumped on him, all thought of the tapestry forgotten. "What did he say?"

"He said to meet him in his office," said an already familiar voice from the corridor. I bit my lip, wishing I didn't feel a physical response to his nearness.

"What are you doing in there?" Teddy attempted to peer over Bertram's tall shoulder. "Is this the other part of your suite, Millie?"

"Yes, I'm putting Isla in here," Millie said. "In case we get word to ride out in the middle of the night or something."

"Excellent! All the better to keep her under close surveillance." Teddy winked, inviting me into his light-hearted jest, but I couldn't help swallowing and reminding myself, yet again, to watch my step.

As the three of us started off down the corridor, I glanced back over my shoulder and saw Sara directing Bertram toward the tapestry. He was grinning at her as they spoke, and she was gazing up at him with a look I found all too easy to interpret. Biting my lip, I forced myself not to glance at the tall young man by my side. I only recognized the expression because I knew how it felt to wear it, and I hated making a fool of myself over this handsome prince.

It had been one thing when I had been a princess and thought him a regular land dweller, but now I was the commoner and he was the prince. I could only imagine how sad it would appear if people saw me mooning over him.

As soon as I walked into the captain's office and saw his serious expression, however, all such thoughts fled to be replaced with fear for Ray.

"What is it?" Teddy asked as soon as the door closed behind us. "Did he talk?"

The captain sighed and sat back in his chair. "Once I made it clear what we knew—or at least suspected—and the safeguards we were willing to undertake on his behalf, he was more than cooperative." He nodded toward me and Millie. "You ladies were entirely correct about their strategy."

"But that's good news!" Teddy's hand strayed down to his sword hilt. "When will we be off after them?"

The captain shook his head. "Unfortunately, the prisoner had less information than I would have liked. He was able to tell me where the raiders were camped as of this morning, but he thinks —as do I—that they will have fled to a new location in the wake of his capture. And the hostages are held in a second camp entirely. The conscripted raiders are only allowed to see their friends and family once every couple of weeks, and he hasn't been to their camp for ten days. He said they will have moved location for sure by now."

I grimaced. "They're no doubt as eager to keep the hostages' location a secret from their own men as from your guards."

The captain's measuring eyes turned to dwell on me, and I immediately wished I'd kept my mouth shut.

"Yes, I can easily believe this man wouldn't be kept abreast of their location."

Teddy collapsed into a chair. "Which means we're no better off than we were before."

"It's not as bad as that," the captain said. "He still had valuable information on their general patterns of behavior and on the characteristics they look for when choosing a new camp. Plus, they may have left behind something valuable in their haste to move."

"But we need to tread carefully in our 'discovery' of their abandoned camp site," Millie reminded him. "And in following up his other information."

"Indeed." The captain nodded. "We'll make sure we give it a bit of time before one of our patrols 'stumbles' on the site." He grinned. "I can think of a couple of guards who would be more than happy to put on a dramatic show of an accidental discovery."

Teddy grinned back, as if he thought such a task sounded appealing. "You know if Gabe were here, he'd somehow convince Father to let him do it. And he'd be brilliant at it, no doubt."

"It is perhaps a fortunate thing for everyone that Prince Gabriel has returned to his own kingdom," Captain Flint said wryly.

Millie gave a short chuckle. "We all certainly get into less trouble now he's gone, so perhaps you're right. Certainly we won't make any such attempt to convince Father."

"For which I thank you," the captain said gravely.

"In terms of helpful information," Millie said thoughtfully, "we also now know we're looking for two separate camps. One of which needs to be within reach but also secret from the other camp."

Teddy nodded, becoming serious again. "And that knowledge will be even more helpful when we eventually locate them. If we free the hostages first, we won't find much of a fight when we storm the raider camp."

The captain rubbed the side of his face. "I'll admit I'd hoped for more, but I think we can congratulate ourselves on being in a significantly better position than we were yesterday." He looked over at me. "And the prisoner said he doesn't think they're likely to kill your uncle, either. He said if they can't convince him to join them, they'll probably try for a ransom. So if he plays his cards right, he should get through unscathed."

I nodded. I had no way to pay a ransom, but neither did I think Ray likely to need one. As long as they didn't kill him outright, he would find his own way out of the mess.

Still, I couldn't help but feel subdued at the thought of his situation compared to my own, and I took no further part in the conversation. Not that my input was needed. The three of them were far better equipped than me to know how to distribute their resources and the most likely areas to send the patrols to search. None of them thought to send me away, however, and eventually I found myself following the two young royals back to their family's private dining room.

I hesitated on the threshold, even though no one else had arrived yet, but Millie pulled me inside.

"It's not as if this room is only for family, you know," she said as she filled her plate. "We've had plenty of guests join us here over the years. And Gabe ate here for eight entire years."

"Gabe wasn't a guest," said Daisy hotly from behind us. She pushed forward and took a plate of her own, glaring at her older sister. "Gabe is family."

"Funny," Millie said, with a teasing twinkle in her eye. "You didn't say that when you had a crush on him all those years."

Daisy stuck her nose in the air and swept past us both. "That was when I was *little*. I don't have a crush on him anymore."

Millie opened her mouth, but I nudged her with my arm before nodding at Daisy's retreating form with a sympathetic expression. I knew what it was like to be the youngest. Millie subsided with a silent chuckle, while I hurried to my own seat, belatedly remembering that a princess might expect less familiarity from a commoner. Thankfully Millie didn't look in the least offended, however.

"I should hope you don't," Teddy was saying to Daisy. "Given we've barely returned from his wedding."

"Were you there, Isla?" Daisy asked me suddenly. "Maybe we saw you in passing and never even knew." She looked pleased at the idea.

"Uh…" I looked quickly between Millie and Teddy.

"We mean Prince Gabriel, your own prince, of course," Millie said in a friendly voice. But I could see the slight confusion in her eyes that I hadn't been able to put that together for myself.

If a Talinosian prince had spent eight years here in Trione, it seemed the kingdoms of the land still continued the ancient tradition of cementing alliances by sending their children as wards to other courts. Although all of these three seemed to have been here during that period. Perhaps it wasn't a widespread custom.

"Of course," I said, trying to cover my lapse. My throat tightened, threatening to close altogether, and I chose my words carefully. "My people live in an extremely remote location, so I'm afraid we're not abreast of all the latest happenings. And you definitely wouldn't have seen me at the capital, or at any royal weddings."

All three immediately looked sympathetic.

"You poor thing!" Daisy said.

"In that case," Teddy said, with a look of interest, "I would love to hear how you came to be proficient with my sword."

"She learned from a book," Daisy announced.

Teddy raised an eyebrow at me. "Very impressive."

I laughed. "Don't speak too soon. You haven't seen me do anything but hold off a raider who was more interested in retreating than attacking."

"That can be remedied," he said with a grin.

I tried to look away from his dimples but failed.

"What do you say to sparring with me tomorrow in the practice hall?" he asked.

"I—"

Before I could think of an excuse, the king and queen arrived, and the conversation was dropped. But as I left the room for my new bedchamber after the meal was finished, Teddy held the door open for me.

"See you in the morning." He winked at me. "And don't forget my sword."

"I think that's *my* sword," I said, unable to resist.

"Ah, we'll see about that tomorrow," he said, his smile deepening, before he bowed and closed the door behind me.

CHAPTER 14

I slept deeply and woke with a start, my mind grasping at the unbelievable fact that I slept in a castle on the surface, across the corridor from the boy I had dreamed about for so long. But almost immediately it flew guiltily to Ray. How had he spent the night?

I glanced around at the casual excess of wood that surrounded me. Even as a prisoner, Ray must be eating entirely new food and seeing unbelievable sights. I slipped out of bed, my feet luxuriating in the thick rug across the floor, and ran to throw open the curtains. I needed to see the sky and feel the sun through the panes of glass before any of this would feel entirely real.

"Oh, you're already up," said a surprised voice.

I turned to find Sara edging into the room, a large tray carried carefully in both hands. Pushing the bits of clutter I had already accumulated from the surface of a round table, I made room for her to put it down.

"Her Highness thought you would be tired after yesterday," Sara said, "or I would have brought it earlier."

"I was," I admitted, leaning over the tray to breathe in the tantalizing aromas of the breakfast. "But I went to bed so early."

Sara gave me a slight smile. "In truth, Her Highness is no early riser, so she finds it hard to imagine anyone else could be."

I smiled back. "I'm not one for lying in bed, to tell the truth. My two closest sisters could never understand it."

"Have a lot of sisters, do you?" Sara gave me a warmer look than she had done thus far. "That's something I can understand, right enough. I have nine."

"Nine!" I gasped. "Oh gracious."

She chuckled. "You should ask my brother about it one day. He has ten. Five older and five younger, and him sandwiched in between."

I snorted. "I can only imagine."

"Likes to spend long days fishing, he does," she said, removing the various lids and covers from the dishes on the plate. "Unless one of us girls hosts the other young ladies of the village." She winked at me. "Then he's suddenly needed about the house."

I laughed. "Well, I suppose siblings have to be good for something, don't they?"

"If you say so," she said dryly, and I laughed again.

She turned for the door, only to pause when I spoke hesitantly.

"Thank you for bringing me my tray. I don't like to put you to so much bother. I understand you're Princess Millie's maid." I knew servants had their own hierarchies and could be quite put out if asked to take on additional responsibilities.

But Sara just laughed as she continued back toward the corridor. "I've been Princess Millie's maid for enough years that I've grown accustomed to far odder requests than accommodating a strange girl from the beach. You should hear some of the things they got up to when Prince Gabriel lived here." Still chuckling, she pulled the door closed behind her, leaving me to my food and my thoughts.

For some time, those thoughts were focused on the tart, tangy orange liquid that filled my glass—entirely unlike anything we had at home—and the hot, sweet, brown liquid that filled a ceramic cup. Between the two drinks, I wasn't sure if I'd have room for the more familiar eggs. But I soon discovered that even eggs were different when eaten with toasted bread and something that had to be a roasted tomato.

But even the incredible food couldn't keep my mind from wandering to my last interaction with Teddy. He wanted to spar with me. Up here in Trione, they didn't seem to think that princesses had no place among the guards. But the giddy grin that kept wanting to slide across my face was soon tempered by nerves.

If we were planning to spar with tridents, I would have no qualms, but I had never actually crossed swords with anyone before. And as hard as I'd trained, I couldn't imagine I would hold up long against someone used to bouts with real people. And Teddy was a crown prince—so no doubt his usual partners were master swordsmen.

As I strapped my sword belt over one of the more practical gowns from the selection that had appeared in my wardrobe, my concerns filled my mind, following me as I made my slow way down to the long practice hall. Just as at home, the practice hall was a long colonnade—except here the elegant marble columns supported arches that looked out over the sand toward the waves.

I halted in the doorway to take in the stunning view and breathe deeply of the salt-scented breeze. The screeching cries of the seagulls wheeling overhead completed the surreal picture. No, this was nothing like the practice hall at home where Ray and I sometimes sparred or crossed tridents with other nobles.

Teddy stood beneath one of the arches, talking quietly with a slim, older man, but they both turned at my arrival.

"Isla!" Teddy called in welcome before saying something quietly to the man beside him, who bowed to the prince and slipped away.

"Oh, I'm sorry," I said, as I approached Teddy. "I didn't mean to chase him away. You didn't say what time to meet you here."

Teddy laughed ruefully. "No, I can only imagine I didn't." He grinned disarmingly at me. "I'm afraid I'm not the best with details. I'm just glad to see you're not a lay-abed like my lazy sister. I'm always trying to convince her of what she's missing. There's nothing like the beach in the morning."

I closed my eyes and took another deep breath through my nose. "I couldn't agree more," I told him with perfect sincerity.

When I opened my eyes, he was watching my face, and I felt the heat rushing to my cheeks.

"So, do we mean to spar, or were you just poking fun last night?" I asked quickly.

His eyes laughed at me, as he patted his sword hilt. "I am always perfectly earnest, I assure you. I merely thought you might prefer not to have an audience."

I bit my lip and nodded. For all his laughter and talk of thoughtlessness, it was a considerate gesture since I was sure to be utterly outmatched.

"I think that might be for the best," I said ruefully. "Since Daisy already revealed my secret, I can openly admit that I've never actually attempted a practice bout before. No one else I know ever owned or trained with a sword, so I had to stick with the individual training exercises I found in a book on swordsmanship."

"Oh, don't back down now!" he said. "I've seen you face down raiders single-handedly. Surely you're not worried about a lone prince."

"Who said anything about backing down?" I asked, swiftly drawing my sword from its scabbard.

"That's the spirit," he said, the laugh still in his eyes.

He drew his own sword and gestured for me to move back toward the center of the colonnade. I rubbed my free hand nervously down the skirts of my dress, and then dropped into the familiar posture.

Teddy looked me over critically before nodding in an approving way and taking up a similar stance opposite me.

"We can just do a series of exercises if you prefer," he said. "We don't have to start with a proper bout."

But I shook my head. I had spent countless hours going through the exercises with my sword, and I had spent even more hours training properly with a trident. I had been curious for a long time as to how I would fare in a bout with a sword, and I wasn't about to pass up my opportunity to find out.

"En garde," I said in response, and lunged forward.

Teddy skipped back out of the way, an answering light leaping into his eyes, before he lunged forward with a return attack. My mind urged my body to defend, and without thought, my muscles responded, my legs pulling me back while my arm moved across and up, to drive his blade away. The two lengths of steel met with a loud clash, the ringing filling the air around me and setting the seagulls screaming.

The shock of the impact traveled up my arm, just as it did when my trident met another guard's, and then my feet were responding with the prescribed counter move.

Teddy managed the first three hits—polite, light taps, achieved when I momentarily forgot what weapon I wielded and tried to block as I would with a trident. But my mind was catching the rhythm of his movements, and I started to combine the familiar positions into long sequences of attacks, parries, ripostes, and feints. When I broke through his guard to score the fourth point, only just pulling my blade back in time so that the tip rested gently against his arm, we both fell back, panting lightly.

"Well done!" he said warmly. "I wouldn't guess you to be so inexperienced."

I bit my lip, feeling once again guilty at having misled him. I might be inexperienced at fighting with a sword, but I wasn't exactly unfamiliar with the pressure and cadence of a practice bout.

Teddy examined me, his gaze curious. After a moment, he strolled over toward me, and I dropped my blade as I waited for him to approach, wary.

He stopped just within arm's reach.

"What do you say we see what a bout is like with some real pressure?" he asked.

"Real pressure?"

He nodded. "Let's add some stakes. Aren't you curious to see how you could do?"

"Name the stakes," I said before kicking myself internally. I needed to be more cautious.

"My sword," he said.

"You mean *my* sword," I said coolly back, forcing more confidence than I actually felt.

He grinned. "Precisely."

"You mean the winner gets to keep the sword?" I felt a pang at the idea of losing the weapon, but I reminded myself that it was no longer my only link to the surface or to Teddy himself. Still I hesitated. The odds were high I would lose.

"Oh, no." Teddy stepped closer, now only a breath away, the laughter in his eyes sparking into something more intense. "I've already told you that you intrigue me, Isla." He reached up and gently touched a single strand of my hair. "If you win, you gain the right to keep my sword. If *I* win, you have to answer a single question of my choice."

I gulped. I should have been more cautious, but it was too late for that now. If I refused, it would look like I was hiding something. He had trapped me—and from his expression, he knew it.

He stepped back with a challenging smile. "Well?"

"En garde," I replied.

I attacked fast and hard, hoping to catch him off guard and

win quickly. His sword flashed faster than I could follow, though, always ready to clash against mine and drive me back. I could tell I was getting better with each bout, but I was outmatched, and we both knew it.

I tried a long, desperate lunge, but he flicked my blade aside and counter-attacked, his reach longer than mine. The tip of his blade came to rest gently above my heart.

"Hit," he said in a calm voice.

"Hit," I acknowledged before stepping back.

But he pursued me, coming much closer now that both of our blades had dropped. When he reached nearly as close as he had stood before, he stopped and scrutinized my face.

"Well?" I asked at last, my voice coming out more breathy than I had intended.

"Where did you find my sword?" His words were low and soft, but I felt them as intensely as if he'd shouted.

"I…" My throat twinged, and I searched for the right words. "I found it on the bottom of the ocean while I was swimming." I glanced sideways at the blue of the lagoon. "I couldn't tell you exactly where. But I've been keeping it wrapped in oiled leather ever since."

Teddy leaned back, an odd look on his face almost like disappointment. Almost like some part of him had still wondered if I might be his ocean girl, after all.

"That would certainly help to keep it in excellent condition."

I slowly slid it back into the scabbard on my hip before looking up at him, a crease in my brow.

"You won, but it's still my sword."

Teddy's eyes smiled at me. "It looks far too good on your waist for me to steal it away now."

I hoped he didn't hear my soft intake of breath as he stepped away from me.

"Oh, great," Millie's unimpressed voice rang out from the other side of the room, and I started guiltily. "You're another morning person, Isla. Am I always going to be surrounded by them?"

Teddy strode over and slung an arm around her neck.

"Unless you plan to kill me in my sleep, yes. You're stuck with me for life, I'm afraid."

Millie rolled her eyes and pushed him off, but I could see her amused smile. She looked between us questioningly.

"Who won?"

"Prince Theodore, of course," I said quickly, hoping he wouldn't say anything about the stakes of our game.

"Call me Teddy, please, Isla," he said quickly. "I get quite enough Prince Theodores from the servants. I don't know how Daisy has tricked everyone into calling her by her nickname, but I wish she would share her secret."

"Just be glad your real name isn't Millicent," Millie said tartly. "And you're perfectly well aware how she managed it—by resolutely ignoring anyone who called her Margaret and pretending she didn't know who they meant. Behavior—I feel compelled to point out—that is beneath the dignity of an heir to the throne."

Teddy groaned. "One day Daisy is going to grow up and marry some heir to the throne of her own—and then she'd better watch out."

Millie shook her head. "There aren't any crown princes left—as you are very well aware if you'd only think about it for more than one second. Not even in the Four Kingdoms—unless one of us wants to wait twenty or so years for our intended to grow up."

"Don't worry, Mills." Teddy slung his arm back over her shoulder. "I could never rule without you anyway, so you're better off staying here and being my First Advisor like we always planned."

This time Millie didn't push him off, instead laying her head briefly on his shoulder before straightening again and looking briskly around.

"Are you two finished here? Because I heard Captain Flint has news."

We both assured her we were done, and I trailed behind the two of them as we left the colonnade behind. I loved my sisters, but I had never had the easy relationship with any of them that Millie and Teddy shared. Did it come from being twins? Or was it something missing in my own family?

My eyes lingered on Teddy's back. He strode forward with energy, not seeming in the least tired from our bouts or from any sparring he might have done beforehand. His golden hair had worked itself into a disheveled tumble of locks that somehow did nothing to make him look less princely. Already I was starting to wonder how I had failed to guess he must have rank the first time we met. He wore the air of comfortable command so effortlessly behind the laughing mischief of his eyes.

Teddy suspected I was keeping secrets, but they seemed to intrigue rather than disturb him. And I couldn't help but wonder what he might think of me if his ocean girl didn't stand between us. A bubble of determination rose inside me, pushing away my weak efforts to tell myself it was a bad idea.

Because it didn't matter if it was wise or not. I had to find out if I could drive his phantom ocean girl from Teddy's mind and heart. If I couldn't be her, perhaps I could destroy her completely. If I didn't at least try, I would always regret it.

hatever strategy Captain Flint and the twins had come up with worked better than even they had hoped. One of the patrols had found the abandoned camp and made a show of looking astonished and riding back to the palace. But two of the guard's best scouts had slipped away and followed the raiders' trail. The fleeing raiders had been sloppy in their haste the day before, and we finally knew where to find them.

Teddy had looked ready to bolt for his horse, but one look at Millie, and he deflated. We couldn't attack the raiders when the majority of them were hostages just as effectively as their family and friends. Any such attempt would only result in a whole lot of unnecessary bloodshed—on both sides. And even if we won, it might lead to the massacre of the hostages in the second camp.

"And so, we wait," the captain said. "We wait and we keep them under surveillance. Eventually they'll lead us to the hostages. And then we strike."

Teddy and Millie had been somewhat deflated to have such exciting news end in nothing but more waiting, but I was elated. One of the scouts had been with Teddy when he chased after the raiders on the beach, and he had recognized Ray among them this morning. He was alive, and no longer a captive even, moving among them freely.

I could feel the captain's eyes resting heavily on me when he delivered this news, but not even his suspicion could darken my relief at the confirmation that Ray was unharmed.

"I wonder how they've compelled him to cooperate?" Teddy mused aloud.

I watched the captain's eyes narrow, but he voiced no alternate theory. Whatever concern he felt about Ray, he apparently hadn't forgotten that within a day of my arrival, they had already found the raiders' camp.

Teddy hadn't forgotten it either, apparently. Because as soon as we made it out to the corridor, he picked me up and spun me around and around. When he put me down, I stumbled back, unnaturally breathless, but he didn't seem to notice.

"Thank goodness for your arrival in Trione, Isla," he exclaimed. "Apparently you were just what this island needed."

I couldn't resist smiling at his infectious enthusiasm. But as his words sank in, my joy over Ray dampened. My arrival might have been good for Trione, but so far I had achieved little for Merrita. I couldn't even consider returning home while Ray was still with the raiders, but the memory of the tremors made me shiver.

If one thing was clear it was that the kingdoms of the land weren't as consumed by darkness as my father thought. Which meant there was every chance that he was wrong about the warning the High King was sending. In which case, what exactly were we being warned of? And if we were being told to flee—or rise—how much time did my kingdom have left?

Millie insisted I stay close as we whiled the day away, saying that both she and Teddy needed a distraction or they would be driven wild by the waiting. The two of them took me to the stables for what they called the beginning of my journey toward appreciating horses. Apparently, I needed to learn to be a little less unnerved around them before they would let me actually try mounting one.

And in the afternoon, Millie produced her own elegant blade, saying that now that it was a civilized time of day, we could do some real sparring. Teddy and I had assented readily enough, and we spent some time running through various exercises. None of the bouts had the intensity of the morning match when Teddy and I had been alone, but there was a great deal more laughter. And I was pleased to note that I was much more evenly matched against Millie.

The princess confessed that she had never had the interest to dedicate herself to the weapon in the same way her brother had.

"No," Teddy had agreed, "because you're far too good a sister. You've been learning a great many things that will be of far more use to us when we rule Trione one day."

I hid a sigh. I wished Oceana had ever shown the least interest in having my assistance in her future rule. Perhaps I wouldn't have felt so out of place, if she had. Although I admitted to myself, somewhat grudgingly, that it was natural to feel differently about your twin from how you would feel about a seven-year-younger sister.

The next day, my door swung open while I was still halfway through breakfast, and Daisy swept into the room, pulling up a chair beside me. She took a triangle of toast and took a loud bite, her eyes boring into me.

"Good morning, Daisy," I said, sipping at the brown drink which Millie had told me was called hot chocolate.

"I need your help," she told me. "You have to save me."

"That sounds dramatic," I said, moving on to the orange juice.

She groaned. "Mother said I could have the day off lessons, but Baron Hargin is coming to court to petition Father about something horridly boring…and he's bringing his children with him." The last part of her sentence came out more like a wail, and Teddy appeared in the doorway that Daisy had left open.

"Did you say Baron Hargin, Daisy?"

"And his children," she moaned.

He came over, swiping an apple from my tray, and threw himself down onto the rug. "Gracious, yes, we must escape at all costs."

"That's just what I was telling Isla," Daisy said.

Teddy turned his sea-green eyes on me with an admiring expression, and I tried to suppress the flush that raced toward my cheeks at their weight.

"Brilliant, Daisy!" he exclaimed. "Isla is just the escape we need."

"I am?" I asked, looking between them.

"What are you doing here, Teddy?" Millie asked, thrusting open the door connecting our rooms and poking her head into my unusually crowded chamber. "Oh, and Daisy, too."

"Baron Hargin," Daisy said glumly.

"And his children," Teddy said with an exaggerated shudder.

Millie's eyes widened. "Today? What's our plan of escape?"

"Isla!" Teddy announced triumphantly, gesturing toward me.

Millie looked me over. "Yes, that could work very nicely. But we'll have to move quickly."

"I still don't understand." I looked between them all, but Teddy had moved on to a cluster of grapes, and Daisy had already dashed from the room calling something about the cook over her shoulder.

"She's the best one to take care of that," Millie said. "Cook will give her whatever she asks for."

Teddy nodded absently, selecting another grape, and Millie descended on him, shoving and pulling him to his feet.

"Get out of here," she said. "Do you want us to get caught? Isla still needs to get dressed."

141

I glanced down at my dressing gown, as did Teddy, and for once it was his turn to flush before hurrying swiftly from the room.

"Well, that takes care of that," Millie said, shutting the door firmly behind him. "Just don't take too long." She was already back in her own room before she had finished speaking, but she stuck her head back through the door. "Wear that white and gold one from the first day. The short one."

"But Millie…" I called, but the door had already closed.

I shoved a final forkful of egg into my mouth and hurried to follow instructions. I was a little afraid that if I took too long, one or more of them would come barging back in to harangue me on my state of undress.

Minutes later I was knocking on the connecting door and passing through to Millie's room. The other princess gestured me ahead of her into the corridor, stopping to look around suspiciously, as if we were fugitives in her own home.

"Am I allowed to ask what's going on?" I asked meekly.

"Of course not," said Teddy cheerfully from behind me. "There's no time for such nonsense."

He gave me a grin as he passed Millie and took the lead, directing us back toward the practice hall.

"Should I have brought my sword?" I asked uncertainly.

Millie shook her head. "You won't need it today." She paused mid-stride and frowned at Teddy's back. "At least…you did order us some company, didn't you, Teddy?"

"Of course," he said, and she resumed walking. "A whole squad, in fact." His face looked serious now. "I wouldn't risk asking for less when the raiders have gotten so brazen and we'll have Daisy with us."

When we reached the colonnade, Daisy popped out from behind one of the pillars, a large basket in her hands. She looked barely able to lift it, and Teddy took it, swinging it easily from one hand.

"Come on!" Daisy hissed, before I could once again ask what was going on, and I found myself propelled under an archway and down some steps to the sand.

My toes sank into the fine grains, and I hopped a couple of times at the unexpected warmth. Now I understood why Millie had told me to wear the shorter dress. I would have tripped in a longer skirt.

"Running helps," Daisy assured me before taking off down the beach, her hair flying behind her, and her arms out like a bird.

The twins laughed and ran after her, their long legs quickly gaining ground. I shook my head and followed. We dropped to a walk after a while but didn't stop until we were out of sight of the palace. Looking back, I saw the squad of guards, just as Teddy had promised. They kept their distance, staying out of earshot but close enough to intervene should any danger appear.

"So," I said when Daisy at last collapsed onto the sand. "I take it Baron Hargin is someone to be avoided?"

"Always," Daisy assured me.

"He's a minor noble with an estate far too close to the palace," Millie told me, beginning to scoop sand into a pile. "And on his own, he's merely tedious. Plus, he usually comes to see Father, so it isn't so bad. As long as we stay out of his way, we can avoid his boring lectures on the duty of rulers to their people and the correct behavior of princes and princesses."

"As if we don't already know," Teddy scoffed, his hand inching in to the top of the basket while Daisy was distracted helping Millie with her sand pile.

I smacked his hand lightly and gave him a look that made him laugh.

"Protocol isn't what makes a good ruler," he said. "Whatever Baron Hargin thinks. And the rest of the nobles and the whole populace know it, even if he doesn't."

"Which is why Father is so well-loved," Millie said. "He knows ruling is about putting the people first."

"But Baron Hargin has children," Daisy said, maintaining her focus on the central point, despite her efforts with the sand. "A sixteen-year-old son and an eleven-year-old daughter." She made a face. "His daughter smiles prettily and says sweet things when the adults are around, but whenever we're alone, she's always lecturing me about how a princess should act. As if she would know!"

"Be grateful that's all you have to put up with," said Millie darkly. "His son is always trying to kiss my hand and drop hints about what a wonderful royal he would make." She gave me a pained look. "He's three years younger than me, heir to a tiny estate, and utterly insufferable. I can't imagine what he thinks I'll find so appealing."

"His good looks, naturally," Teddy said promptly. "How could any woman resist?"

"How indeed," Millie said dryly before turning back to me. "So you can see why we needed an escape. Once they found us, there wouldn't be any way to get rid of them without being horribly rude. And despite what the baron and his daughter seem to think, we generally try not to do anything to embarrass Father."

"No," Teddy said, his cheerfulness undimmed. "We just run, like the cowards we are."

"Perhaps the words you're looking for are skilled strategists," I suggested, and Millie nodded her approval.

"Exactly! And since we were able to leave word that we had taken our new guest for a tour of the island, they can't even be offended with us."

"Masterful indeed," I said with a chuckle. "And I must say, it's a lovely tour."

Teddy smiled up at me from where he was now lounging on the sand. "We really can take you on a tour, if you like."

"Just nowhere near the palace," Daisy cut in quickly.

"But surely there could be nothing to see more glorious than this." I gestured at the lagoon, the sand, the sky, and the greenery behind us. "I'm more than content, I promise you."

"Excellent. Then you can help Daisy and me with this sandcastle," Millie said.

"Sandcastle?" I gazed at the pile of loose sand questioningly. "It doesn't look like much of a castle, I'm afraid."

Daisy gave me an odd look. "Well, they don't have to look like castles, do they? And we're just getting started, anyway."

I nodded quickly, wishing I'd held my tongue. Yet another opportunity for me to give away my unnatural ignorance.

"We'll fetch water," Teddy said, hauling himself to his feet and offering me a hand. "Then you'll be able to start shaping it."

He produced two small wooden pails from inside the basket and handed one to me. Together we ambled down toward the gentle waves. I cast a single glance back toward his sisters. They accused Teddy of being a dreamer, just like my family accused me, but he fit here in this place, with them, in a way I never had in Merrita.

"It's been too long since we took a day to enjoy the beach," Teddy said. "Maybe it's for the best Baron Hargin came for a visit since we're stuck waiting anyway."

I grimaced. "Yes, I can't say patience has ever been my strongest attribute."

The sand had turned cool and firm beneath my feet, but I still jumped as the first wave crept smoothly up over my toes. The second one followed in its wake, and already I had adjusted a little to the change in temperature.

I glanced down quickly but could still see ten toes and smooth skin. A human reaction, then, like adjusting to the water of a bath. I took a deep breath, smoothing the concern off my face before looking up.

But for once Teddy wasn't watching me, his face instead pointed out to sea, while his feet were firmly planted in the water. He wore a dreamy expression as he gazed at the horizon, and I didn't have to guess what he was thinking about.

Earlier, this sign of his devotion would have thrilled me. But now I felt a surge of dissatisfaction. I wanted his attention on me, not some dream that had my hair and voice.

Reaching down, I let my fingers trail in the water before flicking a shower of drops toward his face. He started and turned toward me, for a brief second a frown flitting across his features, before I flicked him again and it transformed into a laugh. He might be a dreamer, but he was also kind and friendly and didn't seem to hold on to offense.

He took several deeper strides into the still ocean, ignoring his clothes, before attempting retribution. The water he sent in my direction was more of a wave than drops, and I jumped back shrieking. Millie and Daisy both looked up at the commotion, Daisy jumping instantly to her feet and rushing down to join us. Millie followed a little more sedately but with an eager enough gait.

As soon as Daisy arrived, she charged straight into the water, tackling Teddy around the waist and sending him flying backward full into the water. I gasped, but Millie had reached me, and she only chuckled.

"You might have noticed that Daisy is not one to be trifled with," she said.

A wave of water came racing toward us before I could respond, and we ducked in different directions. I aimed a retaliatory strike toward Teddy, hitting him full in the face while he was focused on splashing his sister.

He turned to me while Daisy pursued Millie, approaching with a mischievous gleam in his eye. I backed away slowly.

"You can't visit the beach and stay dry, you know," he said.

I put my hands up and backed away even further. "Oh, I think I can."

A loud splash behind us signaled Daisy's triumph, and the

sight of a sopping wet Millie distracted me from Teddy's approach. Panic burst through me. How much of me had to be submerged to trigger a transformation to my mer-form? Once I was in the water, the process took only seconds to complete.

Teddy, not reading my face, took a final step forward and scooped me up around the waist, half-throwing me over his shoulder as he turned toward the water, ready to dump me in.

CHAPTER 16

I erupted into violent motion just as I had done when the raider threw me across his horse, thrashing wildly and trying to push myself free of Teddy's grip. Whatever happened, I couldn't let him throw me in the ocean.

At the last moment I realized my mistake as my efforts met with success. Having twisted myself free, I began to slip toward the water. But Teddy moved even more quickly than I did, scooping me back up and depositing me safely on the sand, just past the level of the incoming waves.

"Thank you," I said, breathless and trembling.

"No, I'm sorry, Isla." He reached out as if to touch my arm and then quickly drew his hand back. "I should never have grabbed you like that."

My heart twisted. I wished I could tell him that in normal circumstances I would have enjoyed the half embrace a great deal more than I should. But that would involve telling him that this was no normal circumstance, and I couldn't do that.

"No harm done," I said instead, wishing we could return to the joking, happy mood of a few moments ago.

But before I could think of anything to say, the crashing

thunder of a wave rent the air—so different from the gentle lapping that had been a constant background to the day. I looked up in alarm. But the breaking white of the wave was against the distant reef, and only ripples of its fury spread across the lagoon toward us.

"What was that?" I asked.

Teddy shrugged. "It happens from time to time, although I'll admit they've been more frequent of late. You needn't worry, though. The reef keeps us safe from bigger swells than that. You should have seen the last wave that hit four days ago. It was a monster compared to this one."

Four days ago? I froze, counting rapidly in my mind. If they were more frequent recently, and the biggest had been four days ago…It lined up perfectly. And surely a disturbance on the ocean floor might cause a wave that was big enough to be noticed on shore.

Relief flooded through me. I had been afraid that while I waited here, my home might have already been destroyed. But Teddy was saying this tremor had been smaller than the last one. And that there hadn't been any others in the last four days.

I picked up one of the buckets which had been brought in by the water to bob against the sand and scooped up some of the clear liquid.

"Come on, then," I said to the others, a bright smile on my face. "Let's build this sandcastle." But as I walked back up the beach, I wasn't thinking of palaces of sand, but of the one I now knew was still standing beneath the waves.

It turned out Millie was right—the royal cook clearly had some sort of soft spot for Daisy who had managed to cajole a veritable feast for our impromptu picnic. It also turned out I had a previously unknown skill for sand sculpting.

When Teddy had announced we would have a competition among ourselves, and Daisy had chosen mythical creatures as the theme, I had been unable to resist sculpting a mermaid. And when Millie called the lieutenant leading the squad of guards over to judge for us, I couldn't help the swell of satisfaction at being pronounced victor.

I was still enjoying the honor now, with Daisy insisting that I receive all the most enticing treats from her basket as my prize. Teddy accused me of keeping them all in the dark about my extensive skills, and I had nearly retorted that it was, in fact, my first time making a sand sculpture. I only just bit the words back in time. I could hardly make such an admission when he believed me to be from a small, coastal village.

After lunch, I had thought we might return to the palace, but all three siblings assured me that we were far from safe yet. Daisy then insisted we all visit a rock pool which lay further around the curve of the beach, where a section of rock jutted out from the trees, across the sand, and into the water.

I was hesitant at first about anything called a pool, but I soon discovered it was shallow—the water reaching barely above ankle height. Small fish darted through the crystal waters and small pieces of dead, bleached coral drifted around.

"Oh look!" Daisy cried, pointing at a bright orange sea star draped across the softly waving fronds of a yellow sea anemone. I splashed over toward her, taking care not to step on the repulsive body of a round sea cucumber, its dark green color broken up with brown lumps.

"Very pretty," I agreed once I had closely examined her find.

"Sea stars can regrow their limbs. Did you know that, Daisy?" Teddy asked, eyeing the poor thing with far too eager a gleam in his eyes. Almost as if he was tempted to pull one off to see what happened.

"Obviously." Daisy rolled her eyes. "Since you've told me before."

Teddy turned to me instead.

"Are you familiar with sea stars?" he asked. "I know the northern current hits the Talinos coast, so the water is quite a bit colder. Do you have them there?"

"Ah..." I said elegantly, scrambling to remember if sea stars lived in the northern waters.

"But really it's the sea cucumbers you have to watch out for," he said, pointing at the one I had just avoided. "Don't ever step on them. They can make you really sick."

I nodded, unsure what was safe to say.

"Sea stars can be poisonous, too. And coral," Daisy announced with relish.

"But don't be nervous," Teddy was quick to reassure me. "It's perfectly safe to swim around here—especially in the lagoon. Just don't touch anything but sand if you can avoid it."

I had to bite my tongue to keep from telling him that I had been well versed in the dangers of various forms of sea life from before I could walk. Irritation rose inside me as he kept talking, oblivious to my obvious disinterest.

"Obviously don't swim past the reefs. It's deeper and colder out there, and the currents can catch you up before you know what's happening. But you'll be safe enough in here if you stick with us."

He gave me a charming smile, and I tamped down on my annoyance, smiling back. He thought I came from a coastal village, did he really think me so ignorant about the ocean? Or did he think I seemed like the kind of person who was afraid of everything?

I reminded myself that I had been forced to behave a little like it earlier—he was just trying to help me after my apparent nervousness earlier about being out in the lagoon. I was standing here with the boy I had been dreaming of for years, and I couldn't let the sort of silly irritations that passed back and forth between me and my sisters intrude on the moment.

But still, my enthusiasm for the rock pool had waned. I stepped back out onto the sand. It wasn't until I stepped free of the water that I felt the wrench, though. I had never gone so long without being fully immersed before, and wading in the ocean felt like a relief and a strange torture at the same time. I glanced up at the clear sky, looking unsuccessfully for a glimpse of white. Maybe I wouldn't feel so parched if the sun wasn't constantly beating down on us without relief.

"I'm going up to the tree line," I said. "I want to get out of the sun for a few minutes."

"Good idea." Teddy followed me onto the sand. "We can pick a coconut or two while we're there. I think there was a knife for the purpose in the basket. I'll meet you there."

I skipped awkwardly across the hot sand further up the beach. He hadn't asked me to wait for him, or to take guards with me, as if I needed careful coddling. Which showed my irritation had been entirely misplaced. He hadn't doubted me, he had merely been swept up in his own excitement about the ocean and missed the cues that I had no need of his information. He had been attempting to care for a stranger who might be in danger—it was sweet, even if it displayed a certain obliviousness. I shook my head, starting to feel slightly dizzy from the heat. What was wrong with me?

"Ahhhh..." I sighed with relief as I stepped into the cool shade of the trees, the grass soft beneath my feet. It was different from the sand but pleasant in its own way.

Glancing up the tall, bare trunk, I stared in bewilderment at the distinctive green fronds. There were coconuts up there—I could see them—but how was anyone supposed to get up to them?

I was still looking upward, pondering this question, when rough hands grabbed me around the waist, propelling me through a clump of some sort of thick bush or low hanging tree. It brushed against my face and bare arms, making me gasp and panic, and then we were through into open air again, no longer in sight of the beach.

My hand flew to my waist, but I wasn't wearing my sword. I whirled around anyway, arms raised to defend myself, and my eyes locked onto a familiar sight. A trident. I faltered. A moment later, my eyes caught on the man holding it, and I gave a quiet scream.

"Ray!"

He gave me his customary lazy smile.

"Greetings, Princess!"

"Shhh!" I glared at him. "Don't call me that here! And goodness I've been so worried. Are you hurt? Did they just let you go? I've been feeling terrible about it all. What happened?"

"Whoa, whoa." He held up a hand. "That's a lot of questions."

"And where did you get a *trident?*" I added, not helping the cause. "Are you sure you should be carrying one around openly like that?"

He shrugged. "Apparently some of the men from small fishing villages use them. This particular one saved my life, so I have no intention of relinquishing it."

My eyes widened, and I was about to prod him to hurry up and tell me everything, when someone moved behind us through the vegetation. I turned, backing up toward Ray, but it was only Teddy who burst through to confront us.

Ray immediately swept me behind him, bringing up his trident in a defensive posture. Teddy's face turned thunderous, and his sword leaped from its scabbard.

The two young men faced each other, all hint of laziness vanished from Ray's face and body, just as Teddy had shed both his light-hearted cheer and the dreaminess that sometimes seemed to disconnect him from the world. Both of them looked deadly serious, and the loud clash of their weapons sent a spike of terror through me.

I darted out from behind Ray.

"Stop! Stop it at once! Teddy, I'm not in any danger. This is my uncle." I turned to face Ray. "And this is Teddy. Prince Theodore. The one whose family has been generously hosting me. *The last person I would ever want you to attack.*"

I overdid the emphasis and watched Ray draw back, amused understanding spreading across his face. Heat flamed in my cheeks, and I kept my face determinedly turned away from Teddy until I could force it back under control.

"Well then, that changes everything," he said. "Did you say *Prince* Theodore?"

I nodded slowly, giving him a warning glare, and turned back to Teddy. The prince was watching us with confusion on his face, the point of his sword lowered, but the weapon still tightly gripped in his hand. I stepped toward him.

"Teddy, this is—"

But I didn't manage to finish the introduction before more rustling sounded behind us. All three of us swung around in time to see Millie come bursting through the greenery.

She stopped, her eyes growing round as she looked from Teddy's naked sword, to Ray's trident, to me, hovering in the middle.

"What in the kingdoms is going on here?" she asked. "Daisy wanted to stay in the rock pool, so I told the guards to stay down there with her. Only then you all disappeared, and I thought I heard..." She frowned, looking again between the sword and the trident.

"It was just a misunderstanding," I said quickly. "They were both just trying to protect me."

Millie raised both eyebrows and turned her full attention to Ray. I didn't need her to voice any words to understand her question.

"Teddy, Millie, this is my uncle. Nereus."

Millie gave a choking cough. "I'm sorry, did you say your uncle? The one who was abducted, I assume?"

I nodded.

"I thought that's what you said earlier." Teddy slowly returned his sword to his waist, but I noticed his eyes stayed fixed on Ray's tall form, and his expression didn't grow any friendlier.

"Your uncle?" Millie said in faint tones. She shook her head and addressed Ray directly. "I have to admit, you're not what I've been picturing."

I bit my lip. Neither of them had managed a good look at Ray, slung across a raider's horse that was galloping down the beach, and it had never occurred to me to clarify Ray's age. But something in Teddy's eyes made me rush to explain the situation.

"I suppose he's actually my half-uncle," I said. "He's thirty years younger than my mother. Her father married again in later life. By blood he's an uncle, but in reality, he's more like a brother." I shrugged. "I only have sisters, so…"

Finally Teddy relaxed and offered Nereus a small smile.

"I'm glad to see you're alive and well. Isla has been extremely concerned for you."

"I can see she's been wasting away with grief and fear," Ray said, regarding me with a slightly caustic expression.

I put my hands on my hips and glared at him. "I *was* worried. But I also trusted that you could take care of yourself." I gestured at him. "As you clearly have been able to do. Plus," I added triumphantly, "we sent out spies, and they reported back that you were in good condition."

Ray's eyebrows lifted.

"Spies at the raider camp? Within the raiders, you mean?"

I shook my head. "Just observing from outside. We only just found you all."

Ray nodded. "I'm glad you managed that much. When the rumor reached us that your prisoner was proving uncooperative, I thought I had better come and find you. Plus *I* wanted to check on *you*, at least."

I rolled my eyes at the mocking gleam in his. "No doubt you knew I was just as likely to land on my feet as you."

He chuckled. "More likely, I imagine. Plus," he added in a more serious tone, "it was fairly clear you were in good hands once it became clear what had the raiders so worked up."

"So you've managed to escape them?" Millie asked.

Ray hesitated. "Not escaped, precisely, since I'm no longer a prisoner."

"But that's wonderful!" I said. "Now you can come back to the palace with us, and we can—"

I paused, arrested by a sudden thought. I glanced between the twins. They had promised to house me until my uncle could be rescued, and now he was free. They would be expecting us to bid them farewell and continue with our plans. Except we didn't have any plans, and I'd already found my ocean boy. The last thing I wanted to do was leave.

"The situation with the raiders isn't good," Ray said, lines of concern appearing on his face. "They've been—"

"We know," I said, cutting him off without thought. "They've been using hostages to force men to join their number." I smiled proudly. "Millie and I worked it out. And then the prisoner confirmed it. The rumor about him being uncooperative was spread by us so we wouldn't endanger his family."

Ray looked impressed, glancing from me to the princess, who had yet to contribute to the conversation.

"Then you know that we have to find that hostage camp," he said.

"We have patrols searching right now," Teddy said.

Ray nodded slowly, and I could see in his eyes that his thoughts were far away, analyzing every angle of the problem.

"Once you know where they are, you'll free them, and then come for the raiders." He said it as a statement not a question, but I still nodded confirmation.

"Unless they move again, and you manage to lose them." Ray's grip on his trident tightened. "I need to stay with them."

"Stay with the raiders?" I grabbed his arm. "What are you talking about?"

"If they move, I can get away again and let you know where they've gone," he said. "And when you eventually come to attack, I'll sow confusion and rally those who want no part in it."

"We can't risk alerting them to our efforts too early," Teddy said quickly.

Ray gave him a flat look. "Of course not."

I bit down hard on a grin at seeing the prince and Merrita's youngest captain size each other up. I glanced toward Millie, expecting to share my amusement, but she still looked stunned.

"Ray's been trained as a guard," I said, deciding we needed some sort of explanation for his competence. "And he basically grew up with one of those in his hands." I waved at the trident.

Ray grinned, his posture relaxing, and hefted it into the air. "They're good for fighting and fishing, so there's not much more you could ask for, really."

"If you're sure you want to take the risk," Millie said slowly. "It's not something we can ask of you."

Ray nodded once, decisively, and I shook my head at him. I knew better than to suggest he pursue a less risky course. Just as he would never have told me to stay back if our squad confronted a leopard seal, or even a shark.

"But you're not leaving again until you tell us what happened," I said. "Otherwise I'll die of curiosity before I see you again."

He lifted his eyes heavenward. "Well, we couldn't have that now, could we? It's not such a complicated tale. They hauled me back to their camp, but since they were eager to be gone from it, they hauled me along to their next destination without stopping to discuss my fate. By the time they got set up somewhere new, the leader seemed to have ransom in mind. But I rapidly disabused him of the notion that he would be able to find anyone with coin to pay in exchange for me."

"I'm glad he didn't decide to dispose of you on the spot," Millie said.

"Well, they had something of the sort in mind, I'll admit," Ray said.

A rush of belated anxiety swept over me, and I had to remind myself that he was here in front of me, clearly alive and well.

"I realized I needed to do something decisive," Ray said, "so I declared I wished to join them. I said I was sick of being dirt poor, and ready to carry someone else off across a horse instead of being the one carried. That seemed to amuse the leader, but he said men who joined his crew had to prove their worth."

Ray shook his head. "It was obvious they didn't think much of me after seeing how inept I was on a horse and that I didn't carry a sword, so I demanded a trial by combat. Their leader laughed and agreed, no doubt thinking he would get an amusing show before his champion finished me off. They brought out two swords and the biggest of their own men, but I pointed out that in a trial by combat, I got to pick my own weapon. And, fortunately for me, when they showed me their pile of accumulated weapons, I found a single one of these."

A slow smile spread across my face as I pictured the scene, and the looks on their faces once they saw Ray with a trident in his hands.

"How fortunate," I said. "Obviously you couldn't lose once you had that."

Teddy raised an eyebrow at me, but he'd never seen Ray fight.

"Once I won, I demanded a place among the raiders," Ray concluded. "And their leader has taken quite a shine to me." His voice turned grim. "I don't think he gets a lot of willing recruits."

"It seems Trione has cause to thank you," Millie said. "You have taken our people's well-being to heart most swiftly."

Ray shrugged. "It is the job of a guard to protect the vulnerable—wherever they may be found."

"Speaking of guards..." I glanced back toward the beach, invisible through the trees. "I don't think we should let any of them see Ray. And we shouldn't tell anyone except Captain Flint himself that Ray is working for us. Just in case."

Both twins nodded rapid agreement.

"They'll come looking for us soon enough," Millie said, sudden alarm in her eyes. "You must be gone at once, Nereus."

He nodded and gave them both a half-bow. Before I knew what was happening, he was striding deeper into the trees. I ran after him, throwing my arms around him in a farewell embrace and taking the opportunity to whisper in his ear.

"A tremor beneath the ocean causes a big wave here. There's only been once since we left, and it was a small one." I tried to add that our people were safe, but my throat closed over, reminding me that I couldn't directly reference Merrita now, even when we were alone.

He got my message anyway, though, nodding once, before hesitating.

"Your ocean boy?" he asked softly, and I nodded, not quite able to meet his eyes.

"Don't get lost in a dream, Isla," he said softly.

That made me look up swiftly, but he was already half gone. I stared after him, concerned.

I wasn't the one I was worried about. It was all too like him to wish to help the people here—but I had expected him to be more concerned about the people we left behind. It was almost as if it was more than a fleeting fit of pique that had driven him to join me on the surface.

When I finally walked back to the twins, however, Millie's expression immediately distracted me. She pulled at my arm, drawing me close, and letting Teddy outpace us as we wove back through the trees to the beach.

"Isla!" she said reprovingly. "You told us he was your uncle. None of my uncles look anything like that."

I laughed. "I guess I'm so used to it. He's the only uncle I've got. But I do have an aunt, and I will admit, she's nothing like Nereus." No one had ever thought of Nerissa and the word lazy in the same sentence.

Millie looked at me with a horrified expression. "No, I should imagine not!" As we stepped out onto the sand, I heard her grumbling to herself. "An aunt indeed!"

CHAPTER 17

$\mathcal{T}$wo nights later, a summer storm hit, sudden and ferocious. Peals of thunder kept me far from sleep, and I found myself straining to hear the faint sound of the crash of the waves on the reef. Finally, I gave up attempting to hear through layers of marble walls and pulled a light wrap around my shoulders. It was long and green, and trailed on the floor around my feet as I padded down the corridors toward the practice colonnade.

When I reached it, I moved to stand in an archway, gazing across the sand toward the ocean. Here I could clearly hear the drops of water hitting the surface of the lagoon as the rain curtained down, and the crash of the waves. I breathed the salt air deeply, strange smells of dirt and green mixed in that I didn't recognize. It was like the storms at sea, and yet unlike in so many ways.

And—as always—it reminded me of *the* storm. I planted my feet, trying to hold firm against the call of the ocean. Up here the storm was almost frightening, but I knew that once I dove beneath those waves, it would transform just as I did.

Lightning flashed, illuminating my surroundings, and—as if

brought into being by my thoughts—I made out another figure among the arches.

Slowly, on silent feet, I walked the long length of the colonnade, the call of the water overridden by a stronger pull. He stood right down the end, where a section of white marble jutted out to meet the curling edge of the bay. Marble steps led downward, and the waters of the lagoon actually lapped against the stone.

The moon dove out from between clouds, and for a moment, the water almost drew me forward, but the light also fell across Teddy's hair—strangely colorless in the moonlight—and I resisted. He was staring out to sea, his gaze distant, and his bearing straight and still.

Another flash of lightning threw everything around us into stark relief, and he stirred at last and glanced back at me. I had expected him to start, or show some surprise, but he didn't. Almost as if he had known I would come.

"It's mesmerizing, isn't it?" he said, speaking right into my ear to be heard over the crashing clamor of nature around us.

I shivered at his breath on the side of my face and pulled the wrap more tightly around me.

"I can never stay in bed on such nights," he said. "I feel the pull to be closer to it all." His eyes returned to the distant, roiling sea.

I bit my lip as I followed his gaze. Isla of Talinos had no business knowing what he was talking about, but Princess Isla of Merrita knew all too well the allure and the memories that swirled in those clouds and darted down with each drop of rain.

"There's something so wild about it," I said. "So free."

He nodded without looking down. "A man might forget anything in the midst of such mighty chaos." He paused. "Or imagine anything." He sounded as if he was trying to convince himself.

"Oh no," I said without thinking. "Some things are too real to be imagined."

This time he did glance at me, although the moon had slid back behind a cloud, and I couldn't make out his expression.

"Yes, you are right, of course. Some things are beyond what I could imagine. And out here, in storms like this, I feel close to…" He shook his head. "I'm sorry, I must sound a little mad."

"No." I rested a hand on his arm without thinking, and he didn't pull away. "I understand. There is something about both a storm and the ocean that is just…bigger than us."

"Yes, exactly," he said, looking at me with a hint of surprise. I suspected from what I'd seen of his family so far—and what I'd heard of the absent Gabe—that he wasn't used to anyone understanding this side of him.

A fresh peal of thunder rang out, and we both fell into silence. After a moment, I sat down on the top step, bundling myself in my wrap and gazing out at the dark water. A minute later, Teddy sat beside me. Neither of us spoke.

Whether one hour passed, or three, or four, I couldn't be certain. But at last the storm spent its fury, and passed on, the air already starting to warm again.

I started at the strangeness of silence, only to realize I had dozed off at some point, my head nestled into Teddy's shoulder. I pulled back, horrified, but he was smiling at me.

"I can't seem to stay away from storms, but I've never had company for one of these vigils before. It was more pleasant to have a companion than I anticipated."

"I'm sorry to have disturbed you," I said. "I couldn't stay away either."

"Please don't be. I, of all people, understand."

We fell back into the silence, although it was slightly less comfortable than before—on my side at least—and when he bid me goodnight, or rather good morning, at the door of my room, I hurried inside as fast as I could.

Lying in bed, staring into the darkness, I decided that I couldn't risk going back there at night again. No matter how the sea called me. It was too dangerous—to my heart and my secret.

But two nights later, I couldn't resist. My skin felt stretched and dry, parched almost, in the constant heat and wind. The water called to me. I could almost hear it lapping against those steps.

I reasoned that there was no storm, and so I needn't fear meeting Teddy there. All I wanted was to walk down the marble steps and dip my feet into the water that I had been so carefully avoiding during the day.

This time the moon shone brightly, lighting my way, and allowing me to clearly see the prince as he walked down the long colonnade only minutes later to join me on the stairs. He offered no explanation of his presence, and neither did I. Instead we both gazed across the water, illuminated this time as it had not been during the storm.

Though I had told myself I couldn't risk meeting him here, a thrill raced through me. He had said he came here to watch storms, but there was no storm tonight. Had he come hoping to see me? Had our connection the other night drawn him from his bed just as his dreams had done previously?

We met many times after that among the arches. During the day we received reports from the spies and the searching guards, and an air of impatient tension seemed to follow me wherever I went. But at night that drained away, and my only regret was that I couldn't slip into the water, don my tail, and lose myself in the vastness of the ocean.

Sometimes we were silent, more asleep than awake, but sometimes talk sprung up between us while we watched the waves. We talked of what it was like to be the youngest compared to the oldest—if only by a few minutes—and what it was like to have a twin. His description of his connection with Millie made me despondent. Perhaps if I'd had a twin, I wouldn't have felt so out of place beneath the waves.

He told me about the many adventures they'd all had in the years Gabe lived with them, and I wished I had been around to join the fun. It was clear Teddy loved his foster brother and missed him.

"Although sometimes he exhausted me," Teddy admitted one night. "When he was here, we were always on the go. I wouldn't have dreamed of missing any of the adventures, of course, but I need some time to myself at night."

"I'm sorry," I had said, "you must be desperate to have your private retreat back."

But he had merely cocked his head, gazing at me as if taken by surprise.

"You know, it's a strange thing. If you'd asked me a month ago if I wanted someone else here at night, I would have said I would hate it. But you're so comfortable to be around, Isla. Your presence doesn't tire me at all."

It wasn't the most romantic of comments, but it filled me with pleasure all the same. While he was with me, Teddy didn't miss the time he used to spend dreaming of his ocean girl.

It was harder to reciprocate with stories of my own childhood, but I managed as best I could, modifying them as necessary. I understood what he meant about being comfortable because my throat closed over far too often as I slipped and tried to say something the enchantment wouldn't allow. It was too easy to forget to be guarded here in the moonlight with no one but Teddy around.

I told him I had always felt different from everyone around me, that I felt things they didn't feel. I was thinking of the pressure of the water, although I couldn't say it. He had still seemed to understand, though, talking of a different kind of pressure that had weighed him down since birth. In his case, it was the pressure of knowing that he alone would sit on the throne one day. Behind his words, I could hear a trace of guilt at the knowledge that he was to have the crown merely because he had been born a few minutes before Millie.

Did Oceana ever find her position as heir to be an unwanted burden? Now it was my turn to feel guilty that I had never thought to ask.

I was always looking for openings, and finally one night, I managed to turn the conversation in a natural way to the other kingdoms and the darkness that plagued them.

Except, to my surprise, I discovered that darkness no longer held sway in any of them.

Joy rose within me, drowning out any other emotion. The Old Kingdoms respected the ways of the godmothers again and had brought life and hope, not darkness, here when the way was opened.

"It all started with the Tourney," Teddy explained, in answer to my carefully considered prompting. "We expected an invading armada when three of their princesses got pulled into it against their will, but somehow instead, we got a turning of the tide. Most people seem to think everything changed after Palinar, but it was really Marin that was the key."

"The Beast, you mean?" I asked, tentatively. I had heard enough casual talk to associate him with Palinar.

Teddy grinned. "Well, he was the flashy one. And Palinar had suffered the original curse, of course. They let the darkness in, although almost everyone else succumbed quickly enough. But the twins were more than a match for Dominic, of course. And he's only going to be more outnumbered soon."

"Twins?"

"You didn't hear that they're twins, too?" He laughed, and though I didn't understand the reason for his humor, I found myself smiling anyway at the familiar sound of his throaty laugh. "Two of the princesses who came are twins—and now they're both pregnant with twins of their own."

I still didn't understand why this struck him so humorously, but I could find no trace of my father's fears in the domestic picture this painted.

"And everyone else is free, too, as you've no doubt heard. Celine took on Oliver and the icicle that Eldon had become," he continued. "And I don't know where Snow found the courage, but she rose up out of nowhere and overthrew her stepmother. That woman was going to bring Eliam to ruin, and we all knew it, although we didn't know how to stop it. Snow got herself engaged to some woodsman as well. She's young, so they've had a long engagement, but they'll be married in the winter."

He glanced sideways at me. "Perhaps, if you're still with us then, you'd like to travel with us to the wedding? It will be in Eldon naturally, since she's queen."

I stayed silent, feeling a pang at the invitation. I wouldn't still be here in winter, of that I was sure.

When I didn't reply, he hurried on, as if trying to cover the momentary awkwardness. "I still can't quite imagine Snow as a queen. Gabe must find it even stranger than me—he was always a little disgusted with her timidity." He chuckled. "Gabe doesn't have much patience with fearfulness, which is rather ironic as you would know, given your own kingdom's plight."

I tried to look knowledgeable, although I didn't know what fear had to do with Talinos.

"We all miss him here." Teddy sighed and gazed out over the water. "I think at some point my parents might have been thinking he and Millie would make a match of it, but after eight years, he's too much of a brother for either of them to think of such a thing. And we hardly need any strengthening of our ties now. So it's probably a good thing he married Addie."

He laughed again. "It's too bad you weren't able to be there for their wedding. In typical Gabe fashion it wasn't quite like anyone else's. They had an honor guard of white swans—and one crotchety black one who tried to bite the official as soon as he declared them married. You should have seen the poor man's expression, although one of the bride's attendants rescued him at the last moment. But the best bit was when I saw Addie's godmother giving the bird a stern talking to later on in the evening. A very strange sight, I assure you."

"Godmothers," I breathed, and Teddy nodded.

"Yes, all the rumors are true. They really have returned. As each kingdom has fought free of the darkness, their godmother has returned to assist them. I keep waiting for ours to show up because our troubles have only come now at what should be the end of it all. Father was always unusually faithful to the ancient laws, and we thought we'd escaped the darkness completely. Until these raiders showed up. I'm not even sure they're from Trione."

He shook his head. "But we probably shouldn't be surprised. If there were mercenaries willing to take on cursed Palinar and its Beast, then you can be sure there will be men attracted to the riches of our island. They've gutted three whole villages already." He smiled at me in the dim light. "But thanks to you, we will soon be able to turn the tide on them as well."

I chewed on the inside of my cheek. So everything was reversed. All the kingdoms of the land—even the Old Kingdoms—followed the ancient ways again, their godmothers returned to them. While in Merrita, our calls were no longer heeded.

The news that so much had changed since the last report Merrita received should have been uplifting. The surface was safe again. Which meant my father was free to blow the royal conch and allow Merrita to rise again.

But the joy I had felt earlier had all drained away at Teddy's mention of the godmothers. The tremors were getting worse, and it was clear now my father had entirely misinterpreted their message. Whatever warning they contained had gone unheeded, and now the godmothers had withdrawn from us. It seemed, despite everything, we had strayed from the right path ourselves, and my people were in danger.

But my despondency didn't last long. I finally had the proof I needed to convince my father that the tremors were warning us to flee the ocean bed. And my father possessed the means to bring us up, safe and intact. As soon as Ray and I were free to return to Merrita, we could help ensure our people's safety. And hopefully when we finally obeyed the warning, our godmother would return.

In my agitation, I considered spilling my secret to Teddy. But then I remembered I could not, thanks to the enchantment. And a moment later, I remembered I also should not. I could still clearly see my father's face as he upbraided me for my foolishness in speaking out to the court, only for him to still turn around and trust me with his greatest secret. I couldn't betray his trust. When Merrita rose to the surface again, the godmothers' old enchantment of protection would be lifted, and my tongue would be free again. And my vow not to sing would lift also. Then I would come to Teddy as a princess—his equal—and tell him everything. He had come to know the real me now, and I longed to tell him I was his dream girl, also.

But none of that would happen unless I could convince my father my report was not the wishful exaggeration of a rebellious child. And for that I needed Ray. Which meant there was nothing to be done but keep waiting.

"Would you like to go to the market?" Millie asked, sticking her head through the door that connected our rooms. "The moon will be at its thinnest tonight, so it's the big one."

"I'd love that," I said eagerly.

I had already heard plenty of talk about the market that occurred each month just outside the palace. Queen Juliette had promised Daisy that this time she might choose her own material for her next gown, and Daisy had spent a long time considering what to select.

"Don't worry," Millie said with a twinkle in her eye. "We'll only spend about half the day at the cloth merchant's stall while Daisy deliberates."

I laughed. "What a pity it would be if we were accidentally separated from her by the crowd."

Millie rolled her eyes. "I'm the fool who already promised I would help with the choice, so you'll have to convince Teddy to help you with that one."

"I don't know what you're talking about," I said with a straight face. "Naturally if I get lost it would only be by total accident."

"That's good." Millie nodded approvingly. "But not good enough for Daisy. We could never fool her, even when she was shockingly young. I think she spends too much time observing people—or should I say spying on them? Her governesses are always telling her it's not ladylike, but I can't help feeling it's a practical occupation for a princess. Knowing people—and what's going on in the kingdom—is sort of the role of a royal."

I bit my lip as I hurried to change into a practical dress for a day at the market. Was that the role of a royal? The memory of that disastrous ball once again surfaced, and I winced before pushing the image aside. I was going to come back with a way to save my people—hopefully that would make up for a lifetime of not really knowing them.

In Merrita, the palace sat amid a city, one almost as large as the city-state of Marin, according to the ancient history books. The palace of Trione, however, was the center of a group of sprawling villages, all within a day's ride of each other. And, once a month, the villages gathered in the large clear land that extended west from the palace.

Traveling merchants from further flung parts of the island and even the other kingdoms would also attend—making the most of the chance to access so many people at once. The crowd had been swelled in recent months by the presence of a large number of guards—their protection ensuring the raiders didn't get any ideas about attending themselves.

I heard the noise first, a low, chattering rumble that could be heard as soon as we stepped out into the palace courtyard. But as we walked through the open gates and toward the assembled wooden stalls, it was the smell that nearly overwhelmed me. The sound had reminded me of our markets at home, but here the overwhelming smell of horses and livestock mixed with the delicious aromas of roasting meat to create something entirely unfamiliar.

I made a small gasping noise as I clamped my arm over my nose and mouth.

"Don't worry," Teddy said, stepping up beside me. "You get used to it. And then all you can smell, wherever you go in the market, are the pies." He lifted his nose into the air and inhaled deeply. "There. I can smell them now."

"Pies at this time of the morning?" I shook my head, still covering my nose.

"It's never too early for pies," he said with a grin.

"No pies until I've chosen my material," Daisy said with a glare at both of us. "I'm not finding the perfect one only for you to get berry stains on it."

We followed along obediently toward the largest of the stalls selling lengths of cloth. My head swiveled in every direction, taking it all in. It was still strange to see a replica of my home with no city around it. And most jarring of all was the lack of a Hall of Meeting, balancing the palace. But I had known I wouldn't see one, since it had been built after Merrita sank. When our people realized they were trapped together, with nowhere else to go, the king had declared they needed a place to come together in unity and know that their voices would be heard. Did the people of Trione feel their voices were heard? Perhaps one day—when I was free to talk about my home—I could suggest that one be built here.

We approached the cloth stall, but just before we reached it, a group of men in home spun clothes with the distinct smell of fish lingering about them crossed our path. Teddy instantly grabbed my hand and pulled me away, darting behind the screening wall of fishermen. A moment later we had passed behind a stall and out of sight of the cloth merchant.

Teddy didn't drop my hand, and I tried to pretend it wasn't the only thing I was thinking about as we strolled through the stalls. Did he even realize he still held it?

"No one who thinks cloth should take priority over pies is a fit leader for our day," he said as we walked. But he must have read discomfort in my eyes because he added, "Don't worry. I'm quite sure she forgot all about us as soon as she saw all her options spread before her."

Another couple holding hands passed, heading in the opposite direction, and I realized with a smile that I recognized them. From the way Bertram was looking down at Sara, I could see that the emotions I had observed in her previously were reciprocated. I was pleased for them both. But seeing them made my own hand throb strangely.

Did Teddy even realize he held it? The gesture certainly seemed to mean much more to me than to him.

He finally noticed my abstraction and followed the direction of my gaze.

"Excellent," he said in an under voice. "I was a little afraid his courage would fail him, which would have been a pity since I gave him the day off specifically."

"You gave Bertram the day off so he could take Sara to the market?" I stared up at him, a little surprised he would notice the romantic interests of one of the general footmen.

He grinned after them, not seeming in the least offended by my tone of surprise. "She already had the day off, so it seemed like a perfect opportunity. Not that I would have known anything about their interest in each other if Millie hadn't pointed it out, of course. But once she had, swapping his day off seemed like the least our family could do. And now it means their rest days will line up in the future, too."

Of course Millie had been the one to see the budding romance. I should have guessed that. Still, it had been a kind thought from Teddy.

"Your Highness!" A piercing call halted us before we could reach the pie seller's stall.

A man in elaborate robes hurried over to us, a young girl and a youth in tow. The girl's eyes fixed on our joined hands, and Teddy instantly pulled his free, his eyes focusing on the man who was now bowing. The youth followed his father's lead while the girl dropped into an elegant curtsy. She continued to watch me, however, through narrowed, judging eyes, although she only looked about Daisy's age.

"Good morning, Baron," Teddy said in a relaxed voice that somehow didn't carry his usual friendly tone.

I regarded the three before us with more interest. This must surely be Baron Hargin and his unpleasant children.

"But is it a good morning?" the baron asked, frowning. "I fear it is hard to think of it as such when I live in constant expectation of being set upon at any moment."

I could almost hear Teddy's jaws clenching together, although he spoke with admirable restraint.

"As you can see there are more than enough guards present to ensure the safety of everyone at the markets."

"Ah, but who will protect us in our beds, Your Highness?"

"I assure you that the crown is taking active measures to protect the people from the raiders," Teddy said, his voice noticeably more strained.

"Is Princess Millicent enjoying the markets today?" the baron's son asked, craning his head to try to see through the crowds around us.

"We were sorry to miss you all when we visited the other day," his sister said in a simpering voice that set my teeth on edge. Escaping people like her was half the reason I signed up to train as a guard.

"I suppose this is your visitor," the baron said, his eyes focusing on me and clearly finding me wanting. "Most unusual."

Teddy stiffened beside me, going from merely irritated to haughty and commanding in an instant.

"I think," he said coldly, "that you will find it is far from unusual for the royal family of Trione to extend hospitality to those visiting our fair home. Or are you suggesting my father has become derelict in his duties, including that of hospitality?"

"No, certainly." The baron looked alarmed. "I certainly meant no such thing."

But the glance he cast his children suggested it was exactly what he had meant. No doubt he thought the royal family derelict in their duties for not sending a small army to fortify his estate. At least that had been the demand he made on his visit earlier in the month. Our dinner the evening after our beach adventure had been a great deal enlivened by King Edward's caustic comments on the matter which Queen Juliette informed me in an aside were a necessary outlet for his frustration.

Better he says it in the privacy of this room than to the nobles directly, she had said, and I had enthusiastically agreed, hoping my words and expression conveyed that I understood her subtle warning. I would never dream of relaying anything they said to anyone else.

But I couldn't help remembering the words as I looked at the baron, and I could hardly blame the king for being as irritated as his son. The man was clearly entirely focused on himself.

"Father," the girl said, pulling on the baron's sleeve, "you said that I might buy a new comb, remember?" She had clearly lost interest in us upon spying a jeweler's booth some way beyond.

"Certainly, my pet," her father replied, appearing almost as eager as she was to remove himself from the conversation.

"He truly is an insufferable man," Teddy muttered as soon as they were out of earshot.

I nodded sympathetically and started to tug him toward the pie stand. At first he resisted, still glaring balefully after the baron, but when he finally saw the direction I was moving, he relaxed and looked more cheerful.

"Now that's what a market is supposed to be about," he said.

I let him make the order, gazing absently over the milling crowd while the seller collected our pies. Being out here felt almost like being back in Merrita's bustling streets, almost bursting now since we had no way to expand our city. But the overarching blue sky, the soft touch of the ocean breeze, and the brightness of the sun made it impossible to forget I was on the shore not beneath the ocean.

As my eyes idly slipped over the people strolling past, they fell on two men I recognized, walking calmly through the crowd. I stiffened, feeling a shock as strong as if I had brushed against a stunning eel.

CHAPTER 18

A sound, half cry, half gasp, squeezed out of me, and I started forward, only pulling myself back at the last minute. Ducking behind the stall, I peered out to follow their progress, relieved that they didn't appear to have seen me.

Because I had no idea how they would react if they did. Just like I had no idea what two Merritan guards were doing strolling calmly through the middle of a market here, above shore. They didn't carry their usual tridents, but there could be no mistaking them. Connor and Dante had been full guards before I started as a recruit, but I had done patrols with every guard in Merrita at some point or other.

I drew back once they walked out of view. Should I leave the market immediately? They would no doubt recognize me just as easily as I had recognized them—more so, probably, since my status had always made me stand out among the guards. Would they attempt to intervene if they realized I was here? Perhaps drag me back, willing or not, to my father? I froze.

Had he sent them here to find me?

But surely not. They had not appeared to be searching partic-ularly, just making their way through the crush of people. I thought again of the ease of their manner. These two men had not just splashed out of the ocean for the first time. Sudden understanding washed over me. Of course. Father himself had told me that guards were sent to the surface.

A giddy smile burst over my face. How surprised and delighted they were about to be when they heard what changes had been wrought on the surface in the last two years. Everything had changed since last we checked on the land dwellers, and it would no longer rely on just my testimony—or even on Ray's. I wanted to dance in place.

"If you've got your eye on those two merchants, you're out of luck, young lady," said an amused voice.

I looked around and realized I had somehow inched down to shelter behind the next stall over, one covered with various creations in lace. An older lady sat behind it, her hair graying but her eyes sprightly as she eyed me with interest.

"Merchants?" I asked. "What merchants?"

She pointed in the direction the Merritan guards had taken. "Those two strangers who just walked past. The ones in brown leather who you couldn't seem to take your eyes off. They're just passing through."

I frowned. "How do you know?"

"I'm good with faces." She shrugged. "And those two come through regular as clockwork—they just don't stay for long. They're traders all the way from Eldon, I believe."

My frown deepened as I considered her words. I supposed it made sense that they would need some sort of cover story and a background that put them far away from Trione. It would give them the chance to ask the questions they needed to ask. But her words still bothered me.

"How often do they come through?" I asked.

She laughed. "You're a patient one, are you? I've never seen them linger to chat with the young ladies, though."

"How often?" I repeated.

"Only once every six months. So I'm sure a pretty thing like you will have found a more friendly young man by the time they visit us again."

"Oh, there you are, Isla." Teddy appeared around the back of the stall, an individual berry pie balanced in each hand. "I wasn't sure where you'd gone for a moment. What are you doing back here?"

The stall holder's eyebrows rose sharply as she looked between me and the prince.

"Well, well, well," she muttered. "That's unexpected."

But I heard both of them through a haze, my mind having slowed to a crawl. I kept trying to remember my father's exact words when he had told me of the guards visiting the surface. I couldn't seem to recall him saying how often they came, but given Teddy's account of the recent changes across the kingdoms, I had assumed they must only come once every few years.

But this stall holder had recognized them easily enough, and she had no possible reason to lie to me about such a thing. Which meant these guards had been here only six months ago. And six months before that. Which meant they knew that the darkness had lifted from these kingdoms—knew it and had never reported it.

Everything swirled around me as I tried to make sense of it. Why would these guards be hiding the truth from their king? I could think of no possible reason for it.

Teddy continued to chatter away, but I couldn't make sense of his words. Eventually he took a deep bite into his pie and gave a satisfied grunt. When I glanced blindly in his direction, he tried to thrust the second pie at me.

"Go on!" he said. "Try it. And tell me it isn't the most delicious thing you've ever eaten. Not even the palace chef makes them quite this good."

I shook my head, my thoughts a whirl of tridents and guards

and my home and my father. Real fear gripped me. These guards must have a reason to lie to their king, and they must know the consequences of being discovered. Which meant the last thing they would do was drag me back to my father. In fact, they might be determined to make sure I never made it back at all.

I swallowed, everything coming back into focus as my thoughts crystallized. I needed to get somewhere out of sight.

Teddy had dragged me a short way from the lace stall without my noticing and was still attempting to push the pie on me. I shook my head, my stomach churning. Should I go straight back to the palace? The so-called traders could hardly start wandering around there.

"Come on," Teddy coaxed. "At least try it. You'll love it, I promise. Absolutely everyone does."

I had felt so light-hearted as I entered the market, and now everything had changed. Darkness seemed to have descended on me from nowhere. Why couldn't Teddy see it on my face? Why did he keep pestering me about a pie, of all things?

Tension simmered inside me, threatening to erupt. Teddy was the boy from the storm—the one who had looked into my eyes and seen deep into my soul, the one who knew me, the real me, better than anyone. Why couldn't he see my distress now? Why wouldn't he leave me be!

I whirled around, my elbow catching the pie Teddy was still offering me and knocking it to the ground.

"I don't want the pie," I said through gritted teeth. "Can't you see that?"

I strode away from him and plunged into the surrounding trees. As soon as I was out of sight—although not out of hearing —of the market, I sank down onto a convenient rock and took several deep breaths.

Something was wrong—very wrong—with everything. My father's guards were lying to him. My own life might be in danger. Ray was in the middle of a raider's camp. And Teddy had suddenly changed—no longer sensitive and caring, no longer the one who truly knew me.

Tears burst from nowhere, streaming down my face. I took a couple of gulping sobs, but already the pressure was easing at the sudden release.

"Isla!" Millie's voice sounded concerned, and she sank onto the rock beside me, putting an arm around my shoulders. "Don't worry. He knows you didn't mean to knock the pie down. He isn't angry."

My tears instantly ceased as I stared at her in confusion. She thought I was crying because I imagined Teddy was upset with me?

"Why would he be angry?" I asked, my voice tight. "I was the one who was upset and sick—and he didn't even notice! I'm the one who should be angry. He was completely thoughtless."

Millie stiffened, her arm dropping from around me, and a second too late, I remembered that I was talking about her twin.

"You were fine when the two of you snuck away from us not so long ago."

"Yes, well, I saw something…" I said, lamely.

Millie raised an eyebrow. "So, Teddy isn't always the most observant. So what? He's a dreamer at heart, we all know that. Some people just don't see every detail—and some never will, no matter how old they get. But it's not as if the rest of us are so perfect."

She stood, putting her hands on her hips and glaring at me. "That doesn't mean he's thoughtless. Who do you think asked the spies to look for any sign of your uncle if they found the raider camp? Teddy, that's who. He knew you were worrying. And he's gone out of his way to make you feel at home here. Who cares about a stupid pie in the face of all that? And a pie, might I add, that he was excited to share with you because it's his favorite food, and he thought you would love it, too."

I stared at her, my mouth hanging open, unable to form any words. After a loaded pause, she turned and began to stalk away.

Suddenly my mind began to race, moving as quickly as it had previously gone slowly. It had been Teddy who told them to look for Ray?

She was right, of course. I could think of a hundred other examples of Teddy's consideration, and not just toward me. Only today Bertram and Sara had benefited from his kind actions.

But other things came to mind, too. The way he had tried to throw me into the ocean, oblivious to my cues that I didn't want to get wet. The way he had rushed to instruct me about the dangers of the sea, not noticing my disinterest. This wasn't the first time he had failed to read my mood. But they were small irritations, things any normal person would have brushed off. But I hadn't made light of them so much as I had turned my eyes away and pretended they never occurred, which had left them to simmer beneath the surface.

Until suddenly I found myself stressed and anxious, and it all came boiling out in an overreaction to a minor offense. And then, to top it off, I had spoken badly of him to Millie—upsetting someone who had shown me just as much kindness as Teddy had.

"Millie, wait!" I called.

She stopped, almost to the edge of the trees, and turned slowly back around.

"I'm sorry." I stood but didn't move toward her, leaving it up to her to decide whether she wanted to close the distance between us.

After a moment's hesitation, she walked back to join me, the irritation already fading from her face.

"You're completely right," I said. "Teddy—all of you—have been more than kind to me, and I completely overreacted. It was a moment of stress, and it wasn't really to do with any of you. Please forgive me."

She regarded my face, eyes slightly narrowed, before her expression relaxed, and she smiled.

"Of course," she said. "Believe me, no one knows better than me how irritating he can be sometimes. He gets lost in a dream and fails to notice what's going on in front of his nose. But he really does have a generous and loving heart. And I wouldn't be much of a twin if I didn't try to protect it."

I could hear the faint warning behind her words, and I realized suddenly why all those small, unimportant things Teddy had done had annoyed me so much. I had been blushing and losing myself in his eyes all this time not because he was Teddy, or even because he was a handsome prince, but because he was my storm boy. He bore the face that I had spent two years building an elaborate dream around.

And in my dreams, my storm boy knew and loved every part of me. He read and understood every change of my moods. He never said the wrong thing, he never bothered me when I wanted to be alone or left me alone when I wanted company. In short, he wasn't a person at all.

Because real people had flaws. They got excited, and distracted, and absorbed in things other than me. But they also had the capacity for depth and richness far beyond a dream. They had real arms to fold around me, jokes for me to laugh at, and a comforting shoulder for me to fall asleep on. Teddy might sometimes be too abstracted to notice my emotions, but he no sooner thought of a kindness than he acted on it. Could I really accuse him of being thoughtless?

I had told myself I was in love with Teddy, but I had been in love with a dream. And every time Teddy did something that didn't fit my idealized image of him, it needled at me, poking holes in my delusion. But how could I love his ability to sit by my side for hours while we lost ourselves in the wild beauty of a storm, and then turn around and get offended when he got lost in his own thoughts at other times?

I had been treating Teddy like a dream, not a person, and I had nearly destroyed the real friendship I was building with these two actual people because of it.

Overwhelmed, I threw my arms around Millie.

"Thank you," I murmured into her hair.

"For what?" she asked, drawing back and staring at me with bewildered eyes.

"For understanding," I said. "For defending your brother because that's what siblings do. For everything."

"You're welcome?" she said, the words coming out like a question.

"Isla!" The rough voice interrupted us, and I whirled, my hand dropping to the hilt of my sword—which I had made sure to wear this time—before my mind caught up.

I had heard that voice say my name enough times to recognize it even here.

"Ray!"

"I don't have long," he said. "But when I heard about the market, I knew it was my best chance to find you."

"Don't tell me the raiders mean to attack the market?" I cried, aghast.

"No." Ray shook his head. "They're not big enough fools."

"They've moved camp, then?" Millie asked.

He nodded approvingly at her, as he had not done at me, and I had to squelch down a renewed surge of irritation. Toward Ray, at least, the sensation was familiar and almost comforting.

"But not before letting their forced conscripts see their loved ones," he said. "They were starting to get agitated, so it had to be done. And between that and the move, they got sloppy enough that I can tell you exactly where both camps are."

"Both camps?" Millie leaned forward, clutching at his arm in her excitement.

He stilled, his eyes dropping to her hand, and she pulled it quickly back, her eyes widening. I watched them both with a quirked eyebrow. I had often clutched at Ray in anger or excitement, and it had never elicited that reaction...

"Yes," Ray said, seeming to recover himself. "The raiders' camp and the hostage camp. And if you can free the hostages, fully three-quarters of the raiders at the main camp will turn on them with more ferocity than your guards are likely to show."

"Tell me where," Millie said, determination on her face.

Ray quickly outlined the distinctive details, none of which made much sense to me. But Millie nodded, asking a couple of questions and seeming satisfied with the answers.

"I know the spots," she said.

"Good. Then I have to be going." Ray stepped away and offered her a small bow.

I noted with some amusement that he made no effort to include me in the gesture. But as he began to stride away, I lunged forward and grabbed his arm.

"Isla, I don't have time," he said.

"I know," I whispered. "But I saw something. Something important. Connor and Dante are here! In Trione. And they've been coming every six months."

He frowned at me, his attention finally focusing on me instead of the trees.

"They didn't see you, did they?"

I shook my head, remembering that I hadn't had a chance to tell him about my conversation with Teddy yet.

"No, but the two of them come every six months. And I've recently learned that these kingdoms have been pushing back the darkness and returning to the godmothers for *two years*. Wait," my mind caught up with my mouth. "Did you see them too?"

He nodded once, but a sound off in the trees made his head whip up, and he shoved me lightly away from him.

"I can't stay. You two need to go. Now!"

And he took off before either of us could say a word.

I grabbed Millie's arm, and the two of us hurried back toward the market, only pausing on the edge of the trees to glance back. There was nothing to be seen but vegetation, however.

CHAPTER 19

"But Father," Teddy said through gritted teeth, "this whole operation is under our command. We can't let everyone else bear all the risk for us."

"Yes, it's your command," King Edward said calmly, "and part of command is knowing when your job is to issue orders and when it is to get involved. This is most definitely an issuing orders situation."

Teddy looked away, clearly still displeased, and the king sighed.

"I'm not doubting your capability," he said. "But if you take part in the actual attack, then you're making yourself a target—one the rest of the guards will have to protect. And that will just distract them from their real job—and might end up getting people killed."

"But while it might not be wise for us to attend the attack on the main camp of raiders, it's different with the hostages, surely?" Millie asked cautiously. "We'll need clear and strong leadership with so many innocent lives at stake, and we'll need to take supplies and doctors beyond the guards' own medics in case some of the hostages are injured or ill. Perhaps we can wait with them back behind the fighting?"

King Edward surveyed her for a moment. "That sounds like a sensible suggestion."

Teddy opened his mouth, but Millie moved slightly, and Teddy jerked before falling silent, no doubt the recipient of a swift kick under the table. Millie's study of both people and politics were clearly telling her they didn't have a hope of winning this one. She'd done well to negotiate a compromise—I only wished I had shown as much sense with my own father.

We all retired to our beds shortly after to get a good sleep before the early morning raid, but I, for one, struggled to sleep. My skin felt stretched and dry—parched, although I had drunk three glasses of water at dinner, earning myself some strange looks from Millie. Tonight wasn't a night for staying up late and talking or dreaming, but this time it was the ocean itself that called me.

When I reached the steps leading down into the water, I was alone. I told myself I would just dip my toes in, but I couldn't resist sliding a step lower, and then another one. The moonlight glinted on the constantly shifting surface of the water, and in a moment of madness, with a single glance over my shoulder to check I was still alone, I abandoned my wrap and let myself slip all the way in.

The water enveloped me, not deep, but cool and refreshing. The tingle swept down my body, transforming the long skirt of my nightgown into scales and giving me breath and vision again. The night no longer looked dim and dark, and the whole of the lagoon opened up before me.

I twirled and spun, letting the water rush past me before stopping suddenly and floating, suspended weightless above the sand. Here, in the shallow water, I didn't feel the pressure of the deep sea, the subtle reminder that the ocean could be a heavy weight. Here I only felt light.

I was a princess of mermaids, and yet I had spent so many years looking toward the surface and believing I would find my true home there. But here I was, on the land at last, and the sea still called to me. Why did I feel something akin to a physical sigh of relief at the feel of the water rushing up to cradle me? Was I just the foolish, dreaming child my father thought me after all?

I gazed up at the moon, visible through the clear, shallow water above me. But as I did so, my eyes swept across the edge of the palace, and I stiffened. A familiar figure now stood there, and he looked to be frowning down at my discarded wrap.

With a flick of my tail, I shot across the lagoon, away from him. Reaching the coral that bordered it, I swam along beside it, careful not to brush against its bright surface, dimmed a little in the moonlight. When I reached the stone of the promontory, thrusting out into the water, I followed it back around to the palace once more. Hidden around the corner of the building, I approached carefully. Peeping past the edge, I stayed beneath the water, although I counted more on the darkness than the clear lagoon to hide me.

But I strayed too near the surface, and a faint splash—more ripple than anything—accompanied the tip of my head breaking through into the air. Teddy started, turning toward me, and I immediately pushed myself back down, flattening against the sandy bottom.

I yearned to swim all the way up to the steps and reveal myself to him. But I couldn't imagine how such an encounter would go when I was prevented from telling him anything about my people or my history. And he needed a clear, focused mind for our raid in just a few, short hours.

Rejuvenated by the water, I knew my swim had done more for me than extra sleep would have. But I wished for his sake that he would return to his bed.

His image became clearer, larger, and I only just caught myself in time as I drifted unconsciously toward the surface. He looked so alone standing there. Did he feel lonely after so many nights of my company? Did he miss our conversations? Or was he glad, after all, to once again have the peace to dream of his ocean girl?

But whatever he was feeling, he didn't remain long. With a final lingering look up and down the colonnade, and another searching one across the surface of the water, he carefully folded my wrap and placed it on the top step before disappearing back into the palace.

I gave him five long breaths and then another five. And then, unable to wait any longer, I pushed my head back up into the air, gazing at the empty stairs. Well, not completely empty, my folded wrap a reminder of his presence.

My desire to play in the ocean seemed to have drained away, leaving exhaustion in its place, and I heaved myself up onto the steps, propelling myself far enough out of the water that my legs re-formed. I hurried up the steps, my nightgown dripping puddles around my feet, and snatched up my wrap. But by the time I had made it back into the main corridors of the palace, it was almost as wet as the rest of me.

"A midnight swim?" a voice asked. "That's a strange way to prepare for battle."

I spun, my eyes searching through the half-light for the speaker. When they fell on only Daisy, my racing heart slowed again.

"I'm not going to be part of the battle, remember?" I reminded her.

"Close enough," she said, her voice sour. "While I have to stay here and miss everything."

A shot of alarm rushed through me. Was she hatching plans to follow us?

Daisy sighed. "Mother has even informed me she's assigning two guards to watch me all day to make sure I don't go after you."

I heaved my own soft sigh of relief. A highly sensible measure by the queen.

"I'm sorry," I said, able to be sympathetic now that I knew she would be safely away from any fighting.

She shrugged. "It's hardly your fault."

Her gaze dropped down to the small puddle that had started to accumulate at my feet, and I hurried out a quick goodnight and dashed for the safety of my room. Dry and tucked in bed, I told myself I couldn't risk returning to the ocean in such a way again. But even as I thought it, I didn't know if I would be able to resist.

~

We gathered at dawn. Five squads of guards on horseback or foot, a wagon with three doctors and a range of supplies, and me and the twins. I had been on a couple of practice rides by this point, but no one wanted to put me in a saddle on such a serious and dangerous occasion, so I rode with the doctors.

We had to take a roundabout route due to the wagon, our numbers, and our need for secrecy. Our path took us well beyond the range of our regular daily excursions, and despite the solemnity of the occasion, I enjoyed seeing more of the island. The coconut trees—which I had learned were called palms—seemed to grow everywhere, sometimes in clumps of two or three, and sometimes among much heavier vegetation.

We moved south and slightly west, heading for the southern coast where the raiders had found shelter among a collection of irregular rock formations. Ray had explained that they were looking for somewhere that wouldn't leave tracks. And certainly nothing out of the ordinary could be seen as we approached.

The sandy soil ended abruptly where the porous black rock began, the end point for the animals and the wagon. I could see Teddy and Millie restraining their frustration as they held a quick consultation with Captain Flint before giving final murmured directions to the guards. I felt it too, my hand constantly straying to the sword I had wrapped tightly around my waist. It felt wrong to come so far and then linger behind, keeping ourselves safe. But it didn't matter how we felt, we had to think of the captured children and let the guards do their job.

Within minutes, the guards had left, Captain Flint at their head. The doctors busied themselves unpacking supplies which they lined up on the floor of the wagon. A single squad had been assigned to protect our position, and they spread out in a circle, their eyes focused outward for any sign of movement.

Teddy, Millie, and I drew together. All of us threw wistful glances at the doctors, and I knew we were all wishing that we had something useful to occupy ourselves with, just as they did. But soon enough they had done all they could to prepare and had joined us in the waiting.

The plan relied heavily on the element of surprise and of overwhelming numbers. But the captain had instructions to scout out the camp first, seeing if he could interpose his men between the captors and the hostages from the start of the conflict. I knew it was critical that they approach slowly, but the minutes ticked by at an agonizing crawl. How could it possibly be taking so long?

Millie wandered over to consult with the doctors in quiet tones, and Teddy turned to me. I could see a storm in his eyes, and his frequent glances toward the steep rocks in front of us gave him away. But he still forced a smile.

"It feels like it's taking them forever, doesn't it?" he said. "But it would actually be a worse sign if we'd heard something by now. If they're taking this much time, it means they haven't been discovered by the raiders."

I smiled back at him, touched by his efforts to reassure me, although the truth of his words obviously wasn't doing much to reassure him. I was about to thank him, when a sound in front of us made me cut off, both of us tensing instantly.

Feet scrabbled against the rocks, dislodging small pebbles that clattered away down the steep inclines of the jagged waves of stone. But we still couldn't see anyone. And no distant sound of fighting reached our ears, either.

A small figure appeared at the crest of the nearest rocks, shorter than Daisy, although not by much. An adult followed, her hand reaching out to steady the youngster when he nearly toppled down the surface in his haste. Teddy started forward toward them, but the closest guard waved him back, his face tense.

The woman looked up and saw the guard. She gasped and slowed. But her eyes traveled on to Teddy and then the wagon of medical supplies behind him, Millie still standing beside it.

"Oh, it's true, it's true!" The woman's voice caught on a sob. As soon as she reached the sandy dirt, she dropped to her knees as if her legs could no longer support her. "Your Highness!" she gasped.

Teddy stepped forward again, but Millie beat him to it, rushing to take the hand of the staring child and lead him toward the doctors.

"Come," she said. "Let our doctors examine you."

Teddy reached forward to take the woman's arm, helping her to her feet, but as he did so, he spoke in a quiet, urgent voice.

"What is going on back there? Are there other hostages coming?"

The woman took a deep breath and visibly pulled herself together.

"Yes, oh yes. There are more not far behind us. A large group of us were in a tent on the edge of camp, and your guards cut through the back and said if we ran this way there were doctors waiting for us. Some of the others thought it was a trick." Steel entered her face as she glanced at her son. "But I wasn't missing out on my chance. I said if there was any hope of getting free, we were taking it."

More feet sounded, scrambling across the rocks, and another set of hostages appeared. With a quick glance, they took in the situation, their eyes dwelling on Teddy and Millie's faces, and one of them let out a glad cry. The others whirled on him with angry looks and whispered reminders to keep his voice down, and I realized why we hadn't heard any fighting yet. The captain was attempting to get as many hostages away as possible before the violence erupted.

More and more people arrived, all of them young, elderly, or female. But the first woman to arrive had returned to us, already cleared by the doctors.

"This isn't all of us," she said. "It looks like your guards convinced everyone in the tent in the end, but there were almost as many out and about doing various chores for the camp. Naturally the raiders don't like to do anything for themselves." She spat on the dirt beside us.

Teddy and I exchanged a worried look. I had begun to feel hopeful, thinking we might pull this off without any civilian casualties at all, but her words had dashed such hopes. A second later a single, bellowing cry sounded from the distance, followed quickly by a great many voices and the clash of steel.

The youngest child began to cry, and several older ones rushed to bury their faces in their mothers' skirts. Had that first cry been the captain's signal to his guards to attack, or the raiders' discovery of the guards? There was no way for us to know.

Teddy hurried forward and gestured for the remaining stragglers to move in toward the center of our circle, marked by the doctors' wagon. I rushed to help him, collecting a small child in my arms and depositing her on the floor of the wagon.

Less than a minute passed until we heard feet again, these ones coming faster than the first lot and accompanied by a great deal of grunting. I looked down and realized my sword had somehow found its way into my hand, and I had joined the guards' circle around the liberated hostages.

Teddy stood on one side of me, and Millie was wading toward us through the mass around the wagon. I saw one of the guards throw a concerned look in our direction, but the expression on Teddy's face must have convinced him not to make the futile attempt of remonstrating with the prince.

And then there was no time for such thoughts because a second wave of hostages came into view. This group thankfully contained no small children, but several of them struggled forward despite visible wounds.

I stepped away from Teddy, creating a wide gap in our circle for them to stream through. But the first of them had barely made it between us when a new set of figures appeared across the rocks. These ones bore weapons and ugly expressions of fury.

Several of the guards called warnings, and the fleeing hostages sped up. At the back of the pack was an older man with a long gash down one leg, accompanied by a burly woman who was supporting him on his wounded side. At the warning shouts, she bent down and scooped him up. Throwing him across her shoulders, she leaped down the last of the rocks and jogged toward us.

I raced forward, Teddy keeping pace with me, to meet them.

"Take him through to the doctors," Teddy shouted as we interposed ourselves between them and the pursuing raiders.

I could see now that there were five of them, each bearing a drawn sword. I wished briefly that I had a trident in my hand since it was a longer weapon, and I was more practiced with it, and then a blade thrust at me, and I was too busy defending myself to have time for wishes.

The crash of steel on steel reverberated through the air, and the jarring force of the blow smashed through my arm, nearly numbing it. I gritted my teeth, forcing the man's blade away and lunging forward in a counter-attack. He pulled back, out of reach, and I saw Teddy facing off against another guard beside me.

My attacker regrouped, pushing forward again, and a second raider joined him. I dropped back this time, conscious I couldn't let them push me into retreat or they would come within range of the hostages.

Parrying desperately, I fended off one blow and tried to whip my blade around to reach the second one in time. I realized in the fraction of a second that I wasn't going to make it. But a round leather circle appeared from nowhere, a shield interposed between me and the blow. I fell back another step, allowing the guard carrying the shield to settle into place beside me.

Now my attackers were reduced to one-on-one again, and I pushed my advantage, lunging forward with a feint and a lightning fast thrust that I had practiced on Teddy only days ago.

My sword tip slid past the edge of his leather jerkin, piercing his shoulder with sickening ease. I pulled it free as the man backed away with a bellow of pain.

But I didn't even have time to catch my breath before an alarmed voice called, "Watch your back, m'lady."

I whirled, dropping instinctively into a crouch as a sword swung toward my head. It rushed through the empty air where I had been standing a moment before. I surged back up, my sword raised awkwardly above my head to try to block any further blows, but I didn't encounter the raider's sword.

Instead, the man swayed and then crumpled to the ground, his weapon falling uselessly from his senseless fingers. His collapse revealed the woman who had carried the injured man, her right hand gripping a short wooden plank as if it was a cudgel.

"Is that a splint?" I gasped out between panting breaths.

The woman's look of fury, directed at the comatose man, faded, and she grinned across at me.

"Whatever tool comes to hand, m'lady."

I shook my head. "Thank you. You saved my life."

"What, that?" She gestured at the man with her splint. "*That* was a pleasure." She gave me a big grin that showed her teeth. "And seems to me, we should be the ones thanking all of you."

The guards had converged around us by this point, with the exception of two sentries left on the other side of the wagon. I turned to survey the chaotic scene in time to see a clean thrust of Teddy's take down the last standing raider.

"Let's hope they've been as successful back at the camp," said a gruff-voiced guard, as he bound one of our injured attackers.

I bit my lip, suddenly noticing that the distant sounds of fighting had stilled. Teddy glanced in the direction of the rocks and then back to the shifting crowd of freed hostages and captured raiders. I could see the resignation in his face. He couldn't leave the people here to go and see what had happened to the captain and his men.

But we didn't have long to wait. The sound of many feet was quickly followed by the appearance of our squads. My heart lifted only to sink again as I realized several of them had hastily bandaged limbs, and they carried two stretchers, each bearing a still figure covered by a thin sheet.

When they climbed high enough to look down and see the crowd of hostages and five vanquished raiders, their faces lit up, however. They had clearly been fearing a far worse outcome.

The captain pushed to the front of the crowd of guards, leaping the last section of rock to approach Teddy and me.

"I'm sorry to say one of the raiders got away," he said grimly. "We must move on the main camp at once, Your Highness."

CHAPTER 20

"I'm coming with you," Teddy said at once.

"As am I." Millie stepped forward to join him.

The captain frowned, but Teddy pressed his point.

"We're here in case the plans had to change, and that's exactly what's happening. We can't give you orders in advance if we don't know what you're going to find at the raider camp."

"You can consider it an order, Captain," Millie said. "And we'll deal with Father when we return."

"Very well," the captain said, clearly still reluctant.

"There is no time for debate, anyway," I said briskly. "We need to leave any injured guards plus enough able-bodied ones to protect everyone if the raiders somehow circle around and find them here. How many do you think are needed, Captain?" I didn't know the guards well enough to know how many would be required for such an assignment.

The captain frowned, his eyes running over the large group of hostages, and I could read in his expression that the number was a great deal higher than he would have liked. We had initially intended to see the hostages safely back to the palace before going after the main raider camp. But we had likely already lost the element of surprise, and we couldn't risk waiting around to see whatever response the raiders might make.

"If you're counting heads, count us in," said the woman who had saved me. She still gripped the base of the splint like a cudgel, the length of it resting against the open palm of her left-hand. Arrayed behind her were approximately twenty women and older men.

"We'd appreciate weapons, if you've got spares," she said. "But we're going either way, and you can't deny us. We spent long enough under their thumbs, we'd like a chance to get our own back. And we've got loved ones to rescue."

I could see from the light in her eyes that she was motivated partially by the desire to hit some more raider heads, and partially by a desire to ensure we didn't end up killing whatever man was serving with the raiders to keep her safe.

"She's capable enough even just with the wood," I said quickly. "She took down one of the raiders and saved my life. I'll vouch for her."

The captain gave me a somewhat skeptical look before turning to eye the oldest of the men. It was true he didn't look overly strong, but he just chuckled at the captain's scrutiny.

"Don't you be worrying about me, boy," he said. "I was bashing heads before ever you were born, and I don't think I've lost the skill of it yet."

"Ha!" The woman at the front snorted. "Those raiders be fools the lot of them, only interested in young men. If they only knew it, I'm as handy with a weapon as my husband ever was, and almost as strong. I would have been out of their camp quick enough if I wasn't worried for what they'd do to him." She gave us a significant look. "And given I saw one of them escaping off toward the raider camp with my own eyes, I'd say it's time we stopped jabbering and ended this."

Teddy nodded immediately and turned to the captain. "With

this lot to swell our numbers, we can afford to leave a full three squads behind, wouldn't you say?"

The captain still looked less than excited about exchanging his own trained men for unknown civilians, but he nodded assent and started barking orders. As his guards hurried either to the horses or to form up around the mob of people surrounding the wagon, he turned back to Teddy and Millie.

"They'll prove their worth regardless of their skill, I'll warrant," he said quietly. "With them at our sides, we'll be saved the task of convincing the blackmailed raiders their loved ones truly are free. Because you can bet that runner won't have blurted out his news to the whole camp."

No one in this conversation had paid me the least heed, and I decided the safest course was not to bring attention to myself but merely to take one of the available horses and manage the best I could. The attack team would all be mounted, and I didn't want to give the captain the chance to decide that my poor horse skills meant I was better left behind.

Those of the hostages who were determined to join the attack were outfitted with spare weapons of one sort or another. And, to my dismay, enough of them claimed competence with horses to take all of those remaining after the two guard squads were mounted. Those hostages left without a horse were soon pulled up in front or behind someone else—even some of the guards taking a passenger. It wasn't a long ride, and they would appreciate the numbers when they arrived.

Except it looked increasingly as if I was not to be going. My thoughts flew to Ray and then the twins, and my heart raced. It had been bad enough waiting at the wagon while the guards freed the hostages, I couldn't bear to be left so far behind, wondering if the three of them were injured, or even dead.

But just as I was determining I would run behind the horses if need be, a hand reached down to me. I looked up with relief into Teddy's eyes.

"Come on, Isla, time to be off."

I took his hand, put my foot on his, and swung myself clumsily up and over the horse's back. Teddy had to steady me, helping me twist and turn until I was secure.

"Thank you," I said as soon as I was settled.

"You didn't think I'd leave you behind, did you?"

He gave me a distracted smile, and I knew his thoughts were on those already injured and the danger still ahead. And yet, he had reached for me as a matter of course. He had been thinking of me when I was otherwise forgotten, and he knew me well enough not to suggest I should stay behind where it was safe.

Some things hadn't changed—I was still all too aware of sitting with my back pressed against his chest—but in other ways everything was different from the last time we had ridden like this, my first day in Trione. Then I had been wrapped up in a dream which had finally taken solid form. Now I thrilled to be held so close by Teddy—a prince who truly cared for his people and took his responsibilities to lead and protect them seriously, but who could also laugh in the face of a storm and accept his sisters' teasing with a grin. Teddy had shown me that you could lose yourself in dreams of far off places and people and still belong completely in your home and family. And, in the circle of his arms, I finally felt that belonging, just as I had always dreamed.

The ride down the coast passed in a blur, possibly due to my concentration on the task of not falling from the horse's back. I gripped the mane with white-knuckled hands, determined not to embarrass Teddy and slow everyone down by tumbling off.

The captain had sent two scouts after the escaped raider before bringing his wounded guards back to the wagon, and the two men wheeled out of the trees to meet us far sooner than seemed possible.

"Your Highnesses. Captain." They saluted briskly.

One of the horses stepped closer. "We didn't manage to catch him, I'm afraid. He made it into camp."

"Have they moved on?" the captain asked.

"No." The spokesman shook his head. "Not yet. They've been in something of an uproar. We didn't think it worth the risk to get close enough to find out why. Not when you told us to avoid being seen at all costs."

The captain nodded his approval and turned to Teddy and Millie who had been riding on either side of him.

"What would you advise, Your Highnesses?" His voice was neutral—almost too carefully so, as he sought the commands of young people at least two decades his junior.

I tried to make myself as small as possible, not wanting to intrude uninvited. Millie cast an anxious glance in our direction, her eyes seeking out her brother's.

"What do you think, Captain?" she asked.

His expression softened somewhat.

"I'd say the horses give us an advantage in combat, but if we just go charging in there, we won't have the chance to get the lay of the land and find out which way the raider chief is trying to spin this."

Teddy ran an absent hand through his hair.

"It's a tricky situation," he said. "It would be so much simpler if they were all true raiders, and we didn't have the complication of sorting out the coerced from the willing."

The captain hesitated for a moment, glancing back at the riders behind him before lowering his voice. "Exactly how strongly do you feel about the need to avoid any accidental deaths of the wrong raiders?"

"Extremely strongly," Millie said stiffly.

The captain looked unsurprised, but also unrepentant.

"Don't be forgetting they've been raiding all across the island, regardless of why they've done it."

"But we cannot disregard why they've done it," Teddy said in a stern voice. "And neither can we disregard that they've stuck to looting and abducting. Bad, yes, but there've been no killings thus far."

"Likely the chief knew his band might mutiny if he took it that far," I muttered, and Teddy nodded his agreement.

"In that case," the captain said with a sigh, "we'd better take the cautious approach."

"Perhaps we can do both," I said without thinking. All three of them turned to look at me, so I straightened. "We have Ray in the camp, as well as the twenty hostages with us, to assist in the task of sorting out the true raiders from the blackmailed ones. If I can get into the camp to Ray, I can tell him to spread the word that the hostages are free and for anyone there against their will to lay down their weapons. I'll pass on your word that anyone who's laid down arms will be unharmed. Then we'll give the call, and the cavalry can come streaming in. Fight anyone who's still bearing arms or trying to flee, and round up anyone who's laid down their arms. Between Ray and the hostages, we'll soon have anyone who doesn't belong in that group weeded out."

"An excellent plan," Teddy said promptly. "With one small adjustment. I'm not letting you go in there without me."

"Absolutely not, Your Highness," said the captain.

"I'm not asking you, Captain," Teddy said coolly. "And it makes sense anyway. If the promise of amnesty comes from me, it will be more likely to be believed."

A loud throat clearing from behind made us all turn to confront the hostage woman who even on horseback still bore her makeshift cudgel.

"If someone's heading into camp, then I'll be going along with them, if you don't mind."

I looked between Teddy and the captain. "She'll certainly go a long way toward confirming our claim."

Teddy shrugged. "Why not?" He looked across at his sister. "Millie?"

She looked torn but gave a resigned sigh. "I'll remain behind with the captain as a sop to Father." She glared at him. "But if I hear the slightest sign you're in trouble, I'm leading the cavalry in without waiting for your signal."

The captain gave a small groan, but he seemed to have resigned himself to the fact that the twins did not intend to stay out of the action this time, and the king was not around to gainsay their orders. I narrowed my eyes at Millie as the thought occurred to me. Had this been her plan all along? Had she gambled on the fact that something would go awry, and they'd have the opportunity to get involved? Politics, indeed. Clearly there was more value to life at court than I'd ever realized.

"We'll work our way in closer while you're gone," the captain said. "But slow enough to keep it quiet. Just so we're within hearing distance of your signal."

Teddy lowered me from his horse's back, following me down with more grace than I had managed. The hostage woman dismounted as well, and Captain Flint waved for the two scouts to also dismount and join us.

"The name's Ellen," the woman said quietly as we waited for their approach.

"I'm Isla," I replied. "Glad to have you with us."

The woman regarded me for a moment and then gave an approving smile. "Seems you actually are, which is something. I'd say old high-and-mighty back there—" she jerked her head back toward the still mounted captain, "—would gladly replace me with one of his own."

"The captain knows your value," said Teddy. "As do I."

"Do you now, Your Highness?" The woman gave him the same assessing gaze, although this time it was accompanied by a small bob and head nod.

"Isla said you saved her life," Teddy said, "and that's not something I'm likely to forget."

I went pink, looking quickly away. He had gone out of his way to cheer me up, had been the only one to think of me back at the wagon, and now this. It was hard to remember why I had ever allowed myself to get so worked up over a pie.

The scouts joined us, and the five of us took off without further conversation. We hadn't picked our way through the trees long before we could hear the uproar that the scouts had reported.

The trees and vegetation were thick enough to screen us, although not so thick that a mounted company couldn't ride through—as long as they didn't attempt to hold any sort of formation. Which meant it was also clear enough for the raiders to get out if they decided to mount up and flee. As far as I could see, that would be the biggest hurdle to our plan's success, and I half expected to see them all in the process of doing so by the time we arrived.

Instead the scene we found was so unexpected that it took me several seconds to absorb. As soon as I did, my stomach flew up to lodge as a ball in my throat.

The horses all stood to one side of the large clearing, still picketed in place, although several of them were completely or partially saddled. A number of dirty looking tents stood in random formation, with three others in states of partial dismantlement, completing the picture of preparations to leave that had been interrupted.

The cause of that interruption was readily apparent, the raiders all being gathered together around a flat-surfaced boulder that rose to about waist height. Multiple people were yelling at once, but it was easy to pick out the only familiar voice to me.

Ray, clearly the center of the disturbance, stood atop the boulder, his trident swinging dangerously in a circle to keep back the raiders who circled him. One darted forward while I watched only to have his sword knocked aside by Ray's weapon.

With the numbers against him, they could easily have rushed

him en masse and dragged him down, but many of them seemed hesitant, hanging back with looks of uncertainty. And none of the ones who had circled in close appeared willing to be the one to take the hit from the three sharpened prongs that would allow their fellows to safely pass.

A moment later my mind made sense of what Ray was shouting, and I understood the hesitance and confusion of those hanging back.

"I'm telling you, that so-called messenger came from the hostage camp! Didn't you recognize him?" he called loudly. "And I can tell you right now what he was here to say: your people have been discovered and freed by the crown."

As he spoke, clearly repeating a message he had delivered before, the chief of the raiders attempted to shout him down. Several of those closest to the stone jeered loudly as well, but I noticed more than one of them casting nervous glances over their shoulders as if they realized that their backs were vulnerable if the coerced raiders changed sides.

A couple of the braver ones among those hanging back yelled questions at the chief and called to let Ray speak.

"Where is this so-called messenger?" One of them yelled, and Ray fell silent to let him be heard, although his trident still whirled in a defensive circle. "Let him come out and be seen and relay his message in person, if it's true he doesn't come from the hostage camp."

Several of the others were heartened enough by this demand to call out their support. Ellen, beside me, whispered proudly, "That's my man."

The chief, his expression ugly, began to push his way through the crowd toward the dissenter. Ray's voice picked up again, his tone even more urgent.

"See, he has no defense! Because it's true! Now is your chance. Honest men to me!"

"Lies! All lies! From this snake in our midst," the chief cried, still thrusting his way through the crowd toward Ellen's man.

"He speaks the truth!" The female voice rang out, bringing a single moment of deafening silence as everyone present swung around to stare in our direction.

Ellen stood alone and defiant several steps into the clearing, her cudgel now clutched in her left hand while her right held a long dagger.

"Ellen!" cried her husband. "That's my Ellen! It must be true."

"Well, that's done it," said Teddy, almost cheerfully. "So much for the plan."

He put his fingers in his mouth and let out a whistle that made me clutch my hands to my ears. Then he stepped out to join Ellen.

"Every hostage has been rescued," he yelled. "And every raider who is here by force is offered amnesty by the crown. Lay down your arms, and you will be spared."

There was another second of ringing silence, shock on everyone's faces, and then the chief changed course. His gaze swept the clearing, and when he saw no one else coming forward to join the prince, he clearly thought he saw a way to salvage some of the situation. I could almost see the calculations in his mind as to how much ransom a crown prince might be worth.

Both guards and I scrambled forward to join Ellen and Teddy. There was so much hubbub now that it was hard to make out distinct sounds, but I thought I heard a thunder that could be hooves behind us. We just needed to hold off the raiders long enough for the guards to arrive.

Staring forward at the mass of raised weapons, however, my heart sank. Almost no one had laid down their arms, after all. We would never be able to hold off so many.

Ray, his eyes latching onto me, leaped from the rock, his trident driving forward. He landed on one knee, his hands still gripping the weapon which now sprouted from the chest of a downed raider. It was hard to be sure with everything going on, but he looked like the one who had held the knife to my throat so many days ago.

Within another second Ray was up and running toward us, but even with all his skill, he wouldn't be enough against so many.

The chief reached us, Teddy stepping forward to meet him himself. Another raider rushed to his chief's aid, and I thrust out my sword inelegantly, apologizing silently to the beautiful weapon for using it like a stick to trip someone. It worked, however, the raider going down hard.

I whipped my sword back up, expecting to need to fend off another attack immediately, but no weapon greeted my ready blade. I stared around in confusion at a clearing that was still a chaos of weapons and realized my mistake.

I should have known from the response of the able-bodied hostages that the coerced raiders weren't likely to throw down their weapons and stand meekly by. Few of them had responded to Teddy's offer because most of them had chosen instead to fall upon the true raiders. Small clumps of fighting men spread out across the space, and one of the tents had caught on fire, the flames already leaping high.

The thunder of hooves was now unmistakable, and with a rush of air, horses swept into the clearing around me. Ray, who had just reached me, took one look at them and raised his voice to deafening volume.

"The guard have arrived! To me, honest men, to me! Throw down your weapons and run."

Once again, the action around the clearing paused as everyone stared in shock at the latest arrivals. But this time, everywhere I looked, men were breaking off to sprint in our direction. Most of them had thrown down their weapons, in obedience to Ray's direction, and the opponents they had left behind were already being engaged by the mounted guards.

"Teddy!" I cried. "Where's Teddy?"

My eyes searched through the chaos for the prince, eventually finding him still locked in battle with the raider chief. I ran toward him, but someone else got there first.

A chestnut mare bore down on the two combatants, a slim figure leaning precariously sideways to run the chief through with her sword. The man collapsed, blood streaming from his right shoulder, and Teddy saluted his sister.

"Magnificently done, Millie."

"Well, I couldn't let you have all the fun, could I?" she responded quite calmly, although I could see the way her hand shook.

Two guards who had been following Millie slid down from their horses to take charge of the chief.

Moments later, it was all over, the true raiders all either killed or subdued, and the honest men gathered into a shifting mass on the edge of the clearing. Ray emerged from among them, many of them patting him on the shoulder as he passed.

Millie dismounted to join Teddy and me, and the three of us hurried over to join him.

"Excellent timing," Ray said with a grin. "I knew there was something up as soon as I saw that raider run in here, white as a sheet and covered in sweat. Snuck up close enough to the chief's tent to hear his report, and that was that. The chief was all for driving everyone out of camp as fast as they could go, but I couldn't let us leave if rescue was about to arrive."

I shook my head, my relief making me irritable. "You're a foolhardy—"

But my insult was cut off by a cry from the middle of the mass of unarmed raiders.

"Hey! You ain't one of us!" the rough voice said.

I spun in time to see a true raider, hidden among the coerced ones, erupt from the crowd, drawing a long dagger from inside his boot as he did so. He lunged wildly at Teddy, who had already returned his sword to his scabbard, aiming for his chest.

I had no time to do anything but throw myself bodily at Teddy, knocking him down and out of the way of the lunge. As we both fell, Ray spun, sweeping the man's legs out from under him with the pole of his trident, bringing it around to press the sharp tips against the man's chest.

"I wouldn't move if I were you," he said in a voice as cold as the sea.

From the edge of my vision I saw Millie gazing at him with wide eyes before my entire attention focused on the fact that Teddy lay flat on the ground, while I lay sprawled full-length across him. His eyes were so near, I could make out each long eyelash. And my suddenly malfunctioning brain mused on the fact that their color was even more like the sea up close.

Then my gaze caught on his lips, so close I could feel his breath, and everything in me froze.

"Not that this isn't pleasant," Teddy said, his voice light and amused, "but do you think I might get up now?"

Gulping, movement and thought suddenly returned to me, I pushed off him and scrambled to my feet. Mortified, I would have turned away, but he stood almost as quickly and grabbed at my wrist.

When I turned and met his eyes, his face was still so close and utterly serious now.

"Thank you, Isla," he murmured quietly. "But I want you to promise you'll never throw yourself toward danger for my sake again."

Caught in his gaze, I couldn't look away. But neither could I say what he wanted to hear.

"I can't promise that," I whispered back.

His brow creased. "Why not?" His grip tightened slightly. "I couldn't bear it if anything happened to you because of me."

"And that's the problem," I said. "I couldn't bear it if anything happened to you at all." I finally succeeded in tearing my eyes away, pulling my arm free too.

I had revealed more than I meant to, but too many emotions had passed through me in the last hour to leave room for circumspection.

I glanced over my shoulder as I moved toward Millie and Ray. Teddy stood where I had left him, staring after me with an odd, startled look in his eyes.

I hadn't meant to say anything, but I didn't regret it either. It was time Teddy stopped thinking of a dream girl and started thinking of a real one instead.

CHAPTER 21

The trip back to the wagon and the freed hostages took a great deal longer in the other direction. Between the joyous reunions of the hostages who had come with us and the coerced raiders, and the need to load up all of the raiders' stolen bounty onto their horses for transportation to the palace, I thought we would never get away.

My impatience stemmed from the discovery that Ray had taken a deep cut to his side at some point and had been quietly bleeding into his shirt. Millie helped me craft a makeshift bandage and secure it in place, but I was anxious to have him seen by an actual doctor.

Thankfully Captain Flint surveyed the chaos and ordered the wounded loaded onto the raiders' cart and taken back, escorted by those raiders whose loved ones had not been with us and who were ready to mutiny at all the delays. I was determined to stay with Ray, and the twins offered to lead the party.

Ray made no complaint at the many bumps on the road back, but by the time we reached the edge of the rocks, he had lost consciousness. My fear had risen to sickening levels at this point, and I pounced on the first doctor I saw, dragging him over to my uncle.

The man, frowning at me, immediately turned business-like when he surveyed Ray. He cleaned and bandaged the wound, telling me it had been a clean thrust that had avoided any major organs. It should have been good news, but he delivered it with such a somber air that I felt only the slightest lift of my anxiety.

"But he's lost so much blood," I said.

"Indeed," the doctor replied. "But he is young and strong, and we may hope for a recovery yet."

And with that he moved on to the next patient, leaving me to turn to Millie.

"Is it just me or was that not exactly comforting?" I whispered to her, my eyes seeking out Ray's pale form.

My friend gripped my hand hard, tears in her eyes.

"Oh, I know he'll be fine, I just know it! Don't lose hope, Isla."

I had worried the first time he escaped from the raiders that Ray's return would signal the end of my welcome at the palace. But there seemed to be no thought of any such thing now. Instead Ray was installed in a large guest suite across the hall from Millie and me and attended by the royal doctors.

To my relief, he regained consciousness before we even got him back to the palace. But I knew how weak he must be when he made no effort to rise or gave any protest at being moved from the wagon to a stretcher to the bed.

I suspected Teddy and Millie were reprimanded by the king for their active role in the attack on the raiders, but I wasn't there to see it. I barely left Ray's side for two days, meals for both of us being delivered on trays by the servants.

But at the end of two days, I no longer feared for his life. He was still weak and couldn't do more than lie or sit, but he was definitely regaining strength. Enough strength to order me back to a more normal life, at any rate.

"You weren't made to sit at a bedside for days on end, Isla," he told me irritably. "You're chafing, and it's making me twitchy."

"What are you talking about?" I gave him an offended glare. "Of course I want to be here for you."

He sighed. "I appreciate your nursing, oh dutiful niece, now please go and harass someone else."

With an eye roll, I departed, secretly glad he was feeling well enough to needle me. Teddy pounced on me before I'd gone far, politely asking for an update about Ray, and then giving me the latest report of the aftermath of the raiders.

"All the families have been reunited now, and we've redistributed what we've been able to recover. We've lost one village completely, unfortunately—the raiders had razed it to the ground—but we've relocated the residents. You and Ray are becoming famous, you know, since the hostages are spreading back out around the kingdom and telling tales about it all."

I shook my head. "I'm sure it's you and Millie they're talking about."

"Never mind that." Teddy smiled. "Will you spar with me? I feel like it's been an age."

But we had no sooner begun our first bout than a resounding crash sounded around us, making me flinch and look toward the distant reef, our fight forgotten. My defense dropped, and Teddy barely pulled his blade back in time, his face going pale.

"Isla! Don't scare me like that!"

"Sorry." I shook myself, trying to refocus, but my eyes wandered back to the sea.

"It's too soon," Teddy said quickly. "You're still shaken, and that's natural enough."

"Shaken?" I frowned at him. "No, it's just tiredness. I've been sitting up at night by Ray's bed."

"Yes," he said quietly. "I've missed you."

I swallowed and met his eyes.

"There you two are!" Daisy bounced into the colonnade, her

voice piercing the moment between us. "Have you told her, Teddy?"

"Told me what?" I asked.

"Mother and Father are holding a ball," Daisy said with great relish.

Teddy narrowed his eyes at her suspiciously. "Since when have you been so excited by a ball?"

"Since never," Daisy said, with airy unconcern. "But this one is to celebrate your great victory."

Teddy's disbelieving expression didn't lift, and she laughed.

"Fine. Mother said that if I behave like a proper princess at the ball, she'll convince Father I'm old enough for lessons in swordsmanship. And it's only a week until the ball."

I couldn't help smiling at Daisy's obvious delight, but only half my mind was engaged. The other half was thinking about the wave and what it had meant. The raiders had been dealt with—the darkness beaten back in Trione—but my own kingdom was still vulnerable. I should be returning beneath the waves. But I could hardly leave Ray behind.

He had been agitated when he first awoke, but I had taken pains to tell him there had only been two more smallish waves in all my days at the palace. He had understood my message that Merrita must still be safe, even if I hadn't been able to say it directly.

He hadn't seemed entirely convinced, but neither had he seemed enthusiastic about the idea of my returning on my own. And eventually he had to agree to wait until he was recovered from his injury. But how long would that take?

Considering how ill he had been, surely it would take at least a week or two? And one more wave hardly signified that Merrita was in urgent need of us. Still, the delay chafed. I kept wondering if Connor and Dante had already returned, and what report they had given.

But there was nothing I could do to find out. All I could do was wait. And if I was forced to be here, then I could admit to myself that the idea of a ball was all too alluring. I glanced surreptitiously across at Teddy. I had never been so eager to be present for a ball before, but I also didn't spend my days imagining myself in the arms of any of my Merritan acquaintance. And besides, with Millie's example, I was becoming a great deal more reconciled to the value of spending time among the court. And the Trionian court seemed a safe place to start.

Millie herself seemed a great deal less interested in the ball, although her excitement grew as the date approached. She had kindly organized for a gown to be prepared for me, one she had ordered previously but never worn and which only needed a few adjustments. And on the morning of the ball it finally arrived.

I went searching for Millie in her room, but it was empty, so I roamed around the palace to her usual haunts, not finding her anywhere. At last I stalked into Ray's room, knowing he would be a far less satisfying recipient of my gushing. But all thoughts of my dress were forgotten when I saw that he was up, out of bed, properly dressed, although still pale, and playing chess by the window with the missing Millie.

She was flushed slightly, looking up at him with laughing eyes, and he was gazing down at her with a humorous, satisfied expression, a chess piece twirling between his fingers.

"Mi-lli-cent of Tri-one!" I said, and she started, jumping up guiltily.

I entirely ignored Ray, marching over to take her arm and drag her back to my room. She came without protest, collapsing onto my bed once I got her inside. I faced her, hands on hips.

"Does your sudden interest in the ball have anything to do with the fact that my *uncle* has recovered enough to attend, if not exactly dance the night away?"

"Ugh." Millie stuffed a pillow over her face and collapsed back onto the bed. "I wish you wouldn't call him that. It sounds so, so…wrong."

"Millie," I said, no longer entirely able to keep the laugh from my voice, "are you, by any chance, interested in becoming my aunt?"

That made her sit bolt upright, the pillow tumbling to the floor as she regarded me with wide eyes.

"I...hadn't quite thought of it in those terms," she said, her voice choking.

But I noticed it wasn't exactly a denial. And I realized with a start of guilt how absent she'd been in the last week as I'd ridden with Teddy, walked on the beach with Teddy, sparred with Teddy...

I had been too happy to notice then, but I was noticing now. And I was fairly sure I could guess where she had been spending that time—and why Ray hadn't complained at my neglect. If anything, he had delivered caustic lines about my uselessness as a nursemaid, designed to drive me away. My eyes widened.

"He likes you, too!" I said with astonishment.

Millie flushed, a hopeful look entering her eyes only to be replaced by something a little accusatory.

"You needn't sound so surprised about it," she said.

"Sorry." I took a deep breath. "It's just that it's *Ray*. He's never been romantically interested in anyone. All the girls among the guards have been interested in him at one time or other, but he's never given them any return attention. I've never been quite sure if it's because he's too lazy to be bothered with it all or too driven to want to be distracted..." My voice trailed off as I considered this question.

"He hasn't said anything," said Millie uncertainly. "Maybe..."

"Maybe nothing," I said decisively. "I saw how he was looking at you. And Ray would never have put up with you being there all the time just to be polite." I raised an eyebrow at her. "You *have* been there every day, haven't you?"

She nodded her head before flopping back down onto the bed.

"Please tell me I haven't been making an utter fool of myself," she said to the ceiling.

"Of course you haven't," I said briskly. "And we now have the rest of the day to make sure that we both make an unforgettable impression at that ball tonight."

Millie instantly sat up again, her eyes alight.

"Now where do we begin..."

As princess, Millie got a formal announcement as she entered the ballroom, and I watched from a shadowy corner as she swept gracefully in. Ray stood, tall and assured despite his pale face, near the long table of delicate confections. He turned as the herald spoke her name, and I knew in an instant that Millie had nothing to fear.

Except perhaps the opinion of her parents. I couldn't imagine they would be content for her to marry a poor traveler from Talinos. Of course, once my father raised Merrita to the surface again, Ray could reveal his true identity, but even that might not be enough if they had their hearts set on her marrying royalty.

We would just have to convince them that the Vasant Family were as close to royalty as it got in Merrita—except for the Rennons, of course.

Millie, dressed in layer upon layer of soft blue, seemed to float across the floor toward Ray. He moved to meet her, looking oblivious to everyone else in the ballroom. I watched them for a moment with a grin of satisfaction. Finally his turn had come—and I was never going to let him forget it. Family loyalty meant I wouldn't go blabbing about it to all the guards, of course, but that didn't extend to my sisters. They would be delighted to hear that untouchable Ray had fallen hard at last.

But the thought of the guards and my family cast a shadow across my mind. Something was wrong at home, but I still didn't know what. And I was stuck here, waiting, because I had no hope of convincing my father and saving everyone without Ray. Because at home I was a nuisance, not taken seriously by anyone, but Ray was a valued member of my father's court. If we reclaimed our place among the kingdoms of the land, then my father would no doubt be delighted for me to make a marriage alliance with another kingdom. But it was different for Ray.

Ray had been raised from birth to succeed his sister and one day take his place as Merrita's future general. While Millie was devoted to her brother and her plans to become his First Advisor. And the twins certainly made a good pair, balancing out each other's strengths. So even if everything worked out as I hoped for our kingdom, what future was there for the two of them?

A song struck up, and Ray took her hand, leading her out onto the dance floor despite the presence of many of higher rank who might have claimed precedence to dance with Trione's princess. The knowledge that such a thought had probably not even occurred to him brought the smile back to my face. If there was one thing Ray had never lacked, it was confidence.

Teddy swirled around the floor with an older lady possessed of an elegant air and an abundance of white hair. She said something that made him laugh, and the sound filled me with a warm glow of affection. It didn't matter if I had started out loving a dream, I loved the real Teddy now. I loved all the little things about him that I had known nothing of for all those years beneath the water—like his throaty laugh, his kindness for others, and the sense of responsibility that lay hidden beneath his sometimes abstracted air.

Perhaps the weight of my eyes reached him because as he straightened from the short bow he was giving his dance partner at the end of the song, his eyes somehow found me, half-hidden at the edge of the room. He froze, the look on his face sending delicious shivers all through me. My misgivings about the dress instantly dissipated like foam from a wave.

Millie couldn't have chosen something more perfect for me if she'd known the truth. The aqua-green clung to me, fitted until the knee where it flared out in an effect that was eerily reminiscent of my mermaid's tail. I suspected that, for once, Avalon would have approved of my choice of gown. It felt thrilling to wear it, like an allusion to my other self, an open acknowledgment of my secret for all to see.

I blinked and somehow Teddy was in front of me, bowing lower than he had before.

"Isla," he said in a strangely thick voice. "Dance with me."

CHAPTER 22

*H*e held out a hand, somehow both imperious and entreating at the same time, and I placed mine in it, my heart racing faster than seemed healthy. And then his arms were around me, and it turned out it could beat faster still. He swept us both onto the dance floor, and I suddenly knew how Ray had felt. Was there anyone else in the vast room? I couldn't be sure.

We didn't speak, although our eyes remained locked, as if the moment were too significant to be broken by words. My heartbeat had slowed, and an unfamiliar strength filled me, as if I could fight a whole gang of raiders alone or lift from the floor and take flight. Was this what it felt like to be in love? It was nothing like the false imitation I had been dreaming of for so long.

Our dance seemed to go on and on—I didn't know if it had been one song or five, and I didn't care if it lasted all night. Occasionally I spun away from him, but always our hands tethered us together, spinning me back to him.

But eventually we slowed, and then stilled, and cold air

rushed in where his arms had been. He bowed, and I sank into a deep curtsy.

He shook his head slightly as if struggling to come back to reality, just as I was. "You dance beautifully, Isla."

"Beautifully? That doesn't quite cover it," said a slightly shocked sounding Millie over my shoulder. "How have we never seen you dance before, Isla? You're so…elegant! It was exquisite."

I blinked, taken aback by her praise. My singing voice had always won me admiration, but several of my sisters danced more elegantly than me.

"Thank you?" I said, still unsure what to make of her extreme response.

And then my eyes finally focused on the rest of the dancers, and my brow creased. There was something strange about them, although I struggled to put my finger on it. They moved too slowly, I decided at last, and their movements weren't fluid, like the dancing I was used to seeing at home.

I bit my lip. I had never had any comparisons, so I had never known that mermaids in their human form kept some of the elegance of movement that came from our mer-forms. Perhaps I should have tried to hide it, but I didn't know if I was capable of doing so. Certainly not with every thought focused on Teddy. I didn't know how to move any other way.

"You really need to dance with the countess," Millie said to Teddy in an under voice, giving a significant head nod toward someone outside my line of vision. "You're going to make a scandal if you monopolize Isla and ignore your duties."

Teddy made a rueful face but didn't argue, going determinedly off toward the unknown countess. Millie looked like she wanted to drag me into a corner—either to ask about my dancing, ask about me and Teddy, or tell me about Ray, I wasn't sure which. Had she noticed that he also danced with unnatural grace? But any such designs were foiled by the sudden appearance of a young man I didn't recognize.

He begged me for a dance while two other young men lingered a few steps back, looking disappointed that he'd beaten them to it. Millie chuckled and leaned in close.

"Now that they've seen you dance—not to mention that dress —you're not going to sit out a dance all night."

I couldn't imagine dancing with anyone but Teddy, but somehow, before I knew what was happening, I had been swept back among the dancers. And to my surprise, after the initial shock wore off, I found I enjoyed it. It bore little resemblance to the intense moments I had just shared with Teddy, but I enjoyed dipping and gliding and spinning to the beautiful music. I hadn't even realized I'd been missing it, but I had. If I couldn't swim, at least I could dance.

And a less noble part of me had to admit I enjoyed swirling past Teddy on the dance floor, as he danced with the middle-aged countess, and seeing the glare he directed at my partner. When the dance ended, I extricated myself with murmured thanks but was immediately pounced upon by another eager supplicant, just as Millie had predicted. I had never been so popular at balls in Merrita, despite my true rank being known there. It no doubt had something to do with the fact that I was the youngest of six princesses and known for being too much of a fighter and too much of a dreamer—not a combination that endeared me to anyone.

After that dance there was another and then another. At some point I realized I hadn't passed Teddy on the dance floor for a while. But it took me several circuits before I finally located him. He stood beside the refreshment table, gazing down into his crystal goblet with a less than pleased expression. I spun, and when my eyes found him again, he was looking at me and my current dance partner, his free hand balled into a fist.

He looked as if he wanted to murder the man guiding me through the dance, and yet he was no longer dancing himself. If he had asked me to dance again, he was the prince, and none of the other young men would have tried to gainsay him.

As I watched, he placed his glass down roughly on the table, the goblet nearly toppling to the floor, and strode away into the crowd.

My gut roiled, reflecting my confused emotions, and when the dancing finished, I could barely hear my partner's polite words over the chaos in my mind. Someone else approached us, but I shook my head, brushing past them all and heading for a wide doorway that stood open, letting in the cool sea air. I rushed through to the outside, stopping to take a deep breath. The long crystal wall of the ballroom allowed the light and movement of the party to shine out onto the sand, and my gaze caught on a familiar figure standing on the sand past the edge of the ballroom.

I drew a sharp breath, trying to decide if I should join him or flee. But he heard the sound of it and turned toward me.

"Isla."

I stiffened, still undecided if I should flee back to the safety of the ballroom.

"Isla," he said again, and this time I couldn't resist stepping forward to meet him.

Enough light still reached us here that I could clearly see his features. As he looked at me, a strange light leaped into his eyes, and he closed the remaining distance between us. I tried to swallow and couldn't as he gripped both of my arms, staring down into my eyes.

His breath was ragged, as was mine, and fire leaped between us. I swayed toward him, and he leaned down, his eyes dropping closed as his lips hovered no more than a breath from mine.

"Teddy," I whispered, everything inside me trembling at his nearness.

A wave hit the reef with enough force for the sound to reach us, and he stiffened. His eyes sprang open as he pushed me away to arms' length, his gaze shifting over my shoulder to the ocean.

"I...I'm sorry...I can't," he muttered, and then he was gone, and I was standing alone.

Shock washed over me in waves, hot and cold flushes chasing themselves through my body. What had just happened? But I knew what had happened.

My knees gave out, and I sank down to sit in the sand, heedless of my dress. Something important hovered just at the edges of my mind, but I couldn't seem to grasp hold of it.

Floating blue layers of material approached me, but I couldn't bring myself to look up at my friend.

"Teddy is an idiot," Millie said brutally, making my eyes fly up to her. "I've been watching him all evening, and he needs to ask himself why he clearly can't bear the thought of anyone else dancing with you." She sighed. "But he's a dreamer, he always has been. And some dreams are hard to let go."

"His ocean girl."

"Yes." Millie plonked down beside me. "His ocean girl."

I opened my mouth, and in the shock of emotion, I would have told her the truth, but my throat closed over, blocking off the words. Instead I laid my head on her shoulder and let two tears slide out.

I had treated chasing away Teddy's dreams as something of a game, always knowing in the back of my mind that I was his ocean girl—the one he had pinned all his dreams on. And, if everything went to plan, soon enough I would be free to tell him.

But suddenly I found the thought brought no comfort. I didn't want Teddy to love me because I had rescued him once, and he had built up an impossible dream around me that I could never match or fulfill. I wanted him to love me because of me as I really was—just as I had come to love him. But I had failed. Me—the real me—was not enough, just as I had not been enough in Merrita. I had hoped that here on shore I could find the place I belonged. I thought I had found my home in his heart and his arms. But I had been wrong. There was no place for me here.

A tremendous boom sounded, and I whirled to stare at the distant reef. The earlier wave had been barely large enough to register, but this was the largest I had yet heard. I pulled myself away from Millie, my eyes widening. In all my time here, there had never been two so close together or one so large as the second one.

"Did you hear that wave?" I asked, my voice breathless.

She looked at me with a confused expression. "I think everyone heard it, what of it?"

"It was larger than the usual ones, wasn't it? Was it as large as the one just before I arrived here?"

Millie frowned at me. "I don't think so. Although it's hard to remember specifically. That was a long time ago now. Why is it important?"

"Never mind why." I leaped to my feet, my broken heart pushed aside in the urgency of the moment. "I need to find Ray. Where did you leave him?"

"I..." Millie actually blushed, as if embarrassed at my assumption that she had been with Ray up until coming to find me. Meeting my gaze, she let a little giggle slip out. "He was getting some refreshments."

I raced toward the crystal wall of the ballroom, my dancing slippers abandoned behind me in the sand. That wave had been much bigger than the other recent ones. What did it mean for Merrita? How much destruction had it wrought? Here we were, eating and drinking and dancing, when our people might be dying below the waves.

I pushed through the crowd heedlessly, my eyes roaming everywhere looking for Ray. He had left the refreshment area, and I couldn't see him on the dance floor or among any of the knots of chatting people standing here and there. I had lost Millie in my haste, so I switched my search to her, in case she had been more successful in locating him.

Her blue dress stood out, and I found her quickly enough. But even as our eyes met, Daisy appeared from nowhere and grabbed her sister's arm. She was dressed in a frock of deep rose—made from her chosen fabric, although I knew the style had been a compromise made with the promised sword lessons in mind. Millie tried to pull free, saying something to Daisy and looking toward me. But Daisy just hung on tighter, her face setting into familiar, stubborn lines.

Millie sighed and gave in, letting her sister tow her into a small recess away from the crowds. I frowned and turned back to my search. It was probably for the best not to involve Millie, anyway, given my reason for searching out Ray.

I spotted him, finally. He sat, half hidden by a potted shrub, his head resting back on the wall behind him. His face was white, and his eyes closed, and I gasped, trying to push through the people that stood between us.

But my steps slowed as I saw his chest rise and fall and his hand raise to rub his temple. The entire pose was so uncharacter-istic of him that I knew the ball was taking more of a toll than he wanted anyone to know. His hidden position behind a shrub made that clear. In his state, in the midst of the noise of the ball-room, had he even heard the wave?

If I rushed over and told him my concerns now, he would feel duty bound to act immediately. And clearly he was in no condi-tion to do so. He was in safe hands here—I glanced back toward Millie but could no longer see her—more than safe hands, in fact. And his convalescence was going well—as long as I didn't destroy it now.

Certainty swept over me. We couldn't delay our return any longer, but I would just have to find a way to convince my father on my own. Ray needed to stay here.

I turned and ran, filled with an urgent need to act, now that my mind was made up, and eager to be away before Ray opened his eyes and spotted me. He had always been able to read me too easily.

I broke free onto the sand, running past my discarded shoes. I hadn't seen any sign of Teddy, and I fiercely told myself I was glad. I didn't need any distractions now. But inside my heart was crying. I had wanted him to love me, Isla—not me, the face of his dream—and yet I hadn't been able to share the truth of myself with him. Everything had been a hopeless tangle since the beginning.

The godmothers' protection prevented me from telling him the truth directly, and my own impetuous vow had robbed me of the only part of my voice he recognized. And now I had to leave, and I realized I had never told him how I felt. I had been waiting for him to come to the same realization I had, and now he never would. I would never again get to see the burning fire in his eyes that I had seen that first morning on the beach—the fire he had come so close to directing at me in the sand only moments ago.

My bare feet hit the water, but I didn't pause. Taking several long steps, I threw myself forward to fully submerge. The shock of the cold and wet lasted for only the briefest moment, as the old tingle raced over my body. How easily I returned to my old skin, leaving behind the new life I had started to dream of owning forever. I turned my face toward the reef, only to pause. Reluctantly, but unable to stop myself, I rose to the surface for one final glance back at the land king's palace.

I emerged from the water, my eyes searching for the familiar building. But instead I saw two figures at the waterline, their faces bearing identical looks of shock—as visible in the bright moonlight as my own clearly was to them.

Millie and Daisy.

PART III
THE MERMAID PRINCESS

CHAPTER 23

"*I*sla?" Millie's voice carried easily across the water, my name uttered in a tone I hadn't heard from her before.

I knew I should turn around and swim away, but I couldn't do it. This family had taken me in, had cared for me as if I was one of them. And I couldn't pretend they didn't deserve an explanation—even if I couldn't give them one.

They had both stepped forward into the water, heedless of their ballgowns, but both of them had stopped when the water reached their shins. Almost as if they were afraid of me.

That thought propelled me forward. I swam as close to them as I could, resting my stomach against the sandy bottom and pushing my arms straight to lift my head and shoulders up into the air.

Both girls regarded me with round, wide eyes, and the painful silence stretched out. Daisy was the one to break it.

"See! I told you so!" Her voice sounded odd, as if she wasn't sure if she was more shocked, excited, or nervous.

"You did not say you thought Isla was a mermaid!" Millie replied. Her eyes kept flicking down to my tail and then back to my face.

"Well, no," Daisy admitted. "But I did say that something strange was going on with her. And it does make sense."

"You think Isla being a mermaid makes sense?" Millie asked in a faint voice.

"Well, it does," Daisy said. "Think of all the things I just mentioned to you that were worrying me."

She threw an almost apologetic look in my direction. "Sorry, Isla, you know I like you. But even after all this time, we don't really know anything about your background. Or your uncle's. And I could hardly be in that ballroom and not notice that *both* my siblings are in love with mysterious strangers. So I couldn't stay quiet."

She began to list her concerns, tapping against each finger on her left hand as she did so, as if checking off a list. "You retrieved Teddy's sword from the ocean, but then you didn't seem to know what a sandcastle was. Almost as if you'd never been to a beach before. We know you're not royalty or nobility from any of our kingdoms—because we know everyone—but you don't act or talk like a commoner, either."

Daisy paused to look at Millie. "You have to admit it's true."

Millie nodded, her face thoughtful. Daisy resumed checking off her points.

"You told us Nereus was trained as a guard, but clearly you have been too—but not with a sword. And, Millie, you yourself gushed to me about how Nereus fought with a trident."

She gave her sister a significant look, and Millie paled, as if it had only just occurred to her that if I was a mermaid, my uncle must be merfolk too.

"You never seemed to find it strange to call us by our first names, either," Daisy added, her triumph growing. "Plus, I saw you coming back to your room dripping wet—in the middle of the night. And, on top of all that, you came here knowing nothing about horses, as if your family were too poor to own one, but I snuck into your room the other night and looked through your bags and you have enormous jewels hidden at the bottom of an old canvas sack!"

"Daisy!" Millie looked shocked. "You didn't tell me that before! I suppose that's what *you* were doing up and roaming the corridors in the middle of the night."

Daisy didn't look repentant. "I knew you would get mad at me if I told you. But it was easy because she wasn't even there." She lowered her tone as if imparting something suspicious. "She's often not in her room at night, you know."

"I think you're forgetting something," Millie said. "You just told me in the ballroom that Isla and Nereus are both unnaturally familiar with the palace, and that they must therefore be spies."

"Mermaids, spies...the point is I *knew* something was wrong." Daisy flushed slightly, again looking at me with an apologetic expression. "It's not that I don't like you, Isla," she hurried to add. "I do. But then, I suppose they would pick likable people to be spies, if they want them to infiltrate palaces."

I hadn't interrupted her litany since the godmothers' enchantment made it impossible for me to offer explanations for any of her points. This one, however, I had to question.

"Who did you think I was spying for?" I asked, my curiosity overwhelming everything else. "And for what purpose?"

"She didn't know," Millie said, looking me straight in the eyes. "But perhaps you can tell us."

"Millie!" I stared at her, aghast. "You can't believe I'm a spy, surely!"

"I don't know," she said. "Right now, I don't know what to believe. But I do know that you haven't been honest with us."

A sick, trembling feeling swept over me. I had already lost Teddy tonight, I couldn't bear the thought of losing Millie as well. This was just what I had feared happening if they ever saw me transform.

Tears filled my eyes. "I would have told you if I could!"

"And why couldn't you? Because you thought we wouldn't believe you?" Millie asked.

I shook my head frantically, but when I opened my mouth, nothing came out. Apparently the enchantment also prohibited my talking about the enchantment. My hand flew to my throat and Millie's eyes followed it, a crease appearing on her forehead.

"Are you a spy?" she asked me directly.

"No!" I said, able to answer this question at least.

"And have you at any point meant Trione or my family any harm?" she asked, her voice softening slightly.

"No!" I said, just as strongly. "Ray and I risked our lives to help you with the raiders. Why would we do that if we wanted to harm you?"

"That's what I said to Daisy." Millie glared slightly at her younger sister. "And then I dragged her out here after you so you could tell her yourself."

"Please believe me, Daisy," I said. "I never meant anyone any harm. Quite the opposite."

"The opposite?" Millie asked, jumping on my words, but I could only shrug, unable to explain further.

"What I don't understand," Daisy said, wrinkling her nose, "is how Teddy's sword is so perfect. He couldn't understand how you had it when he lost it in the middle of the ocean, and being a mermaid explains that. But it doesn't explain his other question —how had it not rusted away in all this time?"

"I think there are a few other missing explanations," Millie said, throwing up her hands in exasperation. "Like how mermaids exist—and *no one* knows about it!"

They both turned inquiring looks on me, and my heart sank. Neither of those were questions I could answer.

"I have to go," I said, "I'm really sorry, but it's important. You'll just have to believe me."

"But you'll come back?" Daisy asked, already seeming to have forgotten she had convinced herself I was a spy.

"I..." I paused. I wouldn't lie to them if I had a choice. "I don't know. But I hope so. Could you tell Teddy..." My voice broke down, and I tried again. "Could you tell Teddy that—"

"Tell me what?" called an achingly familiar voice across the sand. "What are you all doing out here? Are you *swimming* in your dress, Isla?"

When he got no reply, he strode toward us. Whether the other two were frozen in startled surprise like me, or just didn't know what to say, I didn't know.

"I know it's a warm night," he said as he neared us, "but really..." His voice trailed slowly off, replaced by a strangled sound.

For a moment he stared down at me, his eyes tracing the length of my tail, fixating on the green scales, and then he took two long strides and dropped to his knees in the water, facing me.

"Isla." His whisper was rough, his face full of swirling emotion. "You're a mermaid. *My ocean girl.*"

I swallowed, not sure what I was allowed to say—not sure what I wanted to say. This was exactly what I had hoped and feared—to see that look in Teddy's eyes again just because of what had happened all that time ago. But I couldn't make myself turn away from it, not when I wanted it so badly.

I opened my mouth to speak, no idea what was going to come out. The enchantment seemed equally confused, not cutting off my voice entirely, but transforming the sound that emerged into an inelegant croak. A sound I'd made in the presence of these siblings before.

"Don't be foolish, Teddy," Daisy said in a practical voice, "she can't sing, remember?"

The light went out in Teddy's eyes, not all at once, but slowly, as if he needed time to absorb the truth of her words. My heart broke all over again.

He lurched back onto his feet, water streaming off him. Turning to his sisters, some of his earlier excitement returned.

"Isla might not be my ocean girl, but at last you have to admit that it's all true! I know you've all thought I'd run mad these last couple of years. But I was saved by a girl—and she must have been a mermaid. It all makes sense. Isla can't be the only one!" He turned to me. "There are other mermaids, right?"

It hurt in a strange way to hear him addressing me so calmly. To know that the revelation about mermaids and what that meant for his ocean girl filled his mind to the exclusion of all else —like my deception and betrayal, which had so agitated Millie and Daisy.

I took a deep breath and reminded myself that I knew what it was like to be misunderstood and scorned by the ones closest to you. Even in my grief, I could understand some of the vindication and excitement he must be feeling. If I could succeed in convincing my father to raise Merrita, maybe I would have the chance to feel the same feelings one day when my family saw the truth of the surface.

"She doesn't seem to be able to talk about it," Millie said.

"As in an enchantment?" Teddy frowned, looking down at me in concern, although it was hard to read if it was concern about me or for me. "I suppose that might explain why word of their existence has never gotten out. You would think it would have if they make a habit of coming on to land to mingle with us."

He glanced at me questioningly. "Do your people do so in general, Isla, or are you unusual?"

I wanted to tell him I was unusual, but my mind flew uneasily to Connor and Dante. What did I really know about how often my people had walked among them? I shrugged hopelessly, and he seemed to accept that as proof of his sister's claim.

"An enchantment would explain it," he said. "I'm sure Isla wouldn't keep something like that from us otherwise."

Despite everything, a warm glow filled me. Perhaps he had ignored my apparent betrayal because he didn't believe it. He might not love me, but he still seemed to value my friendship. My mood instantly dimmed again. It wasn't his friendship I craved.

"Unless she had a good reason to…" His eyes jumped to me. "Isla, are your people in trouble? Do they need help?"

He looked ready to leap into the ocean and start swimming toward the reef. I found his concern touching, although there was nothing he could do for us. And I couldn't answer anyway. I couldn't even confirm that I *had* people, let alone anything about their current state.

"Millie? Are you down there?" called yet another familiar voice, and I instantly regretted getting caught up talking for so long. Everything about my attempted escape had gone wrong.

"Have you seen Isla?" Ray asked, apparently having recognized Millie's figure, although she hadn't said anything. His voice came closer as he repeated himself. "Have you seen Isla? I can't find her anywhere, and someone said she was looking upset."

He stopped beside Millie, looking down at her with a quizzical look. But the look she was casting back up at him was one of devastation. His expression faltered and dropped, his eyes glancing from Millie to Teddy, and at last to me. His eyes widened, and he made a strangled sort of coughing sound in his throat.

"Isla! What are you…?"

"Nereus," Millie whispered, and his attention instantly shifted back to her, his color paling further. I watched as his face closed up, his emotions locked away.

"Millie, I'm sorry," he said, his voice pitched just for her, although we were all so close we heard anyway. "I wish I had never—"

"Never what?" she asked, a spark appearing in her eyes, but he didn't answer.

"Ray," I said, putting all the urgency into my voice that I could manage. "There was another wave. A big one. I have to go."

"So that's what you were trying to do," he said in an approximation of his normal long-suffering tone, although I could hear how much it cost him. "I'm not so weak I'm going to let you go alone."

I bit my lip. I still wasn't convinced he really was well enough to come, but neither did I think I had any hope of convincing him to stay behind. And with the exposure of our secret, I wasn't even sure it was a good idea. The twins would have to tell their parents the truth, and when Ray couldn't answer any of their questions…

"Fine," I said. "But we have to go now."

Ray raised an eyebrow. "What? You're not going to fight me about it?"

I rolled my eyes. "Come on!"

Still he hesitated, looking back at Millie. But he had no more words than I did. So, with a shrug, he took two long strides into the waves and dove cleanly in. He didn't resurface.

"Goodbye," I said. "Thank you for everything. We—" I shook my head. We had already established there was nothing to be said. "Goodbye."

I turned and disappeared beneath the surface myself.

CHAPTER 24

For a long time, we swam side by side in silence. Only my concern for Ray distracted me from my misery, and I cast him assessing sideways looks whenever I thought he wouldn't notice.

"You can stop looking at me like that, Isla," he said at last. "I'm not going to suddenly grow so weak I can't continue, or so heartbroken I lose all will to live, or whatever romanticized nonsense you're coming up with in your head." He turned and gave me a piercing look, his voice dropping. "And neither are you."

My irritation faded, and I managed to give him a weak smile. For all he condescended and criticized me, Ray believed in me. Perhaps that was even why he did it. It was certainly why I had always liked him best of all my relatives.

His words opened up all the emotions sealed within me, and my thoughts swam ahead of us through the lengths of water still to go.

"It was a big wave, Ray. And it came right after a smaller one. Do you think Merrita is still standing? Do you think anyone is—"

"Nonsense!" Ray scoffed. "It wasn't *that* big a wave. I would have heard it in the ballroom if it was. Our home will still be standing." He paused, and I knew that despite his efforts to reassure me, neither did he want to give me false comfort. That wasn't his way. "I don't know what we'll find, though."

I swallowed. "Because of Connor and Dante? You don't think we'll be able to convince my father now that we know there's someone actively feeding him lies? Or do you think they'll try to stop us reaching him at all?" My hands balled into fists, and I swished my tail faster through the water. "With the two of us, we can fight our way past them if we have to."

"It's more than that," he said, and I had never heard his voice so grim.

I faltered, trying to think what could be worse.

"You don't think they're working alone?"

"There's something I never told you," he said. "I told you part of it that day outside the market, but there's more. We were interrupted then, and after the battle, I decided not to mention it. It's a piece of information that needs a proper conversation—the sort of conversation the enchantment wouldn't let us have on land." His voice turned cold, laden with self-recrimination. "And, if I'm honest, I didn't want to talk about it. And especially not when I was crippled in bed, unable to act."

"No." I reached over and squeezed his arm. "You can't blame yourself for being badly wounded. Too badly wounded to be doing this swim now, most likely."

"Actually, I feel stronger than I expected to," he admitted. "I think the ocean is doing me good. It's been so long since I swam."

I remembered my own feelings when I finally gave in and took a dip in the lagoon. I should have thought of that while Ray lay so deathly ill. If it had occurred to me it might help, I would have dragged him down to the water myself.

"But that's not the important point," he said. "I told you I saw Dante and Connor myself. What I didn't tell you was who I saw them talking to."

"Who?" I stared at him, nearly swimming straight into a drifting piece of loose kelp in my distraction.

"They were talking to the raiders. The ones I'd just managed to separate myself from. Two of them were there, on the edges of the market. I had leaped at the chance to accompany them, but they never fully explained why they were going in the first place. They clearly weren't planning a raid. All they said was that they needed to collect some information and supplies. And then just after I managed to slip away from them, I saw Connor and Dante. I followed them, of course, and they led me straight back to where I'd just left."

"Did you hear what they said?"

He shook his head. "Unfortunately there was no way to get close enough to them without being detected. And at that point I was starting to worry about running out of time to find you before they got suspicious. But the more I've thought about it since, the more I can't believe that Connor and Dante would not only be lying about the state of things on the surface, but also actively instigating trouble. Not unless they were acting under orders…"

I gasped. "You think my father ordered them to do it? I don't believe it! Why would he do it?"

Ray stared straight ahead, his body stiff and his face set. "Not your father."

I stared at him. "Then who…" My voice drifted off as I realized his meaning.

"Oh Ray! No! Not your sister! But she's done so much for Merrita! Why would she do such a thing?"

"I don't know for sure," he said grimly. "Although there are sides of her you've never seen. But I can't think of anyone else with enough sway over those two that they never let a single word slip in all this time."

"But she's so…" My eyes stung, although if they were producing tears, the ocean made it impossible to tell. I had always admired my aunt, always striven to fight like she did. Surely she could not be involved in something so nefarious?

"She's so, what?" Ray asked. "She's never been the saint you always thought she was, you know."

"What's that supposed to mean?" I asked, stung despite his revelation.

"Well, why wouldn't she speak up for you to your father? She saw you at training often enough. She could see you were as competent as any other recruit."

"What do you mean?" I asked hotly. "She did! I know Father would never have agreed to let me join the patrols without convincing—he would never have let me join the recruits in the first place!"

"No, he wouldn't," Ray said, sounding strangely uncomfortable.

I frowned at him. "But I don't understand. You just said..." Enlightenment dawned. "It was you!" I gasped. "You were the one who convinced him!"

Ray just shrugged, but his face gave him away.

"But why didn't you ever tell me?" I asked. "Why did you let me think it was her all this time?"

"Now I can see that might have been a mistake," he said. "But she inspired you so much, that I didn't see the harm in letting you hold on to your mistaken belief. So many fewer girls join the guards as it is—let alone a princess. I knew feeling like you had her on your side, advocating for you, was a comfort and an inspiration. She'd spoken up for you, so you couldn't let her down."

"You should have told me the truth," I said, although with less heat.

"Yes," he said. "It seems I should have. And then perhaps you wouldn't have overlooked other things that I chose to ignore because she's my sister."

He shook his head, anger all over his face. "I couldn't believe my sister would be working against the good of the kingdom. I told myself if she concealed things, or misled anyone, it was merely to preserve the honor of our Family, of the throne, and of the guards themselves. Not to mention the safety of the kingdom. I told myself it was a task I would one day have to steel myself to do as well, when I took over as general. In short," the words burst explosively out of him, "I was an utter fool. As if lying to my monarch or deceiving those around me could ever be for anyone's good but my own."

"But you wouldn't do that just to benefit yourself," I said quickly. "You know you wouldn't. That's why the idea of having to do it one day was so difficult for you. You told yourself it was weakness that you couldn't stand the idea, but it was strength."

His shoulders slumped. "Thank you, Isla. You have more faith in me than I have in myself."

"But I still don't understand." I battled against the fear spreading through me. "How has she deceived us?"

"Not big things," Ray said quickly. "If it had been big things, I couldn't have fooled myself in such a way. Just things like saying that there were already cracks in the Hall of Meetings before the quake. I told myself my sister was taking on the burden of the necessary lie so that your father could reassure the people with a clear mind and conscience."

His expression made it clear he had fallen back into internal self-recrimination. But I could understand why he had told himself that. If it had been my sister, maybe I would have indulged in the same self-delusion.

"But we don't know for sure it was her orders behind Connor and Dante," I said.

Ray cast me a withering look, but I glared back at him. "Well, we don't!"

"We shall see soon enough," he said before settling back into brooding silence.

I cast him another sideways look. He had clearly been faster to understand the significance of Connor and Dante's presence than I had because he had already had suspicions—however vague. It had been more than hurt pride that sent him to the surface with me, then. I could imagine something of the complex tangle of emotions that must have driven him—the urge to escape his increasingly uncomfortable position as her heir no doubt hopelessly tangled with his drive to uncover if there really was any wrongdoing and protect our people.

As my initial shock passed, transforming into simmering outrage, I considered every angle of Ray's revelation. According to Teddy, Trione had escaped the darkness until the recent appearance of the raiders. And now I learned that those raiders were connected with our own people. Despite all my father's fears about the surface, the darkness in Trione had come from Merrita. I felt sick. At least my father would have to listen to us now.

Time passed strangely, and I didn't even try to track when dawn arrived, here beneath the reach of the sun. Weariness dragged me down, but I pushed against it. There was no time for resting.

And, eventually, the great shimmering bubble of Merrita's barrier came into view. By silent accord, we had taken the same roundabout route we took on our departure, so we made it all the way to the edge of the city without meeting anyone. I led us the last little way, casting a single longing glance at my secret room as we passed it.

We had agreed that we would go straight to the palace, so it made sense to enter the city in the sculpture garden. I hoped that by entering the palace from the back, we might find my father before our return became known.

I swam forward through the barrier, my tail reaching for the ground even as it transformed into feet. I gasped a single breath of the strange air of my home—so different from the clear air of the surface—and then a shout went up.

Ray had been a beat behind me, so we barely had time to lock startled gazes before a whole squad of guards rushed forward and grabbed Ray by both arms.

"What are you doing?" I cried. "Unhand him!"

"We can't do that, I'm afraid, Your Highness," the lieutenant said uncomfortably. "He's been charged with treason, and we have our orders."

"Treason!" I stared at them in dismay. "For what? Leaving the city? Then do you intend to arrest me as well?"

The guards—every one of them known to me—looked between each other, but I couldn't read their expressions. Sudden anxiety gripped me. They couldn't arrest me, could they?

I drew myself up to my full height and injected confidence into my voice that I didn't feel.

"I should hope you know better than to lay a hand on a member of the royal family. I'm going to see my father, and I'll soon have this straightened out."

Ray's eyes bore into me, heavy with silent warning, but I just lifted my chin. I couldn't believe that my father truly thought Ray treasonous. It was all a misunderstanding. I would explain that Ray had gone to the surface to protect me—that he had been a hero—and then he would have to let him go. And once Ray was free, we would break the news to my father about General Nerissa.

My heart seized at the thought. I could no longer question Ray's interpretation. Clearly my aunt must be terrified of the truth being exposed if she would go so far as to falsely accuse her own brother of treason. How long had she had squads lying in wait around the grounds, poised to arrest him at first appearance? No doubt if it hadn't been for my rank, she would have whisked us both out of sight before we had a chance to speak to anyone.

I hurried away from them, telling myself to be strong. When I had entered the ocean, so many hours ago, it was with the intention of leaving Ray safely on shore. So I was no more alone now than I would have been if my plan had succeeded. But my encouragements failed to inject any confidence. Ray's absence at my side was too noticeable to be so easily overcome. I had been relying on him to be the convincing, believable one.

I rushed through the corridors, hurrying for my father's office. It appeared to be early morning, and various servants moved hither and thither, although I saw no sign of my sisters or any of the court. I preferred it that way because while the servants might stop and stare at my sudden reappearance, they didn't try to question me.

My father had always been an early riser, so I directed my steps to his office rather than his vast suite. The corridors of my own home felt strange now, everything about them an uncomfortable echo of a different palace and a different life.

Outside my father's study, I paused. On instinct, I pressed my ear to the door rather than pushing it straight open as I would normally have done.

And, sure enough, I heard voices. They were too faint to make out the words, but I recognized the speakers. I swallowed audibly and backed away, eyeing the door as if it might bite me.

My aunt was with him. I couldn't approach my father with my tale while she was there to dispute every word I said. I needed the chance to explain everything and convince him, if need be. My back hit the opposite corridor wall, and I stopped, still staring at the door. What should I do? Leave and come back later? Was there somewhere nearby I could hide so that I would be able to see when she left?

But while I was still making up my mind on the best course of action, the door sprang open, and my aunt stepped out, pulling it promptly closed behind her. I stared, frozen in place, as she looked up and saw me.

For a mere second, she was equally still, although her face didn't show the shock I was sure mine did. And then she leaped forward and grasped me around the upper arm, dragging me—as if I was a recalcitrant child, in need of a sound scolding—down the corridor and through a nearby doorway.

CHAPTER 25

I sprang to life before the door could close behind us, trying to twist myself free. I struck out at her head, but her grip was like iron, and she easily blocked my blows. Only when she had kicked the door closed and taken up a firm stance in front of it did she release me.

We stood in a small internal meeting room which didn't even offer the hope of escape that might have been afforded by a window. I kept my attention firmly focused on my aunt and the door behind her.

"So, you've returned at last from your little jaunt." She surveyed me coldly. "The surface, I assume?"

I glared at her. "You know you can't keep me locked in here."

She gave a harsh bark of laughter. "Of course I can't. I just wanted to talk to you." She arched an eyebrow. "Is that a crime?"

"I don't know," I snapped back. "Is it? You seem to be inventing them left, right, and center. At least you must be if you think your own brother suddenly guilty of treason."

A stronger emotion crossed her face, although I struggled to read it. But then, had I ever actually been able to read her?

"Nereus is a fool who has always been far too attached to his nieces. But I didn't think he would actually throw away every-thing he has worked for—everything the Vasants have worked for."

"Ray is a far better person—a far better Vasant—than you will ever be." I let all my betrayed hurt spill out into my voice.

But none of my anger or scorn seemed to throw her even the slightest bit off balance. I certainly saw no shred of regret in her eyes.

"Neither you nor my idiot brother have any idea what I have done for the Vasants," she said. "And I didn't have to make up a single one of the stories my guards have been telling your father. If it hadn't been for those interfering godmothers, they would still be true, and there would be no need for lies."

Sick horror rose inside me. "Interfering godmothers? You mean the ones who even now protect our kingdom and people from the ocean above us? I'm the one who's been a fool. Father was wrong when he thought the tremors were a message for us to stay beneath the ocean, but I was also wrong when I thought they were a message that we needed to flee. The tremors were trying to warn us that the darkness had already arrived. They were warning us about you!"

I pressed a hand to my stomach, trying to control its churn-ing. "Father said guards died up there! What did you do? Kill them yourself to maintain your lie?"

Real fury crossed her face for the first time. "How dare you, girl?" she spat at me before forcibly calming herself. "Those men died for the good of their kingdom, and the guards still honor their death. We may have claimed they died keeping sharks from our waters, but in truth they died for a more noble cause."

All the guards killed fighting sharks had actually died on the surface? My mind tried to grasp it. This went far beyond Connor and Dante. And it had begun before the raiders appeared in Trione. Teddy's stories sprang into my mind. Darkness had come to each of the kingdoms, and in most of them, when good people tried to resist it, mercenaries fought against their efforts. Mercenaries who had been bolstered by Merritan guards. No wonder when she wished to stir up trouble in Trione, Nerissa knew just where to find the remaining leftover, unsatisfied malcontents from across the kingdoms.

The darkness might have started up there, but it had taken root here, deep below. And while the kingdoms of the land had lopped off its branches and trunks, it must be uprooted once and for all here in Merrita.

"Noble cause?" I hurled my words at her like projectiles. "You call it noble to send out Merrita's loyal guards as mercenaries for evil? How could you! No wonder you never included Ray in anything to do with the so-called scouting trips. He would have discovered the truth and found a way to stop you."

Still my aunt showed no hint of shame. "You needn't worry about Nereus. Some time in the dungeons will no doubt give him a chance to reflect on his folly and see the wisdom of showing his sister more respect."

How could she know her brother so little? "He's not going to forget all your lies—or what we saw on the surface."

"Ah, but what did you see on the surface?" she asked with amusement in her voice. "A pretty prince, perhaps? One who spun you all kinds of tales to try to lure you to remain at his side? One who shielded you from all the true horrors of his world while he reeled you in?"

I gaped at her. "It wasn't like that!"

"Wasn't it? You don't think your father will see the wisdom in my words?" She cocked her head to the side, her expression changing to one of sympathy, and her voice taking on an indulgent note. "You're so young, Isla. Really, no one can blame you for being taken in. I'm sure you meant no harm by your little excursion, and we can merely be grateful that you returned before those land dwellers managed to infect you with their evil."

I stumbled back a step in horror. It had all been so perfect.

The tone, the expression, everything undermining me while appearing to support me. On the surface, her words suggested my father accept me back without punishment while, underneath, they laid the insidious seed that would ensure he never trusted me again. The king's greatest fear was of the darkness of the land infecting the kingdom entrusted to his care. Too bad he didn't know the darkness was already here.

"He won't believe you," I said, because I had to say something, but my voice no longer sounded convincing.

"Won't he?" Nerissa asked with a smile. "He always has before. Because he knows the Vasants are loyal to the crown above all else."

Was there something mocking in her expression as she said that? It was gone so fast that I couldn't be sure.

"One Vasant is, at least," I said. "And you've got him locked in the dungeon. But even without Ray, I will never give up. I'll convince Father to go to the surface himself to see, or at least to send a scout of his own. Someone truly loyal to him. One way or another—if it takes me my whole life—I will convince him. And if I can't, the tremors will!" I said, using my only trump.

For the first time, the general looked the tiniest bit unsure, as if the tremors produced cracks not just in the city, but in her certainty as well. Had she always known she was the cause of them? Had she been living in fear all this time that someone else would work out their true warning?

I pressed against her hesitation, trying to undermine her further. "Once my father sees how the darkness he fears already controls you, he will blow the golden conch and bring Merrita back up into the light. And darkness cannot withstand light."

"Golden conch?" Nerissa leaped on my words like a shark in a feeding frenzy. "*That's* what he has to do to raise us back to the surface? Blow on some special conch? Of course the godmothers would come up with something so ridiculous!"

A different kind of tingle started at my scalp and trickled

down my body, sucking the blood away with it and leaving me trembling.

"You didn't know about the conch? I thought surely you…"

"No, stupid girl," she said. "I didn't know. And the fact that your father would entrust such knowledge to you over me just shows everything that is wrong with this kingdom.

"But where does he keep it?" she asked—half to me, half to herself. "In his chambers, or his study, or…"

Relief strengthened my trembling legs. She didn't know where it was, and I wouldn't be tricked into divulging that. But my stomach continued to roil as if I had eaten rancid fish. My father had trusted me, over anyone else. He had trusted me, and I had let my assumptions and my headlong emotion lead me into betraying that trust.

I would have to tell him what I'd done, of course. And at least try to tell him everything else. But I could already see how my efforts to put him on his guard against his sister-in-law would likely fail. The sick feeling intensified, inching up my throat. She would no doubt pledge her loyalty once again, swearing never to reveal his secret, and it would all confirm her practiced words. I was the flighty, irresponsible child whose opinions couldn't be trusted, while she was the solid, dependable counselor.

No, my aunt wasn't going to try to keep me locked in this room. She had no need to.

As if sensing the last of my fight leave me, she opened the door, leaning out into the corridor. Someone must have been passing because she barked a command, and a guard appeared behind her.

The man gave only a single curious glance at me before nodding his head at whatever command she whispered and trotting back out of sight. She then closed the door again, leaving us alone once more.

I couldn't even muster the interest to ask what that had been about. What did it matter? Ray was locked away, Teddy was out of reach, and my aunt knew exactly how to render me impotent. Her lies were too practiced, her influence too deep. The darkness would destroy my home just as I had once feared the tremors would. But for all I had never truly belonged, I couldn't abandon my family and my kingdom. Especially not now that I knew how the darkness here could reach out to all the other kingdoms, too. I would have to keep fighting, trying to gain my father's trust, however long it took. And that meant I could never go to the surface again.

I would never again feel the wind or the sun on my face, or the sand beneath my toes. I would never build a sandcastle with Daisy, laugh with Millie, or feel Teddy whirling me around the dance floor.

A knock sounded on the door, jerking me out of my depression. It opened immediately, and my second-oldest sister stepped in.

"Where is she?" Coral cried, her eyes falling on me. "Oh Isla! Thank goodness you're safe!"

"I caught her just before she made it in to see your father," Nerissa said, exchanging a loaded look with Coral. "So I thought I'd better send for you to talk some sense into her."

"Thank you," Coral said, her voice heavy with gratitude. "I'll do my best."

I gaped at them, my mind trying to reject what my ears were hearing. Coral? My sister in league with Nerissa? And not just any sister but Coral—the one who was almost like a mother?

My aunt crossed to the door but paused before opening it. Looking back at me, she spoke in a serious, concerned voice, although her eyes mocked me.

"Do listen to your sister, Isla dear. Think carefully before you go blurting anything out to your father."

Then she was gone, and I was alone with Coral. I wasn't sure I could feel any part of my body anymore. I certainly couldn't move.

Coral, however, had no such compunction, rushing across the room to scoop me into her arms.

"Isla! I've been worried sick! Where have you been?"

"Coral," I said through numb lips, unable to form the questions burning on my heart.

"Wait, no!" My sister laughed and held up a hand. "Don't tell me, actually. That way I can tell Father quite honestly that I don't know where you were." She laughed again. "I'm sorry, I'm just so relieved to see you safe."

She gave me a little shake. "And angry at you for leaving, of course. At least you took Ray with you. That gave me some comfort."

I frowned. That seemed a strange thing to say in the circumstances. Almost as if she didn't know Ray had just been hauled off to the dungeons.

"Coral," I said slowly. "What exactly shouldn't I be talking to Father about?"

Her face dropped. "Oh, Isla. Maybe we protected you young ones too much…" She sighed and met my eyes earnestly. "If you —hypothetically—had gone to the surface, on no account should you mention that to Father. Oceana somehow convinced him that since Ray was with you, you had most likely gone off in search of some great feat of daring that would prove Father should make you a full guard. Given you'd just embarrassed yourself in front of the whole court and then had an awful row with Father, she managed to make a convincing case that you had decided to abandon court and fully embrace being a guard."

She sighed again. "Of course, our sisters and I had no such false hope, and Waverly has been worried sick. Avalon was convinced you were never coming back."

"And was at least a little glad for it," I muttered.

Coral didn't try to deny it, merely shaking her head with a look of long-suffering.

"Coral, I have to tell him the truth," I said.

"No," she said sharply. "You don't! Not unless you want to have at least three guards with you, night and day. If Father thinks you've been up on the surface—actually on land—for weeks on end, he'll be terrified of letting you out of our sight."

"But I need to convince him he's wrong!"

"Oh Isla," she said. "You'll never convince him of that. Not after mother."

The hot rebuttal faded from my lips at her unexpected words.

"What does mother have to do with any of this?"

Coral sat down on one of the three chairs that sat in a row along one wall, gesturing for me to sit in another. I hesitated before giving in and taking a seat beside her.

"Mother has everything to do with it. Because you are just like her."

"What? No I'm not. Everyone knows Mother looked just like Oceana and Waverly."

Coral shook her head. "Not in looks. In other ways. She was adventurous like you are. Hot-headed sometimes, and always full of so many hopes and dreams." She pinned me with her gaze. "Dreams of the surface."

"Mother dreamed of the surface?" I could hardly believe the words. "How could I not have heard that about her before?"

"No one told you because we didn't want to encourage you," Coral said. "It was hard enough trying to stop you constantly talking of the surface and your wish to go there. And we knew how Father would react if he ever realized how bad it really is with you. He was already getting worried when you were three years old. Why do you think he chose Mother's shell collection to give you when he decided we should all have something of hers?"

"Yes, but what about her shell collection?" I asked. "It's proof that Mother loved life at the bottom of the sea."

Coral shook her head, looking guilty now. "Mother inherited that collection herself, from Grandmother. I think she handed it on with the same hope Father had when he passed it on to you—

the hope that it would help Mother see the beauty of the ocean. Which of course means Father should have known it wouldn't work."

I stared ahead, trying to wrap my mind around this new version of my mother. I wasn't the only member of my family to look upward and dream of a different world, then. Fresh grief filled me. How different my life would have been if she'd lived. Had she hated the shells as I had done? Would she be glad to think they were all broken?

But not even my grief could distract me from the current danger for long.

"I still don't understand," I said slowly. "What do Mother's dreams of the surface have to do with Father's obstinacy now?"

Coral licked her lips, clearly trying to force herself to say something she didn't want to say.

"Mother was killed by a shark because she traveled outside the safety of our waters. She tried to go to the surface—all the way to one of the kingdoms of the land. When they realized what had happened, Aunt Nerissa went after her, but she was too late. Father had been holding on to hope because Mother's two personal guards went with her, but Aunt only found pieces of the three of them."

"I..." I pressed my hand against my head, trying to make sense of it all. I had always known Mother was killed by a shark, and that Father feared letting the six of us roam too freely, but this changed everything. No wonder Father feared the surface. Just dreaming of it and attempting to reach it had been enough to kill Mother.

A horrible certainty followed this revelation. Father blamed the surface for Mother's death. He hated it with a passion undimmed by the passing of fourteen years. I had no hope at all of convincing him that Nerissa was lying to him. He wanted to hate the surface—to believe it evil—because it had taken his beloved wife from him. Lies that confirmed something you wanted to be true were the most beguiling.

"So you see, Isla?" Coral was still pleading with me. "Just tell him you're sorry for going, and you won't leave again. Let him go on believing that you were merely roaming around looking for trouble. Trouble that thankfully didn't find you."

"You make me sound like a heedless fool!" I snapped.

She raised an eyebrow at me. "Aren't you one?"

I collapsed in on myself. At least Coral wasn't in league with Nerissa. That was something to comfort myself with. She was only trying to protect me—and our father at the same time. I thought back to Nerissa's face as she left. She had enjoyed tormenting me, knowing how I would interpret her words.

"And the first thing you have to do," Coral said, "is go straight to your room and change out of that admittedly incredible dress."

I glanced down at myself. I had almost forgotten I still wore the green ballgown, the skirt returned to me when I passed through the barrier and lost my tail.

"Father's never going to believe you were out looking for a feat to prove yourself if he sees you wearing that."

"Very well," I said slowly. "I'll go now."

Coral walked me back to my room, fussing over me, although I barely heard her. At least she left me when we finally reached my familiar door. But I only had a few moments alone in the quiet of my room before it swung open again.

Avalon rushed through, only to pull up short, her eyes bulging.

"Where. Did you get. That dress." She eyed me up and down, going so far as to circle me in order to see it from every angle. "When do I get to go to the surface?"

I laughed. I couldn't help it. "Hello to you, too." My sister was dressed even more oddly than usual, her hair wrapped in some sort of lopsided turban that completely obscured whatever color hair she was currently sporting.

Avalon ignored my return scrutiny, all her attention on my gown. Only when I'd stripped the dress off was she able to focus on anything else.

"So, you're back after all."

"Sorry to disappoint you," I said lightly.

She merely shrugged. "I'm going to convince you that I'm the true owner of that dress, and then all will be forgiven."

I didn't reply, and she seemed to take that as an opening, launching into a passionate explanation of why I should give it to her.

I held up a hand to stop her, rubbing my temple with the other one.

"It's been a long night, Avalon. A very long night. I can promise you one thing, and that's if you don't give me some space right now, I will certainly never give you that dress."

She jumped to her feet and instantly fled the room, glancing back over her shoulder at me with expressive, beseeching eyes. As soon as the door closed behind her, I sighed, overtaken with a wave of guilt for letting her think she might convince me. I would never give her that dress. Not when I had danced with Teddy in it. For the first and only time, most likely.

But even as I thought it, a small kernel of hope lodged in my mind. I might never be able to convince my father, but did that mean Merrita could never rise from the waves?

Royal blood, royal conch, my father had said. And my father wasn't the only one in Merrita with royal blood. I could blow that conch myself and raise our kingdom. Once it was done, and we were on the surface, Father would see the truth and forgive me. Together we could bring my aunt to justice. Avalon could have as many dresses as she wanted. And I could have Trione back.

I pulled on a plain gown, picking one at random. I had to get to the conch first, before Nerissa could use her new knowledge to somehow find and destroy it—which was no doubt her aim since she seemed determined to keep us from the surface.

I dashed from my chamber, hurtling down the corridor toward the royal reception room. Surely Nerissa couldn't have discovered its location yet? No one would be watching it. I would take it and hide it out in my secret room—the hiding place that had safely stored my treasures for so long. And if I couldn't pry it open in there, I would find a way to get the key from my father. Surely I could come up with a plan if I only had time to think about it.

Inside the room at last, I saw with relief that the tapestry looked undisturbed. Pushing it aside, I revealed the alcove, drawing out the wooden casket. The gravity of the moment hit me, and I paused, gazing down at the huge, glinting ruby. Could I really do this?

But I already knew I could. For the future of my kingdom I could do more than this.

I turned to leave, the casket tucked under my arm, and found I was no longer alone.

CHAPTER 26

"*I*sla!" My father's anguished voice cut through my heart, and I nearly dropped the chest and ran to him.

But then I saw who stood beside him, barely concealed triumph on her face, and the urge passed. How had Nerissa known I would come here? Because somehow it looked like I had played right into her plan. This was why she had called for Coral, seeking to delay me in that room while she arranged things to her benefit.

"I trusted you—my own daughter—and this is how you betray me?" My father sounded old and weary and broken.

"Father," I said, but he cut me off before I could go further.

"I don't want to hear it. When the general came to me, saying there was a plot to steal my most valuable possession, do you know where my thoughts went first? To you and your sisters. Because nothing is more valuable to me than my daughters. When she clarified she meant the conch, I thought it impossible, since no one knew of it."

His eyes blazed now, his wrath mounting. "Except the general pointed out to me that since she herself knew, that proved the information had leaked. I brought her here, under strictest promise of secrecy, and I told myself it couldn't have come from you." His voice dropped. "It never even occurred to me you might be the thief."

Tears dripped unheeded down my face, but I could think of nothing to say in my own defense. Nerissa's cunning had been complete. She hadn't accused me to my father, knowing such accusations might sour him against her. Instead she had brought him here to be shocked and heart-broken. Every way I thought to turn, she was there to foil me.

"I'm sure she didn't mean harm," Nerissa said, right on cue. "I'm sure she doesn't realize the gravity of what she's doing."

"Not realize?" My father roared, his anger whipped into a white hot fury by her moderate response. "I told her myself what value that casket has to our Family and my throne. Isla is so desperate to be taken seriously, to be viewed as an adult—well, she must accept the consequences of her wrongdoing."

Nerissa gasped. "Surely you don't mean to lock up your own daughter, Your Majesty!"

My father blinked, and I could see that he had not, in fact, meant that. But now that the seed had been planted, I saw it take root behind his eyes.

"Certainly she must be locked away," he said. "As any enemy of the crown must be." He strode forward and removed the chest from my unresisting hands, tucking it away out of sight beneath his cloak.

"Guards!" He roared the word, and four guards poured into the room.

"Father," I pleaded, my voice trembling despite my best efforts. But he turned his back on me, issuing a stream of orders to the guards.

As two of them took my arms, gently but firmly, and led me from the room, I got a final glimpse of the general. I had underestimated her desire to neutralize me. Or perhaps this entire plan had been about nothing more than finding the location of the conch. She had certainly succeeded in doing so without casting any suspicion on herself.

Either way, I had taunted her, saying she could not lock up a royal, and she had found a way to manipulate my father into doing it for her. She could not have more clearly stated who held the real power in Merrita.

The guards escorted me down several corridors and into a nondescript, seldom-used guest suite. This room had no furniture beside the bed itself, and a cupboard built into the wall beside the single window. Neither guard said anything to me, but I heard the key turn in the lock behind them before their footsteps retreated.

I tried the door, just to be sure, and then went to the window. It had cross panes which removed any hope of smashing the glass, and there was nothing to use to smash it anyway. I certainly couldn't pick up the bed and use it as a battering ram.

Only once I had gone through the motions of checking for a means of escape did I finally allow myself to collapse on the bed and cry.

After crying myself out, I fell into an exhausted slumber. When I woke, there was both an untouched breakfast tray and a lunch tray on the floor. I tried to remember the last time I had eaten and could not. Ravenous, I consumed all the food on both trays, an act I immediately regretted.

The long afternoon passed with ceaseless pacing, my body unable to be still while my mind raced. But it didn't matter how fast it moved, it always came back to the same spot. I was stuck, and there was nothing I could do.

I had begun to think of my evening meal, wondering who might bring it and if I had any hope of turning them to my side, when the tremor struck. It went on and on, sending me staggering across the floor to crash against the wall.

When the ground finally ceased shuddering, I remained, pressed against the wall while I gathered my breath. This time my room had no possessions or decorations to be tumbled around, though my mind flew to the single shell I had saved last time. Had it been destroyed too by now? My conversation with Coral had transformed my feelings toward the keepsake. In a perverse way, it had become a connection between me and my mother—an item we had both owned and both resented.

And then I thought of the Hall of Meetings—which had not been cracked—and I could think of nothing except what damage had been wrought this time. How far would the High King go in his warnings? Had this one finally been enough to make my father take note?

I didn't even consider trying to call on my godmother. We had been sent warnings, and we had failed to heed them. Merrita was responsible for fighting against the godmothers across the kingdoms. We had been given protection beneath the waves, and still, somehow, we had been the ones to bring darkness. I was no longer surprised the godmothers had stopped answering our calls.

I could only hope there was still a chance Merrita could rise up to the light once more. As long as my aunt hadn't yet found a way to destroy that conch.

No meal came for a long time. But eventually a key sounded in the lock, and the door creaked open. I rushed forward, not sure if I meant to attack the guard or try to duck past him, only to stop in surprise. My doorway was full, but not of guards.

The food tray was borne by Coral, and at her back were the rest of my sisters. With the single exception of Avalon.

"Oh Isla!" Waverly rushed forward and threw her arms around my neck, weeping against me. "I don't understand what's happening!"

Oceana rolled her eyes, and if the situation hadn't been so serious, I would have grinned over Waverly's shoulder at her.

"Please calm yourself, Waverly," Oceana said. "That's not helping anyone."

Coral gave our oldest sister a reproving look but put down my tray on the bed and detached Waverly from my neck, putting a comforting arm around her shoulder.

"Is everyone all right?" I asked, focusing on Oceana. "What buildings came down this time?"

"Only a single building in the center of the city," she said. "And we were fortunate again. It wasn't a residence, and at this time of day everyone is home."

I breathed a sigh of relief.

"But whatever did you do, Isla?" Marine asked. "I still can't believe Father has had you locked up."

I bit my lip, my eyes flying to Oceana. So she hadn't told them about the conch. Then I wouldn't either.

"I can't say. But I did it for the good of our kingdom—I swear."

Coral sighed. "I don't doubt you believe that, Isla, or you wouldn't have done it. But I fear you must have done something shockingly rash."

"Never mind what I did," I said quickly, realizing what an opportunity I'd been given. "The important thing is that you mustn't trust Aunt Nerissa. Under any circumstances. And you have to convince Father that Merrita needs to rise back to the surface."

"The surface?" Waverly sounded shocked while Coral and Marine exchanged weighted looks.

But Oceana was regarding me with sharp consideration, and I hurried over to her.

"Please Oceana, you have to believe me!"

"I do believe there is some hope for your situation, at least," she said. "Father has had you locked up here, not the dungeon, and he has not yet told anyone about your arrest. In fact, he has ordered the guards who were present at the time to keep silent on the matter."

"And he's in such a towering rage no one would dream of violating his orders," Marine added.

"Yes, surely he must forgive her, whatever it is," Waverly said.

"Lyon has gone to his grandmother," Oceana said to me. "He's going to ask her to intercede with Father on your behalf. She knows how much Father loves us all, so Lyon believes she will see your captivity as the general's influence at work. And Elda already believes our aunt is overreaching. If anyone can do anything for you, it's the Delaneys."

"Thank you," I said.

"Is it true you went to the surface?" Marine asked. "What was it like?"

"Incredible," I said, trying to keep tears from rushing to my eyes. "I can't even begin to describe it all. The sun, the animals, the birds. They screech so." I chuckled weakly. "And the food! I really have no words for the food. And they have so many clothes and so much wood—everything we lack."

I eagerly looked between each of them. "But the best thing of all was that they follow the ways of the High King again. The godmothers have returned and everything. There couldn't be a better time for Merrita to rise. You have to convince Father!"

"He is in no mood for convincing right now," Oceana said heavily.

"But Oceana," I said. "You felt that tremor. Two big ones in as many days. The godmothers are trying to warn us of something terrible down here. How long can we afford to ignore their warnings?"

"As far as Father is concerned, only one significant thing has happened in the last two days," Oceana said with an apologetic look. "If Father sees a warning in the tremors, I don't think you're going to like his probable conclusion on what that message is meant to be."

I gulped. I could only imagine how delighted my aunt would be to encourage his thinking in that direction.

"We have to go," Coral said suddenly. "Father doesn't know we're here."

I hugged them each in turn and begged them to visit again. When Oceana embraced me, she whispered in my ear for me to check the bed after they left. It was hard to focus on my final farewell to Coral after that, but a part of me still melted inside her warm embrace.

"Give Avalon my love," I said wryly, when she finally pulled away.

"Be patient with her, dearest," she replied. "This is all hard on her. While you were gone, the court has been asking her to sing for them."

"I have no desire to take that away from her." I looked sourly around the room that enclosed me. "And I'm hardly competition for her in here. I'm surprised she didn't come to gloat."

"She feels too guilty to come, of course," Coral said, as if it was the most obvious thing in the world. "She's ashamed of her feelings toward you."

I raised an eyebrow. "Avalon, ashamed? That would be new."

Coral gave me a reproving look. "She might not understand that's what she's feeling, but I know she is. As I said, give her time."

I glanced around my prison again. "Time is all I have right now."

"Don't lose hope," she said, squeezing me one more time before leaving me alone.

I hurried straight for the bed. A short, elegant dagger lay nestled among the covers. I snatched it up, relieved by the solid feel of it in my palm.

The first thing I tried was the catch on the window, but it

refused to respond to the dagger tip, and the window itself resisted my efforts to pry it open. Eventually I gave up and tucked the weapon into one of my boots, hiding it for an opportune moment.

The minutes and hours ticked by, and I kept catching myself tensing all my muscles, waiting for another tremor, although none struck. After Oceana's words, I could only be doubly relieved for the absence. I didn't need more reasons for my father to doubt me.

Horrible images invaded my mind as I remembered all the horrors my father had once listed for me. Beasts and curses, famine and poison, and unnatural infections that could grip an entire kingdom. How deep would the darkness have to take hold before such things became reality here as well?

A tapping drove these despairing thoughts from my mind. I turned back to the door, only to realize the sound came from the other side of the room. I hurried over to the window, trying to peer through the tiny diamond panes. Had Ray somehow escaped and come for me? Or had one of my sisters decided to break me free, after all?

But when I peered through the glass, I found myself looking at an impossibility. My captivity was affecting me more heavily than I had realized. Because those faces could not be here, outside my window.

I fell back a couple of steps, fear filling me at this betrayal by my own mind. But with a loud creak, the window swung open, and I could see, without distortion, the faces of Teddy and Millie.

I gasped their names, remaining rooted in place.

"Isla!" Teddy cried joyously. "You *are* in here. I wasn't entirely sure if we should believe that lady, but we figured we had nothing to lose."

"Wait. You're real?" I asked.

Millie laughed. "Of course we're real. Did you think we were apparitions?"

"Hallucinations, perhaps?" I said, before adding, under my breath, "Beautiful dreams."

"Climb in, Teddy, and help her," Millie commanded.

Teddy hoisted himself up and scrambled inelegantly across the sill while I mused about my good fortune at being imprisoned on the ground floor.

"But how is it possible?" I asked. "I don't understand."

"Neither do we, exactly," Millie said. "All we know is that when we went swimming the morning after you left, something very strange happened."

"We sprouted tails," Teddy said matter-of-factly. "The second we submerged in the water."

"Impossible," I said.

"It was certainly a surprise," he said with a grin that suggested the word was a significant understatement.

"So naturally we called on our godmother," Millie said. "She seemed like the only one who might have answers."

"And she came?" I gaped at them.

Millie nodded. "She explained that you needed us. And then she sent a glowing fish to lead us here. We were not expecting this place, though." She looked back toward the barrier, glistening in the distance.

"You came all this way for me?" I asked.

"Of course." Teddy sounded wounded.

I threw my arms around his neck and squeezed as hard as I could, not even caring that it had likely been friendship that motivated his words rather than something more.

"Thank you, thank you, thank you."

"Whoa, steady," Teddy said, although he sounded like he was smiling. "From what I can gather you've been locked in here. Maybe you should wait until we've actually succeeded in the rescue before handing out hugs."

I shook my head, mopping at my soggy eyes. "No. You came,

and that deserves a hug all of its own." I grinned at him. "But, also, let's get out of here."

He knelt on one knee beside the window, gesturing for me to stand on the raised one and use it as a step up into the window.

"I'm capable of climbing out on my own, you know," I pointed out.

"Of course you are," Millie said promptly, "but you're wearing skirts. And believe me, it's an inelegant enough process without the stupid things getting in the way."

"True," I conceded, hopping neatly down from the sill and watching Teddy struggle back over on his own. "But I still don't understand how you ended up here at my window. How did you find me? Did you say something about a woman?"

Teddy nodded. "A young woman, really, although older than us."

"And very dignified and commanding," Millie interjected.

"I'm afraid it was a rather sad and sorry rescue attempt before she showed up," Teddy said. "We were wandering around, hopelessly lost. We'd managed to find the palace but had no idea what to do from there. That's when the lady appeared from nowhere, asked if we were here for you, directed us to this window, and even provided this very handy key." He waved a small brass key in the air before letting it drop into the grass.

"We're supposed to make it obvious you escaped through the window, so that blame doesn't fall on those with a key to the door," Millie said.

"I'm afraid you're going to have to lead us from here," Teddy said. "Because I think our glowing fish has disappeared."

"But we can't leave yet," Millie said. "What about Ray?" She looked at me anxiously. "I was expecting him to be with you."

I bit my lip, grimacing. "He was arrested as soon as we stepped back through the barrier. No one is supposed to go to the surface, you see. Or, well, not unless…" I sighed. "It's a long story. But suffice it to say, I've been told he's in the dungeons.

Which won't be nearly as easy to break into as this room, I'm afraid."

Teddy gave Millie an uneasy look, and I could see from his face he was trying to decide if he should suggest we head back to Trione without my uncle. But there was no way I was agreeing to that.

"Don't worry, we'll think of a way to get him out," I said quickly. "But even once we have, we still can't run for Trione. Not yet. The godmother wouldn't have sent you here just to save me. My kingdom is in danger, and she sent you because she knew that together we have a chance of saving Merrita."

"Save Merrita? From what?" Teddy asked, but Millie, her expression strangely abstracted, spoke over the top of him.

"You told us Nereus was trained as a guard, so I assume that means he's a guard here. But it's quite obvious you've also been trained as a guard, as Daisy pointed out at the ball. Yet Nereus is in the dungeons, and you were locked up in there." She pointed at the window and fixed me with a piercing look. "Isla, you're not just a guard, are you? I think it's time you tell us exactly who you are."

My eyes stayed locked with hers, although I was burningly aware of Teddy's presence beside me.

"I'm a princess. The youngest princess of Merrita. My father is the sea king."

Millie shook her head, looking dazed. "You're a mermaid princess. I've actually swum with a tail myself and breathed underwater, but it's still a little hard to absorb."

But I wasn't listening to her because my words had sparked a memory and with it, a realization. We needed to free Ray—and doing so might be a lot simpler than I had feared.

CHAPTER 27

*M*inutes later, we were hurrying out of the dungeons with an astonished but silent Ray at our side. My sisters had told me my imprisonment was being kept secret—and that meant I only had to walk into the dungeon and order Ray freed.

I told the guards on duty I was fetching him by the general's orders, and since I was a princess, no one challenged me. We still had to move fast, though. It was an unusual enough event that someone was sure to report it. And there was also the possibility of running into one of the guards who had been present at my arrest.

All I knew was that we needed to get away from the palace as soon as possible.

Somehow Ray managed to thrust aside his astonishment at the twins' presence and focus on the most urgent matters.

"I assume my sister didn't really order you to have me released?" he asked as soon as we were out of earshot of the guards.

"Not as such," I said. "What she did was maneuver me into getting arrested as well."

"What?" Ray asked, and then looked around a little guiltily at the volume of his exclamation.

"Thankfully most people don't know about that part yet," I said. "But we need to get out of here as quickly as possible."

Ray shook his head, wonderingly. "Where are we headed?"

"Ah, we hadn't got that far in our thinking," I admitted.

"The woman who helped us find you said something about trusting a Lyon. Does that make any sense to you?"

"Woman?" Ray looked between us with a creased brow.

"I'm fairly sure it was Oceana," I said. "And the Lyon comment would seem to confirm that."

We slipped out a side door and hurried across the courtyard, leaving through the main gate. No one stopped us, so none of the guards who knew of my transgressions were on gate duty then. I breathed a deep sigh of relief while trying to keep my expression free from guilt.

As soon as we could do so, we darted down a side street, out of sight.

"Isla," Millie said, looking back in the direction of the palace and speaking with a strange note in her voice. "I can see why you were so familiar with our palace."

I smiled. "Yes, we used to be an island just like you. My ancestor called the kingdoms of the land our sister-kingdoms, but she also spoke of a special connection between Trione and Merrita. But when the other kingdoms turned from the High King's laws, Trione believed there was still hope for them to change their minds, while Merrita begged for protection and sank down here. Only now everything's reversed, and we have to find a way to raise Merrita again before we're the ones consumed by the darkness."

Both twins gulped and looked up at the distant shimmering bubble around us. I, however, gazed out over the streets.

"Oh!" I said. "I think I know what Oceana meant. We need to head for the Delaney manor. We need to see Elda."

Ray raised an eyebrow but didn't question me. Instead he produced a dirty rag from somewhere and directed me to put it over my head.

"We've been seen leaving the palace, we can't help that. But I'd prefer there wasn't a trail of people who can point out where we went from here," he said.

I tied the repulsive thing over my hair while reminding him he was nearly as distinctive as me.

"Not with this," he said cheerfully, thrusting a guard's helmet onto his head. I hadn't seen him swipe either item from the courtyard, but it was the only place he could have gotten them.

"Why couldn't I have a helmet, too?" I asked.

He grinned at me. "Because it wouldn't cover all your hair and would look completely out of place with that dress."

We were moving forward as we talked, keeping to the backstreets. Only twice did we have to cross major thoroughfares, and soon enough we arrived at the Delaney manor. It was the largest in all of Merrita, sprawling the full block between two side streets.

Ray led us down one of these roads, approaching a small door in the side wall rather than the great gates that fronted the main street. He rapped twice, and we all waited, tension bouncing between us.

Finally the door opened, and a stiff guard looked out, a lantern in his hand.

"What do you want?" he barked, before his eyes jumped from Ray's face to mine and widened.

"Captain. Your Highness." He bowed.

"Is Lyon here?" I asked.

The man shook his head. "No, His Highness has already returned to the palace."

"Then we need to see Elda," I said. "Now."

"Certainly." The man stepped aside and gestured for us to enter, frowning at Teddy and Millie but saying nothing.

When he closed the door behind us, Ray spoke in his most commanding tone.

"We need our presence here to be held in strictest confidence. Both your Family's honor and your kingdom hang on it."

The man looked surprised, but he nodded, and I trusted his word. The major Families chose personal guards from among their own members. He wouldn't do anything to betray his Family's honor. Unless Elda ordered him otherwise, he would deny our presence to my father himself. Which was just what we needed.

We followed the guard across a wide courtyard and through a side entrance. We climbed what looked like a servants' stair and emerged into an antechamber.

"Wait here," he told us, and disappeared through a door on the far side.

We didn't have to wait long, however. He quickly reappeared and gestured for us to approach. I half-expected him to announce us, but instead he merely held the door open and pulled it closed behind us.

Beyond, we found a long chamber with high ceilings. Floor length windows dominated the far end of the room, although the curtains were now drawn, and several lanterns stood around the room in placements chosen to provide even light. The nearer half of the room had been outfitted like a study, while the other half had been furnished like a sitting room.

Elda—matriarch of the powerful Delaney Family and grandmother of my brother-in-law, a future king—awaited us alone.

"Welcome, Your Highness, Captain." She bowed.

Her pure white hair proclaimed her age, but neither her bearing nor her alert eyes suggested any weakness. And she had clearly already been sitting here, surrounded by lanterns, despite the lateness of the hour.

"We're sorry to disturb you in such a way," I said. "But we are here on a matter of sensitivity and urgency."

"Yes, I can well imagine," she said gravely, although her eyes held a small twinkle, "given my grandson has only just informed me about your imprisonment at the palace. He requested I petition the king on your behalf. But it seems that won't be necessary, after all."

"I'm afraid we've come with a more serious request than that," I said, looking her directly in the eye. "We need asylum—a place to hide. And we need help to defy my father and save Merrita. If you can't help us, please tell us so at once, and we'll be on our way."

Elda hid her shock quickly, an amused expression replacing it.

"Ah, the haste of youth. A distant memory for me, I'm afraid. Please, sit down." She gestured toward the sofas in the other part of the room. "You must tell me your story, and how Merrita can be saved, and then I will tell you if I can help."

I hesitated, and she gave me a serious, sincere look.

"I can tell you now that I have the gravest of concerns for our kingdom and am willing to go to any lengths if I am convinced of a way it can be saved."

I nodded. That would have to be enough to start.

The four of us took seats, somehow ending up with Teddy and me on one sofa and Millie and Ray on another. Elda, who took her place on the third sofa, noted our positions.

"Perhaps," she said, "you might begin by introducing me to these two?"

I glanced first at Millie and then at Teddy.

"We trust you, Isla," he murmured.

Elda raised her eyebrows at his tone of familiarity, the interest on her face growing. I took a deep breath.

"May I introduce you to Prince Theodore and Princess Millicent of Trione?"

This at last shocked her into an exclamation.

"Impossible!" She looked between them with wide eyes. "What foolery is this?"

"No foolery," I said quietly. "And no impossibility, although I would have thought it so myself mere hours ago. But the whole thing is a confusing mess, and I can see I'll need to tell it from the beginning."

And so I did. I told her of my concerns, and my father's refusal to listen to them. I briefly touched on my announcement at the ball, glossing over the details since Elda had been there, and then—with a churning of my stomach so extreme I nearly lost my last meal—I told them all my father's secret. I hated to betray his trust again, but he was a victim of a far greater betrayal, and this was my only chance to save him and Merrita.

Teddy took my hand and squeezed it, giving me strength.

"How fascinating," Elda breathed, her eyes wide with something suspiciously like hope. "I never guessed such a thing could exist. And while I must confess, I had a hand in goading you onto that stage at the ball, I didn't expect such spectacular fruit."

I gaped at her. "You knew I was going to snap and announce my fears to the whole court?"

She smiled primly. "Let us say, rather, that I hoped." Her face softened. "Although I am sorry for the personal suffering you have endured as a result of it."

"I was a fool," I said. "I can see that now. But I can't regret it. Because it drove me to the surface, and I could never regret that."

Teddy, who still hadn't released my hand, squeezed it again. No, I could never regret meeting Teddy. I wouldn't tell him I was his ocean girl—that wasn't the love I wanted from him—but I still couldn't regret my own love for him.

And with the strength he loaned me, I told the rest. How we were attacked by the raiders, and I was rescued by Teddy and Millie. My weeks in the palace, and Ray's weeks in the raider camp. What I learned of the current state of the kingdoms of the land.

That part greatly interested Elda, and she directed a number of searching questions at the twins, seeming greatly pleased with their responses.

I glossed over everything at the ball except for the size of the second wave that hit, and the fact of Ray's and my departure—with the resulting exposure of our mer-forms. It was clear from Elda's perceptive gaze that she knew there was more to it, but she asked no questions.

I related Ray and my conversation on our way back, and our horrified conclusions about General Nerissa. Conclusions that were confirmed upon our arrival by her increasing acts against us. I flushed with embarrassment as I told of my poorly thought through attempt to take the conch, but no one said anything to judge me. And from there I jumped straight to the twins' arrival and our escape.

"And so," I finally concluded, "we broke Ray out, and here we are."

Elda gave a long sigh and leaned back into the sofa. "An incredible—almost unbelievable—story."

I sat forward, but she held up a hand to forestall me.

"Oh, I do believe it. I don't think anyone could hear you tell it and not do so. There is just so much to take in."

For a long moment she gazed into the distance while we all remained silent. When she at last sat forward again, her voice turned brisk, and her eyes gained a determined edge.

"Not least among this news, is the confirmation of Nerissa's treachery." She shook her head. "The Delaney Family has long suspected the Vasant Family." She paused and gave a nod in Ray's direction. "Meaning you no disrespect, young Nereus. But we have long suspected that your sister, at least, no longer had the best interests of either this kingdom or the crown at heart."

She nodded again. "The Delaney Family will risk everything and throw every bit of our influence and resources behind you. The time has come to act, and if we do not seize it, everything we have built will be ashes."

I sank back against the sofa myself, trembling all over. I hadn't even realized how tense I was until the relief of those words. But I forced myself to regain control and sit upright again. I was the only representative of the crown here, and I couldn't afford to appear weak.

"For now," Elda said, "I think we must all get some rest. In the morning we will consult again, with my daughter, Fina, included this time. You can trust her as implicitly as you trust me." She glanced at Millie and Teddy. "She is Lyon's mother."

"I'm sorry," Millie said, "but I'm afraid I still don't know who Lyon is."

"Oh, no, I'm the one who's sorry," I said. "I should have explained. Oceana is my oldest sister—the heir to my father's throne—and Lyon is her husband. And also Fina's son and Elda's grandson."

Elda smiled proudly. "And already I have two gorgeous great-grandchildren. Prince Edmund and Princess Eloise are Delaneys, and one day—when I am long gone from this world—Edmund shall rule as the first of the Delaney royal line."

"Wait. What?" Ray spoke up for the first time, having allowed me to tell the story on my own—even those parts that were strictly his.

Elda raised an eyebrow. "You didn't know? It is not to be made public knowledge until Oceana and Lyon are crowned, but I assumed you would know through your sister. It was part of the marriage alliance that was brokered between the two of them. Upon marrying Oceana, Lyon took the Rennon name. And, when their time comes, he will rule beside her as a Rennon. But," and even now she couldn't keep the pride from her voice, "their children have taken the Delaney name and will rule as Delaneys."

"No wonder my sister was so against the marriage," Ray said. "I assume she is aware of the terms."

"Given her position as general, there can be no doubt," Elda said. "But you might be interested to know that it was your other sister, Queen Nerida, who negotiated the alliance in the first place, not long before her tragic death. She knew that with Rennon and Vasant blood flowing in Oceana's veins, and a Delaney husband by her side, nothing could ever challenge her daughter's rule. And since she was not a Rennon herself, she didn't have the same attachment to the name. I think King Morgan only agreed because he loved her so. And after she died, he would never have repudiated her dearest wish."

"The Vasant and Delaney Families are the oldest, richest, and most influential Families in the kingdom," I explained to Teddy and Millie. "Other than the Rennons, of course."

"With their position as generals, the Vasant Family have had ascendancy for generations," Elda said. "But we bided our time, and now it is we who will be victorious. But do not be concerned," she added quickly. "We will uphold our end of the bargain and throw every support behind both Oceana's reign, and Edmund's after her. Rennon blood will continue to sit on the throne. And since—unlike the other Families—the Delaneys have long believed that Merrita is destined to rise again, we've been quietly positioning ourselves for some time for a return to the surface. I imagine, therefore, both our resources and influence will be considerable."

"Now we know why my sister is so determined to keep Merrita beneath the waves," Ray said bitterly. "Down here, with dangers on every side, she still holds sway. But on the surface, among the now-peaceful kingdoms of the land, Nerissa and my Family will be swept from influence and power."

"Some people take the game too far," Elda said with sadness in her voice. "It has always been the way. But for now, we all need sleep."

I slept far more quickly and far more deeply than I had anticipated. I shared my room with Millie because we had refused to be separated, and a servant brought breakfast for us both on an enormous tray. The food we were served was the best Merrita had to offer—although I knew it would be unappealing to the twins. Millie, however, gave no sign of displeasure, asking with interest about each thing on her plate.

All of which meant that, much to my surprise, I found myself back in Elda's study feeling encouraged, rested, and restored, rather than exhausted and desperate like I had expected. And it seemed I had been right to put my trust in the elder stateswoman.

As soon as we were all gathered, she announced that she already had an answer for us.

"A ball," she said. "There is to be a ball tomorrow night at the palace. And you will all attend among the Delaney party."

"Will that work?" I asked.

"We have already received word back this morning. The king is not advertising your escape, but he has doubled the guards at every entrance to the palace. They have no excuse to comb the city for you, and they can have no grounds for demanding to search our property. You will be safe here until then. And no one will search the guests as they arrive at the ball either. With two such recent tremors, the king will be looking to pacify, not incite, the court. Which means we have a chance of sneaking you past unseen. We just need to ensure the crowd that enters with you is too large and too tightly packed to be easily examined by sight alone. But I'm afraid, after that, it will be up to you to find that artifact."

CHAPTER 28

We passed the day in the Delaney manor, sharing many of the unfamiliar aspects of our world with the twins. Both of them bombarded us with endless questions and observations—from the lack of plants and birds in Merrita to the food we ate. And in between every other conversation, we discussed the various possibilities of where my father might now be storing the conch.

"He's angry and hurt," I said at last. "He'll want it close to him. And that means his study. He spends more time there than in his chambers. He's never liked his rooms—I think they remind him too much of Mother."

Teddy gave my shoulder a squeeze of silent support, and I took a deep breath, pushing aside thoughts of my father and how he was currently feeling about me.

"Once we're inside, we start our search there," I said.

The question of how to acquire the key that would open the box was not so easily solved. And when we concluded at the midday meal the next day that we would have to see what opportunities presented themselves in the moment, I felt deeply uneasy. But we were out of time. If we wanted to slip past the guards as guests, then we needed to look the part. And that meant it was time to prepare for a ball.

Fina had promised us dresses, and I had quietly explained to Millie that she couldn't expect anything like the array of gowns she had at home. The Delaneys somehow managed to produce acceptable offerings in both of our sizes, however.

I felt the slightest pang as I carefully stepped into my gown, remembering the last time I had dressed for a ball. Presumably my mermaid dress was still strewn across my bed back in the palace. Or likely Avalon had claimed it already. That thought made me scowl.

But I knew I couldn't have worn it anyway. Fina had chosen us elegant dresses in a standard style—ones designed to ensure we didn't stand out, either by being out of fashion or by being notable. None of us were meant to create a sensation with our attire tonight.

When the four of us met in the vast entrance foyer of the Delaney mansion, everyone murmured compliments to each other, but it was clear none of our hearts or minds were really in it. Whenever my eyes fell on Teddy and Millie, dressed ready to infiltrate the palace, my heart seized. What was I doing dragging them in to such a venture? And what would my father and my aunt do if they were discovered?

Somehow, impossibly, the twins had both gained mer-forms, and my father might consider that their mere presence in Merrita made them his subjects. Subjects who had been born and raised in the supposed darkness of the kingdoms of the land. Subjects who had no hope of rescue, or even diplomacy, from their own people. If they were caught, he might not hesitate to lock them up and throw away the key.

Either that or he would repudiate them entirely and cast them back out through the barrier. And neither Teddy nor Millie had any training on life beneath the ocean. Last time they had traveled with a godmother's guide—on their own, unable to eat in their mer-forms, would they survive long enough to find their way back to land?

I shook myself and sternly rejected such imaginings. I needed to focus on the task at hand. The best way to help Teddy and Millie was to make sure they weren't caught.

The foyer had filled now, a shifting mass of gowned women and elegant men. It seemed Elda had decreed that the Delaneys would arrive at the ball as a single block, so even those Family members who didn't live at the manor had gathered in preparation for the event.

Many of them cast us curious glances, their eyes skimming over me and Ray to fasten on Teddy and Millie, but no one asked any questions. Elda had made a pronouncement, and they trusted their matriarch. After all, it was her wisdom that was leading the Delaneys to glory.

When we stepped out of the Delaney gates, we made a glittering procession. Glancing up, I could see interested eyes peeping from high windows. Those not fortunate enough to have secured an invitation to the event were admiring the spectacle.

I quickly looked back down, not wanting to draw attention to myself. Teddy's elbow appeared in my lowered vision, and I clamped onto it, grateful for his offered support. But before we reached the palace gates, he pulled gently away, and another, older gentleman slipped into his place.

I glanced up just long enough to see Teddy offer his arm to a young girl, barely old enough to attend balls. She looked up at him with starstruck eyes and whispered something I couldn't hear. I didn't immediately see Ray or Millie, but I knew the same thing would have happened with them. Elda wanted us each entering separately on the arm of a Delaney to give us a better chance of blending in.

The palace loomed before us far too soon, and it was torturously hard not to look up to scour the gate and check who was on guard duty. But I forced my eyes to remain down, and my feet to move slowly, not giving away how my heart drummed wildly.

As I shuffled forward, I nearly tripped over the heels of the woman in front of me, just as someone else jostled at my back. My escort stepped closer, pressing right against me, as people closed in on us on either side. We had reached the gate, and rather than slowing and spreading out, to enter in a trickle, the Delaneys had clumped together, forcing as many people through the gate at once as possible.

My straining ears, trying to do the job my eyes could not, picked out the irritated tones of a younger Delaney complaining to the guards about something a short way back up the street. His tone grew more and more strident, blaming the guards for not having cleaned up whatever mess had offended him. Finally Fina's cool tones intervened. She scolded the man, who no doubt slipped back into the mass of people and gave her calm—but profuse—apologies to the guards.

Despite everything, a small smile tugged at the corners of my mouth. Even without being able to watch it, I could tell the Delaneys put on a good show.

The cobblestones of the courtyard passed beneath my dancing slippers, and then I was swept up the stairs and into the palace, unable to move from the middle of the mass surrounding me, even if I had desired to do so.

We had planned to slip away as soon as we were inside the building, but footmen ringed the entryway and lined the path to the ballroom, making it impossible for us to separate from the crowd without being seen. Elda didn't falter at this setback, leading her assembled Family along the proscribed route. We swept into the ballroom in a block, rapidly swelling the numbers inside.

Music rang through the room, swirling dancers flashed past me, and I had a single glimpse of the long crystal wall—less impressive now that I had seen one that looked out directly onto a beach. Then my escort slipped an arm around me and swept me into the dance.

Nothing could have been further from my mind than dancing, but my body responded instinctively to his lead, skipping lightly through the required steps. Surreptitiously I watched the people whirling past me. If they were scared by the tremors, their faces didn't show it, chatter and laughter ringing out on all sides. And their movements seemed almost impossibly light and graceful after my weeks spent among land dwellers. How long would it take for the darkness to infect everything? How long until it destroyed these people's lives? I moved through them, another joyous dancer to all appearances, but filled with thoughts of death in my heart.

Skillfully, my partner directed us across the ballroom and off the edge of the dance floor, delivering me to a dark corner, half hidden by several shell sculptures that had been brought inside for the event. Millie already stood there, gazing wide-eyed at the dancers, and Teddy and Ray soon arrived.

"This way," Ray said, under his voice, pulling open a door behind us.

I nodded and hurried through it. I knew where it led, and sure enough we found ourselves in a small meeting room, used on occasion for spur-of-the-moment negotiations by ball attendees.

Ray led us straight through the dark room and out its main entrance. The corridor beyond was sufficiently removed from the palace entrance to be deserted in the middle of a ball. I let out a long sigh of relief. We had made it this far at least, which was more than I'd feared as I waited in the Delaney foyer.

I took the lead, hurrying toward my father's study, trying to stop my mind from uselessly running through every possible hiding place for the two hundredth time. We were moving into one of the less frequented sections of the palace, home to many of my family's private rooms, so still we didn't see any servants.

But as we reached a turn in the corridor, liquid notes broke the silence. The wordless song filled the space around us, bouncing from the stone walls which only magnified its haunting beauty.

I stopped abruptly, looking around for somewhere to hide. I knew that voice: Avalon. It sounded like she was warming up as she prepared to arrive fashionably late to the ball. Coral had said they were asking her to sing now, and I knew she wouldn't want anything to mar her performance. Of course Avalon would be the one to run late and ruin everything. And of all my sisters, Avalon was the one we couldn't afford to let see us. Not when she was the only one not pleased at my return. Who knew what she would do?

Pushing open a door beside us, I gestured for the others to hurry inside. We didn't have much time. Millie rushed toward me, Ray on her heels, but Teddy didn't move. He stood in the center of the corridor, as if frozen in place, his expression dumbstruck and his eyes focused on the corner that would soon reveal my sister.

I hurried over to tug at his arm, not wanting to risk speaking, but he didn't seem to notice me.

"Teddy," I hissed, hoping Avalon's continued singing would mask my voice. "We need to get out of sight."

But even my words had no effect. Following his gaze, I looked up in time to see my older sister come into view, her mouth open in song. My hands fell away from Teddy's arms as my own mouth dropped open.

Avalon had stopped short of stealing my gown in my absence, but I could now understand the bizarre turban she had worn the other morning. I was used to Avalon's shocking hair colors, but this was something else entirely.

Rather than decorating her blond hair with streaks of bright, unnatural color, as if mimicking the sea life around us, this time she had dyed her entire head. And the red wasn't the bright red of the coral or a redfin, but a natural shade.

The natural auburn of my own hair, in fact. Apparently, my sister had been jealous of more than my voice, and with my absence, she had decided to take my place.

Teddy started, taking a stride forward, only to hesitate and fall back again, glancing wildly at me before his gaze was drawn back in her direction.

"I thought I recognized that voice," he said in a shaken tone.

Avalon's song cut off, and she stared in confusion at Teddy for a moment before her eyes shifted to me and widened into shock. Teddy, however, seemed oblivious to her response.

"I wasn't even thinking of…" His voice faltered. "With everything else going on…But now here you are."

Avalon ignored his half-formed sentences, focusing instead on me.

"Isla? What are you doing here? I heard—"

But whatever she had heard of my wrongdoings was cut off as Teddy spoke again, apparently too shocked to even notice the interchange between Avalon and me.

"I never had the chance to thank you, you know."

"I—" Avalon looked wildly between Teddy and the rest of us.

From the corner of my eye, I could see Ray watching Teddy in confusion and Millie looking rapidly between my sister and me. But I couldn't tear my attention away from Teddy. He had been so supportive over the last two days that I had nearly forgotten his choice on the beach. He had chosen his ocean girl over me, and I had done my heart a disservice by letting myself forget it. Seeing his shock now brought the memory forcibly home, right when I most needed my focus to remain strong.

Avalon's eyes came to rest on me, and her expression crossed from confused to defiant. For a moment we locked eyes, a thousand pieces of history passing between us that meant nothing to everyone else. She knew me well enough that my pain must have been clear for her to read, because a malicious light filled her eyes, and she looked back at Teddy.

"There is no need for thanks," she said, with no sign of her usual petulance in her voice. "I'm sorry if I seem a little foolish. I'm just so surprised to see you!"

"No indeed," he said, regaining something of his usual courtesy. "I'm the one who has blundered into your home, unannounced."

She cast down her eyes demurely, but not before they cast a lightning-swift look of laughter in my direction. She didn't know what Teddy was talking about, but she knew it upset me, and that was enough for her. My hands balled into fists, and it was all I could do not to throw myself at her.

I cast an agonized glance at Millie, not able to trust myself, and she stepped forward in my stead. Grabbing her brother by the arm, she began to pull him down the corridor.

"Millie!" He pulled his arm free.

"Teddy!" She glared at him.

Slowly he seemed to come back to an awareness of our situation, throwing an abashed look toward me and Ray.

"I'm sorry," he said. "I was just taken by surprise."

"Well, ocean girl or not, we don't have time to tarry," she said crisply. She cast an apologetic glance at Avalon. "Meaning no offense to you."

"And who might you be?" Avalon asked coolly.

"Someone who has somewhere important to be." Ray stepped forward as he spoke, placing himself between Avalon and the twins.

Avalon glared at him, but he ignored her, gesturing with his head for the twins to continue past the turn in the corridor. They complied, Teddy throwing a single torn glance toward Avalon and me as he disappeared from sight. I could only imagine how it pained him to leave now that he thought he had finally found his dream girl.

Ray, on the other hand, strode after them without a backward glance for my sister. Avalon glared after him, clearly furious at being dismissed in such a way. Fear seized me, over-ruling more personal emotions. I darted forward and seized both her arms in a vise-like grip. Thrusting my face into hers, I glared at her with the most ferocious expression I could muster.

"You can't tell anyone you saw us, Avalon. No one! Do you hear me?"

She tried to pull back, but I wouldn't let go.

"You're not supposed to be here, Isla. You must have done something terrible for Father to be so angry with you." She looked at me sullenly. "No one wanted you back anyway."

"This isn't a game, Avalon," I snapped, trying to convey every bit of the seriousness I felt in my face. "Harass me, plague me, laugh at me all you like, but you *cannot* tell anyone that I'm here. This isn't about you and me—the whole of Merrita is at stake."

"What are you talking about?" She managed to wrench herself free. "Who was that man? I've never seen him before." She shook her head. "You should have seen your face when he started gushing over me."

"I'm serious, Avvy," I said, using my childhood nickname for her. "Nothing else matters but that you keep our presence here a secret. Can you think of someone other than yourself for once in your life and do that for me?"

She stiffened. "I don't only think of myself! You're the one always off, distracted in your own little world, not caring about all the gifts you've been given. Who do you think looks after Waverly? Not you, that's for sure!"

I frowned, taken aback. I'd never thought of it like that.

"It's not so easy being different, Avalon."

"It's not so easy being the same as everyone else, either," she shot back.

I gripped one of the long strips of her flutter dress between my fingers, a smile ghosting across my face.

"You—like everyone else? Never Avvy." I kept my voice low.

"But this isn't about you and me. This is about our people. Can you trust me enough to believe that?"

She bit her lip, staring at me uncertainly.

"I trust you, Lala," she whispered finally before hurrying off down the corridor toward the ballroom. I watched her go, shaken by our interaction and trying to remind myself that if she could trust me, then I needed to trust her.

As soon as she was out of sight, I hurried after the others. The moment I saw Teddy, my earlier heartbreak returned, threatening to overwhelm me. He met my eyes, and a strange expression filled his, almost like confusion. Perhaps he was wondering how he had ever allowed me to distract him, now that his dream was finally turning to reality before him.

For a crippling second, I wasn't sure if I could go on, and then a shout from up ahead drove all such thoughts from my mind. The others had reached the door to my father's office, only to find the sharp tips of tridents blocking their way.

CHAPTER 29

"Connor. Dante." Ray's casual voice did little to betray the anger I could read in his eyes. "Run along now, children."

Connor merely laughed. "You're forgetting, Captain. We don't have to follow your orders anymore."

"Not so high and mighty now your sister's seen your true colors," Dante sneered.

Ray gave no visible reaction, his face remaining calm, but I boiled inside at the suggestion that Ray's rank had only been secured by Nerissa's influence.

"He said, step aside." I strode forward to stand beside him.

"Unfortunately for you, we know all about your fall from grace as well, Princess," Connor said. "And we won't be following your orders, either."

"No," I snapped. "It's clear you haven't been following royal orders for some time. I saw you on the surface, you know. And I will bring you to justice for everything you did to create and support those raiders, if it's the last thing I do."

Dante laughed. "Will you now? Or maybe you'll find your

cage not quite so gilded the second time around." He tsked at me. "There are consequences to running away, you know."

I reached for my sword hilt only to remember I hadn't been able to wear it with my ballgown. I glanced sideways at Ray. I still had my sister's knife, now strapped to my leg, but it wouldn't be much help against a trident. Without full-sized weapons, we might actually be in trouble.

"Would these be of assistance?" Teddy asked from behind us. "I found them attached to the wall and thought you wouldn't mind me liberating them." A trident handle appeared by my side.

I grabbed it from him, bringing it up just in time to block the thrust that accompanied Dante's startled yell. Connor also lunged forward, and I twisted my weapon. Leaving the tip of my trident between the tines of Dante's—still barely holding him back—I swung the handle up to whack Connor's thrust off course.

I wouldn't be able to hold them long on my own, though.

Connor pulled his trident back and swung again, just as Dante bore down on me, trying to use his superior strength to twist my weapon out of my hands. I gritted my teeth and pushed back. My arms faltered just as another trident, held by Ray, flashed past to catch against Connor's. Seeing him join the fight gave me a spurt of strength, and I pulled away from Dante without losing my grip on the long handle.

I circled around, leaping in to thrust at Dante's side, my sole goal to keep him from joining the fight Connor and Ray were now waging. He came back at me with a series of attacks, swinging his trident almost faster than my eye could follow. But while I hadn't held a trident in weeks, neither had I been idle.

My bouts with Teddy had helped me learn a different style of fighting and a different way of thinking from the attacks and blocks our training masters had endlessly drilled into us. I gripped my trident like a spear, driving it forward in a feint and whisking it around his weapon when he tried to block. It was too finicky a movement to suit the heavy weapon, but Dante wasn't expecting it, which was what I had gambled on.

Whacking his weapon aside with the length of mine, I drove my tines all the way up to his throat. He lunged back so fast he fell, and I followed him down, pinning him to the floor with my trident's tips.

Risking a glance sideways, I saw that Connor was now on the floor as well, bleeding heavily. Ray stepped over him to move toward me. I looked up at him, my attention wavering.

Dante took the opening, grasping my trident just below the tines and pushing it aside while he scrambled to his feet. Ray dropped into a crouch, his weapon ready, but Dante was already running, leaving his fellow guard behind without a second look.

I straightened and let my trident swing into rest position, drumming my fingers against its length as I gazed thoughtfully after the escaping guard. Ray cocked a single eyebrow in my direction.

Teddy, however, gazed down the now empty corridor in dismay.

"I'm sorry," he said. "I let myself get distracted again and was utterly useless. I should have been able to stop him."

"Don't trouble yourself," Ray said. "Isla has been training with the guards for years, and we do all our training with tridents. She's far past such beginner mistakes. Dante got away because she left an opening for him to do so on purpose."

"On purpose?" Millie looked between us. "Why would you do that, Isla?"

I snapped back to business, pushing open the study door that Dante and Connor had been guarding.

"Because there's one thing we haven't worked out yet—how to get hold of the key. And my father will most definitely have the key on him. So, either we have to wade into the middle of a ball to get it…or we need him to come to us. I suppose you could say I just sent a messenger after him. But it means we need to move quickly."

Teddy stood just inside the doorway frowning around the room. "But didn't you say those two are Nerissa's pets? Won't he run straight to her?"

"Oh certainly," I said. "And that's why I let him go. Nerissa desperately wants to destroy that conch, and I'm betting on her seizing her chance. She'll take the news to my father—she's used the strategy before. She'll have realized by now he won't give the conch into her keeping, even to protect it, and so now she'll try to convince him to destroy it himself. She'll bring him here to see us trying to steal it in an effort to prove that it's not safe anywhere."

"And how does that help us?" Millie asked doubtfully.

"My father believes this conch is our family's greatest responsibility. I don't believe he would ever destroy it. Nerissa is bringing him here to see us trying to steal the conch, and I'm bringing the two of them here together so that he can see her trying to have it destroyed. I have to believe that if I can goad her into revealing her true self, he'll finally recognize her lies. I just need to get the two of them alone in this room with us."

"Alone?" Ray frowned at me. "You don't think she'll bring a squad of guards with her?"

I shook my head. "If someone else had seen us and notified the guards directly, they'd have dragged us off before we ever got a chance to convince him. That would have been a disaster. But Dante will go straight to Nerissa, and Nerissa needs my father here, not her guards. And my father won't want guards in here to see the conch. They've ambushed me trying to steal this once before, remember, and they left the guards outside the room until my father had secured the chest."

"The chest we don't have." Nothing in Ray's bearing gave away if he approved or not of my split-second decision. "We need to find it, and we need to find it fast."

I nodded, letting my eyes rove over the room. Did anything look different from last time I had been here? Anything at all that might indicate where we should look?

I had expected to need to tear the room apart, but as soon as my eyes reached the spot on the wall directly across from my father's desk, I knew.

My fingers trembled so badly that they wouldn't support the weight of the large portrait of my mother as I tried to remove it. Teddy's hands appeared, lifting it from me and placing it gently against the ground.

"She was beautiful," Millie said softly behind me.

"And she sang like the ocean and the sky, and like light and hope," I said. "At least that's what they tell me."

Everyone had gathered around us now. The portrait didn't cover an open recess like the one in the reception room, so I ran my finger along the exposed section of wall.

"There," I said and retrieved the dagger from beneath my skirts.

Slipping the tip between two stones, where a small gap was already visible, I prized the lower of the stones carefully out. Once that one was free, the rest were easy, and I had soon exposed a small opening in the wall.

Drawing a deep breath, I reached inside. For the second time, I withdrew the small wooden box from its hidden home. This time the ruby seemed to glare balefully at me, accusing me of double treachery. I ignored it.

In a fit of hopefulness, I tried to pull the lid open, but it didn't budge. Dropping to my knees, I put the chest on the floor. With a grimace for all the misuse Oceana's blade was enduring, I worked the tip in under the lid and tried to force the two halves apart.

When I couldn't do it, I let both Ray and Teddy try, telling myself that at this point it was no more or less treasonous to allow them to actually touch the artifact. Neither of them had any more success than me, however.

"I don't suppose any of you have any undisclosed skills at picking locks, do you?" I asked, hopefully.

Resounding silence met my question. I frowned down at the casket. An ax would surely split it open. Even the tridents might do the job. But, unlike my aunt, I didn't want to risk damaging the conch inside.

I was still kneeling on the floor, staring at it, when the door to the study burst open. My father strode through alone, without an escort of guards just as I had predicted. A flash of movement behind him told me they were there but remaining outside the door. I looked past him again, but no one further entered. My heart sank. I had miscalculated, somehow, and my father was alone.

"So, it is true," he said, his burning eyes falling on me. "You will see my heart completely broken."

Instead of falling apart, like I had feared I might do when confronted with him, I felt something inside me shift and strengthen. I might not have his years of experience, but I knew a little something of broken hearts and of pushing through them for things that really mattered.

Clasping the chest in both hands, I slowly stood, stretching to my full height. Looking my father firmly in the eyes, I shook my head.

"No, Father. I'm not here to break your heart. I'm here to save it. Because I know that the people of Merrita are your heart. Our kingdom is your heart. And when we rise to the surface, you will see all the lies that have taken root in your heart wither and die. And you will be the king to lead Merrita into a new golden age."

"These are naive dreams, daughter," he said. "And it is time you stopped dreaming them."

He glanced at Ray, still gripping a trident in one hand, and at my own weapon, discarded on the carpet. "Do you mean to try to force me into giving up my key? You must know I have a squad of guards outside the door."

"No, I'm hoping you will *choose* to do the right thing," I said. "Because I've realized that the only way to ever wrest that key from your chest would be with a blade, and I would thrust a dagger into my own heart before I would ever thrust one into yours." I threw the dagger in my hand down onto the worn carpet.

"You have already done so," he said coldly.

"No, she hasn't," said a new voice, strong and commanding.

Teddy stepped forward to stand beside me. "And I hope that she never stops dreaming."

"And who are you," my father asked coldly, "to interrupt the king of the sea?"

Teddy didn't falter. "I am Theodore, crown prince of Trione. And I have seen your daughter stand alone against raiders and risk her life to save innocents. I have seen her stand vigil by the sick bed of one she loves and stand strong in the face of rejection from those who should love her most, all in order to protect them. I have seen again and again that she never gives up. I see nothing but strength and beauty in her, even if you are somehow blinded to it."

He turned his head and stared at me, his earlier expression of confusion amplified, as if he saw me for the first time. For a heady second, I forgot everyone else as I watched wonder grow in his eyes and a smoldering fire far stronger than the bright sparks he had shown me twice before. Then he turned back to my father, and the rest of the world came rushing in again.

"I know first-hand what it is to live in a false world. I've been living in one for far too long. But I find suddenly that it has lost its power over me. Reality is worth more than an empty fantasy, and I for one am choosing to open my eyes to the truth in front of me. My truth is that your daughter is more worthy of love than any dream woman. But you have a reality of your own to accept, Your Majesty. Because I can tell you with utter certainty that darkness no longer thrives in the kingdoms of the land. We have faced the darkness, we have stood against it, and we have overcome it. We follow the High King again. And now it is your turn. Please, Your Majesty. Blow the conch and join us. Save your kingdom."

CHAPTER 30

Slow clapping sounded from the open doorway, and Nerissa strolled into the room.

"A pretty speech from a pretty boy," she said. "But how exactly did a prince of Trione make it down to Merrita?"

"With the help of his godmother," I said. "Because his godmother comes when he calls her, unlike ours. Have you tried calling our godmother recently, Father? Because I did. And she didn't come. Does history teach us that's a good sign for a kingdom?"

My father frowned, looking from me to Teddy to Nerissa. My aunt shook her head.

"Her delusions are even worse than I feared, Your Majesty. I don't know who these people are who she has coerced into joining her, but I see that the circle of those who know of the conch's existence only grows. I don't see any other way to be sure of our protection than to destroy it. Once it is gone, we have nothing to fear from anyone."

My father's frown deepened.

"You know me, Your Majesty." Ray stepped forward, ignoring his sister and keeping his eyes on the king. "And Isla has never coerced me into anything in her life. I have been to the surface, and I have seen the truth of the prince's words with my own eyes. I have eaten in his palace—an exact replica of this one—and I have seen everything the surface has to offer Merrita. I will accept the punishment for breaking your laws, but I hope you can believe that I only ever wanted to help this kingdom and your daughter."

I held my breath while my father weighed his words.

"You have always been one of the finest guards I have ever seen, Nereus," he said after a long pause. "And I will admit that I blessed you for defying me in protection of my daughter. Only your presence with her gave me hope I might see her again."

"With respect, Your Majesty," Ray said, "you have always underestimated her. It is Isla who nursed me back to health, delaying her return here because of my injury. Already at least one of the kingdoms of the land holds Merrita in goodwill. I believe they will welcome us back to our rightful place in the sun. And that is just as much your daughter's doing as mine."

"More than goodwill," Teddy said swiftly. "I would seek your permission to court your youngest daughter, King Morgan. And it would be my dearest wish that your return to the surface might be sealed with a marriage alliance between Trione and Merrita."

I swayed slightly at his declaration, refraining from throwing myself into his arms while we remained in such a precarious position. How had everything changed so quickly?

"You—a prince of the land—wish to court my daughter?" My father looked horrified, but something else showed in his eyes as well. A look almost like wonder. As if, for the first time, he saw me as something other than a child dreaming of impossible things.

"I do, Your Majesty," Teddy said. "More than I have ever wanted anything. More than two years ago, I was lost overboard during a storm and rescued by what I now believe was one of your people. A mermaid. I have dreamed of her and your impossible kingdom ever since. And yet, now that I'm here, I realize that reality far outstrips my dreams. Isla is more to me than any girl I invented in my dreams ever was, although it took me far too long to realize it. If she will have me—and if you will release her—I will never stop treasuring her."

"One of my people rescued you? Two years ago?" My father stared at Teddy before turning dark eyes on me. I winced.

"Then I can assure you," he continued, "that the girl of your dreams and the girl standing beside you are one and the same. No one but my own flesh and blood would dare to defy me in such a manner—going to the surface without sanction and actually interacting with a land dweller. And none of my other daughters would ever think of such a thing. No, it has only ever been Isla with her eyes fixed above."

"Me and Mother, you mean," I said, and it was his turn to flinch. "What choice would she make now, Father? She would hate to see her people bound down here in the depths on her account."

"You know nothing of what my sister wanted," Nerissa spat, a fury in her eyes I had only ever seen once before.

"I don't know about that, it's true," Teddy said lightly, dispelling the power of Nerissa's tone, "but I know you must have more rebels than you realize. The girl who rescued me sung like no one I have ever heard." He smiled at me, the expression transforming his face. "Though I love Isla with all my heart, singing is not one of her strengths."

His words actually startled a laugh out of my father. "Singing, not one of Isla's strengths? She has a voice that could charm a leviathan from the deep. As her mother's could before her." His brief amusement faded away, pain taking its place.

"I don't understand." Teddy frowned.

"She took a vow," Nerissa said. "A foolish, thoughtless vow that robbed her of her voice. Because she is a foolish child without knowledge of the world or of court. But I can see how she has beguiled you. You have fallen for her pretty face." She made a derisive sound. "They say love makes fools of us all."

She turned to my father. "Your Majesty, we are too old and wise to be taken in by the tempests and passions of youth. Long years we have kept sorrowful vigil together over the grief in our hearts. What more proof do we need of the dangers of dreaming of the surface than we already carry with us every day?" Her eyes traveled to the portrait which now rested on the floor, the rest of our eyes following hers.

But one person didn't look. One person didn't take his eyes from her face.

Ray stepped forward, his usual calm mask falling away to reveal a blazing fury that matched Nerissa's own.

"You say love makes fools of us all, sister, but what would you know of that? Have you ever loved anyone at all?"

"You have no idea what you're talking about," she snapped, although I noticed she didn't meet his eyes. "I have given my life to serving our Family."

"That's not what I asked," Ray said implacably. "Did you ever *love* Nerida? Because it seems to me you can't have known her very well. I may have only been six when she died, but I can remember her clearly. And she would have been sickened to the core to see the death and destruction you have wrought on the surface, all to feed the dreams of your ego."

He stepped forward and then forward again.

"Nerida's loving husband is your king, her daughters—your nieces—are your princesses. And yet you lie and scheme as if they meant nothing to you. I say you never loved her at all. I say you never loved anyone."

"Careful, son," my father said, resting a gentle hand on Ray's shoulder, preventing him from taking the final steps to put him face to face with the general. "You were only a child, but I saw first-hand how Nerissa suffered over Nerida's death."

"Did she?" Ray asked, his voice so cold I actually shivered.

"Because I have thought all my life she loved me, too. And yet I see now how she has used every situation, every circumstance to her benefit. I no longer believe there is anything she wouldn't twist. Didn't she gain the generalship after she led the guards against the sharks—apparently to avenge her sister? And yet who is to say it was ever a shark who killed Nerida at all? Were there any witnesses besides Nerissa?"

"What are you saying?" Father asked, his hand on Ray's shoulder tightening.

Ray didn't flinch. "I'm saying I no longer believe a word she's ever said."

My father's attention was on Ray, but I was following Ray's lead and keeping my eyes fixed on Nerissa. And there could be no denying the change that came over her at his words. She paled, and her eyes darted to the door, as if assessing her means of escape. Horrifying sick dread filled my stomach.

No. It couldn't be true. I was letting my well-used imagination run away with me. But I had seen her reveal her true emotions only twice before now. Once moments earlier, when she said Ray knew nothing of what my mother wanted. And once two days ago, when I accused her of killing her own guards. And now a third time. When Ray challenged her long-standing story of how my mother died.

"No!" My hand flew to my mouth, and I stumbled back a step.

Teddy reached out to steady me, murmuring words of concern, but I couldn't hear them through the ringing in my ears.

"You said you've given your life to serving the Vasants," I said. "But tell me, is it actually my mother who gave her life for your twisted cause?"

"Isla!" I had never heard my father speak to me in such a tone, not even when he thought I had betrayed him. "What are you saying?"

Nerissa stared at me, her face paler than before, and I pressed on.

"I learned something in the last two days. I learned that young Edmund will one day rule as a Delaney."

Nerissa's eyes narrowed at my words, and I could see the hatred in their depths. They looked unnaturally black, as if the darkness was now physically residing inside her, twisting her from the inside out. How had I not seen it before?

"And," I continued, "I learned that it was Mother who negotiated the treaty. Mother who was willing to make such a concession to see her daughter marry the heir of the Delaneys. Tell me, Aunt, did you think her alliance would die with her?"

"Of course not!" Nerissa spat, her eyes widening a second after she said the words.

Every eye in the room was now trained on her, and my father had started to go an alarming shade of red. Pushing Ray aside, he strode forward, and pinned my aunt's arms, lifting her and slamming her back against the wall.

"What is that supposed to mean, Nerissa?"

"N...Nothing, Morgan. It meant nothing," she stammered, the last of her confidence gone.

"Like the life of my wife?" my father said in a deadly voice. "Did that mean nothing to you, too?"

"No, of course not!" Actual tears slipped out of her eyes. "She was my sister! I loved her! I only wanted to make her see that she couldn't betray our Family in such a manner." Her voice rose to a strange pitch. "It was her fault for being so stubborn." It dropped again. "She was always so stubborn."

Everything in the room froze. Our limbs, our breaths, my heart. It all suspended in time as we absorbed the meaning of her words.

And then my father roared so loudly it hurt my ears as he slammed her against the wall again.

"You killed her! You killed your own sister! My Nerida!"

"And she killed our father!" Nerissa roared back, suddenly finding her own fury again. "She killed him when she went crawling to the Delaneys. It is the Vasants who are supposed to rule in Merrita. Nereus should be your heir. The Delaneys are nothing. They have done nothing to earn such a place."

She let my father take her full weight, pushing off the wall with her feet and kneeing him in the stomach with both legs. He staggered back, gasping for air, and she landed on her feet. Somehow a long dagger appeared in her hand, and she dropped into a crouch, her eyes going past my wheezing father and fastening on Ray.

"It was supposed to be you," she said. "It was supposed to be your crown, not Oceana's. And yet, you're the biggest disappointment of all. You're as much a traitor to our Family as she was. If the Vasants are never to see the honor they deserve, then perhaps it is better if we cease to exist entirely."

She ran, her blade leaping for him while a scream clawed up my throat. For once in his life, he wasn't faster and more aware. He seemed utterly shocked at his sister's attack, his trident raising agonizingly slowly.

But another trident appeared, thrust in front of him, the dagger's blade turning aside against the long handle of my discarded weapon. Millie had seized it from the floor and rushed to Ray's defense.

"You have done him enough damage!" she cried.

She held the heavy weapon awkwardly, though, and the dagger turned aside to glance up her arm, the sharp point slicing her skin. Blood welled up, but Millie didn't drop the trident, hanging on with grim determination.

My father, his breath finally recovered, roared for the guards, and several poured into the room, staring wide-eyed at the scene before them.

"Arrest the general!" My father roared again, and his fury pierced their shock.

Two of them fell on her, prying the dagger from her hand as another approached from behind, to pin her arms to her side.

Millie let her trident drop and sagged gracefully down into a sitting position, her skirts billowing around her.

"Millie!" Ray paid no attention to his sister, all his focus on the princess. "You're hurt!"

He knelt beside her, frantically tearing lengths of material from her skirt to bind around her arm.

"You shouldn't have done that," he said. "You shouldn't have risked yourself for me."

Millie glanced across at me. "Why are men such fools, Isla?"

One side of my lips curved up. "Only in love, remember, Millie. And we're all fools in love, apparently."

"So the kingdoms of the land want to steal my future general as well as my daughter, I see," my father said in a slow voice. "I assume you're the boy's sister? You look too alike not to be."

"Her name is Princess Millicent." I looked at his face and then had to look away, unable to bear the brokenness and raw emotion there.

My father drew a deep breath, straightening his back. "Tell me, Princess Millicent, what did you mean when you said that Nerissa had caused her brother enough damage?"

"I think she might have been referring to the dungeons, Your Majesty," Ray said. "Since my sister had me arrested and thrown into them as soon as I stepped back through the barrier with Isla. I'd be there still if these three hadn't rescued me."

"In the dungeons?" Father shook his head. "She told me you were injured protecting Isla on your journey back, and that the doctors had prescribed strict rest. Was there anything she didn't lie about?"

I went to him and slipped my hand into his.

"I know it's a lot to absorb, but there is hope in those words. Because she did lie about the surface. You can get the greatest possible revenge on her and save our people. All you have to do is sound that conch."

Still he hesitated, but his eyes found Millie and Ray on the floor together, and then Teddy who was watching me.

"I have been the fool it seems," he said. "And I have nearly brought my kingdom to ruin with my willful misinterpretation of the tremors' message. What more proof could I want that it is possible for love and peace to exist between the kingdoms of the land and Merrita than the four of you? If the darkness is gone from the lands above, as you say, and has taken up residence here instead, then it is clear what the High King has been telling us. The tremors are warning us it is time to rise again, and we must waste no more time in obeying. Bring me the casket, and I will blow the conch."

Now that the moment had come, I trembled nearly as badly with joy as I had trembled earlier with sick dread. It took me two tries to scoop the small chest from the floor where it had been abandoned.

My father had already retrieved the key when I reached him again, and he wasted no time inserting it in the lock and exposing the purple satin and cream and gold shell.

Lifting it carefully, reverently, he held it for a moment, gazing at it. It felt like the sort of moment that should be made formal and honored in some way, but we had no time to waste. Merrita was past due to rise again.

He brought it toward his lips, but it never reached them. Instead the ground shook, sending us all stumbling, and the conch flew from his hand. I tried to follow its progress, but the shaking and writhing of the earth went on and on, sending me crashing to my knees.

A flash of cream and gold caught my eye as it rolled toward my father's desk. But a flurry of movement distracted me. The guards holding my aunt had also stumbled and lost their balance. One of them now lay, red staining the rug beneath him, while my aunt ran with jerking steps toward the rolling shell.

She had managed to retrieve her dagger, and she held it hilt down, reaching for the conch. I gave up on crawling and threw myself forward in a desperate, full body lunge, landing hard as my reaching fingers curled around the edge of the shell.

My aunt's blade slashed toward me, and I rolled. There was no time to think, only time to act. I pressed the point of the shell to my lips and blew every last bit of breath I possessed into it.

A low note sounded, only to abruptly cut off as the hilt of the dagger smashed down, raining shards of shell over my face. The tremor stopped as abruptly as the note had.

CHAPTER 31

I pushed myself up to face my aunt, but neither of us made a move toward the other. We both seemed frozen by the same thought. Had it been enough? The silence and stillness stretched out, and my head began to buzz as horror filled me that it had not.

Except that the buzzing wasn't in my head, it was in my hands. And my arms, and my knees, and my feet. And it wasn't so much a buzzing as a vibration. This movement was nothing like the rolling tremors, but it was coming from the ground just as surely. And then my stomach dropped, as it sometimes did when I raced as fast as I could, straight up for the distant surface.

Now the sensation of movement was unmistakable. Several of the guards cried out in fear, and anyone who had not been felled by the tremor now dropped to their knees. And still we rose.

When the room at last came to a shuddering stop, no one moved. We all seemed to be too shaken to know what to do next. All except for Ray. He appeared, looming above me, to pull his sister up off the ground. She looked slight beside him in a way she never had before. But some of her old fire returned.

"Don't look at me like that, Nereus," she snapped. "It's not as if

I'm the first to break my promises or my vows of loyalty. The Vasants have only ever followed in the great steps of the Rennons." She sounded bitter now, and defiant, although she made no attempt to fight the guards who came at Ray's signal to haul her away.

"Don't worry," Ray said to my father. "I'll have those loyal to me guard her until you decide on a sentence. She won't get away."

My father nodded, but his attention was on the window. I looked too. It was in the full-length style, with a door that opened into the sculpture garden. As if Ray's words had released us all, we hurried over to it, bursting outside in an undignified scuffle.

The ascending layers of rock remained, the outcropping still sheltering the rear of the palace. But many of the sculptures had toppled over, some broken in multiple places. No one was looking at them, though. Instead we were all looking upward.

Where before we had only ever seen the pearly shine of the barrier, now we saw unbroken blue sky. A seagull flew past, screeching its surprise at our appearance, and one of the remaining guards pointed upward.

"Look! A fish!"

"Actually, it's a bird," Millie said, admirably keeping any hint of a laugh from sounding in her voice.

I scooped my skirt into my arms and took off up the winding, zig-zag paths of the garden. Someone followed me, but I didn't pause to see who it was. Only when I reached the top, panting but exhilarated, did I stop. From this height, I could see in every direction, and I slowly spun on the spot.

The sun peeked above the land, dawn already broken, although it seemed impossible it could be morning already. Merrita must have been rising far longer than it had seemed. Already I could feel the warmth of the new rays on my head and bare arms. It was going to be a hot day.

All across the city, I spotted the distant figures of my people emerging from the buildings and gazing upward in shock. I hoped Elda was among them.

Behind me, in the direction of the sunrise, where before the rock had met the sea, a new land stretched out. The kelp had transformed into forests, and the reefs into dirt and fields. We were a proper island kingdom again, no longer a single stranded city in a vast sea. Our population—straining against the limitations of the barrier—could once again stretch out into villages and towns and smaller cities.

On the other side of the city, I could see a long stretch of sand and then the glittering blue of the water, hard to look at, it shone so brightly.

Without conscious thought, I opened my mouth, and a joyful torrent of song poured forth. My voice! Merrita had risen, and my vow had released me. The notes rose and dropped as I flung them to the wind, releasing every bit of joy evoked by this vision of the surface.

I sang of my people's freedom, of the death of the darkness, and of my golden-haired storm boy telling my father of his love for me—a golden, soaring melody that bared my heart.

A sound behind me made me break off and twirl around to see Teddy watching me with a look of shock and wonder on his face.

"I don't know how I mistook your sister's voice for yours. Isla, I've never heard anyone sing like you do."

I shrugged, slightly awkward after everything that had passed between us. I didn't want Teddy to love me for my voice—something I had done nothing to earn.

But Teddy seemed not to notice my hesitation, stepping forward to take both my hands in his.

"You heard what I said in there. I've been worse than a fool. I've been blind. Please don't tell me I've lost any chance with you. And not because of your voice—incredible as it is."

311

My smile belied the tears in my eyes. He might not have noticed my discomfort, but he had still understood my heart.

"More than a chance. I've loved you since the moment I saw you on that ship laughing at the storm."

A fresh wave of wonder crossed his face, and I nodded.

"While you were looking to the sea and dreaming of your ocean girl, I was looking to the surface and dreaming of my storm boy."

"Incredible," he breathed. "And somehow we found each other."

I chuckled. "Well, to be fair, I did come looking for you. Although I didn't expect to find you within minutes of stepping onshore."

"Clearly we were meant to be," he said softly.

He gazed at me for a moment, his eyes bright with emotion, and then he pointed across the blue ocean, broken by small caps of white tossed up by a playful wind, to a distant smudge on the horizon. "And now our kingdoms can be joined again, as they were long ago."

"Sister-kingdoms," I murmured, and my heart sank. "I'm sorry, Teddy. I came to find you because I believed you could tell us how to keep the darkness away from Merrita. But the truth is that Merrita was the one bringing the darkness to Trione."

He shook his head. "None of that was your fault, Isla. And I still owe you my thanks. For saving me all that time ago. From everything I've heard, other merfolk might have let me drown, believing me an evil land dweller."

"I don't believe they would have," I said. "Not if they'd been there and seen you."

"I'm glad it was you," he whispered. "Now that I know the real you, I could never want anyone else. I'm just sorry it took me so long to understand that."

"Don't feel bad," I said. "It took me a long time to separate fantasy from reality as well." I grinned. "But I've loved *you*, the real Teddy, since our first fight."

He looked bewildered, but adorably so.

"We had a first fight?"

I nodded. "The market, remember? That pie."

He frowned and then laughed. "I still have no idea what was going on there. Millie said to forget about it, and with the news of the raiders, that was easy to do. But they really are incredible pies. One day I'll get you to try them."

I rolled my eyes, but I was chuckling too. "Of course I'll try your pies. It was never about the pies."

"Wasn't it?" He looked slightly alarmed.

"It was about how much I loved you," I told him solemnly.

"Oh. Well, then." His arms reached out and gripped my waist, pulling me against him before sliding around to hold me tight. "Do you think we could avoid fighting about that in the future? Because, for my part, I intend to love you until the day I die, so that could mean a lot of fights."

I pretended to think about it. "I suppose that sounds fair enough." My eyes laughed up at him. "I daresay I'll be able to think of something else for us to fight about, every now and then."

Teddy gave a half-playful, half-frustrated growl and pressed his lips down over mine. And I forgot all about fights—real or imagined—and remembered only that I got to spend the rest of my life in the bright light of both the surface and his love.

Millie had to fetch us in the end, or we might have spent the whole day up there, alternating between talking and kissing. I hadn't decided which one I liked better yet, so I felt I needed a great many more examples of both.

But she dragged us down, grumbling until I suggested that

perhaps she should stay up there, and we could send Ray after her. That made her flush, and Teddy gave her a startled look.

"Millie! What does that expression mean? Don't tell me you've been kissing down there in front of all those strangers?"

She flushed even harder. "Well, what was I supposed to do? He just grabbed me."

I laughed, shaking my head at the idea of Ray, of all people, so losing control. "Naturally you couldn't have resisted!"

"Could you?" she asked me.

I gave her a look of revulsion. "He's my uncle!"

She giggled. "I meant if Teddy kissed you, of course."

"Oh." I cupped his cheek with my hand and smiled into his eyes. "Well, that's a different thing."

"No, it's exactly the same thing. And I hardly think you two are ones to talk."

"Do you think Mother and Father will approve?" Teddy asked, worry in his voice.

Millie frowned, her joking good humor dropping away. "I'll have to make them approve. Because I won't give him up." She chewed on her bottom lip. "Unless he doesn't want to come. I don't quite understand all the complexities of your Families, but I take it he has an important position here."

"He's essentially heir to the generalship—a position that just became vacant. And with Nerissa disgraced, he's head of one of our most influential Families. As far as alliances go, he's the strongest we have to offer, given Lyon is already married, and I have no brothers. I'll do my best to explain all that to your parents, if you'd like."

"Yes, but…" Millie's voice trailed off, and I saw the anguished look she gave her twin as she weighed whether she would leave her kingdom and her brother for Ray.

"He would never ask that of you," I said quietly, and she glanced at me sharply. "I know Ray well enough to say that with certainty. If he kissed you in front of everyone, then he's willing to give everything up to go with you. And you couldn't have someone better supporting your throne. He's one of the most talented people I've ever met."

"He's your uncle and Millie's love," Teddy said promptly. "He'd be welcome in my court if he was dull as a dotard."

Millie shook her head affectionately at her brother. "I would hardly love him if he was as dull as all that."

"But he would still be Isla's uncle," Teddy pointed out triumphantly, as if he had won the point.

"You're ridiculous," she said.

"But you love me," he said back with a grin. "Both of you do. You can't deny it."

"Goodness," I said. "I don't remember him being this insufferable."

"Oh, just watch out," Millie told me. "Now that he's got his head out of the clouds, he'll no doubt be driving us both distracted. Oh!" She stopped, clearly struck by a sudden thought. "*What* is Gabe going to say when he hears there really is an ocean girl?"

"They're all going to get their comeuppance at last," Teddy said with great satisfaction, and a certain hint of his old dreaminess. "I can picture it now. It's going to be glorious."

"Don't worry," I said. "I think they might be a little distracted by a new island appearing off their coast."

Teddy gave a low whistle. "She makes a good point, Millie. Do you think any of our fishermen have seen this place yet? We need to get back to Father and Mother. They're probably going distracted worrying about us by now, and that was before a new kingdom popped out of the ocean."

"You didn't tell them where you were going?" I asked, shocked.

"We had *tails*," Millie reminded me.

"But they go away when you leave the water."

"There was a glowing fish," Teddy said, as if that fully explained the matter.

"That is hardly an excuse for being inconsiderate, young man." An older lady with dark gray hair stepped out from behind a still-standing sculpture, giving Teddy a stern look.

"Godmother!" Millie dropped into a curtsy, and I quickly followed her lead, surveying the woman with interest. "We weren't sure if we would get a second chance with the tails if we left the water," she added by way of explanation.

The godmother looked slightly startled. "You'd seen Isla popping in and out of the water like a clown fish in an anemone, hadn't you?"

"It wasn't as bad as all that," I muttered.

"Yes, but we're not merfolk," Teddy pointed out.

The godmother frowned. "You are now."

"You didn't mention that," Millie said, a little timidly.

The godmother frowned. "Didn't I? I suppose I didn't. Well, I've told you now. You're welcome, and enjoy."

"You mean we get to keep our tails?" I asked. "When we're in the water, I mean? We get to remain merfolk?"

"Of course," she said. "You're merfolk now, and there's no taking it back."

I beamed at her, my happiness complete. Surely that would ease the transition for many. And it would give us an advantage the other kingdoms didn't possess while we rebuilt to our old strength.

"Thank you for making Teddy and Millie merfolk," I said to her. "They saved us all."

"Oh, I didn't do that," she said. "I merely showed them the way to Merrita."

"What do you mean?" Millie asked. "We hardly did it to ourselves."

"Of course you did," said the godmother. "In part at least. Isla and Nereus were involved as well, naturally. If a land dweller and one of the merfolk fall in love, their love confers a tail on the land dweller."

Teddy grinned. "In that case, it sounds like my heart knew the truth before my head did."

"As is often the way," said the godmother. "Now I really must be off. I have six rulers to visit to inform them not to be terrified of a giant landmass rising from the water with a long-forgotten kingdom of merfolk residing on it."

"Please will you tell our parents we're safe?" Millie asked. "Because I don't imagine there are any boats in Merrita. I don't know how long it will take us to get home."

"Boats? Millie, we have tails!" Teddy said, shaking his head.

"Oh, of course." She flushed, but the godmother looked at her with kindness.

"Of course I'll tell them, lass. It's the sort of news we godmothers love to impart. I'll let them know you'll be there as soon as you're able. For now, I think there are some matters still to be cleared up here." She looked significantly down in the direction of the palace.

We all followed the direction of her eyes, only to look back again and find her gone.

I led the way down, eager to tell my father the news from the godmother. He received it with pleasure and began issuing a stream of orders to the guards who had gathered around him.

He was walking off, still giving commands, when he paused and looked back at the four of us.

"I would like to see the four of you in the reception room in an hour." His eyes dwelled on Ray. "There are things we still need to talk about."

We all nodded, and he left, the guards trailing behind him.

"There are things we need to talk about too," Millie said quietly, her eyes on Ray. "You know I love you, Nereus, but I don't want to tear you away from everything you've worked for here. And I have responsibilities of my own back home..." Her lip trembled although her voice remained steady.

"Millie." Ray took her into his arms, gazing tenderly down into her face. "If your father will let me marry you and come to Trione, I will never once look back at what I've left behind with regret. And it's not such a great sacrifice, after all, since I take it I'll have my best friend with me."

"Best friend?" My eyes bulged in my head. "Did you both hear that? Ray just said I was his best friend!" I moaned. "Oh, why weren't any of my sisters *or* any of the guards around to hear it! After all these years complaining what a pest I am!"

"Naturally I wouldn't have said it if they were here," he said with a straight face.

"Why, you..." My glare dissolved into laughter. "I'm glad you'll be coming, as well."

He grinned at me. "Of course you are."

"Insufferable, arrogant..." I muttered the words, my voice trailing off as a group of people emerged from the palace, eyes wide and mouths hanging open.

"Over here!" I waved at them excitedly.

Four of my sisters—only Oceana had not appeared—moved in my direction, their speed varying as they stopped to gaze around them.

"I'd like to introduce you to Prince Theodore and Princess Millicent of Trione," I said, gesturing at the twins. "Or Teddy and Millie, rather."

That got all of their attention. Coral, in particular, inspected them minutely before nodding her approval.

"Teddy and Millie," I said, "these are most of my sisters. Coral, Marine, Avalon, and Waverly." I gave Teddy a significant look. "Avalon's hair is usually blond, but apparently she's trying out a new look since my departure."

Teddy had the grace to look ashamed. He gave Avalon an elegant bow.

"I'm sorry for the misunderstanding. It was all a mistake on my part, I'm afraid."

"I can see you've sorted it all out now," she said, eyeing his arm as it looped around the back of my waist and pulled me to his side.

Coral raised both eyebrows at us, but I just grinned.

"He's already asked Father permission to court me, and promised a marriage alliance, so you needn't look so disapproving."

"Father has agreed to you marrying a prince of the land?" Marine blinked at me. "And here I was, concerned he must be going into an apoplexy at Merrita rising like this."

"Oh no," I said. "He was always the one with the key to bringing us back up."

"You mean *Father* did this?" Waverly shook her head before once again gazing up at the sky.

I nodded, not feeling the need to explain my part in it as yet. "Now you can see plants and feel the breeze without ever having to wear your tail, Waverly. In fact, there won't be any more processions, so you won't have to wear it ever again, if you don't want to."

"You mean we *can* still wear them?" Coral asked. "We're not land dwellers now?"

"Well, in the strictest definition we are, I suppose," I said. "But we'll still take our mer-forms in the water."

I turned to Avalon. "And you'll be able to have as many dresses as you like. There's this incredible silk…it's hard to describe, but Millie showed me one of her dresses. They wear them on formal occasions, and it's like they're wearing the ocean itself."

Avalon's eyes lit up before her face closed over, her expression turning suspicious.

"I didn't tell anyone. Like you asked," she said.

"Thank you," I replied. "Everything had to happen just as it did. If Father had come without Nerissa—or if Oceana or Coral or some of the guards had tried to intervene before Father ever arrived—I don't know how things would have ended." I paused. "I hope we can make a new beginning, Avalon."

She also paused, examining my face before replying.

"I would like that."

"I heard they've arrested Aunt," Coral said.

My mood changed in an instant, and I looked up at Teddy. He squeezed me gently, telling me without words that it was my choice whether I told them now or not.

"I'm afraid I have some bad news," I said, trying to keep my voice steady. "It seems...it seems Mother wasn't killed by sharks."

I ended by telling them everything that had happened in the study—they had as much of a stake in the revelations as the rest of us—and at the end of it, they all insisted on accompanying us to meet Father.

CHAPTER 32

He was already in the reception room when we arrived, as were Oceana, Lyon, and Elda. From the red around my sister's eyes, she already knew what I had just shared with the others. As the oldest, she had the most memories of Mother, and she had also worked most closely with our aunt. The news had to have been doubly hard on her.

"I have sent guards around the city to reassure people and let them know what to expect. I will hold a grand audience tomorrow, and every Family has been instructed to send a representative. Already, I have scholars scouring the history books. We will work out a just and reasonable way to spread the people out and divide up the land. We have a new life waiting for us here. But things could have turned out very differently, given what we now know of Ncrissa's interference with the kingdoms of the land."

He turned to me. "We must all be grateful to you, Isla. Thanks to your efforts in Trione, we are well-positioned to have our story believed. We will plead for their mercy, and if all you say is true about the new state of things here, we must hope they grant it."

He crossed over to me and took both my hands in his.

"I'm sorry, my daughter, that it took an outsider to recognize your strength and value."

Tears hung unshed on my eyelashes.

"And I'm sorry, Father, that I defied you at every turn. I can see now how much of value I missed in my dreaming. Just because I didn't belong in the old Merrita, didn't mean that there was no good there for me to respect and learn from. Teddy has taught me that it is possible to dream of far off, unfamiliar places without rejecting your home. And now that I have found the place I truly belong, I intend to remember that lesson. Though I hope to make my future in Trione and the waters around it, I intend always to keep my connection with my family and my first home."

My father gave a wry smile. "The words every parent longs to hear—and never gets to hear without a great deal of pain first. But matters have sorted themselves out, and if there's one thing I've learned, it's that life always comes good mixed with bad. We must simply choose to be thankful for all the good we are left with in this instance."

He let my hands drop and turned to Ray whose arm was around Millie's shoulders.

"I think I already know the answer, Nereus, but I must ask the question anyway. Do you intend to take your sister's place at my side, as my general?"

Ray shook his head, sadness on his face.

"I do not. And not just because I intend to return to Trione to seek Millie's hand in marriage. There is a history to my sister's betrayal, and I think when you hear it, you will understand why it is better off if I leave the court."

"I don't hold you responsible for her crimes in any way," my father said quickly. "You will always be welcome here."

"Thank you," Ray said gravely. "I hope I may visit often. And at least I can still serve you in Trione by watching over Isla. You need not fear for your daughter alone in a foreign kingdom."

Father nodded his acknowledgment and thanks before turning to the matter at hand. "Your sister spoke of a Rennon betrayal that preceded her own. Do you know what she was speaking of?"

Ray sighed. "I believe I do. Although I didn't know I knew. Ever since I learned of my sister's betrayal, I have been searching my mind—every interaction I can remember—trying to understand why. When I heard the truth of Oceana's marriage alliance, a suspicion formed. And Nerissa just confirmed it."

He dropped his hand from Millie's shoulder, his face pained at the words he had to relate.

"I'm afraid my story involves speaking ill of a number of the dead, including your father, the old king."

"You're saying the betrayal was my father's?"

"In a way. Although it's all a matter of perception. And it seems Nerissa's perception was...unhealthily skewed. You see, when I was very young, my father used to tell me stories. And there was one story he liked to tell above all others. He used to say it was a feat of imagination, imagining the world as a different place. But I suspect now that he was already trying to plant the seeds in my mind he later meant to reveal as truth. Except then he passed away when I was only five, and then Nerida died and Nerissa became general, and the stories stayed as a distant memory of a non-existent past."

"And what was this alternative past?" My father asked, his brow creased.

"This is the story I have managed to cobble together in my mind based on his old tales, and the facts I know to be true from indisputable history. I believe, Your Majesty, that it was not King Donovan, your father, who defeated the orca, but rather his young general, my father, Jason."

My father's frown deepened, but he didn't protest. Ray continued.

"He defeated the orca and saved the king's life. But the young king didn't want the people to know of his weakness. So he asked his friend, the young general, to lie to the people with him and say it had been the king who defeated the predator."

"And you believe his loyalty to my father was such that he did so?" the king asked.

"I don't think it was just loyalty, although I believe they were truly friends. King Donovan didn't have any children at that point, remember, although he had been married for many years. He and the queen had just about despaired of ever having children. But Jason was younger, his marriage newer. He still expected sons and daughters to follow him. And so, he and King Donovan agreed. Without siblings, Donovan was already to be the last of the Rennon Family line. So he swore that he would name Jason's first son as his heir, and that one day, when he died, the first of a Vasant royal line would rule over Merrita."

Out of the corner of my eye, I saw Elda shift uncomfortably at hearing such an echo of her own words.

"And so, they returned, Donovan as a triumphant warrior, and Jason as his loyal friend, advisor, and general. It was a scheme that might even have worked since the Vasants were powerful, and Jason was beloved of the people and might expect his son to be also."

"Except, after they returned, the queen finally became pregnant—with me," my father said.

"Yes," said Ray. "As did Jason's first wife. I can imagine it was a rather fraught nine months for them all. Except then the children were born, and the queen bore a son while Jason's wife bore a daughter. And no more children seemed forthcoming on either side. That changed everything. Somehow King Donovan must have convinced my father that it was enough to see his daughter as queen and his grandchild as a future monarch, even if she bore the Rennon Family name."

"And even when, ten years later, his wife unexpectedly got pregnant again, it was another daughter," my father said. "Still he had not managed to produce a son, so my father had not actually broken his vow."

"Except then his wife died," I said slowly. "And Jason married again. And his new wife bore him a son, thirty years younger than his oldest daughter. One the same age as his granddaughters."

"Yes," said Ray, clearly uncomfortable now. "Everyone thought it wonderful, that I was a perfect successor to my sister who had chosen not to have children of her own. But my father, and at least one of my sisters, knew that I had been promised the throne. And, through me, the Vasant Family line. I don't think my father ever meant to do anything about it. He had already made his deal, and his daughter sat on the throne because of it. It can't have seemed like much of an option to try to rip the throne from one of his blood to give it to another. But it didn't mean he didn't remember. And I think it festered."

"I wonder if Nerida knew," my father said. "Surely she would have told me..."

"If she knew, she didn't feel the same way," Elda said. "The Vasants and the Delaneys have long been rivals, yet she was the one who approached us about Lyon."

Ray nodded. "I think that alliance is what changed things. Nerissa seems to believe the shock of it killed our father. She always hung on every one of his stories, dedicated to the idea of Vasant glory and Vasant honor. That's why she pushed herself so hard. It was one thing for the two of them to accept the continuation of the ancient Rennon royal line, infused now with Vasant blood. It was another thing altogether to see their rivals receive what had been promised to them."

"And so, Nerissa pursued Nerida when she was isolated, and in her anger killed her." The words were clearly still hard for my father to say. "I keep going over and over it in my mind. Her grief seemed so real." He swallowed. "But the godmothers tried to warn me. It took nearly a day after the tremor for Nerissa to get back to Merrita bringing the news of Nerida's death, so I never connected the two as I should have."

"Her grief most likely was real," Ray said, his own voice less steady than usual. "And I also imagine some of the emotion you saw was actually guilt. I believe that she must have felt penitence—and even told herself it was right that Nerida's daughter take the throne, after all. The tremors died down again and went quiet for many years. But then the marriage actually occurred, and children were born—children bearing the Delaney name."

He shook his head. "It has become clear now how much power she actually wielded from the shadows, and I think she tried to tell herself it was enough. That the Vasants were the true power of the throne. But she began to see the Delaney star rising, and she was desperate to keep things as they were, to maintain the status quo. I think she knew that if Merrita resurfaced, the upheaval that followed would sweep the Vasants away."

"It would have helped that she had such awful things to report from us all," Teddy said. "If you're talking about four or five years ago."

Ray nodded. "And when things started to improve on shore, she got desperate enough to actually intervene and attempt to maintain the destruction. She must have realized Your Majesty might eventually send up a scout more loyal to the crown than to her."

"Did mother know of the royal conch?" I asked.

"Of course," Father said. "I had no secrets from her."

"Nerissa knew that something existed, some way for you to raise the kingdom, but not any details. It was my fault for thinking she knew and blurting it out. I think it angered her that her sister knew and wouldn't tell her."

Ray gazed at me thoughtfully. "Yes, she may have started to feel that our sister had defected—become a Rennon in more than just name." He looked at my father. "I think you can feel secure that my oldest sister, at least, always remained loyal to you."

"And paid for it with her life," he said, drawing a hand across his eyes. "Thank you for sharing this information. I would like to be alone now. Tomorrow we will build a new life—starting with the Hall of Meetings. It is time I heard the true voice of my people instead of Nerissa's twisted lies. But today I must grieve what I can never recover."

We all exchanged heart-broken looks, but no one could think of anything to say. As we left, each of my sisters and I stopped to place a kiss on his cheek. It was all we could do for him.

We grouped together out in the corridor, the mood somber.

"You're a good man, Nereus." Millie stood on tiptoe to kiss him on the cheek. "I hope you know that."

"He does," I said before I could stop myself. But then I turned to him in all seriousness. "But she's right. You could have reacted to all this very differently. And my father won't forget it. You may have banished yourself to Trione, but he will always welcome you back, just as he said."

We drifted apart after that, the two couples choosing separate directions to walk and talk over the many startling events of the last few days—as well as the equally fascinating topic of our own hearts.

Inside, under the weight of such revelations, I had forgotten that the sun shone and outside the sky was blue. But on the beach, with the crash of the waves, and the sand beneath my toes, it was hard to remember anything else. The Merritan beach had no protective ring of coral, and the waves actually crashed and foamed as they reached the sand. I smiled as I faced them, their steady cadence soothing me.

Teddy's arms slid around me from behind as he rested his chin on the top of my head and gazed out to sea as well.

"You're going to have to take me exploring out there, you know, my mermaid princess."

"With pleasure." I leaned back into him with a sigh of delight. "And I want to explore all of Trione. And the other kingdoms.

And try every different food ever devised. Starting with your pies."

Teddy laughed. "At that rate, I'll have to get rid of my poor horse and replace him with a carriage as we'll be far too round to ride."

"Oh yes, and I want to learn to ride as well as you do," I said, ignoring his teasing.

He spun me around so he could look down into my face. "What I want, is to always be with you."

I shivered with delight and reached up toward him. When he didn't lean down to meet me fast enough, I made an impatient noise in my throat and pulled his head down to mine.

He laughed against my lips before deepening the kiss, and I melted against him. Exploring the world could wait. For now, I had Teddy, and that was all I could desire.

"Millie and Teddy are mermaids now." Daisy's voice sounded from a short way down the corridor. "I told our godmother I wanted to be one, too, but she said it doesn't work like that." She heaved a loud sigh.

A wordless sound of protest told me my betrothed was with his sister. I looked up toward the open door of my sitting room. I had been given a whole guest suite for this visit to the Trionian palace—no doubt because this time I came as a princess on the eve of marrying their crown prince.

Three figures came into view in time for me to see a tall, unfamiliar young man clap Teddy on the shoulder. His skin was already browned by the sun, although summer had not yet begun, and he looked as if he would be equally at home running on a beach or striding through a forest.

"A mermaid, hey?" He grinned at Teddy. "Sounds charming."

"I believe the term Daisy meant to use was merfolk," Teddy said with dignity.

Gabe—because it had to be the famous Gabe—just laughed as he followed Teddy through my door.

"You know in truth we're all terribly jealous," he said. "Not that I'd trade my Addie for anyone, of course, but I'd love to be able to explore the seas. I can imagine the wonders you must be finding down there." He chuckled. "Mother and Father have begun to talk about a marriage alliance for Percy, and he was most disappointed to hear that Isla is the youngest of her sisters. I think he had all sorts of dreams of becoming a prince of the sea."

He turned his attention to me and delivered a charming smile.

"And you must be the ocean girl who I've heard so much about." He swept me a bow. "You're just as lovely as Teddy has been claiming."

I watched him with an amused eye. "For my part, I'm with-holding judgment on whether you're anything like Teddy claims."

Gabe chuckled and looked across at his foster brother. "I won't attempt to defend myself. It's most likely all true. I was rather fond of leading them into trouble during my eight years here. I'm just sorry I don't have Addie with me to introduce to you. Teddy was too impatient to wait, and she was busy trying to explain to the maid in charge of our room why seven large birds have taken up residence there along with us."

"Addie brought her swans?" Daisy cried.

Gabe nodded. "The wretched creatures refuse to be left behind, and Addie worries about them too much to insist on it."

"Why didn't you tell me earlier?" Daisy asked. "I wouldn't have come here if I'd known that." She took off without any farewells, dashing out into the corridor.

Teddy shook his head ruefully. "Hopefully Addie remembers Daisy well enough not to be too shocked when she goes cata-pulting into your rooms without so much as a by-your-leave."

"Adelaide did marry Gabe, didn't she?" I asked. "Handling Daisy should be well within her capabilities."

The Talinosian prince laughed. "I like you." He seemed exactly the easy-going character Teddy's stories had led me to expect.

"We missed seeing you both at Snow's wedding," Teddy said

to him. "Daisy was hoping the swans would be there. And you, of course...but at a distant second, I'm afraid." He grinned shamelessly.

Gabe and Adelaide had remained in Talinos while the rest of his family traveled to Eliam for Queen Blanche and Alexander's Midwinter wedding. I had attended, as well, along with a large Merritan delegation. The cold had been a shock to us all, but I had enjoyed every moment of it—not least because Teddy and Millie had been there, too.

Despite the continued complications of my kingdom's return to the surface, my father had left Oceana and Lyon in charge and taken all the rest of us to Eliam for the wedding. He had been delighted to receive the invitation and was determined to make the best possible use of the chance to meet all the other royals at once. And since every other reigning monarch, save for one, had also attended, it had been an unexpectedly good opportunity for us.

But while my father had conducted a series of productive meetings with the other kings and queens, I had been disappointed to find that many of the younger royals who populated Teddy's stories were noticeably absent. It had hardly been surprising, though, given that Gabe and Addie were newlyweds themselves, and both Prince Jonathan and Princess Lily and King Dominic and Queen Sophie were new parents.

I felt like I knew them all a little already, however, both from Teddy's stories and from the tales of Princess Celine. I had taken a great liking to the princess from the Old Kingdoms, now crown princess of northern Eldon. And my liking for her had only increased when I discovered she could warm a room as effectively as any fire.

The unexpected sound of her voice jolted me out of my thoughts. "There you all are." Celine strolled into the room as if summoned by my thoughts. "I've been looking for you everywhere." She paused and surveyed the room. "Oh. No, I take it back. It's just you, Gabe. I don't want you. Where's Adelaide? Oliver said one of the footmen told him she brought her swans. And since I was stuck in Eldon and missed out on meeting both the famous missing princess *and* her swans at your wedding last summer, I'm determined to meet them now."

"See." Gabe looked plaintively at Teddy. "This is the problem."

"Oh, well, at least your wife must like you better than the birds, even if no one else does," Teddy said before pausing and adopting an exaggerated look of concern. "I mean, she does, doesn't she?"

"Thanks for the loyalty, *brother*," Gabe said, shaking his head sadly. "Does Isla know what she's getting into, marrying you?"

Teddy, his eyes full of laughter, looked across at me, and for a moment I forgot everyone else and let myself fall into them. Finally there were no secrets between us, and we both knew exactly what we were getting into. Waiting for spring and our wedding to finally arrive had taken a supreme act of patience, and it had been hard to treasure my final months with my family when I missed Teddy so much.

We had seen each other as often as we could, of course, usually escorted by Millie and Ray. The two of them had used their lesser ranks, as well as Ray's desire to leave Merrita immediately, to push for a much quicker wedding. The beautiful ceremony had taken place outside the Trionian palace on the beach in front of the crystal ballroom, the sand covered in Trionians, and the lagoon filled with merfolk. I had stood beside Millie, but my father had ordered everyone else attending from Merrita to watch from the water in a purposeful display of our dual nature. He felt that the sooner the other kingdoms got used to the existence of merfolk, the better it would be for everyone—and especially for those of us like me and Ray who were to live among them.

Once married, Ray and Millie had joined Teddy and me whenever the four of us could manage to escape for a day. Ray and I loved introducing the twins to the ocean and all its beauties and true dangers—Teddy having had the grace to laugh over how foolish the warnings he had once given me must have seemed. But it had been hard not to feel the occasional moment of resentment that Ray and Millie didn't have to say goodbye at the end of our excursions.

The two of them were already established together in Trione, Ray working closely with Captain Flint. As an act of goodwill, King Edward had allowed Ray to keep his rank as captain, and it hadn't taken long for him to earn the respect that went with the position. With open relations and commerce between our two kingdoms established, I knew King Edward expected an increase in the number of his people becoming merfolk and had plans to eventually see Ray at the head of a mer-division of Trionian guards.

And now, at last, I had arrived in Trione for my own wedding. Soon Teddy and I would be married, and I was determined there would be no more long separations between us.

"Goodness, she's as bad as him," Gabe said in an audible aside to Celine. "Are they planning to gaze into each other's eyes for the rest of the afternoon?"

Celine gave an undignified snort-laugh. "Oh, they're hopeless if you don't intervene. I'm just hoping they'll recover somewhat after the wedding."

I rolled my eyes, but I could feel a faint flush on my cheeks.

A pale young man with striking blue eyes appeared in the still-open doorway.

"There you are, my love," he said to Celine, with a wry look in his eye. "One of the footmen said I'd find you here, but I'll admit I didn't have much hope it would be that easy. Did you find Addie?"

"No, just these two lovebirds," she said, crossing over to him.

For all her teasing of us, she let her hand rest briefly on his chest, smiling up into his face, and I guessed she had just sent a spark of warmth shooting toward his heart. He smiled back at her before she swooped back over and seized me by the arm.

"I'm not letting you stay cooped up in here just because you're the bride. It's a beautiful day out there." She grimaced. "If a little too warm for my taste these days. Queen Juliette has informed me that all the wedding preparations are in hand, so we should be taking the moment to have some fun."

"Actually, I was just coming to tell you that the twins have arrived." Oliver's lips quivered slightly in apparent amusement. "All three sets of them."

"Lily and Sophie?" Celine gasped. "And their babies?! Why didn't you start with that?"

She took off toward the door with me still in tow. I looked back helplessly toward Teddy, but he and Gabe seemed nearly as interested in the news as Celine. The three princes followed behind us at a pace that was only slightly more dignified than our own scramble.

"Celine's already dragged you across the ocean to visit them both, hasn't she?" Gabe asked Oliver. "Is poor Dominic haggard?" He sounded a little too delighted at the prospect.

Oliver chuckled. "Really, Gabe, you should know him better by now. Of course he isn't. He brought in all his own people from the heir's castle, claiming he couldn't trust his children to anyone else. And now, between them and Sophie, he has to fight to get a turn with the babies."

"A masterful strategy," said Teddy admiringly, and I glared over my shoulder at him.

His eyes laughed back at me. "Not that I would ever attempt such a thing, of course. I will be the picture of doting attention to my future children."

"I don't know what you're all talking about," Celine said. "Whatever Dominic may have been like when you were all young, it's clear to anyone with eyes that he positively dotes on

Sophie and those two children. They're going to be the most spoiled prince and princess to ever live."

"Is it true that Princess Lily had her babies in Palinar?" I asked. "Isn't she the crown princess of Marin? I can't imagine their court was impressed with such an arrangement."

"In the usual course of things you would be right," Oliver said. "But I get the impression they're all growing used to those twins." He paused. "The older ones, I mean."

"Plus," Celine added, "Dominic had already engaged the most experienced delivery doctor in all the kingdoms, and of course Jon insisted that she attend Lily as well. In truth, I feel quite sorry for the poor doctor since no sooner did Lily go into labor than it set Sophie off as well." She shook her head. "Four babies in one night is more than enough for anyone."

At this pronouncement, we all burst out into the entryway. A chaos of moving people greeted us, trunks and bags piled in every direction. A wailing cry cut above the general hubbub, only to be cut short and replaced with happy gurgles.

"Lily?" Celine called loudly. "Sophie?"

The crowd parted, and a slim young lady appeared, a circlet nestled among her golden curls, and a six-month old baby on either hip. I eyed her curiously and the babies doubtfully. I was sure when news of the births reached Trione, it had been announced that Lily and Sophie had each borne a boy and a girl. And both of those babies were clearly girls, although both looked startlingly like the young woman, despite their baby features.

The woman smiled at Celine.

"So lovely to see you. Please excuse our chaos. Normally Grace insists on being with her brother at all times—unless Hope is around. As soon as we are all together, the two girls cannot bear to be separated. And I'm afraid Lily and I are too soft-hearted not to always give in and allow them to be together."

So this was Sophie then. Holding her daughter and her niece.

Another young woman, this one in an elegant light blue

gown, stepped out of the crowd. She cradled a third baby, this one squirming in a desperate attempt to see something over her shoulder. I blinked and stared between Sophie and the newcomer. Somehow, despite increasing age and the burdens of motherhood, the two twins still looked identical.

"Lily has taken pity on us and always wears blue when we're all together," Teddy whispered in my ear. "So now it's not just Jon and Dominic who can tell them apart."

I nodded my thanks, relieved for the tip. A young man, his chestnut hair flopping across his eyes as he tried to keep hold of another squirming young prince, stepped up to stand by Lily's side. The boy she held immediately stopped wriggling and chortled happily as he grinned at the new baby.

Despite the discernible air of command, I had no trouble identifying this young man as Lily's Prince Jon rather than the infamous King Dominic. Somehow I suspected I would know him when I saw him.

"Celine!" Lily thrust the baby she was holding at her husband and rushed toward us, throwing her arms around the princess beside me. "You're here already!"

Celine laughed and disentangled herself to turn Lily toward me.

"Lily, Sophie," she glanced across at Sophie who came forward to join us, "this is Isla. Teddy's bride. And ocean girl."

Sophie laughed, both of the babies on her hips smiling up at her when she did. "I still can't quite believe he was right about that. And that the answer to the mystery turned out to be mermaids! It seems far too much like one of our childhood dreams to be real."

"Yes, well, it's hardly the only fantastical thing we've found in these kingdoms." Celine held out one hand, and a small orange flame flared to life in her palm, dancing forward to her fingertips before disappearing.

"I'm still not used to that," I said, staring at her hand.

Lily shook her head. "Says the mermaid."

I smiled at her. "Exactly. Fire isn't exactly our area of expertise."

"Fair enough, I suppose," said Sophie. "Although, to be honest, I'm not exactly used to it, either. Celine could *not* do that when we were children."

"I'd love to hear some of the stories of Celine's childhood from your perspective," I said.

The twins exchanged a quick glance and then turned to me with matching warm smiles, as if they didn't need words to come to an agreement.

"We would be more than delighted to tell you anything you want to know." Lily's smile had a hint of mischief.

"We're so glad to finally get the chance to meet you," Sophie added with sincerity in her voice. "And we appreciate the opportunity to introduce the twins to everyone." She bounced both of the babies in her arms and grinned. "Both sets of them."

"With so many weddings," Lily said, "we encouraged the other royals to send delegates to the two Christenings rather than attend themselves. But I've been dying to show them off." She beamed at the four babies proudly.

"And with good reason," I said. "I've rarely seen such calm, happy children. They seem remarkably unbothered by all this." I waved at the noise and movement around us.

Sophie smiled even more warmly at me, and I knew I'd said the right thing.

"We're not sure if it's because they have each other or if it's something to do with the Christening gifts from their godmothers. They were rather cryptic."

"A bit like our own," Lily said, with a weighted look at Jon beside her. "I suspect we won't find out the truth of what they mean until the twins are older."

"At least they were gifts and not curses," said a deep voice from behind them.

A tall, commanding man stepped forward to stand beside Sophie, his face set in stern lines. The missing King Dominic. But his expression softened slightly when he glanced down at his wife and continued.

"And we know from experience that the godmothers know what they're doing when it comes to handing out Christening gifts. The twins will find their way."

Sophie smiled up at him, a tender light in her eye. "Of course they will. I just hope they won't have to travel as far from their parents as we did." Her arms around the babies tightened slightly.

I grimaced to myself. I wasn't one to inspire confidence in that area. But then, I was only one of six sisters, and none of the other five had yet shown any inclination to leave Merrita.

"I'm being remiss in my hosting duties," Teddy said suddenly. "You must all be tired from traveling so far and eager to be shown to your rooms."

Several servants appeared at the visitors' elbows at those words, as if they had been waiting for some sign they could intervene. I hadn't noticed it happening, but around us, much of the luggage had disappeared, and the chaos had noticeably lessened. Before I had a chance to say anything else, the newcomers were all swept away.

We reconvened for a late breakfast on the beach the next morning. The spring weather was warm enough that everyone was determined to swim, although I suspected their desire was partially motivated by wanting to see our mer-forms with their own eyes.

We splashed around the lagoon, Teddy and Millie particularly proud to show off their new tails. Teddy ambushed and submerged Gabe three times before the Talinosian prince managed to get his own back, and my respect for Gabe only grew to see how good-naturedly he took his defeats.

His wife, Adelaide, turned out to be nothing like her intimidating older brother, and it was easy to see what had attracted

Gabe to her. I also noticed with amusement that despite Gabe's earlier protestations about his wife's swans, he only managed to turn the tables on Teddy after the black one launched an attack on my betrothed. From the expression in the eyes of the bird as she watched Gabe, I could have sworn she had coordinated with the prince, coming indignantly to his defense. And perhaps she had. After all, the swans were clearly not like ordinary birds, calmly paddling around the lagoon amid splashing land dwellers and merfolk.

Daisy, used to our tails by now, had attached herself to two of the birds and was cooing over them with delight. Adelaide, standing beside me on the sand where the waves could roll over our feet, saw me watching the three of them and informed me their names were Shadow and Sunny.

"You needn't worry about Daisy," she said. "They wouldn't do anything to put her at risk. They understand far more than they have any right to, and they're particularly sensitive around water after seeing me nearly drown once."

I looked at her with shocked sympathy, remembering Teddy submerged in the storm so long ago, but she didn't seem to notice, her eyes on the birds.

"Shadow is the leader of the wedge, so naturally she's accepting Daisy's praise and adoration as her due." Adelaide sounded amused. "I'm afraid they're all becoming quite used to being admired." She glanced back up the beach. "Perhaps I'd better go and give the same reassurances over there. Snowy and Sweetie look ready to make themselves at home."

She hurried up the beach to where two of the swans had approached an elaborate blanket spread out a short way from the others. It was home to the four infant twins and a number of adults whose sole role seemed to be preventing the young royals from succeeding at their dearest wish—eating sand.

But the arrival of the birds was greeted with great interest by the children, and the adults seemed inclined to look on them as a welcome distraction. The two swans settled themselves regally on the blanket while the babies gazed wide-eyed at them. No doubt the birds could count themselves fortunate the children were not yet mobile, or they would have had four babies attempting to climb onto their backs.

I looked back toward the water in time to see the black swan, the humorously named Eagle, swim close to me. Her beady eyes were fixed on Teddy, swimming not far from us, so I splashed out in front of her and gave her my best glare.

"If you bite him, you'll regret it. This is my celebration, and I won't have bruises on my groom."

She swung her head around to eye me suspiciously, but I maintained eye contact until she finally honked something that sounded uncannily like begrudging acquiescence. Stepping back in bemusement at the interaction, I watched her swim smoothly away in a different direction, as if she'd never intended to approach Teddy at all.

My stomach rumbled, and I realized I had been too busy greeting everyone and answering questions about life under the sea to eat. I wandered back to the main set of blankets where the picnic had been spread out and took a seat, watching the others still splashing through the water. Jon, Dominic, Gabe, and Teddy appeared to have launched some sort of race, as if the sun and the water had made them forget they weren't the boys they used to be when they would convene on the beaches of Trione while their parents conducted matters of state. From what I'd heard, though, Dominic wouldn't have been likely to involve himself in such goings on back then. I wasn't sure whether to credit his current participation to his now-broken curse or to Sophie. Perhaps it was some combination of both.

Queen Blanche and King Alexander arrived at the beach as I watched, having only arrived late the evening before. My father had been pleased to hear they would make the journey to honor our ceremony with their presence, despite their own wedding only taking place so recently. He took it as a sign of our increasing legitimacy among the other kingdoms, although I suspected the other rulers' respect for Trione might have more to do with it.

I hadn't spent much time with the young queen on my visit to Eliam since she had been overwhelmingly busy as host, queen, and bride. But she joined me on the picnic blanket with a warm greeting, and a reminder that I must call her Snow, as the other young royals did. Turning her face up toward the sun, she gave a sigh of contentment.

"It's so much warmer here than it is in Eliam yet. You could almost mistake it for summer."

"It's a bit too warm, if you ask me." Celine splashed out of the shallows to join us. "It's good to see you, Snow. How are you enjoying married life?" She selected a nectarine from a bowl of fruit and bit into it.

"It's blissful." Snow smiled at her husband who had bypassed the food to dive into the water and was now steadily swimming out toward the reef, ignoring the race. When she glanced back at us, she made an exasperated face. "I had to wait long enough."

We both winced in sympathy. Celine and Oliver had been betrothed only a short time before Snow and Alexander, but they had been married for almost two years already. Snow, on the other hand, had been forced to wait since she was only my age, having come into her crown young.

I didn't envy her the burden of responsibility that came with her throne. I expected to have many long years getting to know my new kingdom before being called upon to become its queen. And I didn't envy her the long engagement, either. My own, though much shorter, had seemed long enough.

My eyes sought out Teddy, his golden hair and laughing face standing out across the distance. There were only days left to wait now, but it felt like the moment would never come.

"If it's too warm for you here," Snow said to Celine, "how are you going to cope when you finally make your trip back to Lanover? You are still planning to go, aren't you?"

My attention returned to them at the mention of a trip to the Old Kingdoms. I hadn't realized Celine intended to visit her old home.

"Yes, I'm dying to show it all to Oliver," Celine said. "Although I don't know when we'll be able to get away. I don't think it will be until next year, or even the year after, unfortunately. I'll adjust to the heat, it just takes a while sometimes when the temperature change is sudden."

"Are King Leopold and Queen Camille still planning to send Emmeline and Giselle along?" Snow asked.

Celine made a face. "Giselle is determined to come, but I doubt we'll convince Emmeline. So I've already started working on Lord Treestone to let me take Cassandra in her stead. Cassie would appreciate the adventure far more than Emmeline."

"Oh, that's an excellent idea!" said Snow. "And if you succeed in convincing him, please let me know. I'd love to send Daria with you. She still hasn't fully adjusted to her new life, and I suspect it would do her good to travel somewhere completely new without the responsibility of the children or the pressure of her connection to me."

Snow looked concerned, and I could see she cared about Daria and felt responsible for her. I vaguely remembered a self-contained girl with an elaborate bun of black braids who had been one of the attendants at Snow's wedding. Teddy had told me she was a commoner, one of the children who had sheltered Snow when she fled her stepmother. Had her name been Daria?

"She would be welcome, regardless," Celine said. "We would love to have her along."

"Thank you," Snow said warmly, "but I'm not sure I could convince her to accompany you if it's just you and your sister-in-law. But Cassandra isn't a princess, and if my memory serves me, she was always a little rough around the edges." She chuckled.

"She has enough practicality in her to make Daria feel less out of place."

"I feel like there might be an insult to me in there somewhere —if I weren't far too warm to be bothered trying to find it," Celine said in a weary voice.

Snow just laughed again. I didn't remember her laughing quite so much on the previous occasions we'd met and could only be glad Alexander made her so happy. When I first heard her story, it had been another reminder that I hadn't valued my home and family as much as I should. We had both lost our mothers young, but Snow had been alone with no siblings and an ill father, while I had been surrounded by sisters and would walk down the aisle on my father's arm.

My eyes caught on Daisy, abandoned by the swans and trudging somewhat disconsolately out of the water. She stood out at our gathering of royals, so much older than the babies, but so much younger than everyone else. Daisy wasn't an orphan like Snow, she had a family that loved her, but I still saw her reflection in Celine and Snow's words. She was caught between roles, feeling out of place and dreaming of adventure.

"If you're not to go for another two years," I said, my eyes still on Daisy, "perhaps Trione might send a small delegation with you as well."

Celine followed my gaze. "Excellent idea! Us younger sisters need to stick together, you know." She grinned at me, and I grinned back.

Ray arrived, detained from joining us earlier by a meeting with Captain Flint, and I introduced him to the two of them while he filled a plate. Millie spotted him from the water and came straight out. The rest of them trailed behind her until the blankets were full again, most people starting on their second round of food.

I gazed over the chattering heads and locked eyes with Teddy.

The stolen moment made me flush slightly, until Millie bumped me, pulling my attention back to the group.

"We have dress fittings this afternoon, Celine," she was saying. "The seamstress has promised to be as efficient as possible, but with eight of us it will likely take a while."

I had asked all five of my sisters, my two soon-to-be sisters-in-law, and my new friend to be my attendants. Millie, on the other hand, had stuck to just me and Daisy for her own wedding and consequently loved to make teasing comments about large wedding parties.

But she slipped an arm around my waist and squeezed me against her side. "Not that I mind in the least," she told Celine. "All of it is worth it to get Isla as my sister."

"Ha!" I grinned across at Celine. "She's just looking forward to being sisters so she can try to forget she's now my aunt."

"Your aunt?" Lily interjected, looking confused. But then she paused for a moment, a strange look on her face that was quickly replaced with amused understanding. "Oh, of course." She smiled at Ray. "It does seem very strange, but I suppose you're used to it."

"When you're related to Isla, you get used to *strange* very quickly," he said with a straight face. "Millie will soon grow accustomed to it."

Millie laughed and sent him such a loving expression that I had to shove her quickly away from me. "No, no, none of that here," I said. "You're my aunt and uncle, remember."

Millie groaned and shoved me back. "I refuse to be your, or anyone's, aunt." She glanced across at the four babies. "Well, at least until you have children. Then I'll be more than happy to be their aunt."

"Actually," I said gravely, "you'll be their great aunt."

"Isla!" she wailed as I collapsed into giggles.

"It's true, though," Adelaide pointed out. "I'm afraid you're going to have to accept it, Millie." The twinkle in her eye told me there was more to her than just the sweetness I had first noticed.

Dominic joined us from where he had been checking on his children, and the conversation turned to more serious matters. Everyone wanted to hear an update on how Merrita was adjusting to life on the surface, so I spent the rest of the picnic giving a report on our progress.

The autumn had been spent surveying our newly surfaced land and redrawing the maps, and no one had thought it wise to attempt building new settlements in winter. Instead the colder months had given the crown time to navigate the intense negotiations between each of the Merritan Families. By the time spring arrived, the land had been divided up with new villages, farms, and even small cities planned and plotted. Every possible preparation had been made, and the people were itching to go, ready to burst from the city and pour out into the rest of the kingdom. Given their subsequent progress in the early part of spring, they would be comfortably established by next winter.

"The island isn't the same shape as it was when it sank," I said. "It's much longer and thinner. I think the High King realized that everyone would want to live along the coast."

"I can imagine," Dominic said thoughtfully.

The arrival of spring had brought a substantial diplomatic delegation from Palinar, including a suspicious number of young and unattached members. I suspected that, like King Edward, the young king of Palinar was dreaming of his own future merforces.

My father had raised the matter with Oceana and Lyon over the winter, shocking me by including me in the discussions. He treated it like a natural thing, saying my time in Trione and my attachment to a land dweller would give me relevant insights, but I couldn't help thinking how far our relationship had come for him to take me so seriously.

Our conclusion had been that we should do nothing to prevent our people making the romantic attachments the other kingdoms seemed to desire. No other kingdom would be likely to ever equal our numbers in the water, but some presence of merfolk in each of the kingdoms would help them to understand us better and would ease certain aspects of communication. We didn't want the people of the land to see us as a mysterious threat.

My family arrived in Trione the morning after the picnic, my father having delayed their arrival until the last moment since none of my sisters were willing to stay behind and miss my wedding. Lyon had been left in charge of the continuing expansion, but I knew Father didn't want to leave him to manage the task alone for too long.

That night, King Edward and Queen Juliette held an official reception to welcome them, and I sang in public for the first time since Merrita's rise had freed my voice. My eyes lingered on my father, and I sang for my mother, feeling the heaviness of grief that she could not stand beside me at my wedding, denied the chance to see her daughters grow and her kingdom restored. My father's expression, a strange, heart-rending mix of grief and joy and pride, only fueled the emotion of the song.

But my eyes didn't stay on him, drawn irresistibly across the room to where Teddy watched me, his face full of awe and love. Slowly the song changed, hope lightening its notes, and without realizing it, I found myself singing an old, traditional love song of the Merritan people. I poured my heart into it, and his heart looked back at me through his eyes. My song had woven us together, the first time we met, and now it wove us together again.

I could feel it around us, the invisible bonds growing stronger and solidifying as we made our vows two mornings later, in front of all our family and friends. We stood in the crystal ballroom, the dance floor full of visiting royals and local nobles, and the beach filled with commoners, eager to watch the ceremony through the clear wall.

The godmothers of both the Trionian and Merritan royal

families were in attendance, side by side at the far end of the front row, a respectful distance left around them on all sides. My godmother had come to see me before the wedding began, saying the kind words I had no mother or grandmother to say. And she had given me a wedding gift—the one remaining shell from my mother's collection, whether protected or restored, I didn't know.

"Your mother is proud of you," she had said, softly. "She spent her pregnancy with you visiting the surface to float in the sun and dreaming of the day Merrita would rise again. She wished for you to grow up and restore your people, and her dreams have come true. Without realizing it, she shaped you into something different—not a land dweller, because the sea is in your blood, but not a creature of the deep like the other merfolk either. You paid the price of being different, Isla, but you have reaped the rewards as well. Use them wisely."

She had embraced me before disappearing, my attendants crowding in to the space she had left, ready to begin the final preparations.

The royal seamstress had given herself free rein, delighted to be designing a dress for a mermaid princess. Consequently, it took every bit of my extra grace to navigate the length of my train and the voluminous folds of my silk dress. But as I stepped carefully down the aisle, toward my love, I was glad for every bit of the material. Teddy had opened his heart to me when he didn't know my true identity, and I knew that he loved me regardless of my rank. But I wanted his kingdom to be reassured that their crown prince had chosen an appropriate bride, and I wanted everyone to see that Merrita was a kingdom with the same dignity and history as any kingdom of the land. I had come to appreciate my home just as I was leaving it, and it warmed me to think I might do it this final service.

I didn't doubt my decision to leave for even a moment, however. As I placed my hand in Teddy's and raised my face for his ceremonial kiss, I knew I had finally found the place where I belonged. As we turned together to face the cheering crowds, I knew we had a lifetime ahead of us of exploration and adventure, of discovering new places, and of service to these people. And, most importantly, we would do it together.

When Teddy slipped an arm around me and pulled me close, my heart threatened to burst with an altogether different sensation from the restlessness that used to fill it. And when I caught a glimpse of Millie and Ray, standing just behind us, a deep contentment washed over me. Teddy and I weren't alone. We would explore, and we would rule with the best of friends at our side. Together the four of us could achieve anything.

My eyes roamed over the crowd, seeing my sisters and then all of the other young royals in the front rows. We had each had our turn to fight the darkness, and we had reclaimed our lands. Now together we would forge a brighter future than anything that had come before. And maybe one day, we would have the chance to meet the young royals who had done the same in the Old Kingdoms, and we would truly be one people and one land again, as we had been long ago. It was a new day in Trione as it was in Merrita, the green-blue of the water that lapped at both our shores sparkling under the warm rays of the sun.

NOTE FROM THE AUTHOR

More fairytale adventures will be coming in Return to the Four Kingdoms. But, in the meantime, did you miss the original adventures in the Old Kingdoms? Read them starting with The Princess Companion: A Retelling of The Princess and the Pea.

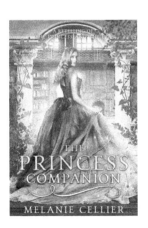

Or for more romance, adventure, and intrigue in a new world, try my Spoken Mage series. In Elena's world words have power over life and death—but none more so than hers. As a commonborn, Elena has always been forbidden to read and write, until a startling new ability thrusts her into the Royal Academy where she finds herself among the mageborn including the enigmatic Prince Lucas. You can turn the page for a sneak peek.

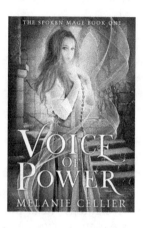

To be kept informed of my new releases, please sign up to my mailing list at www.melaniecellier.com. At my website, you'll also find an array of free extra content..

Thank you for taking the time to read my book. I hope you enjoyed it. If you did, please spread the word! You could start by leaving a review on Amazon (or Goodreads or Facebook or any other social media site). Your review would be very much appreciated and would make a big difference!

CHAPTER 1

I was hurrying home along the dirt road, already late, when I heard the cry. It clearly came from a young child and was too loud to miss and too pained to ignore. With a sigh, I slowed and tried to pinpoint the source. I had spent longer in the woods than I usually did on my herb-gathering expeditions, and the sun was already drawing low. But I was well outside the village now, so no one else was likely to hear or intervene.

An angry voice followed by another cry sent me around some bushes and onto the flat patch of ground bordering the small river that flowed past our town of Kingslee. A small child who I vaguely recognized—not more than three years old—cowered in the dirt away from a boy and girl my own age. I leaped in, placing myself between the child and his attackers, before my brain caught up. I shot a pained look at the girl in front of me.

"Really, Alice?"

She winced. "We had to step in, Elena. He was endangering us all. You would have done the same."

I turned to glance at the boy who now clung to my leg. He didn't look dangerous. Tears ran down his cheeks, one of which bore the distinct red mark of a hand. I turned back to glower at the other two.

"I really don't think I would have."

Alice winced again. "Well, maybe not that. Samuel got a bit carried away, perhaps..."

"No, I did not." Samuel narrowed his eyes at me. "That boy needs to be taught a lesson, and even you should know that, Elena. Isn't your family's house just down the road?"

I rubbed my head. I was too tired today for riddles.

"What are you talking about, Samuel?"

Samuel just pointed at the scuffed dirt beside where we all stood. I looked helplessly across at Alice.

She leaned over slightly, pointing more closely. Reluctantly I bent down as well, frowning at what appeared to be a single short, curving line drawn in the dust, deeper than the other muddled depressions.

"It's a...line?" I picked up the crying child, who was now attempting to climb my leg, and settled him on my hip. "So he's been drawing in the dirt. What of it?"

"Yes, just a line. Thanks to us." Samuel stepped forward, his posture belligerent, and I fell back a step. But only because of the boy. I didn't want Samuel taking another swipe at him.

But Samuel ignored the child, pointing instead at something on the other side of us. It appeared to have been pushed aside and partially concealed by a bush during whatever scuffle had occurred before my arrival. But half a page was still enough to see what it was—a single sheet of printed parchment.

I gasped and jumped back instinctively, nearly dropping the boy.

"What—? Where did that come from?"

Samuel crossed his arms in front of his chest and regarded me again with narrowed eyes. "And now you see. We've saved us all. And that child needs to be taught a lesson."

"He's only a baby," I protested, my arms tightening around him. "He doesn't know any better."

But I could feel the shake in my limbs as residual fear burned through me. How close had we all come to death? I scrubbed at the dirt with my foot, removing even the faint traces of whatever had been marked there.

"Why haven't you burned it?" I asked. "Before someone else sees it. Like a guard. You know the penalty for possessing writing, let alone the danger…"

Samuel shook his head. "We'll burn it once that boy has learned his lesson."

I stepped back again as he leaned forward threateningly. But Alice put her hand on his arm, restraining him.

"I think you've scared him enough, Samuel. Look, he's still crying. Elena is right. We should burn it."

For a moment Samuel and I stood frozen, our gazes locked. But then Alice pulled at his arm again, and he sighed, shaking her off.

"Very well."

As he pulled out tinder and flint, I tried not to look at the parchment. But the firm black marks called to me, and I couldn't resist stealing several glances. I couldn't read what they said, of course. None of us could. But I knew enough to recognize words when I saw them. Their loops and curves and straight edges fascinated me. What mysteries would they unlock, if only I could decipher them? If only I hadn't been born Elena, of Kingslee, daughter of two shopkeepers.

But as the first bright lick of flame ignited the paper, the forbidden letters burning away, I shook myself. I wouldn't trade my family for anything. Not even the wonders of the written word and the magical power it could unleash for those from the right bloodlines.

"Well, that's done then," said Alice when the parchment had

turned completely to ash. "We should be going." She looked over her shoulder at the road, clearly eager to be gone.

But uneasiness stirred in me.

"But surely the real question is where did he get it." I looked down at the boy who had snuggled into my shoulder, his tears finally fading at the mesmerizing sight of flames. "Where did it come from? Kingslee doesn't need that kind of trouble." Not when we stood so close to the capital, in all too easy reach of any number of the king's guards.

Samuel grunted. "Didn't you see earlier? A couple of fancy carriages came rolling through on their way to Corrin." He gestured up the road past my house where the capital lay, far out of sight. "They deigned to stop, and the mages inside even went into your parents' store. I've no doubt one of them dropped the thing, and this idiot found it."

At his angry tone the boy began to tremble, attempting to burrow into me. I hoisted him a little higher on my hip and glared at Samuel again.

"It's not his fault. He's too young to know better. Things like this aren't supposed to be lying around."

"He's obviously a smart one." Alice watched him with sadness lurking in her eyes. "To try to copy what he saw."

"Smart? Ha!" Samuel barked a laugh without humor. "Idiot fool, more like. He could have exploded us all with a single word, you know that."

"Well, he didn't!" I snapped, my nerves having eaten the last of my patience. "And it's getting late. I'm taking him home." I narrowed my eyes, daring Samuel to try to stop me, but he merely glared back.

"Do you know where he belongs?" asked Alice tentatively.

I nodded. "I recognize him. I'll have him home soon enough."

Neither of them moved, so I took off, winding around them. I would have preferred to walk behind them, but I didn't have time to wait around. Not now that I would have to return to town before heading home.

I walked quickly, the boy's weight growing heavier by the minute. I considered putting him down and letting him walk, but the slow pace would have killed me. Instead I pushed on, stopping only once to switch hips.

So someone from the mage families had passed through today. It made sense since no one else would have written words with them. If I hadn't been out gathering, I would have seen them for myself. Spoken to them even, perhaps, if they had come into the store as Samuel said.

What would they have been like? It was one thing to learn the facts of them in school. How they alone could control the power that written words always unleashed, and therefore they alone could be trusted to read and write. About the way they built the kingdom with the power of their written compositions. Even about the different color robes they wore to signify their various disciplines. But that wasn't the same as knowing what they were like as people.

Proud, haughty, and disagreeable? That was how I always imagined them, and how the ones who occasionally rode through Kingslee usually looked.

But what if they had instead looked normal? Friendly even. A person just like me, only wearing fancier clothes. Would that be worse? To know that no more than an accident of birth separated us.

I pushed open the door of a small cottage, set a short way back from the main road, without knocking. A young woman, her eyes red, looked up and gave a small shriek.

"Joseph! There you are!" She rushed forward and snatched him from my arms, wrapping him in her own. I had thought he looked like Isadora's boy, although I had forgotten his name.

She regarded me with wide eyes. "Where did you find him, Elena?"

I shifted from one foot to the other. "Down by the river."

She shrieked again and squeezed him so tightly that he protested and tried to wriggle free. I only just refrained from rolling my eyes. This was a lot of dramatics for someone who hadn't even been out searching for her child.

I wanted to hurry away, but something kept me locked in place. I cleared my throat.

"He wasn't in any danger from the *river*," I said and instantly received Isadora's full attention.

"What do you mean?"

"He didn't show any inclination to go swimming. Perhaps because he'd found something." I glanced around but could see no one else in the small two-room house. I lowered my voice anyway. "A piece of parchment. With words. Samuel thinks someone in those carriages from earlier must have dropped it. Joseph had found it and..." I paused. "He was trying to copy some of it. In the dirt."

I had been sure my revelation would earn another shriek, but Isadora had apparently been shocked into silence instead. She looked round-eyed between me and her young son.

"And..." Her voice wobbled. "Samuel knows of this? He was never one to know when to keep his mouth shut."

"Don't worry," I said quickly. "Joseph is practically a baby still. And we burned it. I'm sure Samuel won't stir up any trouble, no matter what he says." I hesitated. "But you need to make sure he understands—" I bit my lip. "He must be very smart. Has he...has he ever tried anything like that before?"

"Of course not!" She looked offended this time. "He's never even seen words before. Where would he? But he loves to draw. He's always trying to copy the shapes from the pictures at the market, and from the signs..." Her words trailed off, and she dashed her hand across her eyes. "He's smart like you say." She shot me a look. "Like your brother, Jasper."

I smiled, but it felt false, tension still radiating through me.

"That would be fortunate indeed for him. For you all." I refrained from letting my eyes run over the poorly kept interior of the cottage. "But first he has to live long enough."

Isadora shuddered. "It's been burned, you said?"

I nodded.

"Well…" She sighed. "Hopefully that will be the end of it." But I could see the fear lurking in her eyes as she watched Joseph who had managed to work himself free and had run off to play on the other side of the room.

"Yes." I inched toward the door. "I'd better be going…"

"Of course, you'll be wanting to get to your dinner. Thank you, Elena."

Joseph looked up, as if on cue, and repeated, "Thank you, Elena," his high voice mangling the words slightly. His mother's face melted, and even I couldn't resist a smile.

But it fell away as I jogged back out of town. Isadora should have been more careful. Should have been watching her son more closely. He was old enough now to understand. I shivered. Or perhaps he wasn't. I could hardly remember Clementine at that age, let alone what it had been like to be that age myself. Still. A whole village had been lost only last year. One big bang and the whole thing had disappeared. No one knew exactly what had happened, of course. Not after the fact when there was nothing left.

Just that the explosion had been untrained, out of control. Deadly. Someone had been writing. A commonborn without the control to shape the power that flowed out of them as soon as they began to form written words. A commonborn like me and every single other person in the kingdom not born to a mage parent.

And that could have been Kingslee. Nearly had been, perhaps. I swallowed and veered off the path to collect my leather satchel which I had abandoned in the bushes when I rushed to defend Joseph. Not that I remembered doing so. Jasper would scold me as he always did if he ever heard of it, telling me I was far too protective.

"And you're not even the oldest, Elena," he would say, pulling affectionately on my hair. "Aren't I supposed to be the protective one?"

I always smiled and played along, but we both knew the truth. Jasper was our shining light. The one who was going to lift us all out of poverty. The genius with perfect recall who could compete even against the mages when it came to academics.

One day he would secure a lucrative position and take us to the capital. Which meant it was left to me to do the protecting, of both him and our younger sister Clementine. Although he was far away at the Royal University, these days. Too far for either teasing or protecting.

It had always been clear that Jasper would not be accepting our family's conscription responsibility. Any more than there was any question of weak, sickly Clementine being left to go to war.

So if I was to bear the ultimate burden of protecting my siblings, then why not start early? Even if my eighteenth birthday was still more than a year and a half away.

When I pushed open the door to our home, my sister greeted me with a glad cry as she always did. Unlike the house I had just left, everything here was neat and in good order, the furniture sturdy and every surface scrubbed clean. Even the curtains looked newly washed. It was larger, too, with two more rooms tucked away, as well as a loft where Clementine and I slept. The reward of my parents' careful running of their small store. That and their willingness to live out of town where there was room for a bigger house.

I tried to smile, but Clementine knew me too well. Her face fell, and she hurried over to take my hand.

"What is it, Elena? Is something wrong?"

I shook myself. "No, indeed. Don't mind me, Clemmy. I'm just tired." And it was true. Nothing was wrong, now. But still I couldn't dislodge the feeling of unease that had settled over me beside the river.

"Oh, poor thing. Of course, you're exhausted, traipsing through the woods all day." She hurried to take my bag from my shoulder, gesturing for me to sit down while she emptied it, laying the herbs inside out neatly on the table.

"We had some special visitors while you were gone." She giggled. "Well, not visitors exactly. Customers."

I ran a hand over my eyes. "I heard. Mages, were they?"

She nodded, looking a little crestfallen that someone had beaten her to the news. "One of the ladies caught sight of some of our fresh fruit and had a 'hankering that couldn't be denied' apparently."

I rolled my eyes, but Clementine was obviously fascinated by her brush with the upper class. Our oppressors. I pressed a hand to my head. I must be more tired than I realized. Now I was the one getting dramatic.

The mages might wield all of the power and much of the wealth in the kingdom, but they were the only ones able to control the power. And we did all see at least some benefits from it. If only because their growers and wind workers ensured the crops grew, and their creators built roads. Even their healers were available to those who could afford them.

"I hope they paid well," I said.

"That they did," said Mother, bustling into the room. "And extra. As if counting out the correct amount wasn't worth their time." She shook her head in wonder.

"That'll be us one day," said Clementine, pride in her voice. "Once Jasper graduates, and we all join him in Corrin."

"Aye, that it will," said Father, coming in from outside. He picked Clementine up and swung her around, although at eleven she was really too old for such things. None of us protested, however.

When he put her down again, his eye fell on the neat rows of gathered herbs on the table. He raised his eyebrows.

"You did well today, Elena."

I sat up straight and smiled back at him. I had managed a good haul, although the subsequent events of the afternoon had driven it from my mind. I had always been the best at finding the hidden spots in the woods where the rarer herbs grew. The ones that would fetch a good price in the store—either fresh or dried.

My family would miss me when I turned eighteen and signed up to go away to war. I knew they would. But better me than Jasper or Clementine. No one said it, but we all agreed on it. And the law was clear. One child from every family must sign up to join the army when they turned eighteen. And if no one stepped forward to volunteer, then the youngest would be forcibly conscripted on their eighteenth birthday.

I had heard it debated from time to time, but no one seemed able to agree which position was less enviable—to be an older one, forced to choose, or the youngest, without a choice at all. I saw the sadness and the fear in my mother's eyes sometimes, when she watched me. Most families sent their brawniest son and hoped he could survive the three years until he had served his term and was free to return home.

I sometimes wondered if that was why Mother had fallen pregnant again, a full five years after my birth. It had been clear by then that Jasper was special, and that he could not be wasted on the front line of a never-ending war. My parents had already begun to save their coin, in fact, knowing how much tutoring he would need once he finished in the Kingslee school at age ten.

Perhaps my mother had hoped to bear more sons, who might have been better suited than me to surviving in battle. But she got Clementine, the sweetest—and weakest—of us all.

I had never actually had the courage to ask, though, so perhaps that had not been it at all.

"Did any of them drop anything?" The words were out of my mouth before I realized they were hovering on my tongue.

"Who?" Father looked confused.

"The mages, you mean?" Clementine tipped her head to one side, regarding me quizzically. "Why?"

"Oh, them." Father returned to packing up the herbs.

"Not that I saw," said Mother. "Although from the careless way of them, it wouldn't surprise me one bit. Why do you ask? Did you stop by the store and find something?"

I shook my head. "Not me. But young Joseph—Isadora's little boy—found something it seems." I hadn't meant to tell them what happened, but I couldn't keep it to myself—not with the way it weighed on me. The story wanted to escape.

Plus Samuel had been there. I didn't trust him to keep his mouth shut, and once he started talking, it was hard to know how others would react. I just hoped he hadn't recognized Joseph or seen which house I went into to return him. Thankfully he wasn't the sort to pay attention to details.

"Something valuable?" asked Clementine. "Do you think they'll miss it? The mages, I mean."

"I certainly hope not." I sat up, drawing in a breath. I hadn't even thought of that. "It was words. Some sort of printed dispatch or something."

All movement in the room stilled.

"And young Joseph found it, you say," said Father, after a breath.

I nodded. "Samuel and Alice found him down by the river. We burned it. But..." I took a deep breath and finished in a rush. "He was trying to copy it. In the dirt before I arrived, apparently. They only just stopped him in time."

"Trying to copy the...the letters?" Clementine stumbled over the words, her face white.

"If he'd managed a whole word..." Even my father looked afraid.

I swallowed and nodded. "But he didn't. That's what I keep reminding myself. He didn't. And he's only a child, too. Perhaps... perhaps the power wouldn't have grown strong enough in him to do much damage."

No one responded to my hopeful suggestion. Because we all knew the power of words. Words had the power of life—and the power of death. Written words shaped the power, released it from inside us out into the world. But only the mage families could control that power.

Certainly not people like us. Or young Joseph. If any of the commonborn wrote so much as a word, the power would come rushing out in an uncontrolled explosion of destruction. Just like in that poor village up north. In one instant gone forever, wiped off the map. How many letters had it taken? And who had written them? We would never know.

I might hate the system that trampled us into the dirt, but I understood it. There was a reason none of us could ever be permitted the wonders of reading and writing. Without the bloodline that would enable us to control the power once we accessed it, it was just too dangerous. One slip up, and...

The door banged open, and we all jumped.

Thomas, the young boy who sometimes helped in the store now that Jasper had left, leaned against the doorframe, panting.

"What is it, Tom?" asked Father.

"Trouble," he panted out. "Trouble at the store. Something about those mages."

Read on in Voice of Power

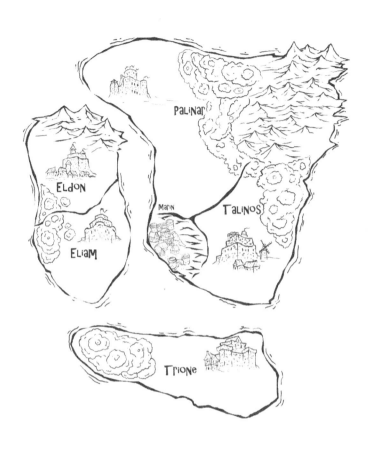

Palinar

Eldon

Eliam

Marin

Talinos

Trione

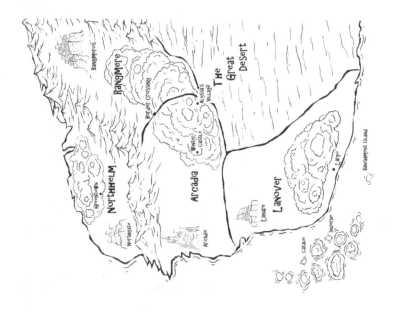

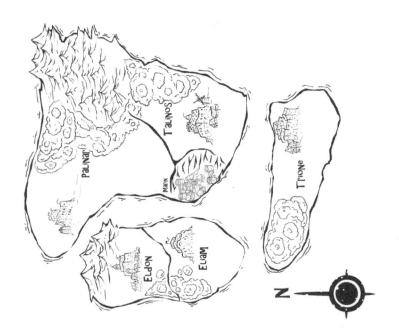

364

ACKNOWLEDGMENTS

Completing A Princess of Wind and Wave feels significant as it's the final book in my third series. It's also my last book of 2019. So while I still have plans for lots more books and series to come in the future, it feels good for this moment to have completed everything I set out to write.

Taking this chance to reflect on my writing journey as a whole, I'm incredibly grateful to the team who have come around me to help and support me in this endeavor. I couldn't possibly continue to write without them, and I couldn't produce at this pace if they weren't all standing by, ready to drop everything to assist me. And whether they help because they're friends and family who love books and believe in me, or because they're part of my paid team, all of them deserve credit for going far above and beyond. I'm not the best at sticking to my own schedules, and I'm so grateful for my team's willingness to work with me anyway and somehow ensure I always hit my final deadlines.

So an enormous thank you, times a million, to:

My parents, Mary, Rachel, Greg, Priya, Ber, Katie, Casey, Kitty, Kenley, Shari, Aya, Brittany, Deborah, and Karri

Every one of you is a star, and I love having you in my life.

And to my family, Marc, Adeline, and Sebastian. I'm so grateful you're willing to shape your lives around my unpredictable—and at times infuriating—schedule. I love being able to live this hectic, stressful, and rewarding life with you.

And to my loyal readers—your love for The Four Kingdoms and its many inhabitants is what has driven me forward and kept me motivated, and I hope you'll journey both onward and back with me in Return to the Four Kingdoms.

As I reflect, I am more aware than ever of the way creativity feeds creativity, and I am grateful to every other creator whose work has entertained, inspired, and shaped me. My ideas have come from your ideas, just as your ideas came from the creatives who went before you.

Which leads me to my final thanks. As always, it goes to God. Thank You for valuing and implanting creativity in this difficult and beautiful world.

ABOUT THE AUTHOR

 Melanie Cellier grew up on a staple diet of books, books and more books. And although she got older, she never stopped loving children's and young adult novels.

She always wanted to write one herself, but it took three careers and three different continents before she actually managed it.

She now feels incredibly fortunate to spend her time writing from her home in Adelaide, Australia where she keeps an eye out for koalas in her backyard. Her staple diet hasn't changed much, although she's added choc mint Rooibos tea and Chicken Crimpies to the list.

She writes young adult fantasy including her *Spoken Mage* series, and her *Four Kingdoms* and *Beyond the Four Kingdoms* series which are made up of linked stand-alone stories that retell classic fairy tales.

CPSIA information can be obtained
at www.ICGtesting.com
Printed in the USA
BVHW031304081021
618558BV00011B/28